Defying Gravity

Defying Gravity

jennifer wynne webber

Edited by Edna Alford.
Cover and book design by Duncan Campbell.
Author photo by Stuart Kasdorf.

Cover image, "Why the World Can Never Be the Same Again – Jill" (1998) by Laureen Marchand. Private collection.

Printed and bound in Canada at Houghton-Boston Lithographers, Saskatoon, Saskatchewan, Canada.

Canadian Cataloguing in Publication Data

Webber, Jennifer 1963–
Defying gravity
ISBN 1-55050-159-3

I. Title.

PS8595.E26D44 2000 C813'.6 C00-920039-B
PR9199.3.W3955D44 2000

COTEAU BOOKS
401-2206 Dewdney Ave.
Regina, Saskatchewan
Canada S4R 1H3

AVAILABLE IN THE US FROM
General Distribution Services
4500 Witmer Industrial Estates
Niagara Falls, NY, 14305-1386

The publisher gratefully acknowledges the financial assistance of the Saskatchewan Arts Board, the Canada Council for the Arts, the Government of Canada through the Book Publishing Industry Development Program (BPIDP), and the City of Regina Arts Commission, for its publishing program.

The Canada Council for the Arts
Le Conseil des Arts du Canada

To Mona, my mother, and Jill and Joan,
my friends on the journey
and deepest source of strength
&
To John Charles, my father,
whose dreams I still carry with me

CONTENTS

"Cry, the beloved country, these things are not yet at an end. The sun pours down on the earth, on the lovely land that man cannot enjoy. He knows only the fear of his heart." – ALAN PATON, *Cry, The Beloved Country*

"I had jumped off the edge, and then, at the very last moment, something reached out and caught me in midair. That something is what I define as love. It is the one thing that can stop a man from falling, the one thing powerful enough to negate the laws of gravity." – PAUL AUSTER, *Moon Palace*

On Top of the World

I was holding Maligne Lake and a Jasper gondola when it happened. Pushed behind the post-card rack by one sharp-elbowed tourist, I had managed to pull out only two of the scenics I wanted before they revolved out of my reach. In seconds, my eyes alternating between the serene turquoise lake and the crowded tramway car suspended high above the earth, the realization hit me. I watched it hit. The very moment it did, my thumbs bent back the skies. Even after I had carefully smoothed them flat again, lightning-forked wrinkle marks remained on the upper corners of each postcard.

Turner had been gone for quite awhile. We were standing outside on the lookout deck when he suddenly went into the Jasper Tram building perched there in the rocks, the destination point for the cable climbing gondolas ascending the mountain. When I followed, I figured he must have headed into the bathroom since he was nowhere to be seen in the gift shop area or even in the little coffee shop. I waited, then stepped back outside and peered around, but all I could see were the gleaming white-capped mountains along the horizon encircling me, the bare boulders before me, the little town of Jasper sprawled down in the valley in a silver J-shape, and the sky above, stretching into infinite blue. And, beside me, the tourists furtively feeding the marmots right behind the sign that said, DO NOT FEED.

I wandered back inside and went to the postcard racks to wait a little longer. Every time the men's room door opened, I glanced up expectantly, with no luck and no Turner. Worrying the clerk might think me a shoplifting candidate, I began to browse with a strongly affected casual air, although a glance at myself in the mirror above the sunglasses rack showed only a stranger looking both anxious little girl and Patty Hearst in the bank after the brainwashing. *Unpredictable,* the look warned. Dark eyes stared just a little too intensely from between strands of short, limply curled brown hair. Thin lips were alternately bitten and pursed. A worried squint lent tension to my whole face. When I reached up to rub the furrow between my eyebrows, the static electricity from my windbreaker made my hair stand on end. The effect was all cornered animal and woman at the end of her rope. No wonder the clerk cleared her throat right about then.

And running through my mind throughout this failed attempt to appear a casual, carefree tourist was a familiar question. What was going wrong now? This time?

Only when I remembered one of the last things

Turner said to me did my anxiety begin to deepen into realization.

"Listen, I don't need this. It's just not for me."

At the time, I thought he was talking about a souvenir shaker toy, the water-filled plastic bubble type, complete with mountain panorama, action gondola lift, and fake snow. But gazing at my chosen postcards and the dusty shaker toys on the shelf, I realized Turner was not in the bathroom and, in fact, was no longer on the mountaintop. A gondola descended every twenty minutes or so and, by this time, I figured Turner was well on his way down to the parking lot.

That is how our engagement ended. Not that I had a ring – it hadn't quite been an engagement of the bridal magazine variety – but I had certainly told people, and so as I paid for the postcards with extra sincerity directed at the clerk, I did wonder how I was going to explain the breakup.

We were just heading in different directions.

Different directions all right. Right down the bloody mountain. Right down a different highway.

And that was another thing to consider. Was the car going to be gone, or would common courtesy replace cowardice once he reached the foot of the mountain? It was my car.

I pushed the door open and walked back outside for another view from the top of the world. The wind gusting into my ears immediately brought an ache to my head. I hoped Turner was not going to leave me a note. The last thing I wanted to find was some sort of *I didn't know how to tell you* note under my bug-plastered windshield wiper. The whole thing actually started to seem funny to me at that point. I wanted to tell someone. Go back to the clerk and say, with a casual chuckle, *You know, you would just not believe it. I've had breakups before but isn't this the most....* The most what? As if getting the clerk onside with a bit of a laugh would somehow reduce the shock and humiliation I felt, the utter, stony coldness that was making it hard for me to breathe right then.

The wind cut through my jacket and prompted me to seek shelter on a bench behind an outcropping of some of the larger boulders. Shivering at a slightly lower frequency, I nevertheless felt an aching cold seep through my limbs and deep into my bones as I sat there. I never have understood the popularity of metal benches.

One stocky little marmot eyed me from behind the guardrails. Another came right to my feet and sat expectantly. More rotund than their squirrel cousins, their inquisitive eyes and shrill whistles make marmots an instant hit with the tourists, particularly those under the age of four. One curly-haired, blond baby stood extending a peanut in a clumsy, balled-up fist. The marmot approached: a careful step or two forward, then a watchful pause on its haunches, then another step forward. The marmot's pattern of movement toward the coveted peanut was irregular in timing but single-minded in determination. Its final dart to the prize was sudden enough to startle the toddler, however, sending her tumbling over in surprise, the peanut falling between two rocks, and the mother rushing to gather up the wailing child.

I did not have anything to offer this little pack of

marmots, hungry after their long hibernation, so I could abide by the posted rules easily enough and simply watch them. As calmly as they surveyed me, I returned their gaze. Without exception they were brown, bushy-tailed, and remarkably unafraid – especially the one at my feet, still staring up at me. As he tilted his head and peered into my eyes, I wondered if animals did have the ability to pick up our feelings telepathically.

Two weeks ago, the segment of our news hour called *lifeSTYLES!* featured a psychic who claimed he could "read" the emotional intelligence of animals. According to him, animals were naturally tuned into people at the level of raw emotion and instinct. One of his examples was that dogs and horses tend to act up when a person feels afraid of them. Because of this theory of his, he had actually started a pilot project for rabbits to be brought into the children's wards of local hospitals. I, however, had squeezed my remote control in disgust and flipped over to check out CBC's five-part series on the legislature the moment he started complaining about lack of government funding for his new psychology clinic in which patients were to voice their troubles to the furry little pet of their choice. The incident had also prompted me to charge into our news director's office the next morning and complain loudly about mindless entertainment taking the place of intelligent news – more specifically, the mini-documentary on family violence I had produced that had been cut short to make way for the dubious Dr. Doolittle character.

But now this one marmot kept staring at me.

Staring.

He cocked his head to the left.

Could this little guy know what had just happened? Did he pick up on some universal animal distress wave I was probably beaming out? To experiment, I thought a little *thank you* at him for his concern and, lo and behold, he darted off the split second I directed the thought to him. Maybe there is an uneasiness when a little critter knows you know.

The belief I could silently communicate with the animal world was probably a sign of shock, but if I were in shock I should not have been. Turner had run out on me before, although never quite so dramatically or effectively.

The usual scenario was Turner simply not showing up after calling to say he was on his way over to my place. The first time it happened, I frantically phoned everyone I could think of and then sat up into the night by the police radio scanner I keep in my kitchen, listening intently for reports of traffic fatalities.

He always had a reason. Something came up. Someone needed his advice. Sometimes a song that had never worked until just that moment started to come and he simply lost himself in the recording studio. And *of course* I understood how he could get so carried away he would forget to phone. This was simply the drawback of dating an aspiring musician and – if I hung in there long enough – possibly a great one.

Other times his disappearances caused my humiliation and hurt to be seen in a more public light. The time, for example, he stranded me at the bar where his band usually played, leaving me with no idea what I had said or done wrong. After finishing the last set, Turner mingled past me, pointedly avoiding my gaze, smiled at some of the reporters I brought to the gig, and disappeared. After waiting long enough to learn that no, he was not in the back room talking to the sound guy about a level problem, I pretended to the others at the table that we had argued earlier and that I had told him, rather rudely, to leave me alone. Familiar with my rough-edged personality around the newsroom, no one there had any trouble believing me when I said I had better catch up with him and make my apologies.

But we had not argued. In fact, I had been looking forward to seeing him. Wrapped up in my purse was a chocolate guitar to celebrate our two-month anniversary of having found each other. Instead of celebrating together, I ended up in a phone booth a few blocks away from the club, realizing as I replaced the receiver that there was no point in ringing phones around the city. Wherever he was, he was not picking up and had no wish to be found this night. Turner had gone *incommunicado* once again.

What I would learn later was how depressed he had been, how sure he was the band had never been worse, and how that feeling had transformed itself into anger directed at me. After all, I was the insensitive lout who brought an entire news team to hear him play the sorry gig.

This fragile, creative being simply had to have time and understanding. Providing him with as much of both as I could was a responsibility I shouldered philosophically, thankful for the opportunity to break my usual routine of dating fellow television reporters who resented me when I broke a few too many lead stories, or who avoided me completely when I became a producer. Turner, on the other hand, when not stricken with bouts of creative *angst,* seemed to enjoy my successes as much as he relished my steady paycheque. At least, that is what was starting to become clear to me, as hurt and cynicism seeped into me like the numbing cold from the bench into my back and thighs.

Admittedly, there were signs our careful accommodation of separate interests had started to show further strain. Over the last few months I was less inclined to sit up and listen for traffic fatalities, more inclined to try to remember the name of the female singer most recently in his company. They were generally talentless young things, well-intentioned but sweetly malleable enough to believe in the grand future Turner laid out for them – if only they followed his lead in *every* way.

The situation was not at all what I *thought,* said Turner.

Said Turner repeatedly.

I chose to believe him. I had my reasons. Desire for him, desire for some romanticized idea of a relationship. On good days, ours truly was that rare TV-movie-style romance, the kind that overlooks any wrong since it is based on the *true love* that conquers any petty hurt, every disappointment. After all, the final scene of the movie always makes all previous betrayal worth the while. I knew it would get better.

Love is not blind; the desire for love is.

My new rule is that if a couple is in counselling together after dating for only three months, then the courtship is probably fatally flawed. Hindsight, right?

My fingers were losing their feeling. Down at the foot of the mountain, the season was definitely a very bearable early June; up here it was a bit more of a mild February. The sky was clear, but the air felt grey-cold and snow still filled some of the crevices between the boulders. I started to shiver, walked back inside, and lined up with my orange plastic tray for some coffee and a shrink-wrapped muffin of indeterminate age. I can only marvel at the focus of our brightest minds; preservatives seem to get more powerful all the time.

The coffee was as flavourful as it was hot. At least the lukewarm liquid did not pose any danger of burning my tongue and at that particular moment I was ready for the pleasantly benign. Probably good that it was so bad; I had given up caffeine three months earlier, and aside from this moment when I felt I deserved a coffee again if I felt like it, I had no desire to pick up my habit again.

For a second the wild idea occurred to me to pop all the pills in my purse, but what effect swallowing all five remaining birth control pills and two lint-covered aspirin might have had is still unclear to me.

There was nothing drastic in what I was going to do. Even atop Whistlers' Summit with all of Jasper to see me plummet, I felt no concern I was going to try to end it all. I did want to sleep though, to tuck my feet up under me in the chair, lean my head against the panorama-view window, and just sleep, with all the clatter and chatter of the tourist-jammed café muffling my thoughts. I took another sip of coffee and stared at my postcards.

I considered writing my sister and explaining what had happened, although for that I would certainly have needed an extra-large scenic. Instead, I thought about Turner and my life and the pointless direction it seemed to be heading. This was the third day of my holiday with Turner and, being Monday, my first away from work. Awaiting me back in Edmonton was a TV newsroom filled with bright, prying minds that would no doubt ask if Turner and I had set a date yet.

Not for the moment, no.

My timing has always been impeccable. An entire newsroom of genetically-created gossips had been none the wiser about our engagement. Had been. Until Friday just after six, when I leaked my good news to one of the friendlier editors and a makeup artist. *This just in.* By now, the word would have travelled not only through news – radio and TV – but right through the building and out past the sales department. It would, very possibly, be working its way across the country via our network's affiliates. And what had loosened my lips? No hard-nosed interviewing style. No pressure. No wheedling. Just hapless editor Ken Ridgway, a sweet balding man with a sincerely hopeful comb-over, and Peg, a woman with more mascara than common sense but with an honest gift for making people laugh. She also has a friendly smile that reminds me of my Mom some days and she, along with Ken, had the misfortune to wish me a good holiday.

They seemed to mean it.

I melted.

Such a sucker I am for anything resembling warmth after a day spent chasing the family of a guy charged with four counts of murder.

Why I hadn't simply nodded and responded with even a touch of my usual sarcasm before safely leaving the newsroom, I don't know. I only know that any random bursts of intimacy in my life have left me regretting them. This would be no exception.

This would also inject some added anxiety into my first day back at work. A place I have had a hard enough time facing lately.

In a way, Turner leaving me on the mountain did nothing but return me to exactly the same precipice I was poised upon when we first met. During my few short months in his company I was able to forget how staring into a TV had become like staring into the void, me feeling like an alien as I watched world affairs coloured by my distorted reflection bent across the screen.

Suddenly on my own again, staring out that mountaintop window smeared with children's fingerprints and my small, shadowy reflection, the feeling was back with greater intensity. There I was in the glass, short wisps of hair standing up at odds with each other, the curl mostly blown out of it, my eyes blurred smudges in a distorted, heart-shaped face, my narrow shoulders slumped. They'd been so sure and square once upon a time, when I was a kid. It made me sad to think of it.

Winded, I thought. *I'm winded.*

It wasn't the first time I'd thought that, either, staring at myself. For too long I had been wondering just what it was that made me feel so removed from the world, even while I spent all my time exploring that whole bloody world and reflecting it back into flickering TV screens. Supper-hour news and the difference it could make. The difference I made every time I sent a reporter off on another story or approved another script. Not to sound maudlin or maybe just a typical newsroom burnout case, but everything I did in the course of a day, or a ratings period for that matter, left me lost, although more incredulous than depressed. How I could be that busy, talk to as many people as I did in a day, or laugh as much as I tended to do around the newsroom, and still feel so pointless inside was an accomplishment I was quite proud of in many respects.

This holiday was supposed to give me some perspective and possibly a new start. The logic of this was straightforward. Maybe all I needed to do was to impress some big shots at one of the Vancouver stations and the malaise would miraculously disappear as I packed my bags and headed toward a new job. Turner and I had talked fairly often about a making a move. He was interested in the coast himself since session work for a good musician was supposed to be more plentiful there. Secretly I wondered if he also thought cocaine supplies would be more plentiful there, although as far as I could see he never had much of a problem obtaining supplies of it in Edmonton.

Turner's predilection for drugs was another little problem between us.

He had been pretty open at first about having been wired to coke "once upon a time." Past tense. But lately the past had been creeping up on him. That alone was a good enough reason for us to have ended things.

To have ended things. *For us* to have ended things.

I could already hear myself. How quickly it had become a mutual decision in my mind, how his daring escape from the relationship had transformed itself into a *for the best* discussion with hard feelings happily resolved.

I love the resiliency of the human animal.

The flexibility of memory.

The whole afternoon is still a bit of a blur to me, as if the first few hours "post Turner" did not register properly. I do remember going up for several refills of coffee. I remember a while later the girl from the till came and took my tray away with an odd look of annoyance. Her hair was light brown with strands falling out of her ponytail and, after she walked away from me, she whispered something through the order window to somebody in the kitchen. I got up at that point, thinking maybe I should order something else to placate the restaurant staff, and that was when I noticed the sunlight hitting the walls at a steeper angle, with a warmer tone to the sharp streaks – like someone had set orange gels on the lights. I had asked my cameraman for that exact effect on my last documentary shoot.

Peeling the plastic wrap from my sandwich seemed to lull me back into my previous numbness, because the next thing I remember was a tap on my shoulder.

"Excuse me."

My eyes realized they were staring out at snow on a distant peak and then turned to refocus upon a tall fellow in a soiled apron leaning over me. The girl from the till stood a few steps behind him wearing a sweater and holding a purse in front of her. She looked watchful. He smoothed his hand back over his black hair.

"It's the last gondola down. We're closing up."

This fact, undeniable now that I could see I was the lone tourist in the coffee shop and that a sliding partition barred my view to the souvenir counter, shocked me. I stood up clumsily, feeling as disoriented as I normally do on mornings when the radio alarm clock blasts the Bosnian situation into my head while I am still dreaming. Picking up my purse, an old favourite I held onto despite its broken clasp, I caught the strap on the side of the chair, sending it flying and spraying the contents of my purse all over the floor. Approximately four lipsticks rolled in as many directions, a dusty roll of throat candies smashed, my change purse flew open, pennies did rain from heaven, and the birth control pill case broke. "You Are in Bear Country" and other National Parks brochures fluttered around me.

"I'm sorry, I can't believe I did this."

I started frantically trying to pick up my things from the floor. The tall, aproned fellow handed me the birth control pill case, along with one of the pills that had fallen from it.

"Thanks," I said, as I looked up and slammed my head into the underside of the table. The whack of my head caused an instant flood to my eyes. I quickly looked down and tried to blink fast enough to guide my hands to a lipstick and hairbrush behind one of the chair legs.

The whole cleanup did not take long. Apron Boy kept handing me various items diligently and even Till Girl set down her purse and picked up some of the change. I nodded a thank you in her direction, but avoided his glance. He had a sympathetic expression that I could already feel too keenly and I was still having to blink an inordinate amount.

We climbed into the gondola along with a few other staff members who appeared from the kitchen. I turned to face the window and watched trees disappear above me as we descended along the face of the mountain. After we bumped past the first tower, I could not blink fast enough anymore and tasted salt the whole, long ride down. Far off, I could see the gondola's small moving shadow darkening the treetops, the only proof I could find that any of this day was real.

Nodding was still my only means of communication by the time we reached the bottom and the door opened to the solid ground of the real world. I stepped out into the smell of oil and the sound of giant gears hauling cable, and walked through the turnstile to the parking lot.

It was there. One ten-year-old grey car complete with last month's dent. The asphalt felt strangely hard as I walked and seemed to hit my feet too soon with each step, as if it were rising up under me. *At least the car's there,* I kept repeating to myself, mantra-like, hoping the words themselves could somehow return me to normalcy. Not that I really thought Turner would have taken it, but then again, I had seen him do some strange things in the few short months we had seen each other. I guess I had the keys anyway, so he would not have had a choice.

The keys.

I checked my purse but, sure enough, no keys. Surely this could not be happening. My head felt thick and I hit that wall where you feel you cannot take one more thing happening to you and you do not know how to cope anymore and there are no tears left to cry and you just want to lie down right there and wait for someone to gather you up and wave away the world. Except there is no one to come and wave it away. There is never anything to do but simply continue plodding along.

I had hit this wall before, once with special force when I was exhausted after a disastrous day at work, with a headache from not eating, and I realized in the express line of the grocery store that I had left my wallet and key card for work on my desk. No cash, no credit card, no bank machine card, and nothing at home but crackers and one packet of instant soup-in-a-cup. But even my head that day could not compare with how I felt in the shadowy parking lot with my smug locked car and the mountain looming up before me.

"Are you okay?"

Apron Boy was back. I was standing, leaning against the car, with my purse at my feet.

"I'm not sure."

The skin under my eyes felt tight from the dried salt

of tears. But the tears had dried, at least. That was something. Time to crack a joke, regain myself. Or maybe simply say a few words without fear of utter dissolution.

"It's just not my day, I don't think. I can definitely say I've had better holidays. Next time I'll go travel agency."

I thought I sounded quite sardonic, David-Letterman-in-trouble.

Apron Boy looked truly concerned.

"Is there something I can do?"

He was not actually wearing the apron any more and his short-sleeved T-shirt revealed a dark-skinned, lean frame. His hair, no longer tied back, was long and curly. A small duffel-style bag was slung over a sharply angular shoulder.

If I hadn't felt so lousy, I would have forced an audible chuckle at what was happening.

Apron Boy is trying to save me. You didn't think of that, did you, Turner? Did you, Evil Minstrel Man?

"Is something wrong?"

I needed a cartoon bubble caption over my head to explain, since once again I could not talk, once again my eyes were brimming.

"My name is Indrin. I'm the guy from the coffee shop. The short-order cook up there?" He waited. I nodded, trying to hold my eyes in a calm and neutral expression, yet wide open since blinking would have sent the tears running again.

"We couldn't help but notice you were in there for a long time today. Has something happened?"

"My keys." I gave up and blinked. Two rolling tears

betrayed the falsity of my previous attempt at Letterman cool.

"They fell out up there. They must have. They're not in here."

I poked at my purse with my foot.

"O-kay."

He took on the air of a reporter who has just been told by a stricken-looking cameraman that the tape ended moments before the Queen went by.

"That is a problem."

"Is there any way of getting back in there?"

He shook his head.

"It won't be open until tomorrow morning."

I thought about this. Hitting the wall had never been so forceful, so utterly devastating.

"I'm not sure what to do."

Indrin's expression brightened. "I have a friend's car today. I can give you a lift to town. Where are you staying?"

All I could think of was the tent neatly packed in the car, the sleeping bags folded together in the back seat, and the meat in the cooler. Tonight we had planned to barbecue.

"Nowhere."

Indrin looked puzzled, but I did not have it in me to explain.

"I have a credit card. You can drop me any place."

I settled into the torn seat of a slightly beat-up orange Volvo. The radio blared a scratchy riff of grunge when he turned the ignition. My cringing at the sound caused him to shut off the radio, so we drove into town in relative silence, except for Indrin's diligent efforts to begin a conversation.

"So, where are you from?"

That I could answer.

"Edmonton."

"Do you mind me asking what happened up there?"

That I could not.

"I don't really want to talk about it."

"No problem. Was that your first time up Whistlers' Summit?"

He would brightly voice a question; I would mumble a one-word answer. Although it felt like I was making an effort, I knew I had become the quintessential lousy interviewee. Maybe I will have more patience the next time I want to deem some accident victim "a lousy talker" because of an inability to describe the demise of friends and family in lively Technicolor clips.

I spent that night at a hotel, after Indrin took me to buy a toothbrush. I ate at a Greek restaurant and had their lemon-roasted potatoes with oregano and decided it was not true you lose your sense perception when you are in shock. Another *factoid* from another poorly-researched TV news item proven wrong. The food tasted good to me; eating it felt wholesome and comforting. Somehow it felt strangely normal to chew, like I had forgotten what it felt like to be human. Mashing up the food in my mouth reminded me what *normal* would feel like when I got there again.

In the morning Indrin came to pick me up so I could check the café before it opened to the public. When we got to the foot of the mountain, I stared at the gondola lift, the long ride up, the distant peak, then asked if Indrin could just send the keys down by themselves in one of the gondolas. When he paused before he spoke I realized I was probably going too far and I should be able to walk up there if I had to and get them myself and stare at the fateful mountaintop with no regrets. I was just about to tell him to forget it and that of course I would go up myself, but before I could, he said it was no problem. He would send the keys down.

I thanked him, and as he sailed up in the gondola, I waved goodbye and felt I had lost my best friend, or had just seen my mother swallowed up by the West Edmonton Mall, leaving me behind, too small to see over the crowd and know which way she turned.

Watching the car clinging to the cable, carrying him far above me, I started thinking about how precarious all of life is, how the links to anything resembling sanity are sometimes so tenuous and you better just hope your cable is strong and there are no electrical storms or terrorists wreaking havoc. What was the movie I had seen about the gondola lift disaster? I could only remember vague images of someone clinging to the outside of one of those things. Was it an accident? Or part of some villain's malicious master plan? Probably just a facile plot twist in another of the lousy late-night movies I watch when I am too tired to get up to go to bed.

Quality has never made a difference to my television viewing habits; never has it mattered to me what the program is, only that something is flickering there on my top-of-the-line Sony box. A television junkie? I admit it. It is not a problem if you can admit it, or so goes the conventional self-help wisdom. Besides, television is my industry and therefore watching it is surely a form of professional development. Most importantly, watching TV takes far less energy than figuring out the baffling world of human relationships.

While I stood by the Jasper Tram entryway, the first eager tourists of the day – a jumping boy, a sleepy-looking girl, and parents sniping at each other – approached the ticket counter and pushed me into retreat. Not knowing just how long it was going to take Indrin to get to the top and to search the floor, I asked the lift attendant if he could please keep an eye out for keys on the seat of one of the cars coming down. His "Sure, lady," had a distinctly patronizing tone to it, but I have long since given up worrying about who thinks I am crazy or at least disturbed, so I did not explain.

Instead I nodded and walked out to look at the interpretive signs and learn handy, little-known facts about gondola safety and cable thickness. Spotting a nearby bench with a view of the summit, I strolled over, sat down, and sent a mental greeting to my marmot friend.

Hello. I hope you scrounge lots of food today. I'm lost – how are you?

I wondered if he were darting away somewhere now, annoyed I was accessing the animal radio band.

I was back at the interpretive signs when Indrin came up behind me.

"They were there," he announced, handing me the keys.

His presence was a surprising relief.

"Thanks. Thanks a lot."

"I hope you have a better day today."

"So do I."

I tried out a smile. This Indrin fellow had been extraordinarily kind at a crucial time, reminding me the world is filled with more than deadbeat boyfriends and disappointments aplenty. My sister is forever telling me not to let TV news crime stories destroy my faith in humanity. "What faith?" is the retort that never fails to annoy her. She would be pleased to see Indrin had tipped the scales for me this day, and I was grateful myself.

"I really appreciate your help."

"Listen, I wonder if you want to chat later or something. If you'll still be in town."

I was surprised he had used the word "chat" in a sentence directed at me. I had been more silent around him than probably any other time in my life and we certainly could not be said to have actually had a conversation. As for whether I would still be in town later, it was something I honestly had not considered.

"I'm not sure."

The idea did have some appeal, although the thought crossed my mind I had better make sure this was not a romantic overture.

"If this is a date, I don't think I'm up to it."

"No, that's cool. I just thought you might want to talk later."

We agreed to meet at the Greek restaurant when he was off shift, and as I unlocked the car door and threw Turner's sunglasses into the back seat, I realized I was truly looking forward to meeting Indrin later. To talking to someone, anyone – especially to someone I didn't know. In my hotel room the night before, I had considered phoning my sister, but decided against it. My wounds did not feel ready for exposure, especially under the bright glare of her common sense. The bandages would remain tightly wrapped around my feelings for a good while longer. A stranger could offer temporary company, a conversation, yet pose no threat to me. There would be no risk of him painfully peeling away the protective layers encircling my heart.

Indrin loped off to the gondola lift. With some coaxing of my clutch, my car nudged into gear and lurched out of the parking lot. Time for a visit to the tourist bureau, I thought. And why not? I did not need a fiancé to breathe in the cool spray of a mountain stream, to watch baby mountain goats licking salt off the asphalt on the edge of the highway, or to watch men with more testosterone than grey matter telling their kids to stand back as they strolled, Camcorders poised, toward incredulous grizzly bears. I drove off determined to occupy myself fully in the long day that stretched ahead, to stop at every roadside lookout, to gaze at every peak, maybe to finally learn their names. Where was my camera? My map?

I would have my holiday regardless of Turner and our previous plans.

Regardless.

∽ ∽

Mount Edith Cavell. As I wrote the words I wondered whether my handwriting had completely reverted to illegibility. *Mount* came out a bit like *Marmot, Edith* looked disconcertingly like *Edible,* and *Cavell* like *Whole.* Since the postcard I was writing featured a close-up shot of a marmot, my notation was all the more confusing.

Without my laptop computer, which was sitting back at work in my desk drawer, I found my writing hampered – and not just by poor penmanship either. The first postcard I had written came out as a news lead:

Announcer intro:	Stranded atop a mountain, a graduate of the school of hard knocks is pummelled again. With one fiancé gone from her life and headed back to the bar, this lone tourist forges on to enjoy her holidays regardless. Our own Miranda Tyler has the story…

Take tape sound up ....(sound on tape)
runs: a lifetime
ends: "Miranda Tyler,
NewsWatch, Jasper"

At first I thought it was humourous enough to send off for the entire newsroom to read on the bulletin board, but I decided against it. Somehow my bravado always betrays too much. I crumpled the card, a shame since it was one of the better scenics, and proceeded with the marmot card.

A list of the day's sights and activities, I decided,

would prove a more neutral postcard message. *Mount Edith Cavell – inspiring; Athabasca Falls – electrifying; the interior of the Alberta Rose Café – vinyl; the interior of George's Garage – expensive.* Figuring that was all I had the energy to explain, I left out the full description of the latter part of my day. No room on the postcard to describe the painfully slow drive along the shoulder of the highway through the picturesque Rockies, my locked emergency brake screeching a serenade all the while. For some reason, it refused to release after my stop at Athabasca Falls. No, the short form message was enough, especially considering the only person I could think of to send the postcard to was myself. It could be a kind of sick reminder of the beginning of my holiday, something to stick up on my fridge with a SMILE! magnet, something to say, *You think you're having a bad day? Just remember this day, honey, and you'll quit complaining.*

Without a stamp, I decided to hold off on sending myself the card. Besides, I didn't need any postcard to remind myself of this particular holiday. I never would.

Stuffing the unaddressed marmot card into my purse, I got up to pour myself another coffee from the grimy pot by the garage's till. The clock on the wall overhead featured a different model of car marking every hour: only two more sedans and one convertible until my dinner date.

∽ ∽

I TOOK ANOTHER BITE of cold potatoes and washed it down with a sip of wine. We had now talked long enough for me to know his full name was Indrin Rajiv Krishnayya, his family was one generation from India, and he was twenty-three years old. What he knew about me was my full name, Miranda Rosalind Tyler; my job, TV news producer on the current affairs beat; my prairie city upbringing, Moose Jaw, and my marital status, single. Especially lately.

He was only slightly surprised to learn I was thirty-three, but apparently I had not needed to worry about romantic overtures. Indrin planned to enter a seminary in Toronto at the end of the summer. A strange choice, as far as I'm concerned, in this day and age, but stranger still about his desire to become a Catholic priest is the fact of his United Church upbringing – baffling to me until he explained his parents were from a predominantly Christian area in southern India and had only turned their back on the Catholic Church sometime in the late 1960s.

Indrin surprised them both when he converted to Catholicism two years ago. His mother was supportive if puzzled, but his father in particular did not understand Indrin's calling. Waving his hand around in mock irritation, Indrin did a lively imitation for me of the way his father talked about his calling, as if he could brush away "Indrin's damnable determination to follow that pope."

Work being my religion, I decided to tell Indrin a bit about life in the newsroom, which, even when overwhelmingly frustrating to live and work in, always makes for exciting stories.

"When the tornado hit in 1987...."

"The time my cameraman nearly killed himself shooting a forest fire...."

"The time my Chinese soundman, on his first Canadian back country shoot, was fooled into thinking the marmots he had never seen before were 'Mar-*mohs,* large and ferocious creatures lurking in the woods, far more deadly than any grizzly....'"

We opened another bottle of wine. For his young years, this fellow had an amazing knowledge of good vintages. This gave away his upbringing in oil-rich Calgary. As for me, even now, if the bottle doesn't have a picture of a duck or a plastic cat or bull on it, I probably haven't tried it. Such was my heritage growing up in the have-not province of Saskatchewan.

We stayed talking until close to 2 a.m. when Napoleon, the restaurant owner, hauled his belly out from under the table top, pushed his chair firmly away from the argument he was having with another heavy-bellied man, and asked if there was anything else we wanted. There was no more coffee, but he *could* put on a new pot.

His message was clear.

Indrin walked me to my hotel. The sidewalk was wet, so it must have rained while we were inside. I could hear a train whistle cut through the trees and it made me feel lonely, reminding me of a night I had lain in bed at my grandparents' farmhouse listening to trains. I was quite small, the attic room felt unfamiliar, and my clothes on the chair looked like an animal in the darkness. I tried to remember why I was alone there that night, but it took me almost to the hotel before it came to me, that was the night my sister was born.

We got to the lobby door, Indrin said goodbye, and when he leaned forward to give me a kiss on the cheek, I started crying and could not stop even after he walked me upstairs, sat me down opposite him, and held my hand for the longest time.

~ ~

THAT WAS HOW I MET INDRIN. We have known each other for just over three days now, although in that way of rare friends it seems much longer. We have not spoken of my tears that night and I have told him nothing about Turner save for the fact he ran out on me, so the protective layers around my heart are still intact. Somehow, though, Indrin's thoughtful gaze seems to beat its way through all of that, the way hot summer sun beats through fabric to warm your skin. His presence feels comforting to me.

Yesterday, I spent a full day roaming the relatively few streets of Jasper while George of George's Garage waited for a part to come in. He got my emergency brake to release the day before when I first showed up at his garage, but as soon as I got in to drive away, my wheels locked again and nothing could budge them. My hand had not so much as touched the emergency brake, I assured the mechanic, who ran back out when he heard my car screech again. The brake was simply holding on relentlessly. George shook his head and clucked, giving me to believe I was in for an unbelievable bill, but it turned out I needed only one reasonably-priced brake cable. A cable that would let go when it was supposed to instead of acting possessed of a bizarre will to hang on tight. A cable, however, that his garage did not happen to have in stock. That meant I was given the treat of spending one more day in Jasper, albeit without wheels to take me exploring.

Instead, I roamed the town and browsed in shops brimming with Mountie souvenirs, handmade Cowichan sweaters, and an assortment of other Canadiana made in southeast Asia. I even walked over to dabble my feet in the icy cold of the sparkling Athabasca River. All of this I did and did again since I had more than a few hours to kill before my car would be ready and before Indrin was off work. We met again for dinner, which this time was followed by flaming Sambucas, compliments of Napoleon, the restaurant owner, who was in a far better mood than the previous night.

Yesterday, then, felt more like a holiday than the day before, more like a purely relaxing, carefree day – as long as I did not stop to remind myself that I was there, supposedly relaxing, only because of one willfully troublesome car. Not to mention the one troublesome, unwilling fiancé who started this detour in the first place.

But if yesterday was a holiday, it was also the beginning of a trek into the unknown. I feel odd and unsettled, as if my body has been exchanged for a new one, a model I'm not used to yet. The air feels fresh and sharp in my nostrils, and I can't believe I never noticed before how strongly scented the world is: pine needles and sap and even the leather of my purse. I think this all has something to do with taking a step into Indrin's strange version of reality.

I'm not sure if I can get back into mine.

I'm not sure I want to.

The plan was to camp on my own for at least one night anyway – to hell with Turner. But, of course, after wasting the day away as a pedestrian tourist, and after catching the late-night bite at the Greek place with Indrin, it was dark before I had even gone to find a campsite. Indrin insisted on following me out in his friend's Volvo to help set up my tent and to make sure I got settled in safely.

We were just turning onto the main highway when I saw something small by the side of the road, half on the shoulder. I couldn't tell what it was, but it was alive and definitely still moving. We pulled over and Indrin ran ahead of me, then stopped and waved for me to stay put. But I could see as plainly as he could, in the blast of headlights, a rabbit with its hind legs crushed trying to pull itself along the pavement.

It was moving steadily forward, with all its strength, even while it had to be dying. The determination in its movements was human only in the most heroic sense, a pure, instinctive grasping toward life, however agonizing the effort. There was nothing for it to do but keep moving, and so it did. It was still alive, and so it kept on living.

There is a kind of helpless panic that makes your body move and your mind race even though neither has any place to go. My feet were stepping from side to side, turning me around, taking me nowhere. I closed my eyes and turned my back when Indrin reached the animal.

When he came out of the woods, his hands were glistening. I poured water over them from the jug in my trunk and then stood by the car while he vomited in the ditch. When he came back, we stood by the car for a long time, saying nothing.

I put my hand on his back, look up at the sky and see the northern lights, greener than I have ever seen them. My hand rests on his thin shoulder blades, damp with perspiration, while he stands with his head down, his hands leaning on the warm hood of my car.

Some moments are different from any others in life. They are moments when time stops and you know who you are and what you feel and nothing else matters or even exists.

I can feel his breathing start to slow down. His body feels fragile to me. I feel him beside me and I feel a surprising and powerful surge of love. The feeling radiates out of me, covers us both like a blanket. I feel my hand on his shoulder blades.

Those moments are what I now call *real life* moments. Moments that do not exist in time as we know it on a clock or calendar. They are moments that transcend time and will always be in the present. For some reason they never completely fade into a memory spoken about in the past tense, but stay alive in a person's heart – newly happening each time they are thought of.

My hand rests on his back. The tenderness I feel concentrates itself in my fingertips. I feel only affection here. The sky dances above us, washes away pain.

One small animal – with all its instinct, all its pain, and all its strength – became the whole universe there under the northern lights. The silent connection it created between Indrin and me was still unbroken even after the mundane task of setting up the tent. Indrin crawled inside to roll out my sleeping bag for me. I watched him moving gently, deliberately, untying the knotted strings, then I walked to the car, grabbed the other bag and handed it to him in the tent.

We fell asleep almost immediately, me feeling his hair fall against my forehead and eyelids just as my mind drifted out of consciousness.

~ ~

MY BARE FEET push their way into gritty running shoes. As I start unzipping the damp tent flap to let myself out, I fumble for my jacket. Slowly, the tent zipper reveals the day, the pale blue sky, the trees, the gravelly earth I step out onto. Against the first light in the sky, I can see my breath. It is not really that cold, just humid. The tent is dripping with dew.

I'm turned around, zipping the tent shut again, when I hear Indrin's calm voice.

"Do you want coffee?"

Indrin asks this already extending me a full steaming mug.

"Thanks."

I sip.

"I can't believe you've got a fire going already. I didn't even hear you get up."

The fire crackles and I can hear the man in the campsite across from us firing up his propane stove. Birds chirp and a little girl's shout carries over the fir trees. We are all of us dwarfed by the mountains thrusting up around us, stretching into the blue overhead, all of us couched among the trees, small, respectful, treading soft as deer.

Indrin pulls his sleeves down over his fingers as he walks toward the picnic table, stops to pick up my torn dishrag from the top of the cooler, and wipes the dew off the bench. He sits down across from me. I am struck by the familiarity in all this, the contentment of this quiet morning moment, the true affection I feel for this boy with the sympathetic eyes. A sharp bird's squawk sends his gaze up toward the treetops, where it lingers now on the sky. His lean Indian looks give him the ascetic air of a Himalayan guru. I imagine him in white robes, sitting cross-legged on the picnic table, entertaining questions from me, John Lennon, and the rest of the Beatles, while sharing a smile with a few bony-kneed Tibetan monks. The mental picture tells me I listen to too much stuff from the sixties, that I should really move on from Donovan one of these days.

Mellow yellow. That is exactly how the morning sun feels at this hour.

"Do you have eggs?" he asks me.

Back from the Himalayas now, I refocus on Indrin. He is no longer the guru, but the short-order cook I met on the mountain, the altar boy.

"Do you have eggs?" he repeats.

"Yeah, we packed them in the...."

We? Turner packed them.

"...Um. In the thing."

I wave my hand until the word comes to me.

"They should be in the cooler."

I take another sip of hot coffee and look up at the pale sky, the tall firs, this hippy-haired being beside me rooting through the food box.

"Here they are. And you've got cheese and tomatoes. Should we make omelettes?"

"Sure."

I open the dew-covered cutlery bag and find a knife to slice cheese. Suddenly feeling a need to mark this morning with proper ceremony, I set the knife down and raise my speckled enamel mug.

"A toast to Turner for the breakfast food."

Indrin turns his attention from poking the fire and looks up at me. I bow.

"A toast to you on this fine morning. Thank you for the truly fine coffee. Here's to the omelette."

"Cheers."

He smiles.

Some people just exude a calm, no matter what the situation. No matter how unsettling or bizarre or frightening the circumstances, their expression alone can make you feel relaxed. As in *This grizzly may indeed be charging us, which is strange considering we're in a little alternative nightclub in Calgary, but I think if we just buy him a drink or change tables everything should be fine.*

A few calm words from them along with a reassuring smile is really all you need to find yourself naturally accepting any situation. Indrin had that ability with me.

This is just a camping trip. We are just making breakfast.

"When are you going to leave for work?" I ask him.

It still feels early, but newsroom deadlines and the constant presence of wall clocks have removed any instinctive ability I might once have had to tell time without a watch. And mine is still in the tent.

"We should talk about that."

A red glowing log falls over, sending sparks flying and Indrin jumping back, holding the hair back from his face.

"To be honest, I think I've quit."

"You think?"

"Well, I guess I have."

He comes back over to sit at the picnic table with me and tells me about his resignation, yesterday, from the short-order cook *biz,* how he took his last gondola ride down the mountain at the end of his shift and folded his last paycheque into his jean jacket pocket. He meant to tell me yesterday, but hadn't quite got around to it before we left for the campground. Then after what happened, well, he'd decided to wait for a better time to talk. But he was done work, permanently off shift.

"Free as a bird. And if you want a fellow traveller, I travel light and I make good omelettes."

He pauses before his big sell.

"I even have a camera strap that says *Kodak – Disneyworld* on it."

"Oh my God, I'm a tour guide."

I crunch a few coffee grounds between my teeth.

"I should have chartered a bus. Printed up an ad in the paper. *Wonderland Cave Tour to Montana. Passion Play Tour of the Western States and Canada. Blue Rinse X-press Bus.*"

He wants to travel with me. To hop in the car and go. Just go.

Go west, young man. Into the wild, wild West.

This type of thing works better in the United States, where stories seem to abound about people throwing a couple of bags into a car and heading off to the Grand Canyon, or Las Vegas, or somewhere else dusty and dry and frontier-ish, New Mexico perhaps.

I have seen more than a few road movies so I realize I really should have a beat-up convertible and a charmingly cynical Susan Sarandon attitude or an ingenuous Geena Davis smile. The latter I could never even pretend, but I am definitely not short on the cynicism, although I would never claim it is one of my more charming qualities. Certainly I do have the most important quality required for living out a road movie: an innate recognition of *point of no return* scenarios. Sometimes you truly do get to a point when you see there is no turning back and, much as I might want to decide this has all been a dream and wake up tomorrow beside Turner in time for a caffeine-charged story meeting and a good row over lead story choices, I think I'm there.

No turning back.

So, while I might not fit the Thelma and Louise

mould exactly, the analogy is working for me. As far as I can figure, my life has already been run off a cliff, and when you are free-falling there is no point in doing much besides watching the world go by and breathing in the cool, fresh smell of the rushing air. Dizzying, but really the only choice.

"What do you think?"

He is smiling, but I can see the earnestness in his eyes. This is the first time I realize how much I could hurt him. An uncomfortable thought.

I consciously fill my lungs, hold on to the air for a moment. As a kid I used to think I could stop time that way. That was before I found out the very act of thinking about time changes it, but never the way you want. It makes it longer. Or shorter. When it comes to time, whatever you hope for produces the opposite effect. Now I try not to think about time, except when I am timing scripts at work. I have actually befriended time, wear the best of watches and check it regularly to make sure I am in step with what it tells me. I have no illusions about who the master is; understanding this reduces conflict.

The morning air is suddenly too quiet. When I exhale, it comes out too loud, too exasperated, too like a sigh.

"I don't even know where I'm going."

I had been thinking yesterday about just going back to work and saving all my annual leave and overtime days for another time. Some winter holiday to an island where I could play chicken with melanoma and watch skinny women being handed drinks by businessmen with paunches hanging over their Speedos. Or maybe a trip next month to Halifax to visit a fellow producer friend so I could drown my sorrows in true British pub style.

The resignation thing is making me feel uncomfortable, slightly panicky.

"I'm not sure what to say here. Don't you have to save money for the fall?"

"I'll be okay."

I'm staring into my mug. Indrin is waiting. Silence is not new to us – in our short friendship it has become a theme – but it is now hanging over us with a weight I have not felt before.

The air is rushing past me. I do not know where I am falling from or plummeting to. I just know I'm falling and floating all at the same time, pulled by a force of gravity that wavers in intensity. Fast or slow? I cannot even tell how quickly I'm falling because all familiar markers have disappeared. Alice in the rabbit hole. But am I off to Wonderland or straight to hell? *Hell* being my new term for all relationships with the opposite sex.

Or maybe this is pure fear blowing in my face, whistling in my ears. Fear of roads I have not yet travelled and an even greater terror of turning back on the ones I have already covered. Suddenly I want to be busy, on the phone – maybe two phones at once – while listening to the police scanner, checking a script, arguing with a reporter and sending a cameraman out on a late-breaking story. I want to fill my head with so many sounds and so many decisions I do not have to think about anything remotely real, like how a heart can implode or why loneliness is the most dangerous of all feelings. I am the small figure in a painting of fog I saw once, closed in upon, surrounded and baffled by something I cannot even touch.

I am falling and his face is still looking at me.

"I have to make a phone call."

He nods.

My feet crunch along the gravel as I walk back to the park information sign where I saw the pay phone. While I dial Turner's number, I need to keep clearing my throat. I test out tones of voice.

"Hello. Hi. Hello."

I get his machine and hang up.

I check for messages on my machine and yes, he did. The bastard actually left me a message.

"Miranda...."

His voice sounds tentative. I swallow hard.

"...I don't know what the fuck to say. I don't know why I freaked out. It was just getting so family holiday and you know how that gets to me. All we needed was a six-seater van, a baby, and a dog. You know what I mean? I couldn't handle it. I mean I thought I could do it, I really did.... Fuck it. You're the one, you know. You really are. When you're back, if you're still talking to me, give me a call. I'm going to play Jerry's gig at the Track after all, so I'll be there tonight through Sunday. So maybe see you, okay, Randi? And if not...well...I know we can work this out. I've just got to get my head together. You know that. I'm sorry, all right, sweetie? Bye now."

Sweetie?

On my way back to the campsite I stop to pump

some water and splash it on my face. The icy water shocks my skin, feels good as it dries.

So Turner figures I will just run back to town and breathlessly phone him. Then I'll hang out at the back of the bar as a starry-eyed audience member just like before. He will apologize for the next week or so, and we will head right back into whatever it was that was normal for us. For awhile I will be tucked back into the dizzying place at the centre of his universe, being adored and needed and revolved around. And, as he tries to make me forget this most recent debacle, the making up will be as sweet as the lovemaking ever was. For too long I'll let myself believe that's the *real* Turner. And then when the other Turner reappears, I'll just go back to believing it doesn't get any better anyway, not really, and that all relationships are more painful than anyone lets on.

Most of the campers are up now. Some are gathered around picnic tables, one couple is already doing dishes. A dog barks at me as I pass one of those silver, lipstick-tube-type camper trailers and it feels like his short, gruff blasts wake me up from a dream. One little girl stands looking very grown-up as she holds a potholder out to her father cooking up their breakfast. I smell smoke on my jacket and in my hair. All of this is real. The cool morning air, the sound of the jet high overhead, Indrin, now visible through the trees, sitting down to his omelette.

I am trying to remember if anything felt this real in the six and a half months I spent with Turner. There had been drama aplenty, sometimes right out of a B-movie if Turner was in a post-coke paranoid state. There had been hilarity and passion and frustration and anger, but, at least as I am remembering it right now, it had never felt like real life. These last three days, the strangest seventy-two hours I have ever wandered through, *they're* real?

Indrin looks up, finishes munching a mouthful.

"Hi."

"Hi, fellow traveller," I say, trying to sound casual as I sit back down at the picnic table.

He smiles.

"Thanks. I figured, you know, that it might be okay with you."

"Oh, you did, did you?"

Who is this strange person?

"I think I'm heading west." My words sound cautionary, maybe even more like a challenge.

"That's cool. I dreamed about dolphins last night."

"I don't remember dreaming anything."

I take a bite of omelette, a swig of cold coffee. No, I did not dream last night, but I usually do. I dream about tidal waves. Huge walls of water that sweep across everything. Sometimes I am swept away, sometimes they just wash on over me while I breathe in the water. They are always unbelievably real.

The sun tops the fir trees and blasts my face with light. *Real life.* If it were about to hit me in the face, I was in for a hell of a blow. I have been free-falling now for much longer than I realized. Falling and floating, dropping from the sky and being buoyed up, sometimes by illusions, this time, I hope, by something real.

Free Fall

The sky is clear; every peak of every mountain is sharply etched against the blue. Snow-capped, the peaks gleam in the sun, tower over rock faces that change from green to brown to purple in the light. Trees rush past me as I lean my head out the car window and breathe in the fresh scent of cedar.

"I want to leave him a message. I'm serious."

I turn back to Indrin to hear what he is saying. My head aches from the wind in my ears.

"Let's stop and I'll leave him a message."

Indrin is driving now and I am discovering that putting him behind the wheel unleashes a fast-flowing imagination. He has written two poems, one semi-rap song, and now he wants to phone Turner.

"What on earth would you say?"

"I don't know. I think the words would come to me."

"Are priests allowed to swear?"

"I'm not a priest yet."

With his hair flying out the window, my flowered sunglasses on his rich brown face, and his open mouth laughing, he certainly does not look like any priest I have ever seen. I picture him as Pope and can hardly wait for the Church foundations to shake. Vatican City, are you ready for this?

"I think I should just say something simple, something intriguing…something that will make him wonder if he ever knew you."

I am starting to enjoy this idea.

"'Hello, is this Turner Mahoney? I would like to tell you that Miranda won't be suing you for paternity after all. She just remembered how she found something better to do one weekend when you were in a back room of the studio destroying your nasal passages.'"

"That I don't think he'd believe. How about, 'Turner, this is Dr. Porter speaking. I feel it necessary to inform you that we believe you may be under some risk of suffering from – name an illness –'"

"AIDS," Indrin suggests.

"Not funny."

"There are funny illnesses?"

He considers this for a moment.

"Gout," he offers.

"Gout? Since when is that funny? Okay, okay – 'from gout… Miranda never found herself able to tell you.'" I stop. "Listen, Indrin, I don't know about the gout."

"It needs to be funny and contagious, doesn't it?"

Indrin is shouting; the wind has changed and the roar from his window is now louder than before.

"'Turner…'" Indrin pauses to roll up the window. "This I think I'll do in a very sophisticated British accent. Ahem… 'I'm sorry for you, Turner old chap. You're missing a super camping trip. The weather is brilliant, the food you packed is delicious, and the company delightful. I really *cahn't* understand why you'd choose to pass it up. My gain really.'"

"Very good. But I'm still glad we haven't hit a phone booth, I must say."

It feels good just to be silly, just to hear the sound of our own voices talking above the roar of the rushing wind.

~ ~

"There. Can't you hear it?"

I stop and listen again more carefully, train my ears.

"No, I can't. All I hear are diesel engines."

Indrin and I walk through a small parking lot lined with majestic fir trees. The ground beneath them is carpeted with dry, rust-coloured pine needles. A big black crow, larger than Turner's cat, Meow, ever was even at his heaviest, stands proudly in the centre of the parking lot, unperturbed by trunks opening and slamming shut, kids running, tour buses unloading, and a person who from the back looks like a sumo wrestler, but turns out to be a very heavy woman in skin-tight black bicycle shorts bent over to reorganize her suitcase. The crow surveys her, as well as Indrin and me, before stepping jerkily aside to let us pass.

Somewhere just down the path are the Athabasca Falls, but they are still impossible to hear above the tour buses. We proceed down the path, my camera bumping against my stomach with every step, and stop to watch a man waving as he works his way to the edge of the falls. He lifts his leg, pretends to slip.

"Oh, that's truly hilarious, isn't it? What an idiot."

I decide I need a bigger audience than Indrin alone. I turn to the silent woman beside me with toddler in tow and tell her about the story I covered several years ago, about the tourist who fell from exactly that spot but whose body could not be fished out until the following spring. The diver I interviewed said the watch on the corpse was still ticking. My cameraman and I laughed about that, I told her, until the diver started describing how they had to smear Vicks VapoRub in their nostrils so they would not get sick at the smell of the decomposing body.

"You'd have to be nuts to climb out there," I shout over the now-roaring sound of the falls to pronounce my story concluded.

"That's my husband," she says.

"Oh my God, I'm sorry."

"No, that's okay," she says, picking up her little boy and turning away.

"Actually, he looks closer to the edge than he likely is," contributes Indrin. "I think he's being pretty careful."

But the woman is not listening to Indrin, she is heading back to the parking lot, her back both to us and to her death-defying husband, and I can almost hear the conversation they will have later as their car pulls back onto the highway.

"Just shut me up, Indrin, if I start running off at the mouth like that again. Okay?"

"Well, you didn't know it was her husband."

We stand, leaning against the concrete railing above the falls and breathing cool mist. The moist air brings a softness to the deepest part of my lungs. I feel muscles in my neck and inside my chest slowly relax; I hadn't even realized they were clenched.

As I feel each breath expand inside me, I pretend I am a part of the shallow, rushing river. My eyes lock onto one ripple in the water and follow it along as it splashes over rocks, rounds the bend, then plummets suddenly into the craggy, cavernous rock world just beneath our feet. I do this again and again, watching how the speed of the water changes depending how I focus my eyes. When they are open wide and are focussed generally on the dramatic scene before me, the water is a foaming wall of white, blue, and sparkling silver. The water is nothing but pure motion, landing the instant it falls and falling again in the same moment. When my eyes play this game, I start to feel overwhelmed with sadness. Instead of water I see one clear, crashing metaphor for life rushing past without me understanding where I am or where I am going.

But when I vigourously train my eyes on one rock and wait for a large splash to follow with my eyes, the clear spray of droplets becomes a slow-motion film. I can see exactly where the arc of sparkling water flies and exactly where it lands before it is swept away again, and I feel comforted.

Indrin is watching intently too and I almost ask him if he notices how the falls change in this way but I stop myself. I also almost reach for my camera, to catch Indrin forever in a freeze-frame against the spray of white, but I realize this picture is already captured in my mind and nothing on film could ever do it justice.

A crow squawks, someone a few feet away yells *Smile!* to an assortment of already widely-grinning kids, and Indrin laughs. And suddenly I am laughing too, and I honestly do not know why, but I am laughing and I think maybe it is because of the water, the wild, rushing water that doesn't try to make sense, just splashes along. And it is roaring so loudly it seems like the loudest sound in the world, even though only steps away it is muffled by the bus engines, and this just makes me laugh harder, because the truth is here and spraying me in the face.

~~

THE COLOUR never fails to surprise me – a deep, opaque aquamarine. Or is it turquoise? Perhaps a colour we haven't a word for. I am standing halfway down a mountain pathway, looking down at Indrin's hair, blowing like dark branches against this jewel colour. This is Lake Louise, the lake I have come to countless times since I was a kid. The lake I have canoed on, walked around, skated on, and gazed at for years, yet each time

I walk up from the parking lot, round the side of the Château, and lay my eyes on that colour, I find myself taking a deeper breath than usual. It is not a sigh, not a gasp; I simply notice my lungs filling more deeply. The lake is the colour of mountain air to me, the exact shade of how it feels to be here.

"I love it here."

Indrin's tone is church-reverent and entirely appropriate.

"Mm hmm."

I have never felt right about talking in churches. Here is no exception. We walk the next few minutes hearing nothing but the thump of our shoes on the damp path and the sound of our voices saying hello to other hikers, other tourists.

"Hi."

"Hello."

"Hi there."

Our heads bob, smiles are exchanged.

"Hello."

"Hi."

We spot nationalities in clothing, in the expressions on the face. The elderly man with eyes like bright lakes in his face who I knew was German even before we saw his *lederhosen.* The two girls, obviously Canadian and from somewhere close enough to be blind to this beauty around them, lost in intense conversation and walking in oversize jeans, their sweatshirt sleeves pulled down over their hands.

"You're kidding. He did that?"

The tone is incredulous.

"Yeah. Right in front of her."

"Omi*gawd.*"

They continue up the trail, discussing the indignities of life as they stare at their shoes.

"Calgary. Definitely Calgary," Indrin whispers to my nod.

The two British ladies standing tall as rocks, catching their breath on the way to the teahouse. The Americans smiling broadly, owning the place with their love of it.

"Nothing like it," I hear one say.

He is Hollywood-good-looking: blond, slim build, suntan, expensive fleece pullover.

"Doctor from Florida," I whisper to Indrin this time.

He just smiles and keeps walking down the path a few steps.

"Or Kevin Costner stand-in maybe?" he adds, but only when he's sure the American is safely out of earshot. My new friend is nothing if not cautious.

"No, definitely doctor from Florida."

"You really think you've got this game down pat, don't you?"

"Yes I do." Putting on the Maxwell Smart voice I carefully learned watching TV rerun after rerun as a child, I add, "Would you believe he's an orthopaedic surgeon from Sarasota?"

"I'd believe anything, Miranda, O mountain psychic."

I enjoy Indrin's smile, our mutual chuckle, and fill my lungs again consciously with this cool, seemingly breathable colour.

"Okay, okay, I can't have you thinking I believe in psychics. I talked to him when you were on your search for Kodachrome. He *is* an orthopaed-"

"-ic surgeon from Sarasota. Of course he is."

He laughs and I beeline for the ice cream stand.

"Want one?"

"Yes, but this one is my treat."

Indrin is pulling out multi-folded bills from his back pocket.

"You're sure?"

This does not feel right. I am the one with the job here. He is the poor kid brother, or so it seems.

"Yes, I'm sure."

Indrin pushes in beside me to check out the flavours.

Soon I am happily licking Rocky Road and chewing frozen marshmallows when out of the blue he brings up religion. Out of the turquoise blue.

"What are you, anyway? What religion?"

"I'm not anything."

"Everybody's something."

"No, I'm not. I'm not anything."

"Okay, then what are you *not?* What did you give up on?"

"I've given up on a lot, but religion was never one of those things. I'm really not anything."

Indrin tilts his head, surveys my face.

"What were your parents?"

"My father believed in Shakespeare. No one else."

"As a stand-in for God?"

Indrin seems to get a kick out of this.

"I'll enlighten you. *'In the beginning was the*

Word...'."

"That's supposed to enlighten me? Are you turning into Billy Graham or something, Ms. Preacher?"

"Not bloody likely. No, my Dad figured if you were going to have a God, you might as well pick one that suited you. He loved all great literature and decided that passage from the Bible was a clue. *The Word.* And since Shakespeare was *the* undisputed master of words and creator of whole universes through his wordplay, well, that solved it. If you were master of the *Word,* you were as close to God as anyone could be. So that was that. God was in his heaven and all was right with the world."

"Talk about respect for literature."

"Too much so. Good job he never met many writers. I wonder if he could have stood the disappointment."

"I take it you have met some."

"I've interviewed a few, but my faith is safe, I guess – I've never met Shakespeare so he's allowed to remain on the family pedestal."

"So your name –"

"You got it."

"And your sister's name is –"

"Juliet. Of course. My dog was Portia. And – I'm not kidding you here – we actually had an iguana named Caliban for awhile. Poor Caliban didn't do too well with me and Julie trying to play with him all the time."

"Poor Caliban."

Indrin smiles, looks back out to the lake.

"Whoa – you're losing your ice cream, there, Indrin."

His double scoop is sliding off the cone he is holding almost horizontal. His fingers catch it just in time.

"How about your mother?"

Indrin is now licking the side of his hand and cone. I am trying to form the words but it is not easy to answer with a mouth full of Chocolate Glacier.

"Nod er eder."

No, in fact it is impossible to answer. I bite into the solid cold, feel an excruciatingly good ache build between my eyebrows. Indrin waits.

"No, not her either," I say when I have lost the numbness in my tongue. "She was a little less for the Shakespeare god than Dad was, and a little more for *God,* but even she didn't get too overly concerned about it. She went to church when I was little I guess."

"What church?"

"What is this? The inquisition? You do come by this priest thing honestly, don't you?"

"I'm just curious."

His eyes are round, his eyebrows raised. Truly sincere, Indrin is. Truly earnest. The unabashed sincerity makes me nervous. I never have liked people to get too vulnerable around me.

"I'm surprised you're travelling with me without having seen a baptismal certificate or something."

This comment of mine brings the sparring glint back into Indrin's eyes. We're playing again, so I continue.

"She was raised Presbyterian, I think. Something fairly rigid, fairly Scotch."

"Okay."

Indrin nods an *I've got it figured out* nod.

"What? What, you define people by their church

membership?"

"No, I'm just interested."

"Well, I'm a mongrel. Presbyterian, some Catholic, some vehement anti-Catholic too in there from Northern Ireland. Way back on my Dad's side was some Jewish background. But someone married someone else whose some other religion won out. One thing cancelled out another and eventually it all came down to nothing."

"And Shakespeare."

"Nothing and Shakespeare. That's me."

I crunch the last bit of my cone.

"Shall we hunt for a campsite?"

"What time is it?"

I check my trusty watch, a watch decked out with time in all zones, worldwide, plus a handy stopwatch. The fact that it even has a compass won me over when I first saw it in the store. The perfect tool: guaranteed to help me find my way in all earthly dimensions, time and space.

"The time?" he asks again.

"Four-thirty."

"Why not ramble some more and see where we end up?" Indrin offers. "We've got time and it'll be light until ten anyway."

On the way back to the parking lot, we pass three more Germans Indrin feels sure are Hungarians because of something about their socks, a group of Japanese teenagers happily posing in the latest Banff Avenue hiking fashions, and an American couple stopped to reload their video-recorder. Then, just before we turn out of view, I look back to drink in one more breath of that colour, of that tangible cloud of turquoise gathered at the foot of the far-off glacier, and I hear Indrin take one slow deep breath of air and exhale it all.

~ ~

We lie in our sleeping bags listening to light rain sputter on the tent. It is a hollow sound, broken only by the crinkle of the cellophane Cheezie bag every time I reach in for another handful. I am wearing two sweaters and my socks are making my feet itch. My head is aching slightly from hunger since we couldn't start a fire, and the mustard-covered bun preceded by cheese-and-cracker appetizer has not filled me up. Although I was too tired earlier to get back in the car and drive in to Revelstoke, I now regret our decision to wait till morning for a proper meal. I also regret driving this far; I knew we should have camped at Lake Louise – or, at the very least, somewhere no further west than Yoho National Park. But after climbing to a still very snow-packed Rogers Pass at Glacier National Park and taking our time in the visitor centre to avoid the wind, we thought we would push on to Revelstoke National Park, more to escape the gathering clouds than anything else. Then, by the time we got that far, Indrin remembered camping somewhere south of Revelstoke once as a kid, somewhere toward the Selkirk Mountains, somewhere that was the *perfect little spot.* His deep brown eyes got that sincere and open and *wouldn't it be great* look they get and suddenly I am ready to sit behind the wheel until we find the very spot. Maybe it is and maybe it's not, but we are now safely tucked into the campground at Blanket Creek Provincial Park. Indrin seems perfectly content. I am perfectly ravenous. My fingers are orange as I brush the last Cheezie crumbs off my sleeping bag. Only now do I think about bears.

"Damn."

I know better. Two grizzly mauling stories last summer alone and here I have turned our tent into a bruin 7-11.

"Why didn't you say anything?" I demand of Indrin.

Suddenly it is his fault our tent has become one big olfactory neon sign.

"I figured you knew something I didn't," he says, "like there were no bears around here or something."

"Bloody hell."

By the time I climb out, shake my sleeping bag into the rain, deposit the crumpled Cheezie bag into the bear-proof trash container, and climb – rain-soaked – into the tent again, I figure the few crumbs might have been worth the risk. Then again, with my luck as of late, I wouldn't want to push it – especially not in grizzly country. Even after learning enough survival skills to cope with evenings alone with a wild and raging Turner when he is messed up from cocaine and too many shooters, I still can't say I'm anxious to face more near-death experiences.

But maybe I'm inviting bears subconsciously, somehow aware that a bear attack might be the only fitting climax to my holiday from hell, the perfect end to the story that someone in the newsroom would no doubt give the slug "DESERTED DIES."

I can even hear the Announcer Voice Over:

AVO

Roll stock video—>	Miranda Rosalind Tyler of Edmonton was fatally mauled by a grizzly
[grizzly bears by highway]	bear last night. Park officials say the sudden departure of her fiancé may have placed her in a state of shock and caused her to disregard the basic safety rules for camping in bear country.
[pics of witness: Indrin Krishnayya]	A future priest at the scene escaped, but not before trying to give Tyler absolution for her many sins. Her last words are reported to have been, 'I'd like a *caffe latte* please," and 'Turner can go to hell.'

I look at Indrin. All my commotion has obviously not fazed him one bit. He is lost in reverie over a map.

"Why are you here?"

He looks up, saying nothing, and studies my face. I continue.

"Why are you here with me? I mean, I know vaguely how I ended up here with you but I don't get your end of it, I've decided. Was your short-order cook job that bad?"

I fight the sarcasm in my voice, try to lower the tone, but the edge in it snaps back with every word.

"It couldn't have been that stressful. I don't even know what you could have cooked. All I remember seeing up there was shrink-wrapped food from some other era."

Indrin raises himself up onto his elbow.

"French fries, onion rings, bacon burgers, fish patties."

"Deep fryer heaven."

"Yup."

"I still don't get it."

Indrin sits up and smoothes back his spiralling hair. It is even curlier in this humidity.

"I don't know why I'm here. Does it matter? Do I have to know for some reason?"

"I'd like to know."

Now I'm studying his face.

"There's not really one answer."

I wait for him to continue, one of the interviewing techniques I have learned over the years. I do not prompt. I do not ask another question. I just wait expectantly. Eventually Indrin speaks.

"Actually, when I quit that day I didn't even know if you'd be at the Greek restaurant. I half-figured you'd have decided to head back to town or would have just headed somewhere on your own already. But you were there. And even before we stopped on the highway and saw what we saw that night, I had already decided to ask you if I could tag along."

Indrin sounds like he is finished, but I am not.

"Why?" I ask.

The rain is coming down harder.

"It sounds ridiculous when you try to explain some things."

"I won't judge what you say."

"We all judge everything."

Indrin's tone is firm, betrays hard-won knowledge.

I move my hand away from the edge of the tent, where water is starting to soak through. Fair enough, Indrin, we all judge, no one understands, why even try to communicate? Everything is pointless, right?

I am just about to turn over and muse on when the mosquito managed to get into the tent when my silent friend speaks again.

"I've known for a long time that I'm going to be a priest. I swear I felt a kind of 'calling' even before I became Catholic, even when I was a kid. It's a strange life in a lot of ways and I guess I just want to make sure I'm doing it for the right reasons and that I'm not running away from my life. Anyway, the day before you showed up in the cafeteria, I went for a walk on my break all the way up to the end of the trail. I was thinking about how when I'm really tuned in, really filled with love – prayerful, I guess – my first instincts are always right."

Indrin's eyes are grave. The sincerity in them makes me feel uncomfortable again, although this time it could be more the use of the word "prayer" that makes me want to thrash around in my sleeping bag and untwist my layers of clothing. But I wanted to know. And the silent one is still speaking.

"I was thinking about that, and the fall, and the seminary and all, and I ended up kind of making a deal with God – a deal that was really just my way of saying, 'Okay, I'm going to go for it.' I decided I was going to follow my heart so fiercely I wouldn't care where it took me. I was going to live on pure instinct from that moment on and refuse to let fear tempt me away to any kind of self-doubt. And I was going to follow my first instincts even if that meant heading in some totally new direction. Even if that meant changing my path completely and becoming, I don't know, a stockbroker.

"I had just decided all of that and made a pact to listen to my feelings and go wherever they sent me – almost as a kind of experiment to see what would happen if I did it, if I truly made that promise. Then you showed up the very next day. And when I went back to work the following morning and looked for your keys, I felt more stranded on the mountain than you were the day I met you. It felt like I should leave, so I did. And there you were with your camping gear. And here we are."

I nod. No argument there. "Here we are."

His eyes are calm. He can stare without any discomfort or self-consciousness, it seems to me. I think about this. His face is lit from the side by the flashlight hanging from the top of the tent and his cheek looks soft. I feel like brushing it with my hand, but do not. No need to add further complication to our already strange friendship.

"And where is this leading you?

"So far all I know is that I'm in the right place."

"Pure instinct, eh?"

"If it's heart-driven instinct – prayer-driven and followed honestly – it's the truest philosophy I can come up with."

"How Christian is that? How Catholic?"

"As far as I can see it's the only thing that's true in any religion."

I think about this too – then reach out my hand and stroke his cheek. He takes my hand and squeezes it, then leans back to study his map of the British Columbia interior.

The rain is slowing down. I fall into sleep and dream of tidal waves, of dead shark bones crumbling into dust under my feet in the sand, and of being washed far and away over the land.

~ ~

He looks quite biblical, actually, with the long hair falling down his back and his head bowed into his hands. I can see the priest thing in him more clearly like this. I'm about ten rows back from Indrin, trying not to let my nylon windbreaker rustle too much as I sit myself down on the pew. I have no idea if it was last night's conversation or just part of Indrin's nature – I have not known him long enough to know – but this morning we had to look for a church. It is Friday, not Sunday, but we had to find a church today, this morning, now. And so, here we are at a church in Revelstoke.

It is not an old church, the kind I have a nodding appreciation for despite the fact I do not believe in religion. If they are old, with dark wood, grandiose organs, and imposing archways towering over complicated stained glass, I can understand how they make people muster up reverence or at least a thoughtful state of mind. This church is new, with simply-sewn banners hung up on plain white walls: a cross and a dove. The carpeting is wall-to-wall beige. I do not feel reverent. In fact, as I flip through the *Catholic Book of Worship,* I am feeling increasingly cranky. *All we like sheep,* the little blue book sings, *have gone astray....* Yeah, sheep. They are certainly sheep, all right.

But I refuse to let organized religion ruin my morning. I close the book just loudly enough to remind Indrin I am here. Then I open my purse and take out a darker lipstick than I normally wear, the Midnight Plum I usually saved for touring the clubs with Turner, and I put it on in silent rebellion. I never have understood how people can pray when they know other people are watching them. After a moment or two, wouldn't they begin to feel just a little self-conscious or find themselves assuming a slightly more sincere and holy expression than they're actually feeling? Posturing truly annoys me. Still, to be honest, Indrin just looks completely lost in his own little world.

The church is absolutely quiet. At the moment I cannot even hear a car outside. My watch says quarter to eleven. The second hand starts its merry way around the dial again and I cough a little bit.

I'm here Indrin, I'm here.

He has been praying for close to forty minutes now so he must be starting to come out of it. I look at my watch again. Yeah, forty minutes because it was five after ten when I dropped him off and went to get another coffee. I am going to say something in a minute if

Indrin still shows no sign of budging.

When does religion stop being someone's spirituality and start becoming someone else's annoyance? I thought we would be on the road by now. Yesterday's rain has turned to hot humidity under today's sun. The air outside already feels heavy with heat. I stare at the tall rectangular windows and wonder if I can figure out how to open one. Nowhere does there seem to be a latch.

I sit back against the hard wood, good for proving piousness I suppose, although I notice there is cushioning on the kneeling bar. Would Sister Bernadette approve? This is the only saint I am familiar with – thanks to the Jennifer Warnes album I like and the song she sings about Bernadette.

So many hearts I find, broke like yours and mine
torn by what we've done and can't undo....

But the chorus escapes me as I sit here staring at the dove on the banner, trying to hum it in my head. I have never been good at remembering a tune.

"Want to get going?"

I look over to see Indrin turned around, leaning his arm on the back of the pew. His voice is normal conversation volume, which sounds loud in here, but he's comfortable with it. In fact, he seems completely relaxed.

"Yes, I've been waiting."

My voice sounds more like a strained whisper.

"I wasn't sure whether to disturb you, I thought you

might be praying."

"Praying? You're the priest, not me pal."

My voice has recovered and the word *pal* comes out too loud and flippant for this shadowed, hallowed hall. I grab my purse and get up.

"I just want to thank the priest," says Indrin.

"What for?"

"For opening up the church. It was locked when I first got here but Father Lowrey was on his way in and let me inside."

"I thought churches were always unlocked."

"Not these days," he says, cheerily leading me through a hallway at the back of the church. He stops to lean into a doorway.

"I'm on my way, Father."

"Oh you are. Well, then...."

I hear a chair screech against the floor and a lean man of about fifty steps through the doorway. He is holding a book in one hand and smoothes his hair back with the other. His hair is thick, looks prematurely white, and seems to stand straight upright. That, along with his somewhat ragged eyebrows raised high above sea-green eyes, gives him the air of a man permanently surprised, if not downright shocked.

"You have a safe trip now."

As he says this, he looks from Indrin to me and back to Indrin. The poor fellow is baffled. He has got a *what's a nice biblical character like you doing with a woman like that?* look on his face. I feel old and rather sinful. Then I feel resentful at having to feel that way. I would bark, *What about Mary Magdalene, for God's sake?* if it were not for the friendly, guileless expression on his face. Do I look that much older than this twenty-three-year-old neophyte? Maybe worldliness shows even more than years.

And so what if it does. The fact is, I am a thirty-three-year-old unmarried woman who has survived too many rotten relationships. I have done more than kiss in my life, with birth control on top of it all, and I cannot believe in this drivel they call organized religion. Incidentally, I gave up believing even before all the news stories broke about the diddling priests in Newfoundland.

So why do I still believe in guilt?

I clear my throat and press my lips together, hoping to blot my Wet 'N Wild lipstick somewhat.

"Hello, Reverend."

"This is Miranda Tyler, Father." Indrin continues. "The woman I was telling you about."

Oh great. Thanks a lot, Wonder Boy. Hope you two had a great chat.

"Miranda, this is Father Lowrey."

Lowrey starts to open his mouth, but Indrin jumps in and revises his introduction. "Right – Father Albert Lowrey. Father Albert."

Lowrey smiles.

"Pleased to meet you, Miranda. Come in, come on in."

He starts walking into his office, still holding my hand in his. "You've got a few minutes, don't you? Sit down, sit down."

Indrin follows us in.

"Would you two like some coffee?"

On a table by his desk is an open bag of coffee beans, a grinder, and a small portable drip coffee maker. Lowrey catches me eyeing the bag of beans.

"It's the Oxfam kind. Politically correct, or more so, I guess. Sister Fran sent it from Vancouver – I used to work there. Guess I've got a bit of a reputation for liking my coffee."

Lowrey pauses ceremoniously before pouring the beans into the grinder.

"Shall I?"

I nod pleasantly enough, but between us Indrin is the only one with a voice at the moment. The religion in the air has winded me.

"Sure. Thanks, Father."

Lowrey flicks the switch on the grinder and grins. He seems to be proud of the way the high-pitched roar fills the room.

"It's a bit loud," he yells.

Indrin smiles. I nod again and look over Lowrey's office. He's got G.K. Chesterton on his bookshelves – one name I recognize from journalism school – but mostly it is bible after bible and lots of namby-pamby-looking books with titles like, *God Delights in You.* Then I notice the *Chronicles of Narnia* by C.S. Lewis, favourites of mine as a kid. He has got the complete boxed set, minus one, on his shelf. I look back to Lowrey and Indrin and see the missing book, *The Voyage of the Dawn Treader,* lying facedown on Lowrey's desk.

The roar of the grinder ceases abruptly.

"So Indrin tells me you're a journalist. How long have you been doing that now?"

"Too long."

In the silence that follows I hear my attempt at sarcasm echo in my ears. It sounds harsh and misdirected, but most of all it feels false. Funny that a tone that serves me so well in the newsroom can sound so hollow here. At work, everyone is as quick or quicker than me in the search for the sarcastic, smartly-worded label. Every story and every person can be, must be, instantly judged and reduced to a two-word *slug* that can be written on a tape box.

SHOCKED PRIEST. ALTAR BOY. WORLDLY WOMAN.

After ten years in the business, I think in labels now, and sarcasm rattles out of me as automatically as wire copy out of the printer in the newsroom. The smart aleck's quick comeback is reflex to me. The one drawback to this is that it has become a struggle to use words that are neutral, to speak them with no guarded posturing. Simple answers to simple questions are as foreign to my mouth as a dead language.

I try another answer, speak it with a mouth that feels distinctly dry.

"I've been in TV news for just over ten years now, actually."

Lowrey nods pleasantly and goes back to making coffee. Carefully opening the filter. Precisely spooning out absolutely level scoops. Ceremoniously pouring in the water. They are very big on ritual in the Church, but I had no idea of the extent of it. It could actually make for quite a humorous visual essay. The tape boxes are already labelled in my mind: CEREMONY PERVASIVE. Or maybe CATHOLIC CAFFEINE.

"Ten years. You don't look as though you could have been out of high school ten years ago," says Lowrey, eyeing me as he flicks the switch on his coffee maker.

Hallelujah, the caffeine is coming. All good rituals have their basis in meaning. *Hallelujah* also for some sense of surprise at my age at last. I do not feel thirty-three and always feel somewhat heartened when someone else is as surprised as I am. I am surprised at a lot of things in my life. Especially lately. I am surprised I am here. On my holidays, having coffee with a priest in Revelstoke. I would like to see the expressions in the newsroom. Over the course of my lifetime in TV news I have ranted about the Church more than once. And, at the moment, that lifetime in TV news seems a long one.

Announcer → on camera	For details we go now to the very heart of the story. Live and on location is Methuselah....
Roll Video→	[sound up]

"Yeah, ten years," I reply. "It's hard to believe."

Lowrey turns to Indrin.

"You're starting at the seminary when?"

"In the Fall. September, actually. And it's hard for me to believe I'm finally going to be there."

Lowrey nods. "It's not for everyone. But there's such a shortage. We sure need good young men these days."

Lowrey drones on with Indrin nodding, but I tune out.

Good young men. Do they hear themselves? Hello. Hello in there. This is what I have never understood about their whole system. *Such a shortage.* Is their ignorance really that all-encompassing, that smug? I was just starting to like Lowrey, but something in me cannot leave this topic unchallenged.

"Yeah, it's too bad, isn't it? We did a story on the priest shortage recently. There's certainly room enough for some women priests. And married priests."

Lowrey turns to check on the coffee. Drips are still dropping steadily from the spout, but he starts filling a mug anyway. He hands it to Indrin.

"That's something I sure don't understand," I say, throwing a bit more into the conversation cauldron.

Maybe I do feel like brewing a bit of an argument. A certain irritability has been building up all morning anyway.

"I mean, what logical argument could the Pope have against priests who happen to be women? As far as I know it hasn't caused the Anglican and United Churches to crumble into instant moral decay."

"There's so much we don't understand," Lowrey ventures, handing me a steaming mug.

"There's a reason not to understand," I counter. "How can you understand the completely illogical?"

I scald my knuckle waving my coffee cup for emphasis. Both Lowrey and Indrin have lowered their eyes. The room is now filled with nothing but the sound of two spoons circling inside mugs. Odd sort of church bells, really. *Clinkle, clinkle, clink.*

"'Look not on our sins, but on the faith of your

Church.'" Lowrey sighs.

"It's true, isn't it?" adds Indrin.

"Pardon me?"

I hate insider jargon. And the bells are still ringing.

Clinkle, clinkle.

Just when I start to think this spoon-tinkling is some sort of monk's meditative exercise, Lowrey sets down his spoon.

"We're called to seek what light we can in this dark world. I'm here in this corner of it; Indrin feels called to enter the same corner. We do what we can."

His tone is friendly, but firm. I have pushed the topic as far as I should. My turn for a sip. Black is just fine for me. I have no need to ring any bells.

I look back to the bookshelves. Then my eyes settle on the rather brilliant column of dust floating in the sunbeam from the window. The silence feels heavy.

"I've just begun 'The Beginning of the End of the World,'" says Lowrey finally.

"Pardon me?"

"In *The Voyage of the Dawn Treader.*"

Lowrey nods to the book on his desk.

"It's one of the last chapters of the book. Have you read them? They're a series, you know. Marvellous books. Hadn't looked at them in years until I saw them at our church sale the other week. I knew I had to buy them when I saw those chapter headings. 'The Beginning of the End of the World.' 'The Very End of the World.'"

Lowrey sets a bookmark into his place and, with just a hint of shyness, smiles as his hands straighten the papers on his desk.

"I'm a bit of a student of the apocalypse. The prophets of doom. Everything from Nostradamus to your modern psychics."

Indrin sits up.

"Is that right?"

Lowrey is nodding.

"Oh, I've done quite a bit of research. The Marian apparitions are a large part of it."

"What's your feeling on Medjugorje?" asks Indrin, suddenly a bright-eyed student with a front-row seat.

I sit staring dumbly until coffee drips out of the mug I realize I have been holding sideways. As I wipe my hand on my jeans, Lowrey moves from the apparitions in Yugoslavia to the miraculous rapture of Catholic schoolchildren in Rwanda and the messages they received. Then Indrin is asking about a place called Zeitoun in Egypt. Did Anwar Sadat really see Our Lady? No, it was Nasser, but Lowrey is clapping his hands together now as he talks about the light, the tremendous light that everyone could see – Christian, Jew, and Muslim, thousands of them, all united in their vision. Has Father Lowrey studied the Kabbalah? wonders Indrin. But it is more the Marian apparitions that interest Lowrey, visions of a wondrous lady bearing warnings for the world, warnings of a dire and urgent nature.

And so they talk.

An apocalyptic priest. What could be more fitting for my journey with a philosophical novice living on pure instinct? I down my mug, but this time Lowrey just waves me to the pot. Social niceties have vanished now that we're on to Marian apparitions in Egypt, bleeding stigmata, Fatima, and the end of the world.

~ ~

WHEN NOT CHEERFULLY regaling us with tales of final battles between good and evil, Father Lowrey makes an admirable tour guide. Maybe it's the sudden heat, maybe the rare opportunity to play mentor to a young priest-in-the-making, maybe a desire, responsibility even, to make sure I don't get in the way of Indrin's holy path – whatever it is, Father Lowrey is leading us on a merry tour of Revelstoke and area. In the old white-domed post office, its sturdy brick standing fortress to the secrets of the city's history, we learn of *once upon a time* paddlewheelers on the rushing Columbia River. On the march to a quaint café for supplementary cups of coffee, we hear of the founding of St. Francis of Assisi Parish by the Scalabrini Fathers who, *interestingly enough,* says Lowrey with emphasis, had a particular devotion to the Virgin Mary. And tucked into my dusty, candy-wrapper-and-potato-chip-crumb-strewn car, we head north of town to stare into the face of nature's raw power safely harnessed: the Revelstoke Hydro Dam. By the time we tour the powerhouse, and the circuit breaker gallery, and snap pictures of the valley from the lookout deck on the dam's crest, my feet are aching and my head is thick with hydroelectricity lore.

Here stretched before us is all the amassing force of the Columbia River, a force that will soon be funnelled through gigantic turbines in one of North America's largest hydro power sites.

Here it all begins to flow together – to send power through a vast web of cable, to ensure society as we know it gets instant light at the flick of a switch or from the nearest, handiest plug-in of our choice. And here it is strangely quiet today. Given the momentous power of such a development, I imagined the roar of water would await us. Instead, I hear only wind.

It's called a concrete gravity dam, all one hundred and seventy-five metres of it – the idea being that the weight of the concrete is greater than the weight of the water. The water, of course, is indifferent to its role in all this. It magnanimously lends its power to the hungry turbines, then continues along, undiminished. The river is held back, then pulled down by gravity, yet triumphs over it all the same.

Indrin is sipping tea from styrofoam with Lowrey over by the cement guardrail when I walk back from another visit to the bathroom. I'm feeling somewhat nauseous but don't want to make a big deal of it. It's the sun, too much caffeine on an empty stomach, and general fatigue. I also think it might be my body crashing from its longtime dependency on the safely-moderated synthetic estrogen I've been taking for too many years. I threw out the last of my birth control pills the day of the breakup, as a symbolic goodbye to Turner in particular and to relationships in general. Now, thrown back upon the uncontrolled avails of my own raw and homegrown female hormones, I'm reeling. My body isn't used to feeling this pure a femininity – or this heavy a period. I feel like I am thirteen again, with all the discomfort and all the honest surprise at my body. I don't feel like me anymore – or the me I have been used to for a long time.

"We were just saying, Miranda, how if you look over this way, it's just like the scene at the end of *Dr. Zhivago.* Remember that?"

Indrin is pointing toward the long cement top of the dam.

"All we need to have is Omar Sharif calling out about the balalaika," adds Lowrey cheerfully.

It's true. I've only seen the movie about a thousand times – or at least ten or fifteen, anyway. Every Christmas, a screening complete with mulled wine follows my now nearly legendary annual skating party. At least it has every Christmas except this last one, since I had just started seeing Turner and he had a bad hangover that day. "Can't we forget the movie?" he wheedled. "You go skating with your friends, sure, but let's just get together later on our own. Just the two of us." It sounded romantic, so I put my prized double-video back in the closet and cancelled.

That was probably the first sign.

In retrospect, it was certainly a clear enough sign, too, but at the time I remained happily blinkered, happy I had finally met someone who wanted me all to himself, someone so thrilled about me he couldn't wait to be alone with me.

Couldn't wait to take away what was part of me.

Suddenly I feel like a kid whose teddy bear has been grabbed. I want it back. And I want it back *right now.*

So, right now, on this sun-baked dam, I determine to

hold a roller skating party when I get home, a Christmas-in-July kind of deal, complete with a make-up showing of *Dr. Zhivago.*

"Have we lost you, Miranda?" Lowrey gives me a friendly nudge. "Sure, you must know the movie. Right at the end there, when they bring up *Lara's Theme* for the last time and the girl runs off with her boyfriend. The young fellow – he's just a boy, really – who runs the whole dam."

"Yeah. The whole dam thing," I announce. "He runs the whole dam thing. And, don't you worry, I know the whole damn movie by heart."

Lowrey's green eyes are suddenly so big they're SeaWorld. I expect to see belugas swim through them. Then he laughs and claps me so hard on the back I accuse him of wanting to knock me over the dam.

"Are you sure you don't want me out of the whole dam picture?"

General hilarity and punning continue as we head back toward my car. Lowrey has decided I am okay as far as Indrin is concerned. I know this despite the fact nothing has been said directly about it. I just know exactly what he's thinking as we walk along, Lowrey's hand now on my shoulder. He can see clearly that I am not a threat to Indrin's path or his chastity and this makes me feel both glad and slightly miffed. I'm in the club. And I'm also safely out of it.

We head back toward town, toward a lunch I am now desperate for. Indrin, charged up with the caffeine from his tea, has offered to drive, and Lowrey is merrily pointing out the softly rolling Monashee Mountains from the front seat. Tucked into the back, I nurse my headache with the last Aspirin in my purse and look back at the great and mighty dam shrinking into nothing. Then I lean into the window and rest my eyes on the glittering river that, even after the dam, just keeps flowing along with us.

Armageddon and Albatrosses

The fir trees cast long, spindly shadows across cracked asphalt; the sun dips behind purple mountains, mountains that in this late light look like mountains from a dream – somehow solid and ephemeral at the same time. Still a couple of hours away from a full sunset, the air is nonetheless finally cooling off and this is a relief. My head still aches. My cheeks are sunburnt. The air blasting from the car window flows fresh against my skin.

For the last few miles the view through the windshield has made me feel like I am on the way back from a news shoot, with the pictures on tape, the script either written or not needed for that night's newscast, and the cameraman and me – our senses dull after a long day – lulled into the soothing sound of the miles disappearing under the van as we drive. And, just as I do after a shoot, I am replaying the day's events in my mind, rethinking my questions, my responses. We are on the highway back to the Blanket Creek campground. Back to set up the tent we just took down there this morning. I am resigned to this idea. Resigned, not ecstatic. Not so Indrin.

Indrin is talking about how peaceful the campground was, how much he enjoyed it last night and how lucky it is we get the chance to spend another night there after all. He sounds over-earnest. I don't feel like being convinced of anything at this point.

"Fine, Indrin. It's fine."

"Fine?"

"Yes, fine. I'm sorry if I'm disappointing you with my lack of back flips. Do I have to love this idea?"

Indrin looks deflated. What an easy boy he is to puncture. Being reminded of this makes me more irritated, not less.

"You don't seem to understand, Indrin, that being a Good Samaritan doesn't come as naturally to me as it obviously does to you. I've never claimed to have taken a particularly Godly path in life."

I'm getting on one of my rolls again. My unofficial audition for a Letterman guest spot.

"I'm sorry. You must be mistaken. Hard though it may be to accept, I am not Mother Theresa. No, I know the similarities are astonishing – at least when I haven't had enough sleep – but I am simply not Mother Theresa. At least I wasn't the last time I looked. And there have been more than a few men who have looked me over fairly well too. I feel confident that any one of them could be called on to testify that I am indeed the sinner Miranda Tyler, not our pal the saint in the making."

"I truly wonder about your sarcasm," Indrin says quietly, more to his pop can than to me.

"What's there to wonder about?"

"Just how angry are you about life, anyway?"

This is too much. My foot hits the brake and I pull onto the narrow shoulder far too abruptly. The car swerves on the gravel and Indrin's pop splashes against the dash. We lurch to a stop, whereupon I am treated to the sound of orange pop dripping onto the plastic floor mat. I contain myself enough to speak.

"What the hell is that supposed to mean? And who here has ever claimed not to be angry, anyway? When I'm angry people know about it; when I'm happy people know about it. But don't expect me to be pleasant and loving and hymn-singing when I'm so irritated I can hardly sit still. I honestly can't believe you sitting there, you with your maybe three life experiences to your name, telling me about anger. The worst thing you've ever had to face in life is a dead rabbit. And I was there to hold your hand."

"I'll walk back," says Indrin, opening the door.

"What?"

"I'll see you at the campground."

He reaches into the back seat for his ball cap and running shoes.

"Oh, this is terrific," I announce to the rearview mirror.

"No, not terrific," cuts in Indrin. "Pretty sad, really. And this is the only thing I can think to do at the moment. It will all be a lot more pleasant once we get some distance on this scene."

"Get back in the car, will you? Go for a walk at the campground, for God's sake. But get in the car. We're still a ways away."

But Indrin is not responding, only sticking his runners onto his sweaty bare feet and starting down the highway, tying his hair into a ponytail as he walks.

"Last chance," I yell, standing half out of the car. "I'm going to take off."

No response.

Fine, Indrin. Fine. I'll put some distance on this scene, all right. The tires spin on the gravel as I pull away. I drive up to Indrin, peer out the passenger-side window, and watch him walking determinedly, his chin thrust forward.

There is an odd phenomenon about my newfound friendship with this stranger walking beside me. The more solemn his young face, the more I feel off balance, even childish.

"This is childish, Indrin," I yell, trying to drive more or less straight while peering out the passenger window. There's nothing behind me on the road anyway.

His feet crunch along the gravel.

"Will you just get in the car?"

When he doesn't answer, my mouth bleats out an apology at last, the volume dropping with every word.

"I'm sorry I blew up. Okay?"

Indrin stops.

"Will you pull over? If a car comes along you'll kill both of us."

Obediently, I pull over. He walks around to the driver's side window.

"Listen, I'm going to walk."

I throw myself against the back of the seat and let out an exasperated sigh.

"I'm going to walk," he says steadily, "because I want to, I need to, and it's not that far. About three miles from here, I figure. I won't be angry when I get there, but I do want to put some distance on this. Distance I can feel with real footsteps, one after another. Okay?"

"Okay."

"I'm sorry, Indrin."

My voice is quiet now. It's me who feels over-earnest, needing his approval.

"I know."

Two quick taps on the roof of the car. That was *see you* I guess, because Indrin sets off again. I pull out, weaving as I look over to catch Indrin's eyes with mine. He nods and waves as I pass him. But right then, in the moment I catch his eyes, I see an old man. Indrin at age seventy-five. Still lean, fluid, determined, but with these old, tired eyes. Eyes that say, "Yes, I know. I know," as they calmly accept news of any disaster.

I know.

Any tragedy. Any sadness.

I know.

As if the knowing tired him slightly, but was simply the burden he had to bear. The price of understanding all too well how life bumps along on this particular planet in this particular universe. As if he had a hint deep inside him somewhere, maybe from a dream, of how smoothly it all works elsewhere.

~ ~

I WIPE MY FOREHEAD with my sleeve. It felt cool enough before putting up the tent to throw on my sweatshirt. But now that the tent is up, I'm only chillier than ever from the sweat cooling my face and back. Putting it up was work, plain and simple, instead of the rather fun "beat the clock" game Indrin and I developed yesterday. We did it in just five minutes flat last night, but then the rain did give us some extra incentive.

Indrin is still not back. The three miles turned out to be more like five, but he seemed emphatic enough about the walk to discourage me from going back to get him. So, the tent is up. The cooler is on the picnic table. And I wait.

The whole mess started with me, so I guess it's only fitting it now sits with me. The true source of my anger was not so much Indrin's comment about my sarcasm as it was having my holiday run off the rails once again. Having coffee with Lowrey at the rectory was fine. So was our tour of town. Even staying for lunch with him at the diner in town was not that bad. I actually enjoy Lowrey's company. There is something of the Pied Piper about him. I have no doubt his *come with me* eyes could lead a few lost parishioners back into the fold because today they led a couple of lost travellers down along green hillsides, merrily humming his tune all the way to talk of doom and doomsday. We lost our way today, Indrin and I. We are no longer on our own happily rambling path; instead, we follow Lowrey's lead.

At lunch, when Lowrey started talking about what a miracle it was we stopped by today, just when there was the worrisome problem about the refugee, it only made sense to ask, "What problem?" "What refugee?" Only after that did the whole thing start to feel like a giant albatross around my neck.

The albatross is a twenty-two-year-old refugee named Edmond Rebero. He is from Rwanda, but he came to Canada a few months ago and is now working on a site planting trees near Prince George.

The problem is his missing brother. That is where Father Lowrey fits in, along with Sister Fran from Vancouver. Sister Fran, gentle nun, giver of politically correct coffee beans, and, apparently, foot soldier in the war against inhumanity to man. Lowrey filled us in on her work with refugees and her search to receive word on the refugee's brother. She thinks she has located him and is now trying to get some confirmation before trying to arrange for his safe passage to Canada. Communications are all a bit tenuous, so it seems she wants Rebero to get to Vancouver as soon as possible to help with this last stage. We're the ticket. The war against inhumanity to man is fairly bankrupt, so miracles are the choice form of transportation. Once again, that's us. Never dreamed I'd be classified a miracle, but the word did keep coming up all afternoon.

"Praise God. You've come at just the right time.

There's always a miracle to be found when we trust they'll be there."

Lowrey couldn't stop going on like that the rest of the afternoon, right through our lunch, and through the long, drawn-out phone calls to a fellow priest in Kamloops, to Sister Fran, and then to Prince George to leave undoubtedly confusing messages for our refugee to try to follow.

For the price of all the calls, I felt like saying, couldn't he take a bus?

Not, apparently, when a miracle has occurred and trustworthy, friendly company for the journey has safely arrived.

The miraculous plan is all very simple. Pick up the refugee tomorrow in Kamloops and drive him straight to Vancouver. Drop him off at the inimitable Sister Fran's. Simple. Straightforward. And that is exactly what I don't like about it. I was just getting used to the relaxed and roundabout route Indrin and I were forging on our now joint holiday. A straightforward trip spells the death of that. The non-linear ramblings of two happy wanderers cut short with one clean burst of speed straight down the Coquihalla highway.

Over the last couple of days, Vancouver has become not so much our destination as an escape route if our journey together starts to get awkward or boring or uncomfortable in any way. It's a kind of an ending we know is inevitable, but that we do not want to hurry by acknowledging. And for me, at any rate, the whole journey is now nothing more than an excuse for talks in the car and sitting long hours in and around a tent. None of this has been discussed. It is simply what has happened and I am quite happy about the arrangement. In fact, as I think about this, I realize the only thing I do not want right now is to arrive anywhere.

But how do you tell a kindly priest, no doubt relieved to be off the topic of the end of world for a moment or two, that you don't very much care for the idea of helping a poor, shell-shocked refugee find his long-lost brother? Especially when it is simply because it puts a damper on your holiday. You're *probably* going to Vancouver, but you didn't feel like going *tomorrow.* This does not have a great ring to it. Sounds maybe just too spoiled-North-American to admit it's how you actually feel. So you say brightly, "That's fine. We can take the refugee. Where do we pick him up? What time do we meet him?" If you happen to be Indrin Krishnayya, you also look truly happy to help out. In fact, your eyes shine with a kindly, holy light. But if you're nasty old Randi Tyler, you'll do the right thing, say the right words, but you resent it inside. And then you blow up at the well-meaning kid who calls you, quite accurately, on your bitterness.

A sharp sting bites into my leg. My instant reflex kills the mosquito with one quick slap of the hand. No thought about it required. Straight, sweet, physical response to the issue at hand. No wonder I bite people's heads off sometimes. Isn't some of it instant reflex? A simple survival mechanism? A little discomfort. Whack. Instant satisfaction. Okay, maybe not complete satisfaction. I reach down to scratch my leg. A welt starts to form. I scratch again.

I'm still scratching while alternately digging around in the supply box for the repellent when I look up to see Indrin walking down the campsite road.

"I think I need new runners," Indrin calls out as he nears the site. "Look." He balances on one leg, holding a foot in the air, flapping a piece of broken sole back and forth.

He is smiling, so I guess the fight, tension, incident – whatever it was – is over.

He sits down heavily on the picnic table bench.

"I owe you," he says as he pulls out his wallet.

"What for?"

"Half the fee." He motions around him. "Half the campground fee."

"Forget it, okay, Indrin?"

"No, I want to."

"Keep your money. You haven't taken a vow of poverty yet, have you?"

Indrin smiles a gigantic, smooth-lipped smile. "That's one that'll come naturally to me. I have no problem being broke."

He counts out some bills.

"Seven-fifty, right? I want to pay my share. I'm serious."

He starts digging into his pocket for the change.

"Forget the fifty cents."

Indrin keeps digging.

"Indrin, forget it. It's getting a bit embarrassing, don't you think?"

His eyes give me a steady, surveying gaze.

"Strange things embarrass you, I've noticed."

"Oh really. Like what?"

"Like you think nothing of bellowing across a truck stop to say the Tampax machine isn't working, but Father Albert saying 'Praise God' a few times over lunch gets you looking over your shoulder like you've got some kind of nervous twitch."

I begin to object, but The Man Who Would Be Priest interrupts me.

"I saw you."

"The whole restaurant thought we were Bible-thumpers setting up a cult," I say in my defence.

"I find it hard to believe anyone in the restaurant took that much notice of us. The waitress even had trouble remembering we were there."

Indrin shakes a few pebbles out of his shoe for emphasis.

"And here, with nothing but fir trees..." His hand waves away a mosquito. "...and insects to pass judgment, it's embarrassing I want to pay you the fifty cents I owe you? Put it toward the Tampax machine loss. Please."

I pocket the coins. His smile is infectious.

"You are an amusing boy, my friend."

"Can we consider the word, *boy,* for a moment. In a few short years I could be a Father Confessor. Yours, even."

"Not a big, bloody chance of that, my boy."

"Seriously. *Boy?* Doesn't it sound just a bit odd, *girlie?*"

I'm enjoying this. Back to our friendly verbal sparring. Playful jests. I like to use the word *boy* with Indrin.

Boy. Not man.

It seems less threatening.

Crouching down to start a fire in the pit, I realize I never have figured out the best way to pile up kindling. And I also realize that I cannot say I have ever dated a man. Guys, yes. Men, no. Men are uncles, certain news anchors, and the suits we get for panel discussions on the economy. Men on an intimately, personal level, however, are not in my realm. Neither are guys – at least since the Turner fiasco on the mountain when I scratched guys off my list for at least the near future. But boys – or rather this one particular boy – gives me just the level of testosterone I can manage. The only dose of manhood I can accept in close proximity to me. It also doesn't hurt that he happens to be Mr. Chastity too. That certainly reduces the risk of any heart-rending brushes with masculinity in its rawest form. Although I can't say I haven't wondered how much would-be priests try to live up to vows they haven't taken yet. It is an interesting thought in Indrin's case.

I watch him setting out the ketchup, mustard, and various bags he pulls out of the cooler onto the picnic table. His limbs are long, his movements smooth, calm. In some ways, Indrin is the most physically appealing creature I have ever met, ever laid eyes upon. His lashes are long. I feel my cheeks burn as I think about this, but more than once I have forgotten what I was saying when I started watching his eyelashes.

What did we call it in high school when we blinked

eyelashes against someone's cheek?

Butterfly kisses.

So daring we were in the back hallway during school dances.

Indrin, I have something to show you. Feel that? Butterfly kisses.

Listen to me. Why don't I write a soft rock ballad for a LITE FM station and be done with it? It's a bit of a comeuppance to find proof my emotions are as vapid and childish as the rest of the radio-listening public's. I feel myself thrown into a sudden, awkward kinship with people I would rather not be linked to. Is this what eastern mystics mean when they talk about "oneness"? All of us collectively humming along to the same Whitney Houston tune in the car?

Oneness.

"It's a small world," I blurt out suddenly, as the kindling catches fire. It's true, after all. I mean, I learned that lesson by heart from the family pilgrimages to Disneyland when I was a kid. And so, I sing out the song now, in full Disney exuberance. My voice gets louder as it soars up, searching for something close to the right note. I carry on with the chorus until I'm sure I've irritated every camper for miles, until I have telepathically united with every small world out there, every Disney doll in every ethnic costume. I finish with some splashy percussion.

Big drum roll on the side of the rusty barbecue pit.

Suddenly I'm chuckling. The world is hilarious. Here in my head anyway.

"Did you have wine I didn't know about?"

Indrin is leaning back, arms folded, watching my Disneyworld pageant play.

"Good idea, my boy. But wrong."

I switch keys and change musical directions.

"How did that song go? 'We are the world' or something like that?"

Suddenly I'm a lounge lizard. "Sing it with me, people."

I break into an interpretive dance as I hum the words I don't know, which is most of them. When I come back to the title line, I stop short.

"How *did* they come up with that bit of egocentricity posing as compassion? Egocentric and ethnocentric. You have to wonder about it."

Suddenly I'm put off "oneness." Cynicism to the rescue. My innate critical faculties have once again saved me from the sweet, saccharine pit of the collective.

"I've never met anyone like you," says Indrin.

Somehow, despite the intended joke, his words break something open inside me.

Anyone like you.

There is nothing in those words that sounds like a "line" when Indrin speaks them. In fact, spoken in his voice the words shape me into someone unique and loveable. His words are as clear, open, and honest as his eyes.

Like me.

He has never met anyone like me. My head spins a bit, slowly, like my insides are turning in two directions at once, and I realize I am perched dangerously over a cliff.

I cannot be falling for this person. It is clearly a classic rebound situation. Besides, I have already broken up with Turner this year and Indrin heads to the Toronto School of Theology in the fall, where they wouldn't be real keen on him having a female roommate, so this would make for two breakups within the calendar year. That's one more than my pattern – and frankly I still have reason to question my mental stability since the first. There are simply too many things to consider, too many thoughts rushing at me.

"I don't think I'm hungry anymore," I say, looking at shrinking orange flames.

I blink my eyes a few times. The spontaneous dance number must have made me a bit dizzy. I watch a rather fuzzy fire die out.

"It's plain to see I should not have quit Girl Guides when I did. After the first meeting."

I add the last phrase after an almost audible beat. Being raised by television has scarred my generation. At least it has scarred me. *Ba DA Bah.* The punchline drum roll. I honestly wait for it sometimes. I listen for laugh tracks.

Indrin is not laughing, though. He looks truly concerned. Suddenly I lose my balance and slam my knuckle into the metal rim of the barbecue pit. He comes over to help me up. Deep-set, empathetic brown eyes. Dark lashes moving. I want to kiss his eyelids. I want to kiss his mouth. To press my lips against his and hold them there just so I can feel his soft breath warm my mouth. His hand on my back guides me to the bench. The care coming out of his eyes toward me shames me somehow. My cheeks feel hot and prickly and this doesn't make sense until I realize tears are flooding my skin with salt.

"I'm sad, Indrin. I can't help it. I'm sad."

"I know."

He strokes my forehead.

"I don't think I can stand it."

I know.

Did he say it, or did I just hear him think it?

I know.

Indrin the boy is gone. A caring, elderly man now rocks me in his arms. I no longer feel hot. Curled inside his embrace, I shake myself to stop shivering. My jaw trembles, my teeth tap an erratic rhythm. The chill in the air is terrible. Just when did the wind come up?

~ ~

INDRIN TELLS ME that's about when I passed out. Or rather, when I got even more delirious before falling asleep in the car on my way back here to Father Lowrey's two days ago. He leaned across the immaculate white bedspread when I was half-awake this morning and said he was glad I was finally back in the land of the living. Then, after he filled me in on my curious exit from consciousness, he also said I should try to go back to sleep and keep getting well since everybody was just so glad the fever seemed to have broken.

Both he and Indrin are gone at the moment. An hour or two ago, I heard a door slam after lots of muffled conversation down the hall, and I haven't heard anyone come back so I figure they must be back at church or touring the town again.

I sit now propped up on some efficiently overstuffed foam pillows in a flawlessly neat room with one chest of drawers, a framed picture of the Virgin Mary, and an array of pleasantly benign books – the tamer mystery stories, *Reader's Digests.* This is the kind of room childhood friends' families had for guests – rooms that always looked strange and exotic to me since our family had no extra space for anything like a *guest room.* It was kids to the couch and onto the floor when Aunt Margie, Uncle Joe, and the cousins came from Saskatoon. But now here I am in a proper guest room, in a Catholic rectory no less, awaiting lunch to be brought to me by a beleaguered-looking church secretary named Jan. She has no business getting my lunch, but I do wonder about the air of overwork. How much Catholic Church business could there be in a community this size?

I shut the *Reader's Digest* on my lap. Laughter does not feel like the best medicine today, at least not when it is supposed to come from jokes that I could swear are the same ones I read in *Digests* twenty years ago on rainy days in my grandmother's apartment. *Plus ça change,* so they say.

My feet kick their way out from under the blankets and I stand up. In the vertical position the killer headache has still not gone, I discover. But the ache feels thinner. Not so much a brick wall as a translucent polypropylene. I can begin to make out my thoughts and I know I am not having any poor woman hauling lunch to my bed. She leaned over me to ask about bringing me a sandwich when I woke up a little while ago, before I could think straight.

Standing in a pair of panties and an old, torn undershirt, I look around for my clothes. Not having packed a peignoir set suitable for this picture-perfect guest room straight out of a 1975 issue of *Good Housekeeping,* I grab up the one sweatshirt I can find at the bottom of my duffel bag. It doesn't smell too strongly of campfire smoke. I catch sight of myself in the mirror. Now I realize it is me who looks the overworked church secretary. Jan, the real church secretary, may actually look more like Sophia Loren. A crucifix looms over my stringy-haired reflection. No lipstick, no hairbrush. No wonder wimples and habits came into popularity. I could certainly stand a little more camouflage today.

I hear what sounds like kitchen clattering so I pick up some speed. Socks, where are the socks I can use as slippers? Jeans? Where are on earth did I throw my jeans? There is a neatly-folded pile of white towels on the dresser. I take the largest, wind it around like a sarong skirt, and open the door.

Down the hall there's a radio announcing *your favourite hits from the sixties, seventies, and eighties!* and I walk in on Jan, the church secretary, leaning against the kitchen counter, taking a long drag on a cigarette. She lowers her hand and waves the smoke away.

"Well, the dead rise again. Some sooner than others. I thought we got all your things into the wash," she says, eyeing my sweatshirt.

"Oh, that's where they are."

A thick, dreamlike memory comes back. I'm sweating and dizzy and I hand my clothes to a woman I don't know, a woman who walks to the window and lets daylight into the room.

Jan sets her cigarette down on the side of the kitchen sink and walks over to flip the grilled cheese sandwich hissing in the frying pan. My mouth waters.

"Sit down, it's just about ready. I'd offer you a coffee but I don't know if that would be the best thing for you just yet. Would you like another apple juice?"

She waves a little cardboard Tetra Pak at me over the open fridge door.

"Yes, thanks."

I puncture the hole with my straw and take a sip. The satisfying, sweet liquid rushes past my teeth, fills my mouth, and sends a cool feeling down my throat and into my chest. This is the only sensation that has brought me relief over the past couple of days. Sweet and cool against my tongue, apple juice is what my mother gave me when I had fevers as a kid. My straw makes a loud slurping sound.

"Pardon me."

I smile sheepishly at Jan who aims another puff of smoke at the open window.

"No problem. I'm glad you're feeling better."

"Where's Indrin and Lowr– and Father Albert?"

"Over at the drugstore. Indrin wanted to make some photocopies and the machine in the office isn't working."

Jan dishes up my grilled cheese sandwich. Beautiful melted cheddar seeping out the sides, dark golden-brown toast. She has even garnished my plate with a pickle. Food has truly never looked so good.

"Oh, this is...."

I crunch into the dill.

"Thank you so much."

It's hard to chew vigourously when you are smiling broadly.

"Not too garlicky, I hope. I like 'em garlicky."

"Perfect, thanks."

This is life, I think. Sometimes you have to get sick to remember just how good it is to sink your teeth into a sandwich, slurp some apple juice. The dill makes another satisfying snap against my teeth. *With relish,* I think. This is what it is to eat *with relish.*

"You want relish?" Jan says, opening the fridge.

"Uh, no thanks."

I didn't think I said it aloud. I was sure I hadn't. Thought is bleeding into outer realms for me now. My pilgrimage with Indrin has either led me into a very strange world – or I'm sicker than I thought.

"I was just thinking how perfect this is, that this is what it means to eat with relish. It's really good. Thank you."

"No problem. It's a nice change from the office. Usually the housekeeper comes in to help with meals or get them sorted out, but she's gone to Kelowna for a few days off so lately it's been all hands on deck."

Jan exhales long and loudly, aiming the smoke away from me.

"Sorry about this. I didn't expect you out here."

"No, it's fine."

In this clear light of day, Jan looks neither church mouse nor Sophia Loren. More Jackie-Burroughsmeets-Annie-Lennox. She looks to be in her late forties, with a suspiciously bright series of blond streaks in her short, spiky hair. An almost crisp tan stretches from her forehead down to the painted toes peeking out the tops of her exercise sandals. She wears a sleeveless tank-style shirt that shows defined biceps. Her slacks are tropical-bright. *Cruisewear catalogue,* I think. There's a slightly sardonic air about her, one that makes me feel right at home.

"Who's Turner? If you don't mind my asking." Jan asks me this as she pulls up a chair and proceeds to crush the last life out of her cigarette stub.

"Turner?"

"Yeah, Turner. I'm sure it's *Turner* you've been saying in your sleep this morning."

"Oh, that would be what I've been saying, all right. Turner. He's my ex."

"Ah. Sorry I asked." Jan pushes her cigarette pack to the edge of the table, out of her line of sight.

"No problem," I tell her.

I manage another bite of my sandwich but it suddenly feels dry in my mouth. Damn you, Turner. Damn you for everything you've put me through. Another round of dizziness spins me inside as I think this, and I have to hold the edge of the table and fix my eyes on my plate so I stay steady in both mind and body.

"It's been a rough time," I say, as much to myself as to Jan.

"I've been there too, don't worry about it. Just eat your sandwich and try to get your strength back. You gave everybody quite a scare."

"Indrin told me this morning when he came in that it's been two days. I can't believe it."

"Well, you've been pretty sick." Jan briefly eyes her pack of cigarettes like a bird of prey then flicks her gaze back to me. "You've had an incredible fever and when Father Albert got the doctor here yesterday – which is no mean feat these days – he told us you likely had a bad flu virus but that he'd want to check you into hospital if you didn't start to improve soon."

"Hospital – God. That truly would have been the icing on the cake."

Jan raises her eyebrows, forcing a series of neat creases across her brow, her very sun-baked brow.

"I'm allergic to them," I explain. "To hospitals. To doctors too probably, but they're even harder to avoid when you have to keep running back to them every time you need a refill on something as simple as a birth control prescription. I mean, it all seems a little archaic to me. They really should have some easier method – not of birth control, I guess – but of refilling prescriptions anyway. You know what I mean?"

"Well," starts Jan carefully. "I'm not sure if I feel that way about doctors and hospitals. The birth control thing is a little more difficult since –"

"Oh my God, I'm sorry. Here I am sitting in a Catholic Church and I –"

"A rectory, actually."

"Church, rectory – whatever. Sometimes my mouth is just too big."

I'm dying at the moment. I feel my face beating even hotter than before, with the blood rushing past my cheeks to burn my ears and chest. This is a full-fledged blush, a full-fledged humiliation. On top of it all, my head feels like it's being slammed with a board. She could be a nun, for all I know, since they don't have to wear the outfits anymore – the habits. There's no way of knowing.

"That's okay. Don't be embarrassed. It's just that I used to teach the Serena method."

"The rhythm method?"

"A much more accurate version of it. It's actually got a far better track record than what you might think. I speak from personal experience."

She offers me a dry, knowing chuckle to cool my searing humiliation.

Thank you, Jan. You're a sport.

Suddenly I'm feeling somewhat better. At least she's not a nun. I thought she seemed too close in character to me, too much my sister in the secular, sinning sense. In utter relief, I decide to build upon our reestablished connection.

"Now you said you *used to* teach it. So obviously it wasn't the greatest method in the world – even for you." I give her a sly smile, before trying another bite of my sandwich.

"Well, not exactly. It's just that…it's just that my husband died and afterwards –" Jan finishes by fumbling with her hands and glancing toward her cigarettes.

"Oh my God. I'm so sorry, Jan," I say. "I can't believe myself today. I'm sorry for saying anything."

I no longer want to eat or talk or in any way acknowledge my consciousness. If I could crawl back into bed, maybe I could convince myself this has all been just another one of the weird hallucinations I was having with the fever. This is no less disturbing than seeing evil-looking faces in the cotton weave of the pillowcase. No less weird than thinking Turner was kissing Indrin behind my back.

"No, please don't worry about it," says Jan. "It's okay. I don't mind talking about it. It's just that you teach it in couples – and I really couldn't have faced my old routines anyway. It's been almost a year now and even though I'm slowly getting back into things, a few Catholic Women's League things, I'm just not there yet."

I allow myself another long, surveying look at Jan. Her sharp edges and piercing eyes led me down the entirely wrong path. What I had first expected was a worldly, wisecracking divorcée – maybe even a lesbian with a mind so laser-focused it could carefully ignore the less tolerant parts of the Catholic Church. Instead I'm talking to a recently widowed woman who is a card-carrying Catholic Women's League member at that. The fact that she has also spent part of her adult life teaching the rhythm method to bright-eyed young newlyweds who no doubt *saved it* until marriage is neither here nor there, it just makes it that much more surprising that I feel such a warmth for her.

Jan's hand twitches toward her cigarettes and this time I assure her it is okay with me, that I won't immediately fall back into my sick bed at the first whiff of nicotine. In fact, I urge her to smoke, hoping she'll feel comfortable again and wishing that breathing it in myself could work as a kind of penance. I also decide that the tiniest swallow of coffee, if it is watered down with a lot of milk I don't normally take, won't kill me.

Our vices comfortably in hand, it takes virtually no time at all for me to learn she met her husband, Brad, at a fitness centre in Kamloops. They were both into body-building – not competitively, but seriously all the same. Something just clicked when they met; neither of them could say exactly what – except that time had proven them right. They'd been married just less than twelve years when Brad was diagnosed with cancer.

And suddenly I'm telling her about my family. Mom and Dad and my sister Julie and how we all reacted when we got the news about Dad's cancer. In my case, I was locked away in my office fighting back tears over some stupid editing problem before the phone even rang.

But it was like I knew.

They found it way too late. It might have been curable earlier – had Dad been a little less allergic to doctors himself, had he been a little more honest about what kind of pain he was feeling, had the world unfolded differently than it did. Everyone reacted normally – denial, grief, anger, acceptance – all the proper emotions in more or less the proper order. Everybody but me, that is. I think I lost it; I just didn't know that I did at the time. So, when Dad went through the worst of the hell with the chemotherapy and then the radiation, everybody was at his side but me. I couldn't get away from work. We had a provincial election going and I was producing the live broadcast. Then it was a documentary that couldn't hold. After that, I think we had hired two new reporters who needed their hands held. It was just such a busy time.

I had planned to come home for Christmas. That much was ritual and I had no intention of breaking it. I would have been there come hell or high water, as they say; I just didn't bank on a cosmic comedy interceding.

"So he didn't make it, the six months he was supposed to have?" Jan asks.

"No."

"Brad was supposed to have had only about a year and he managed to live for another two years after he was diagnosed. We were lucky when it came right down to it."

"I didn't get the luck gene in my DNA. I got the other one, the evil twin version, because – the thing is – it wasn't the cancer that did it. It was a car accident. I lost both my Mom and my Dad."

And suddenly I've said all I can say. I can't talk about it anymore. It shocks me to have said as much as I have. But Jan seems to get this instinctively so there is no strain whatsoever. She just nods and gets up to dump her ashtray. I'd hug her for the non-reaction if I could let myself acknowledge I was feeling anything right now.

I try another bite of pickle, then sandwich, before I blurt out, "You know, I met Turner a year to the day after my parents died."

"It's funny how some things happen," is all Jan says, but it's enough somehow.

I'm saved from further personal disclosure when I hear a car pull into the driveway. Doors slam and footsteps near the house. Batman and Batboy return to the Batcave. I leap up, rewrapping my towel sarong, and start down the hall, sandwich in hand.

An animated conversation dips in volume as the front door opens.

"As far as I'm concerned," says a now stage-whispering Father Lowrey, "I never have seen a successful interpretation of that quatrain. They always ask, 'Is it a future Pope? Is it John Paul the First?' Well, I wonder if that is even the right question. What we should be asking ourselves is whether it's a reference to the very institution – Oh, hello Jan!"

"Hi Father, Indrin."

"How is Miranda?" I hear Indrin ask.

Leaning against the bedroom door, with my towel skirt gaping open and my mouth full of sandwich, I am not in the best position to answer when I hear Jan say, "You can ask her yourself. She's up."

Footsteps start straight down the hall, so I leap back into bed and cover up. Once again I'm the guest neatly wrapped into the white chenille bedspreaded guest room – picture-perfect, except, perhaps, for the toast crumbs all over my face. Handy I did not have a silk peignoir set after all; I am wiping my greasy fingers on my sweatshirt when Indrin taps gently on the door and peeks in.

"Hi. I thought you were up."

"I was," I say, still chewing my last bite, "but I haven't got clothes yet. I didn't feel quite right about greeting Lowrey naked in his own kitchen."

My bare foot kicks out from under the blankets to prove my point. Indrin's smile fills the room.

"I'll bet you are the first naked woman to dine at his kitchen table."

"I can't believe I did this, Indrin."

"Did what? He'll never know about you eating naked in the kitchen, if that's what you're worried about."

I stare at Indrin. When is he being facetious and when does he actually believe I would worry about something like that?

"No, I can't believe I got sick like this."

"You really think it's a surprise?"

Indrin settles down on the foot of my bed.

"I'm surprised you didn't get sick earlier."

His voice becomes quiet, serious. Overly gentle.

"I didn't know you were engaged to Turner."

"Oh, could we forget about Turner? I've been sick enough, haven't I? I'm not anxious to add nausea to my current symptoms."

Indrin is staring at me. I run my hand over my swamp-grass hair to smooth it down.

"I didn't mean to pry, " he says now. "I found an *On the News of Your Engagement* card in the trunk."

"Oh, that. I don't care. I don't care that you know. A breakup is a breakup. It's honestly not worse than any of the others."

I think about a few of the others. The big-fight scenario. The other-girlfriend scenario. The tears. The working it out. The trying again.

This is better. A hell of a lot better. There really is not a lot to rehash with your loved one after he strands you on a mountain.

Indrin squeezes my foot gently. I nod a bit of a smile at him, but pull my foot out of the way. I have now had enough of caring conversations and demonstrative support. Sympathy, even its better cousin empathy, only gets in the way most of the time. How are you supposed to get over something with people hemming and hawing all about you?

Suddenly I see high-school girls clamouring around a fallen volleyball teammate. *Are you O-Kay? Are you O-Kayee??* It annoyed me even then. Some girls seemed to love the attention. Me, I would never let myself fall, just to avoid that whole irritating spectacle. No matter how big the bruise was growing under my gym clothes, no matter how speedily swelling the ankle.

"Could you ask Jan about my clothes?"

"Sure," says Indrin, and he's off.

Faster than a speeding locomotive.

One good thing about my Wonder Boy friend is that he generally takes my cues pretty fast. Superman. I do catch myself thinking of him that way. Skinny student turned superhero rescuer on the mountaintop. Short-order cook turned spiritual tour guide. And when he transforms himself from Altar Boy to Boy Guru in my head, it is never because of anything he says; it is because of what he seems to refrain from saying.

"Sure," is what he said leaving, but I could swear I heard him thinking something about peace, about sending me peace. His presence is probably what makes me think this; something of his calm always seems to seep into me.

The door opens and this time it's Jan. She leans only halfway through the door frame. "Your clothes are still in the dryer."

"Oh, that's okay. Come on in," I say, happy to see my newly-adopted soul sister again.

She waves her cigarette in response.

"I'll find you a housecoat."

With that she is gone, and soon I am seated in the living room in a man's plaid robe, having tea with Jan, Lowrey, and Indrin. Indrin is flipping through some of his freshly-photocopied sheets and asking Lowrey about earth changes.

"Are there a lot of similarities about predictions for the West Coast?"

"Well, they're not like they are for California, but British Columbia could apparently stand to lose coastline, let's put it that way."

Lowrey shuffles a few more pages.

"Look at this. This is a map of one potential scenario."

"Let's just hope the Coast will still be there when we arrive," I interject.

Jan grins between puffs.

"Oh, this is all speculation," Lowrey goes on. "I'm very aware of that. Some of the authors of these predictions will have no credibility at all. Attention seekers, perhaps, who knows? There's quite a range of vastly different scenarios here and they certainly can't all be right. There's also a very big difference between your standard run-of-the-mill New Age psychics and some of the highly documented Marian apparitions. But it is interesting to look at what's being said and at what people are seeing – and fearing. Even the greatest prophets can only speak their dreams and try to explain what they see and feel."

"And pray," says Indrin. "And pray for guidance about what they see."

"Exactly right," nods Lowrey. "The important thing to remember is they don't create events. What happens is up to God. And nothing is etched in stone. We can pray for intercessions; we must. At Fatima, Our Lady asked us to pray, pray the Rosary."

"Fatima?" I ask.

Lowrey searches my face with a certain bewilderment.

"Yes, at Fatima," he repeats. "I mentioned it the other day, remember? When you and Indrin first came by."

"Portugal. Is that the place in Portugal?"

"Exactly right. Our Lady appeared to some little children there. This was in 1917. She told them to pray the Rosary to earn peace for the world and for the end of the war. She promised that special devotion to Her Immaculate Heart would ensure salvation and a place of refuge, although the souls who embraced this path would suffer much.

"The Blessed Mother appeared to Lucia, one of the children, as a dazzling clear light, like a beautiful crystal with the sun streaming through it. I've pondered this image," says Lowrey, "so often. It seems such a lovely thing, such a perfect image. It makes me think of the Prayer of St. Francis."

Indrin smiles. "I like that," he says.

"I don't know it," I remind them. "What's the prayer?"

Lowrey turns from Indrin to me.

"Well, the prayer asks God to make you a channel of His peace, so this image of the crystal with the light pouring through it seems utterly perfect. A perfected channel of love and light. Here we say the St. Francis prayer often, since this is the St. Francis of Assisi parish, after all. Besides, it's a favourite of mine."

His tone of voice is patient and fatherly, which, I suppose, is only appropriate. I feel like I'm in Sunday school. Or rather, since I never went, I imagine this is what Sunday school would have felt like. My body wants to squirm. I'd have been a poor student, I'm sure. A student who would have reached for the crayons and secretly tried to colour instead of properly listening to the Bible story. I look around the room. More neatly shelved books, a vaguely seventies-style green vase filled with dried spirea, a macrame plant holder. No colouring books here, as far as I can see. No escape. But then, it doesn't feel completely stifling. The room just feels insulated, the outside world safely muffled by green shag carpeting and wood veneer panelling.

"This is all documented," says Lowrey suddenly. "You can read about the Fatima apparition if you like. There are many books on it and other Marian apparitions."

My musing about the room was only that. I hadn't

meant to look skeptical, but maybe that expression is one my face assumes by default now. The result of overuse.

"It sounds very interesting," I say as neutrally as I can, swallowing my discomfort and the creepy feeling all this supernatural talk sends through me.

Soothed, Father Lowrey continues explaining.

"Rays of light came from her palms and poured into the earth where she showed them a shocking image of souls in torment. Prayers in devotion to her Immaculate Heart could save them, she promised, and could even end the war. But she warned that unless people ceased to offend God, another war, even worse, would begin. And, as we all know, of course, that other war did come to pass. One other important message was given to the children, but the contents were never made public."

"So that's where the Japanese apparition comes in, then?" asks Indrin.

"Yes, that's right."

"There was a Marian apparition in Japan, too?" I question.

"Yes, in 1973, in Akita, Japan," Lowrey answers promptly. "The statue of Mary there also wept on several occasions. Many believe the message Our Lady gave there is, in fact, identical to the third secret of Fatima."

"So what was that message?" I ask.

"A warning for the entire world, I'm afraid," says Lowrey. "Sister Agnes, the nun who heard Mary's messages, was told that if people did not change their ways, God would allow a terrible punishment to occur. This would be a punishment of our own making, something so terrible all humanity would be affected, and it would be a deluge worse than the flood, annihilating huge numbers. What would happen is that humanity would finally have to bear the consequences of its actions alone, instead of having them mitigated by God. We'd be left entirely on our own to face a calamity we have brought about ourselves through our deeds and our wrong-thinking. I often wonder whether that means some biological warfare disaster. Or whether the nuclear problem is still the biggest threat."

We sit in silence. I no longer feel safely ensconced in this modest living room, but it is not the fear of apocalypse that has got me reeling. It is shock at seeing rational human beings talking like cult members. I wonder when Lowrey will pull out the cyanide pills and suggest a cool drink of lemonade. Sweat beads start to form on my upper lip while I shiver at the same time. Nothing, I'll say nothing.

"This is all preventable, I still believe," adds Lowrey. "It all depends on our trust in God and our determination to change our ways. I don't think I've read anything that makes me think it's too late. We are simply to make our prayers turn the tide."

Indrin picks up several more sheets of paper, setting the previous one back down on the carpet of forest-green shag.

"This account of Mary supposedly speaking through a woman in the States, do you think it's true?" Indrin holds his papers quizzically. "The warnings she writes about are pretty grim. She doesn't think the destruction will come through nuclear war, though. According to her it will be natural disasters like famines and earthquakes."

Suddenly it's too much. End-of-the-world discussions are not a typical part of my day and, as Lowrey starts to respond to Indrin, I'm angry at the casual tones of voice they use for their calm discussion of the annihilation of millions.

"Do you honestly buy all this?" I ask the room.

Jan, silent until now, sighs a cloud of smoky relief from her lips. "It would sure as hell make me nervous if I believed any of it. Pardon my French, Father, but I'm surprised you give it the time of day." Another vigorous drag on her cigarette punctuates her remark.

"The only thing that makes me nervous, Jan, is that our own bishop doesn't understand my interest in Marian apparitions, never mind my reading of modern psychics." Turning to me, Lowrey explains. "It's simply research, of course, but he has trouble with it. I have to watch my back in the New Age book section now."

"Ever since that blabby Madge Martin saw you there with your special order, you mean," says Jan.

"I've said it before and I don't mind saying it again. Some of those staunch Catholic Women's League members could make the Pope nervous about opening his mouth."

This gets a good laugh from Jan.

"Still," adds Lowrey, "I have Saint Paul's advice to rely on – and to back me up with the Bishop. The passage from Thessalonians: 'Do not despise prophecies but verify everything and hold on to what is good.'"

"So you're undercover with all this doomsday stuff,

are you?" I ask in as innocent a tone as I can utter, although it still betrays a certain delight at discovering Lowrey's secret life as a rebel.

"He's just not supposed to bring it up in his homilies anymore," cuts in Jan. "Although Sundays were certainly livelier when all those people roared over to the grocery store to load up on food supplies directly after church. Everybody, but everybody, suddenly out there with shopping carts of canned goods." Jan chuckles as she crushes her cigarette butt into oblivion.

Lowrey moves to the defence.

"That was never my intention. You know that's never what I suggested. Prayer. That's all. But it's always easier for people to think about what they can buy to solve a problem than to look into their hearts."

A familiar dull thud is returning to my head. I tuck my foot up under me and sit higher in my green vinyl throne as I work up the energy to speak. Meeting Jan's eyes in mutual recognition allows me confidence to say what I truly think.

"All I know is if I spent as much time as you did considering the end of the world as we know it, I would either be clinically depressed or decide it's all a bunch of crap. In both cases, I wouldn't bother reading it anymore."

"All I know," says Lowrey gently, "is that I believe we have warnings before us and they tell us to pray. We can choose to pay attention or choose to ignore them."

Indrin looks up from his Nostradamus, or his Edgar Cayce, or whatever psychic or prophet or Catholic saint he happens to be reading now. There seem to be hundreds to choose from strewn all over the floor.

"It's not just a Christian phenomenon, either – all these miracles," Indrin suddenly announces to me. "So you can't pass it all off as some kind of Catholic hysteria. I was telling Father Albert earlier that my Uncle Ashok in Delhi saw the Hindu god Lord Ganesha drinking milk in a temple."

"A statue," clarified Lowrey. "It was a brass statue of their Lord Ganesha drinking milk. Very interesting. I find that very interesting."

"He would suck the milk from dishes and teaspoons offered to him," Indrin explains. "And the interesting thing is that apparently he'd accept it from both non-believers and devoted Hindus. It started a huge craze. My uncle says there was a terrible milk shortage in Delhi." Indrin then adds, "Lord Ganesha is the one with the elephant face," as if Lowrey and I should be up on our Hindu gods.

I almost add a sarcastic, "Oh yes, of course, *that* God. Why didn't you say so?" but I restrain myself.

What Indrin doesn't know is that I am up to speed on this particular phenomenon. We ran a story on it last September when the craze hit Canada. Here there were no milk shortages, but there were still plenty of hopeful Hindus gathered in temples across the country checking to see if the little fellow was thirsty. And, despite what the reporter breathlessly told me when she and the cameraman got back from the shoot, nothing they got on tape made me think any modern miracle had occurred. Even if a few drops did seem to disappear, so did the *miracle* itself when I found a scientist to explain *capil-*

lary action and a bit of elementary physics in a couple of dryly humorous clips.

"'Basic science *milked* by mass delusion,'" I finally blurt out in a fairly good rendition of that scientist's South African accent. My attempt at humour is lost, however, on Lowrey and Indrin, who don't react at all like the guys in the TV control room did.

But don't we all need a little chuckle right about now?

Elephant-headed Gods causing milk shortages in India.

Weeping Madonnas.

I'm lamenting the loss of the logical, enlightened world I used to know, the one I thought was supposed to have begun in the 18th century with lively cynics like Voltaire. *The Age of Enlightenment.* All the real thinkers of the day, weary of an unhealthy, Church-dominated world, were supposed to have put us onto a new path, a path of the intellect, or so I learned in university history classes. Now, today, clearly presented before me here in this living room, the decline and fall of the rigorous mind seems to be the hallmark of the 20th century.

"I don't know why you resist all this so much. None of it has to be frightening, I don't think," Indrin says. "For some reason I'm drawn to all these signs and miracles as much as Father Albert is; I don't feel depressed about any of it – just kind of concerned. Like we're all supposed to wake up and pay attention."

Indrin then sets down a sheet of paper that looks like another map of the West Coast. A drastically different, post-cataclysm West Coast where Denver is clearly denoted as a port city.

"But, honestly, what's the point?" I say in an attempt to appeal to their reasoning faculties. "Why waste time worrying about what hasn't happened and probably never will?"

Indrin opens his mouth to respond but I rush to finish.

"Even if some of this does come true, there's no point in knowing in advance. Unless someone is planning to build an ark here."

Lowrey tips his head, smiles.

"I'm not much of a woodworker."

"I'm serious. What's the point? You don't strike me as a survivalist ready to grab guns to defend your refrigerator, come the deluge." My head is getting worse. I lean back against the chair to try to steady myself.

"Why not be aware simply for the sake of being aware?" Lowrey picks up his pace, continuing in an increasingly excited patter. "Think about the possibility that God is trying to reach us with these warnings. If He is, then we would very rightly ask, 'What's the point?' and 'Why?' But our response should simply be to start searching our hearts. Sometimes our priorities shift and start to drift off course if we're not paying enough attention. Warnings or not, it is always the right time to search our hearts and look for God's guidance. As far as I'm concerned, none of this is really about survival, it's about waking up and starting to live with the right priorities in place."

"Tell her about the Rwanda incident," says Indrin,

getting up out of his chair and picking up his teacup.

"Would you like more?" he asks, nodding in my direction.

"No, thanks. And I wouldn't exactly call what happened in Rwanda an 'incident.' Genocide, yes. 'Incident,' no."

Lowrey leans over to hand his teacup to Indrin. "What Indrin's talking about is the Marian apparition in Rwanda six years before all the violence broke out."

"Like Medjugorje?" I offer suddenly, as the name comes to me. That apparition I do remember them talking about the other day in Lowrey's office.

The elderly woman down the hall from me at home also comes to mind now. She went to Medjugorje with her sister not too long ago. My brows squeeze together as I fight to stay with this memory – and with the conversation. I try to pretend the ache building between my eyes isn't there. The elderly woman with arthritis. Rose. Rose Hazelton. All the way to Yugoslavia and back and when she returned safe and sound, I asked her only about snipers, not heavenly apparitions. Little did I know her pilgrimage destination was only one link in a big gaudy chain of miraculous hot spots.

"So you're trying to tell me Rwanda is another pilgrimage place now? Like Medjugorje and Fatima?"

"Not now, no. No, not given what's been happening there."

"But you mean it's not just Yugoslavia she's been appearing in lately?" For some reason this strikes me as funny.

Now appearing, Our Lady, with a strong supporting

cast of believers. Coming soon to a mountaintop near you.

"Oh no." Lowrey stops briefly, theatrically even, and continues speaking, sitting taller in his chair, with a mounting, high-school-drama delivery. "There are about two hundred Marian apparitions occurring right now – a record number for the Church to investigate. Our Lady seems to have been appearing in a number of places around the world in the last few years. Now I haven't been to Medjugorje, but I did manage a trip to Fatima several years ago as well as to Garabandal in Spain.

"Garabandal was very moving. It's a tiny village in the north of Spain where Our Lady appeared to four little girls in the sixties. It was just beautiful: this little collection of red rooftops in the midst of lush green hillsides, tucked away in such a remote area. There's nothing commercialized at all about the place, nothing that would tell you at first glance that such a miraculous thing happened there – but you could feel it. And there was a lovely little outdoor chapel and brightly-coloured tiled markers showing where each of the appearances took place. Very simple. Very modest. Standing by the pines on the hilltop above the town was one of the most moving experiences I've ever had. I have no doubt something happened there – despite what that rude priest in the neighbouring town seemed to think. Do you remember me saying how rude he was, Jan?"

"I do, Father."

"I travel halfway round the world to visit the place, Miranda, and this fellow couldn't give me the time of day." Still bristling at the thought, Lowrey shakes his head. His eyes are wholly brimming with incredulity.

"There's to be a miracle there too. One day in the future. The date will be given only eight days before by one of the little girls – she's a grown woman now, of course. Won't that be a surprise for everyone who has shown so little faith?"

"Like the rude priest," throws in Jan.

"My thoughts exactly," says Lowrey before going on to fill me in on the rest of the widespread Marian phenomena. Apparently there aren't just apparitions occurring and miracles being predicted. There are countless messages from Mary being received by people from every walk of life, Catholics and non-Catholics, housewives and nuns. Every second seer seems to have been chatting with her lately. Even otherwise conventional priests are getting into the act.

"There's an Italian, Father Gobbi, who has been hearing special messages, *interior locutions* they're called, from Our Lady. I get them sent to me regularly since I'm a member of the group he founded – the Marian Movement of Priests."

Indrin pops his head out of the kitchen and rounds the corner with steaming cups in both hands. "You've got to tell her about Rwanda, though, Father," he says as he hands Lowrey a refilled teacup and settles back down amongst the doomsday papers.

"Oh yes, of course. Yes, in Rwanda, it seems she appeared to seven Catholic students," says Lowrey.

Just when I begin to get visions of a holy robed woman materializing in the middle of a school gym and perching herself atop a basketball hoop to have a frank chat with today's teens, Lowrey changes the picture.

"They would go into a state of rapture, unaware of anything around them. Their eyes were open, but they could see nothing but the Virgin and the light surrounding her."

My headache is worse now, but I'm so sick of being sick I refuse to give in to it. All the same, I'd like to cry. I thought I was over all of this.

"What did she say to them?" I ask, but my voice comes out more like a cracked sigh.

Indrin looks up, searches my face.

"Are you okay, Miranda?"

I start to nod, but that doesn't suit my head too well so I wave Lowrey on. "I want to know what she said."

Lowrey balances his teacup on his knee.

"She showed them turmoil. They saw visions of their country with so many bodies that there was no place to put them. Rivers of blood."

"I'm sorry I asked."

My foot is falling asleep, and as I slide my leg out from under me it squeaks across the vinyl. I sit shaking my leg, feeling the prickle of pins and needles as Lowrey adds the perfect finishing touches to his story.

"What she warned them of turned out to be the very scenario that began to occur in Rwanda six years later. But Our Lady had told them the prophecy was not just for Rwanda, but a warning for the whole world."

Lovely, I think. Does Mary never show up to predict happy events? *Hey everybody, listen up – and relax. I bring you tidings of sunshine, moderate weather, and no real worries.*

This is what gets me about prophecy in general. The

bad things in life just happen and there is nothing we can do about it. So why know in advance? Fat lot of good it did the people of Rwanda. Sure, a few of them had the lovely opportunity to see the horror before everyone else, but who wants a sneak preview of that kind of thing? If I had to know something in advance, I would want to know only the good stuff. Life is tough enough without having to anticipate the worst parts. I want things to look forward to. In fact, if I ever feel inclined to make predictions, I want to be a good-time prophet. I decide this. *Miranda's Happy New Age Predictions. Let the good times roll. Have a nice day. Have a nice life.* I see myself surrounded by rose quartz crystals and chimes in a New Age bookshop and suddenly I am very glad I'm not a prophet. The picture is somewhat nauseating. My forehead is sweating.

"I'll bet prophets in every era have the worst nightmares," I croak out. "All that knowing of the future would make their lives utter hell. That is, if they were, in fact, prophets, and not just losers with troubled REM sleep. Maybe that's the difference between a prophet and a guy who comes to work with circles under his eyes. The prophet thinks his bad dreams are a sign to the world. The other guy just realizes he shouldn't have eaten his supper so late."

Lowrey purses his mouth into a kind of wry smile.

"You do struggle to be a skeptic, don't you?"

"It's not that much of a struggle, I assure you."

Jan laughs out loud at this.

"Sometimes I think I should be the bishop around here. I'd put a stop to this prophecy stuff once and for all." She winks at me.

"It's research, Jan." Lowrey fumbles with his teacup and spills tea onto his slacks. "I don't think you understand how imp –"

"I was kidding, Father."

As she says this, Jan is already in the kitchen getting a rag to wipe up the tea. She hands it to Lowrey and gives his shoulder a reassuring squeeze.

"It's just – you know how I feel about hearing all that doom and gloom."

"Yes, I know," he says as he hands her back the cloth. "Thank you. I don't mean to go on about it."

My leg squeaks across the vinyl as I gather the housecoat around me and stand up.

"Listen, I'm sorry, Lowr – uh, Father Albert – but I think I better lie down again."

"Oh dear. Would you like anything? Anything at all?"

"No, thank you. I think I just need to lie down for awhile."

Indrin, covered with prophecies, quickly starts setting them down in different piles on the carpet. I thank Jan again for the sandwich and head down the hall. By the time I get to my bed, Indrin comes up behind me and gives me a steadying hand.

"I feel pretty stupid. Why can't I shake this?"

"You've been pretty sick."

"And we should talk, Indrin, about when to get going. There's still the refugee to pick up, right? Or are we too late?"

"It's all right. Lowrey phoned. We'll get him when

you're better. Just don't worry about all that right now, okay?"

I'm falling back against the pillows while Indrin pulls comfortingly cool sheets up over me. I'm heavy with fatigue and floating weightless at the same time. Indrin's breath warms my skin as he leans over to kiss my cheek. My hand encloses his and I tuck it securely under my chin as my eyes close and I start to see clouds shifting. They are white, pierced with brilliant streaks of almost blue light, and they tumble over each other. Behind them, like a dark canvas showing behind white paint, is another purple-black bank of clouds. My head pushes into the pillow. One giant white cloud now moves in from the side, obliterates everything from view.

False Starts

Another day of doomsday conversations interspersed with floating in and out of sleep has removed the last traces of flu, although I'm now left with a murky understanding of what I dreamed and what I heard predicted for the world and what may or may not have been the news of the day. Wars, earthquakes, tidal waves, and Revelation-style horsemen were all jumbled together yesterday and they are still tumbling around randomly in my mind today. Even so, I feel normal for the first time in days – normal in that, even though my head is now completely plugged up and my nose constantly running, I actually craved coffee this morning with my usual intensity. Even the weak and watered-down version I had the other day with Jan had tasted too strong to me, but this morning I wanted a nice hit of caffeine, maybe even a double espresso if I could find such a thing in Revelstoke. I wanted to sort out the refugee problem, to get on the road, and, more immediately, to get out of what I now think of as the *sick room.* My neatly folded clothes on the chair went straight into my bag. I was dressed and peeking in Lowrey's kitchen cupboard to find coffee when Indrin entered the room.

He asked me how I slept and I felt a little heat flush my face. Not the fault of any leftover flu, but rather the memory of an all too vivid dream featuring my friend Indrin himself. My friend and, in this dream, lover. It had to be the first real erotic dream of my life: simple, a bit strange, but definitely powerful.

We are standing on a mountain. I am in a nightgown and Indrin is pulling it up over my hips. His hands are smooth and he slides them over my body. Suddenly we are under water, breathing the water in, and fish swim above and around us like birds. When he enters me I feel a rippling. The stone into the lake, the lake responding in ever-widening circles.

Wave after wave.

THE BIGGEST WAVE woke me up, my body still clenched in a deep contraction. I lay there for a good five or ten minutes before that wave stopped and I could come up for air. Only then could waking daytime concerns creep into my consciousness: the craving for coffee, the desire to get organized.

And then he asks me how I slept. Forgive me, Indrin, if I avoid the question. Even a casual *fine* in response I think would give me away today. I have always been far too transparent.

The dream is still with me now as my hands grip the steering wheel and we speed down the highway, Indrin's hair flying out the window. I glance over at him as I reach for my coffee on the dash.

Wave after wave.

Water will never be the same for me again. Not lakes, oceans, or even rushing rivers.

I tear my thoughts away from the dream, back to the road, back to the issues of the day. It took quite a while to get away this morning. Lowrey has become more than a good Samaritan priest and almost a friendly uncle to us, cautious to make sure I was feeling well enough to travel and happily providing Indrin with enough doomsday reading material to take him to the end of the century, or the end of the world, whichever comes first. We have sandwiches, potato salad, and a thermos of tea, and I am now the dubious owner of a book on the Fatima Marian apparitions – reading material which Lowrey says I really should not dismiss without a careful read-through. In return for their kindness, we have left behind a bottle of the best Scotch I could find for Lowrey, another of the same for Jan, and a bouquet of pink and white carnations to brighten the apocalyptic mood of the house – my idea. It was after eleven by the time we left the house and I started loading up the car, and about eleven-thirty by the time Indrin came out of the church after his bit of morning quiet time.

Now we are back on track. At last. Full speed ahead. My giant travel mug is full. Indrin looks content. My foot presses down hard on the gas pedal and sends us speeding directly away from our previous happy aimlessness. There is now a task at hand and I have always been thorough and efficient at tasks, sometimes frighteningly so. The highway pulls me along. I sit up straight, my eyes less inclined to notice mountains, more focussed on a distant perspective point: the highway as a set of converging lines, a gunsight aimed at our point of arrival.

We are to meet Edmond Rebero at the bus depot in Kamloops as he gets off the 4:05 p.m. bus from Prince George. We have more than enough time, but I keep finding myself speeding. Or if I do not catch myself, Indrin does.

"Whoa, there. Where's the fire?"

My foot jumps off the accelerator abruptly. I had not realized my poor old car could even go that fast without hitting some kind of nuclear core meltdown.

"Sorry, Indrin."

"I just didn't see how we were going to make this next curve if you kept it up. Never mind the cowboys."

Cowboys is Indrin's term for the RCMP, for some reason. Royal Canadian Mounted Police. It makes as much sense as anything, I guess. They still ride horses in the Musical Ride.

"Get along little dogies."

Another cryptic warning from Indrin. Once again, I ease off the gas pedal. My foot keeps hurrying us along no matter what I seem to intend.

"You want me to drive instead?"

"Might as well."

I take a careful look at the logging truck in the rearview mirror before I pull onto the shoulder. It roars past us and I wait until the force of its slipstream subsides before I open the car door to switch sides. Indrin settles into the driver's seat and slides it back to make room for his long legs.

"You're a munchkin."

"I'm not tall is all."

Indrin gives me a look.

"Okay, so I'm on the scrawny side. But on a good day, I can get away with pushing the limits. Sometimes I go crazy, forget the Petite pantyhose, and go all the way to Average without batting an eye. The pantyhose size says it all, doesn't it? *Average.*"

He pointedly snorts at *average* but he says nothing since he's holding an elastic in his lips while he smoothes his hair back. All the same, I can tell he's trying to think up a comeback to the pantyhose line. After snapping the band around his ponytail, he waits, signalling while two more cars pass, then a wide smile rolls across his mouth. "How about Queen size?" His voice suddenly affects the lisping, exuberant tone of an over-earnest fashion commentator. "*Queen* size. Exclusively for the hefty man in drag!"

When he pulls out, it is obvious Indrin is in no hurry to break the sound barrier or even to get all the way to the speed limit. I physically push myself further back into my seat, trying to settle into the new, decidedly slower pace of the day.

Turns out Indrin has had different plans all along.

"We've got lots of time today," he says. "Why don't we have a picnic at Shuswap Lake? It's a great spot. I wouldn't mind taking some time to skip stones, just hang out."

Thanks a lot, Indrin. I just got lakes and oceans out of my mind.

This is what I think, anyway. "Sure, why not?" is what I say.

But suddenly I get a mental picture of the two of us skipping stones, Indrin unaware of the ironic humour of it all.

The stone into the lake.

The lake rippling in concentric circles.

Wave after wave after wave.

I take a moment to watch Indrin's long, dark eyelashes.

"Do you think it's weird I haven't tried to talk to Turner?"

This blurts itself out of my mouth. I don't know where it comes from, why Turner has shown up in my head.

"I don't know."

"I mean I did try to get him the once."

"Only you know whether you should phone him."

"I'm not so sure about that."

Why did I bring this up?

I search for a comfortable position in my seat, roll the window down to drown out any further chance of talk. But suddenly I'm yelling.

"I guess I wonder if I'm running away from it."

My mouth shoots these words out of me. I roll the window up in resignation.

Fine, mouth, you want to talk? Talk.

"I mean, maybe there's something I should deal with. What would a therapist say? *Own the pain. Own the anger.* Is that all crap? I mean, I wonder if I'm going to end up with even worse relationship problems if I don't deal with this Turner thing head-on."

"I don't think that's necessarily true. Denial has got a bad reputation these days but I honestly think it's the best thing sometimes. Maybe you just have to put the whole thing out of your mind."

Nearing the tail lights of a slow-moving truck, Indrin responds not by passing, but by easing off the gas pedal and slowing down even more.

"We've got time," he assures me again.

Yeah, right, Indrin. This kind of comment makes me crazy so I snap at him.

"Actually, no one ever knows how much time they have. Sometimes you think you have six months to do something and then the deadline is suddenly moved up – but no one tells you. I have no problem with deadlines. I just need to know what they are."

"Everything is a deadline to you, right? That's what comes from working in a newsroom, I guess."

"Yeah, I guess so."

I don't want to get into it all with Indrin. I don't even want to start thinking about any of it again – not Turner, not the accident, not my mom and dad. Not the fact that my dad and I hadn't been getting along before the cancer. That we'd never had an easy time of it.

Mom said we'd work it out, but I'd had it with my dad giving me his politely distanced and disapproving looks every time he met a boyfriend of mine, right from the time I was sixteen. "He's *fine,* Miranda. He's *fine,*" he'd say. Then would come the carefully weighted beat of silence before he'd add, "If you like that smug, silent sort of thing." It usually took only about another twenty minutes for the whole thing to turn into a shouting match, me screaming that I *did so* have common sense, him yelling that I was rebelling in the most *stereotypical* way possible and that any daughter of his could at least show a touch more imagination. Dating losers, apparently, was a crime, both romantically and intellectually.

Years later, the conflict got quieter, but only because the crevasse between us was deeper, only because the roar of the angriest river sounds muffled when it's that far down in the canyon.

By then, Dad's comments were restricted to random bits of wistfulness that would escape only after a Scotch or two. "He's not half the person you are, Miranda. Not half."

Sorry, Dad, if he doesn't measure up. They never do, do they?

I don't know whether my Dad truly was as much a perfectionist and control freak as I am – but as much as he might have wanted things to be perfect for me, I figured out long ago I would never get the male-female relationship thing sorted out to his satisfaction. It's the one thing I've finally given up trying to push and make perfect. It's the one area of my life where I have become realistic, where I don't believe in idyllic endings – at least for people like me.

Despite the perfect world my parents believed in, where people meet just the right partners at just the right time and make just the right choices to land them in happy Shakespearean comedic endings, I've known since high school that's not the universe where I lived. No Puck would jump out at the end of my Midsummer Night's Dream to "restore amends" and send mixed-up lovers back out to live happy endings. No Prospero could conjure a shipwrecked Ferdinand for this Miranda to marry and live happily ever after with in Naples. That doesn't happen when you're forever stirring up trouble by blurting out just the wrong things – never the soft, sweet things that the men I meet seem to need to soothe their fragile egos, the *I don't minds,* the *whatever you thinks.*

Neither was I interested in living any Shakespearean tragedy, any love ruined by passions-gone-wrong and hopes misplaced. I want to get by. I want to meet guys – a guy – who I can get along with and simply have fun with. I don't want *angst* and melodrama and elaborate stage fights; I don't even want particularly deep feelings. Funny, then, that my supposedly carefree relationships never turn out that way. That even the light, romantic ramblings with Turner turned psychodrama so early on. Our free and easy life together, a marriage of fun and music and good times, wrenched apart by Turner's dark, inexplicable yearnings for emotional roller coasters, for other women, for drugs. Funnier yet that I had resigned myself to it, to a life of it.

All for the sake of company. All for the sake of having someone with me on the biggest road trip of them all.

"I don't care, you know," I suddenly hear myself saying to Indrin. "I mean, I did that day. But I don't miss him or think about him. Right now, I find it even hard to remember what it was I liked about him. He's just so utterly vanished from my mind. That's the odd thing, I guess. How easily I can walk away from it considering I thought he was *the one.*"

Indrin gives me a brief, but unnerving, gaze. For a second, despite his dark skin, curling hair, and elegant arched nose, his eyes are my father's.

Don't you say a word, Dad. I've heard it all before.

"You probably just need time to sort it all out," says Indrin, "before you can think about it much. Don't be too hard on yourself."

This answer is simple. Is it Indrin's inherent spiritual simplicity or the simplicity of men in general? Not that I'm calling them simple – at least not all of them – just a little more straightforward, perhaps. Linear. *A to B to C.*

"I had a dream about Turner and you," he suddenly says.

Exit ingenuous Altar Boy; old man guru speaks. So much for linear.

I stare at him. "So?"

"You want to hear it?"

"Why not? It can't be worse than the real nightmare."

"It'll probably sound a bit weird."

"Please. What's weirder than my life? Go on."

"We were underwater. You and me."

"Just a second. When did you dream this?" I ask, trying to sound conversational.

"Last night."

Now I shift in my seat again. Take a big swig of coffee.

Indrin continues unravelling last night's dream from memory frayed by the day.

"We were underwater, swimming and – kind of floating around each other. I could hear a muffled, echoey sound, like a bumping of a boat hull – kind of like the sound you hear when your head's underwater in the bathtub and you bump the side of the tub. You know what I mean? Anyway, then something happened, either that sound stopped or – no, it just changed. Yeah, it was music. I could hear music. It was coming out of your mouth, but it wasn't like singing – more an orchestral sound. Then I could see Turner hiking – this was still underwater. He was hiking up a mountain that was really a mountain of tiny bubbles that came from your mouth when you made the music. But then, instead of getting to the top of it, he sank into all the air bubbles and disappeared. Then it was like you and I were fish and we swam over to his body."

Indrin pauses, searches the rearview window.

"Fish were feeding on him."

"Well, that's rather horrifying I'd have to say."

As ocean dreams go, I much prefer my morning wake-up call, complete with pleasant physical aftershocks, but this is not a dream I feel like sharing aloud.

Instead, I muse on Indrin's night-time journey.

"I like how it's my fault he dies."

"How do you get that?"

"Well, he sinks into the bubbles coming out of my mouth."

"It was other fish feeding on him."

"Yeah, but I killed him in this scenario. What's that supposed to represent? Those bubbles, are they supposed to be my words or something?"

"Hey, I just dreamed it."

"For you to dream it, Indrin, it has to be in your head somewhere. And in your head, my words are empty air bubbles."

"If you're looking to pick a fight, Miranda, it's no go. I'm on to you."

"What's that supposed to mean?"

"Nothing."

"What do you mean, nothing?"

"Listen, I'm not mad. I'm not trying to pick a fight."

My voice has taken on the affected, saccharine-sweet tone of a girl wheedling a soon-to-be-ex-boyfriend: *I won't be hurt at all. I promise. Just what is it about my body you don't like? Exactly what? I'm just curious, that's all.*

"Come on, Indrin, what do you mean?"

"Okay, sometimes you like to pick fights so you can…fill up air time. I'll use an analogy after your own heart. It's like filler, endless commercial time before getting to the main documentary."

"I fill air time?" This strangely deflates me.

"Yeah, sometimes."

Indrin looks at me. I feel a mental hand on my shoulder.

"I guess that's the air bubbles. That's all."

"Yeah. Air bubbles."

I look out the window. My eyes pick points on the asphalt and watch them rush at me. Just off the shoulder, the grass blurring by looks a dusty grey.

Air bubbles.

"Just tell me, Indrin, if you start feeling any danger of drowning in them, would you?"

~ ~

INDRIN SHAKES a spoonful of potato salad onto my paper plate. Shards of light break through the branches of the tree we sit under and dapple the grass around us. The buzz of motorboats and the shouts of kids carry clear across the lake. Waterskiers, picnickers. We have managed to drive right into high season, to pull up and park in the midst of summer. A couple of pairs of bare feet kick our blanket as they run past; the kids are charged with the full power of summer holidays just begun. They have got wind in their hair, sun in their eyes, and sand on their feet, feet still running from school doors out to the dusty playgrounds of an entire summer stretched before them.

I wonder how long Indrin will be travelling with me. We have not talked about what happens when we get to Vancouver, once we've dropped off our refugee friend, once we are faced with the final result of this spontaneous, rambling trip. The unsettling *what happens next* part of the adventure. For me, the only thing I can see ahead of me is the end of the road, the part of the trip where I wave bye-bye to my new friend and go back to my life.

My life.

Whatever that is or was.

To try to bring that reality closer in my mind, I consider phoning the newsroom and checking up on how things are going. Surely a few familiar voices talking about the perpetual problems in the newsroom could pull me back into my old self, or at least into a mental state I could recognize.

Randi Tyler? I don't remember her. Oh maybe, maybe. Just a minute now. Didn't she used to go out with Turner Mahoney? A bit of a workaholic, wasn't she?

No, I don't remember her.

This is now the longest stretch of time I have ever gone without phoning to check in with the line-up editor or to listen to the most recent complaints of Bill Wylie, the paranoid producer who shares my office. Surely a good rant from Bill could bring the old Miranda Tyler back.

The old me. The wisecracker who would never waste her breath in a conversation with anyone who believed in organized religion, never mind make him a travelling companion and confidant. The skeptic comfortable in her senior position in a newsroom family that only praised her cynicism, admired her for it. The Miranda who would never allow herself to be confused by a twenty-three-year-old neophyte, as well intentioned as he may be, and his peculiar brand of New Age Catholicism.

The old me who not only knew who I was but who was instantly sure of who everyone else was and what was best for them.

The old me who was sure.

It strikes me that I'm mixing up the phone number to the lineup desk. Unbelievable. 6-1-2-4? or is it 6-1-4-2? I honestly cannot remember a number I phone about twenty times a day in my *real* life.

But without even a newspaper in my life for days now, I would not know what to ask even if I got through to the desk.

"I've got to buy a paper," I announce, mid-mouthful of coleslaw.

Indrin looks back from the lake to me. "The news junkie needs a fix?"

"Some news junkie, lately. Quebec could have separated and I wouldn't know it."

"They had the Kamloops paper at the hot dog stand."

"That'll be a start." I get up, brushing the crumbs off my shorts.

On my way to the stand, I catch myself taking a deep breath of relief as I walk away from Indrin.

What am I so stressed out about? Forgetting newsroom telephone numbers? Having had an erotic dream about a guy who would rather stare at statues than me or any other woman? Or the uncomfortable feeling that my old self and my old life were never as real as this, this dreamlike, disoriented self only sure of one thing: the feel of my bare feet pushing deep into the sand as I walk, the sudden cool of the grass blades as I step back across the lawn now, nearing the hot dog stand.

To be honest, I am completely uninterested in Kamloops' news of the day, or in any news. I do not want to read a newspaper, local or national. I would rather not know the headlines. Radios don't interest me and television I would just as soon never see again.

By the time I reach the hot dog stand, I realize I am hoping the paper will be sold out. But there is the stack of fresh, neatly creased newsprint. The sight that normally causes my hand to shoot out, the quarters to be literally slapped down on the counter. But this time I look past it, gaze instead at the array of candy. Pop rocks, candy necklaces, and a freezer full of Popsicles. The flavours of youth.

"Do you have any licorice?" I ask.

"Red or black," says a young blonde in a baseball cap.

She's pumped up, happily snapping gum. Fresh out of school, first day on the job.

"Black," I tell her.

She hands me a rather stiff package of likely well-aged licorice from last summer.

"Thanks. Oh, and a grape Freezie too, please."

When I get back to our spot, Indrin has moved out from under the tree and lies stretched out in the sun. He looks up. "None left?"

"Nope." I throw him the Freezie.

"Cool off, oh sun worshipper."

"This is hilarious. I haven't had one of these since I was a kid."

"When was that, a couple of weeks ago?"

Indrin ignores the comment as he bites the top off the plastic.

"Thanks."

I sit down, crack open my licorice, and start trying to gnaw off a piece. The comfort food gives me a new courage.

"So what's the plan when we get to Vancouver?"

Indrin rolls over on his side, leans up on his elbow. His hair is backlit now and the lake gleams behind him.

"Drop off Edmond Rebero, I guess."

"I just think we should figure out what we're doing."

"A plan."

"Yeah, I guess.

Indrin shrugs, lies back down, face to the sky.

"I thought we were against plans. Pure instinct, remember."

"That's you, Indrin, not me. I've got to figure out what I'm doing. If I'm heading back to work early, I want to let them know. We've got to start figuring some things out."

My fingers twist off another piece of licorice.

"Why would you go back early?"

I stare at Indrin. "Why wouldn't I?"

"Fine." Indrin sits up again, crosses his long legs, and starts shredding grass with his fingers.

"Well, doesn't that make sense? I thought you just needed a ride to the Coast."

"I didn't need a ride anywhere. I just wanted to come

along with you. I want to be here now. Why should I know where I want to be next?"

"Because I'm asking."

"You have been around clocks too much, I'm starting to think. They've got you believing there's such a thing as time."

I look down at my all-powerful wristwatch and stare. The second hand looks unusually slow to me.

"There is only now," says Indrin. "You just have to trust your instinct."

"I forget what my instincts ever were."

"Instinct has no past tense," he answers a little sharply, in a voice that verges on preaching. "It doesn't matter what your instincts may have been once, it only matters what they're telling you now. Now, now, now."

Indrin's voice is a chant, this park suddenly a temple.

"No past, present, future. Only now. There's only one time, only one place we can be."

For a moment the squeals and shouts from the kids on the beach sound far-off and muffled, as if Indrin had covered my ears with seashells. I like this feeling, wish I could crawl into one of those shells or, better yet, into the warm seas they came from. I am lost in a kind of sun-dappled reverie and for this moment alone I wonder if Indrin could be right, if nothing else exists but the moment we are living in now.

I remember far-off feelings of that eternal now, feelings of my seven-year-old mouth chewing licorice with such determination my jaw ached: that was a *now* that had no past or future attached to it. I remember feeling twelve-year-old sun-bronzed legs pounding the pavement around the local swimming pool, the sun prickling my shoulders, the chemical mix of chlorine and sunlight bleaching my hair as I sat dripping on the concrete edge of the pool: moments that still do not feel like memories, but that are simply the *now* of a different person, a little kid, still alive and kicking water into foam in some other universe, some other dimension.

Now.

But suddenly time jolts me like a ringing phone. All at once it is the newsroom hotline from the control room that cannot be ignored; it is the phone ringing with Turner's voice on the other end, asking to meet me for lunch since he needs to borrow a few bucks. It is the phone telling me about a politician who is screwing our story by holding his *newser* at five o'clock, and at the same time it is the phone with the quiet voice telling me to sit down, telling me my parents did not suffer, the truck hit them head-on so it was instant, they never had a chance.

Time is all of these ringing phones. Their insistent sound dictates that I will never be free of the past and that I will never stop believing in what has shaped me and hurt me and led me here. I wouldn't recognize a world that exists only in the present tense, a world that defies all concrete logic and the weight of history. And I do not even want to believe, anymore, in a world that exists only in this one tiny second. I cannot believe in it. I can only hear the phone ringing.

"Pardon me for disturbing your esoteric sensibility, Indrin. I just want to know what we're doing."

"You tell me," Indrin says as he scatters a wad of

shredded grass. "I'm only hitching."

The second hand on my watch looks normal again, ticks with a familiar impatience.

"Okay." My tongue works loose a piece of licorice stuck to my fillings. "Okay, we pick up Rebero, drop him off in Vancouver tonight, and tomorrow nose around the city a bit. The day after I get up early and drive back to Edmonton. That's what I do. You do what your instincts tell you. I can drop you off at the church or ashram of your choice."

"Hey, thanks a lot." Indrin sucks back his melted Freezie. "But, actually, I've got some friends out there. One of them I'll definitely want to check in on. I haven't seen her in a long time."

Oh sure, Indrin. *Her.* You haven't seen *her* in a long time. Make that emphasis clear to me right about now. It's just what I need.

"Yeah, you've gotta check back with all those ex-girlfriends before you enter the seminary. Just to make sure you're doing the right thing." My tone is venomous. It surprises even me.

"Hey, where's that coming from?" asks Indrin. "She's just a friend. Just someone I haven't seen in a while. And if we're in Vancouver, I'm going to say hi, that's all. You might like her."

Yeah, that's going to happen. The three of us happily touring Stanley Park, smiling at the whales in the aquarium, waving to the boats.

Indrin reads the look on my face.

"Or I could just stay on, if you're in that big a hurry to get back."

"So, that's the plan," I confirm.

"If you're heading back, then that's my plan – if I have to have a plan."

Fine, Indrin. I can relax now. Yes, we have a plan. Plans. I have had my holidays, met some interesting people, and can go back to work and have a few laughs about it. Indrin can go visit his girlfriend for a month, for all I care.

"But you really want to go back to work?" Indrin asks as he lies down beside me on the blanket.

"Hey, watch it. You'll spill the juice."

But the apple juice has already overturned, is already bathing my feet and ankles.

"Whoops."

Indrin grabs a handful of paper towels, starts swabbing up my feet.

"Forget it."

My feet swing away. I do not want him touching me, and in this instant realize his physical presence is what is pushing me back to work. No longer can I stand lying with him in a tent, listening to his even breathing. No longer can I take laughing with him and watching him and falling in love with his eyelashes. No longer can I stand the affection and familiarity that my heart follows right up to an electrified fence topped with rolls of barbed wire. The newsroom can go to hell. I have no intention of heading back to work before I have to; I just have to get away from Indrin before I make a bigger fool of myself than I already have.

He is still trying to sop up the juice on my legs as I stand up and grab the paper towel myself.

"I've got it, all right?"

"Okay, okay."

Indrin pulls away and starts putting the leftover food into the cooler. My feet are sticky as I stand up to shake out the juice-soaked blanket. Indrin takes it from my hands and lays it across the backseat of the car to dry.

Can't you hear me?

My mind yells the words.

I want to live on instinct, but my instincts are all wrong. I want to phone the news director and tell him I've quit. I want to drive till I see ocean and sit there until I feel alive again. I want to take your hand and hold it, Indrin, and hold it until you kiss me. I don't want there to be a past or a future, but there are, at least for me, and they're relentless. The second hand on my watch never stops because it's quartz and I just got a new battery and I'll never be able to be free of time. And I'm dying over here, Indrin. I feel like I'm dying and I don't want you to be my lifeline, Indrin, but you are. *Can't you hear me?* Please hear me.

But Indrin just hands me the keys, and walks to his side of the car, and I sit down in the driver's seat beside him. Directly beside him, except for the miles and miles and miles of barbed wire.

∾ ∾

THE FIRST THING I notice about the bus depot is the button hanging by a ribbon on the bulletin board behind the counter. *Together we can stop racism* it announces to the Kamloops bus-ticket-buying public.

"He was supposed to be on the bus from Prince George," I'm explaining to the girl behind the desk. She has small brown eyes, thin lips, and an expression that looks more fifty-year-old unyielding union representative than it does nineteen-year-old summer student. It definitely says *don't bother me, you're pushing your limit here.*

"Just a minute, please." She stops to take yet another phone call in a series that has interrupted my line of questioning. When she hangs up she stops and stares blankly at me.

"The bus from Prince George," I remind her.

"Yeah, right. Yeah, it came in on time." She looks past me out toward the small lobby area of the bus depot. "If he was on it, he's probably here."

I turn around and stare at the rows of empty orange plastic seats. "Doesn't look like it, does it?"

"Then I'm sorry, I can't help you."

It is the exasperated look on my face that makes Indrin come to my rescue once again. He is striding over now in a lanky, quickened gait, no doubt in a hurry to put a halt to any sarcastic scene I am liable to make now that this bus depot gal and I have reached a complete impasse.

"Is there any way you can check to see if he caught the bus in the first place?" asks Indrin with enough politeness to make up for my lack of it.

"No, I'm sorry."

"You're sure?" Indrin glances at me to show me he's pursuing this lead as fully as possible. "I mean, there's no passenger list or VISA receipts or anything like that to check?"

Her wide, heart-shaped face accentuates the smallness of her eyes now as she closes them into slits. "I'm sorry," is what she keeps saying. Her tone says anything but.

"Okay. Thanks for trying."

Little Miss Helpful disappears into the back office and I walk over to sit down in one of the moulded plastic chairs staring at a row of coin-operated lockers. This is great. Absolutely great. A holiday headed nowhere fast, already rerouted, and now with one missing Rwandan refugee to pursue.

"If you were a Rwandan refugee adrift in the wilds of British Columbia where would you go?" This is my attempt to put on a Sherlock Holmes hat, but I've never been much of a fan of mystery stories. Still, this is where my news skills kick into automatic pilot. There's always a way to find someone – anyone, anywhere – if you have enough time and money for long distance calls. "Did Father Lowrey give us the phone number of the camp in Prince George?"

Indrin nods. "But I'll try the cathedral first. He's either missed the bus or had to change his plans for some reason. For all we know, he's already here." Suddenly Indrin leans over to feel my forehead. "Hey, are you feeling okay? You're looking a bit green again."

"I feel a bit green, I guess, so at least my body's consistent."

My laugh sounds weak as Indrin squeezes my shoulder before heading to the payphone by the door. Ever since my flu's transformation into wicked head cold, my ears have been popping because of the difference in altitude between my head and the rest of my body. Other than that, I'm fine, just fine.

I see Indrin fumbling in his pocket for change when my young friend behind the counter shouts out to me, "Hey, what did he look like?"

Her sudden interest surprises me.

"Was he black?" she continues.

"Yes, I guess he would be," I say as I make my way back to the desk. "We've never met, but he's from Rwanda."

"Yeah, he came in then. I just talked to Gary, the guy who was on last night, and he says some black guy came in on the 1:05 a.m. bus. He hung around for such a long time Gary had to tell him there was no loitering if he wasn't catching another bus. So he left. He's probably coming back, though, cause he put some stuff in a locker."

"You kicked him out?"

I ask this amazed at the smug, matter-of-fact expression on the girl's face. At the moment, she looks just like our news director, bitter little man that he is. I'd hate to see her in twenty years time when, just like him, she has managed to find reasons aplenty to blame everything out there – immigrants, women, government – for her own small-minded failures.

"I didn't kick him out," she says. "Gary did. He said the guy was loitering."

I stand, staring at her, about to ask what their policy is if the loiterer is a good-looking white drug dealer when, for once in my life, I bite my tongue and turn my back on her and the anti-racism button hanging above her head.

"You're welcome," she calls out after me. "I mean, I woke up Gary at home to check it out for you."

Midway through my smug, injured stride, I stop, shamefaced. "I'm sorry. Thanks for checking," I call back, this time to someone who appears to be no more and no less than a young girl doing the best she can at a summer job.

Indrin hangs up the phone and shakes his head as he walks toward me. "They haven't seen him at the cathedral," he says.

"Well, he's here somewhere," I say, and tell Indrin the story of the big, bad, black loiterer who arrived in the middle of the night only to be unceremoniously turned out into that night.

"He probably had nowhere else to go at that hour," says Indrin with the first real exasperation I've heard in his voice. "He wouldn't have wanted to bother anyone at the rectory. He wouldn't know anyone here. I don't think he'd have much money on him."

I stand at the door, alternately swallowing, to try to pop my ears back into the right pressure zone, and blowing my nose while Indrin goes back to ask the girl to call the cathedral if Rebero shows up again.

Indrin has always had the look of someone immovable, his calm expression suitable for carving into stone. It would be more likely to see the faces on Mount Rushmore scowl than Indrin, but now, for the first time, Indrin is walking toward me with true anger darkening his eyes. It is an expression that seems to actually cause him pain, as if the anger were a knife stabbing him through the temples.

"Let's leave."

"What happened?"

"Let's just leave." Indrin pushes past me out the door and marches to the car, but instead of opening the car door he paces beside it, his limbs tense and jerky like they are just twitching to kick something or someone.

"What happened, Indrin?"

"Give me a minute, please."

He turns from me, but then glances back to add a few softening words.

"I'm sorry, Miranda. I just need a second."

A feeling of rage wells up in me. Without knowing what was said or just how my guru friend has been offended, I suddenly want to wreak revenge on whatever, whomever, has angered the unflappable, ever-calm Indrin. The feeling is a curious one, flashing through me without direction, but full and powerful all the same. I'm suddenly a lioness ready to kill anything that gets near her cub, muscles taut and adrenalin pumping, but with no predator in sight.

I stand puzzled, ready to march back to the depot and pick another fight, when Indrin opens the driver's side door. Instead of climbing in, he stands motionless, staring at the car.

"I could drive," I offer up to the silent, brooding cloud in front of me.

"Thanks."

A preoccupied Indrin gets up and walks around to the other side of the car.

When we are both in place, seatbelts buckled, I try to calm him down before starting the car.

"It's not her fault, Indrin, the girl in there. Forget it – whatever she said."

"'Has he done something wrong?' she asks me." Indrin's face is still all dark cloud and threatening thunder. "'What do you mean?' I say. 'Like is he running away from the police or something?' When I ask her why on earth she'd ask something like that, she says this Gary wise-ass found him sitting on the floor in the corner with his bags around him and says he was *whimpering.* I ask her what does she mean *whimpering,* and she said that's how this *Gary* described it. Said it was really weird, he was whimpering, sitting there with his eyes shut, so this Gary concludes he's obviously a troublemaker or on drugs or something and he's asked to leave."

Indrin sits staring out the passenger window. "'Has he done something wrong?' she asks me. Fuck."

My hands are on the steering wheel. I stare at the dash. Where to? It is my turn now to be calm and clear, to direct us to the next step. I stab my key into the ignition.

"Where are we going?" Indrin asks.

"I thought the cathedral."

"There's no point. They haven't seen him there." Indrin's head is pressed back against the car seat. His eyes are closed.

"And she'll call if he shows up, right? Or whoever is on shift will call?"

"Yeah. Yeah, any sign of a black loiterer and they'll call the cathedral pronto. No worry about that."

"Well, shouldn't we pop in, just so they know who we are? Then we can always drive around town and see if we can figure out where he went."

"Whatever you think. Whatever."

The starter whirrs when I turn the key but nothing catches. Even my car seems put out and uncooperative by this point. *Come on,* I coax the car in my mind. *Try it again.* This time it sputters into its familiar, overly loud chugging. *Good little car. I'll give you a proper overhaul soon. You'll feel as good as new.*

I turn the car back onto the main road and head down a long, steep hill. I haven't asked Indrin where the cathedral is and now I'm afraid to disturb him so I keep driving toward what looks like downtown in this strange meandering city. Kamloops, the *Crossroads for British Columbia's Three Major Highways* said a pamphlet in the bus depot. *Where the North and South Thompson Rivers Meet.* I look to see if I can find where it all converges. Despite the long, sprawling nature of the place, at the bottom of the hill I ease my car toward what looks like the core of this loosely orbiting city system.

Downtown is generally where cathedrals are found, at least according to my limited experiences as a wedding guest. The theory proves correct when I find the Sacred Heart Cathedral just blocks from what appears to be the urban hub of Kamloops. Surrounded by fir trees, it is a red brick building adorned with a quaint bell tower. I still cannot see bell towers without thinking of Quasimodo lumbering along in grainy black and white, but despite the apparent lack of hunchbacks, it appears to be a Catholic church in the true, old style. To me, this time, it appears a friendly sight. I'm assuming I may as well be our contact man for the Church on this one and am almost looking forward to seeing how I get on with another priest in an all-new parish, when Indrin snaps open his seatbelt. As he gets out of the car, he informs me that he'll be right back, that he'll just let them know we're here and tell them about our search plans. I nod, at both Indrin and his automatic proprietary position when it comes to things Church-related, then I get out of the car anyway. You don't need a membership to stroll around outside a church.

On the lawn there's a statue of what appears to my non-religious eye to be Mary, standing with her heart exposed. This seems somewhat odd to me until I remind myself that the cathedral is, after all, called "Sacred Heart" and that must be what it represents. I just never knew whose "Sacred Heart" Catholics were worshipping. Jesus's? Mary's? Joseph's? The whole family's?

This statue has got itself a quiet little spot, complete with small white bench before it, and flowers laid out at its feet. For just a quick, infinitesimal moment, I get the feeling I wish I had something to say here, perhaps something to pray. I feel myself wishing I believed laying a few flowers at her feet would actually do something. The feeling is a wistful one, the kind that has flashed through me the odd time when watching a movie where some sincerely pious-looking Catholic kneels before a flickering amber-coloured wall and lights a candle to help an ailing mother or a little brother with polio. It's the kind of magic we are encouraged to believe in if we are part of a church. The kind we are quickly taught to outgrow if it is just a childish, secular bit of wishful thinking.

Clink. My imaginary coin drops into the tin for our unmet Rwandan friend. *Flare.* My imaginary match catches the flame from another candle and engorges a new wick in orange light for our finding him.

Clink. Flare. For Indrin.

Clink. Flare. For me.

I start lining up more imaginary coinage and more imaginary candles for my all-too-real concerns about friends and family. For my parents, especially my dad, and for what I hope he knew before he died, what I hadn't been able to show him in years. For my sister who I never let get too close. Even for Turner, who was always so strangely lovable when he wasn't paranoid or wired on drugs or depressed. I light another one to remind myself it wasn't totally his fault, that it could never have worked out for us, that he really did both of us a favour.

The fire is growing, a veritable bonfire of hopes.

But I keep coming back to Indrin, and realize what I want to light candles for would probably not be too well received in this virginal Catholic scenario, so I stop it, shut all imaginary candles out of my mind, and sit down on the bench with my back to Our Lady of the Sacred Heart or whatever she is probably called. This is how I am sitting when Indrin comes up behind me.

"Cynical to the end, when it comes to religion, eh?"

I just give him a half-smile. "It's pretty here, isn't it?"

Indrin sits down on the bench beside me, but facing Our Lady.

"It is," he says. "It really is."

I give the silence a few moments before I break in again with my *get-to-the-point, get-to-the-heart-of-the-matter* approach to life.

"So what's the story?"

Indrin looks like he has just woken up, a bit rumpled but with the softness back in his face. "I just met the one priest, Father Ron Michaud, and he's called the bus depot too to make sure they know it's all kosher – to mix religious metaphors. We could take a look around for him, I guess."

"Did you try Lowrey?" Lowrey grew on me during my sickly stay and I figure anyone in trouble would likely give him a try.

"Father Ron phoned and left a message. There was no answer at the rectory."

"So."

"So."

Indrin pauses for a few beats. "Yeah, it's a *so* situation."

So. Here we sit, the believer and the non-believer, facing and not facing this serenely white symbol of faith. Just as I think this, I realize it does feel like this Mary Statue Lady is peering over my shoulder, but thanks to the stone carver responsible, at least it's a kindly kind of peering.

"I'm sorry, Indrin, about how weird I got in the park today. When the juice got spilled."

"That's okay. You're still not even over the flu."

"I'm fine," I say as I sniff at the same time. "I mean I'm fine, except for this cold. Fine enough to have been a lot less cranky about a bit of spilled juice."

"And it wasn't the juice, either, right?"

"No flies on you. You're sure about this priest thing? Sure you don't want to go into psychiatry or something? Maybe *Indrin's Psychic Readings and Advice?* Or *psycho? Psycho readings and Advice 'R' Us.*"

"Pretty much the same thing, isn't it?"

I give his shoulder a bump with mine and continue.

"No, it wasn't the spilled juice or the lack of newspapers or anything else. I think I'm just feeling a bit panicky about all this ending."

"What do you mean 'ending'?"

"I mean ending. Capital *E.* Capital *N* Capital *D.* And so on."

"My friend the cheerleader. Give me an *E.*"

"Yeah, I'm so cheery," I say, pushing my sarcastic tone to the fore. Indrin smiles.

"Thanks for staying calm at the bus depot."

"My turn, I guess. I had my meltdown earlier."

"I lost it a bit. It wasn't her fault." Indrin is staring at his shoes. In this late-afternoon light, under the fir trees, his skin looks almost red-brown and there are beads of sweat high on his neck, near where his ponytail is gathered.

"What did she know? The guy on the late shift tells her he had to kick somebody out. Why would she think anything of it?"

"I wouldn't worry," I say as I place my hand on Indrin's neck and give it a massaging squeeze. "If that counts as 'losing it,' you've got it all pretty well under control as far as I'm concerned."

I continue to try to work the stress out of Indrin's neck muscles without letting my touch betray any of the tenderness I feel for him right now. To hide it I put on a breezily casual tone. "You're okay, you know. I'm going to miss travelling with you."

"You're sure trying to get rid of me lately, aren't you?"

I give him a smile and bump his shoulder with mine again as I take my hand away. My hand is moist from his sweat and I wipe it on my shorts as I stand up.

"Well, let's get to it. How big is Kamloops anyway?"

"Only about eighty thousand people to go through, I think," he answers. "So I guess we should get to it."

As I stand looking at Indrin still sitting on the picturesque bench in front of the statue, the thing that bothers me is just how easy it is to see him as a priest. As a tall, untouchable spiritual advisor who is there for anyone and everyone at all times and who is therefore completely unavailable to me, at least in the personal and physical way that I understand as close and as intimate. If it were anyone else or any other time in my life, I might precipitate a kiss or take his hand, but he's got me feeling more like a schoolgirl than I ever did as a schoolgirl. As a seven-year-old I was quite bold about taking boys I liked behind the trees to give them a kiss before running away. Now, standing here on this hallowed ground, I'm a thirty-three-year-old too shy to admit I would like to hold his hand, or to leave my hand on his neck for no reason other than to feel it rest there.

"I'm having trouble with this," I blurt out suddenly.

Indrin does not look up, but fixes his eyes more firmly into the white stone feet of Our Lady of Marble and Stony-Faced Virtues. He knows exactly what I am having trouble with, I suddenly fear, and is trying to remain delicate with my feelings. Doesn't want to hurt me. I can literally feel the pure adrenalin of humiliation flood through me, pulse in one burst up to my head and at the same time down to my feet through my stomach.

Idiot, idiot. Why can't I let some things alone?

He answers my fears with a quiet voice, his eyes still locked onto the whitewashed stone. "I know."

My arms feel awkward. I am suddenly a first-time actor on stage whose limbs feel stubbornly alien and resolutely refuse to feign a casual calm. There is nothing to be done with them. My hands are now folded, now swinging, now squeezed behind my back.

"I guess there's nothing to say."

"Sure there is," he says. "That's the trouble. There's too much to say."

Indrin reaches up for one of my floundering hands and pulls it toward him until I step over the bench and sit down beside him.

"This is pretty stupid."

"No, not stupid," he says as he sets his arm down across my shoulders.

"I think I like you a bit too much."

There, I've said it. As bluntly as you'd expect an awkward fifteen-year-old to say it.

"Why did you have to go and decide to become a priest anyway?"

Indrin laughs. "You're interfering with my rules, you know."

"Oh?"

"The rules about following my instincts."

"How am I interfering?"

As I ask this I wonder why the words clump together

in my throat, come out halting and almost mispronounced. This is surely not the most difficult conversation I have had when it comes to relationships. There is not even a *relationship* to discuss here.

"You're reminding me that instincts can conflict."

Indrin's tone sounds like an admission and I hear his words, but this is what I feel him saying inside: *Bless me, Father, for I have sinned. It's been too long since my last admission of feeling something.*

With that, Indrin gives my hand a squeeze and I squeeze back, all the while knowing I don't believe instincts *can* conflict. But I guess we can tell ourselves they do and that's all that counts. His words have opened up something inside me and closed it at the same time. They are an acknowledgment of the direction my feelings have taken, and of his, but also of the onward march of his footsteps down a very different path. I give his hand another squeeze and want to laugh at the ludicrous nature of love in my life, to crack a joke about my hopelessness when it comes to the opposite sex. Instead, I listen to Indrin's quiet breathing, see the breeze play with his hair, and realize there truly is nothing else to say. So we sit, facing the Virgin Mary, listening to birds chirp above us and a motorcycle with no muffler roaring down the block, and I wish my body was a solid piece of stone like Hers. And as we sit, hands clasped, I hear Indrin making the same wish as I am, hear it as clearly as if he'd whispered it to me.

Make me stone. Make my faith in all this solid as stone.

And just as he wishes it, I feel the sweat of his palm in mine.

Infinite Wishes

It has now been about three hours since our heart-to-heart. We have not spoken of it since, and probably will not again. I am starting to learn that my wise young friend is good at many things, but feelings of the personal kind throw a big wrench into the perfectly-timed workings of his universe. I look at him and now I see the careful, quick movements of a tiny windup wristwatch. Ironic for a guy who claims not to believe in time. This is something I'll tell him too, but now is not the right time. Maybe tomorrow when we're on turf a little further from the rumply, tentative marsh of feelings we seem to be treading today.

The north side of the street is mine, his the south. I watch him pull open the door of the café across the street. Do we really expect Mr. Rebero to be hanging around waiting for us in a Chinese restaurant in Kamloops? I don't, but decide I wouldn't mind a bowl of wonton soup so I cross the street after Indrin to suggest a quick break.

We're squeezing plastic packets of plum sauce onto our plates for the hissing egg rolls that have just arrived when Indrin says he is going to call the cathedral again.

"You may as well wait and eat first."

Practicality is something I am never short of when I'm hungry and there happens to be a plate of hot food in front of me. In fact, I don't even have to be that hungry.

"You have a pretty healthy appetite," Indrin says as he chomps into his egg roll.

"A *very* healthy appetite." I raise my eyebrows as I say this and try to look provocative, or at least as provocative as one can look while splashing plum sauce on one's chin.

"Yeah, yeah." Indrin is shaking his head, but he's smiling despite himself. "You know what I mean, though. Most women have a complex about food."

"I don't know why I've never gained weight," I say as I take another bite. "But I'm not about to start questioning it. My high-strung nature has its advantages I guess."

It is only after we have cleaned up an entire platter of Szechuan beef that I decide it is my turn to call the cathedral this time. And, after plugging my quarter into the phone, and a quick conversation with Father Michaud, I return to Indrin and the fortune cookies with a bit of surprising information for him.

"So guess who never arrived?"

"What do you mean?"

"Lowrey called the cathedral. Apparently Rebero phoned him to say he had missed the bus and will be arriving tomorrow morning instead."

"What are you talking about?"

"That's what he said."

Indrin's eyebrows knit together as he absorbs this.

"So what about the guy in the bus depot last night?"

"Good question."

"This is fucking unbelievable," Indrin says as he grabs up a fortune cookie and starts to crunch it into pieces.

"Do you think your bishops and cardinals and all that will mind your language? Or is the Church really that open and liberal nowadays?"

Indrin chooses not to respond to my little jab and simply continues deconstructing the cookie, breaking off one shard at a time.

"What the fuck is going on anyway?"

"I have no idea. What does it say?"

"What?"

I motion to the crumbled fortune cookie in Indrin's hands. He throws me the tiny paper he's managed to crumple as well. I unravel it to read, *You never worry about the future.*

"Some fortune," I say.

"That's okay. It's true. I'm not worried about the future. It doesn't exist, remember?"

"Time still exists in my world." I flail my high-powered wristwatch in his face as my fortune cookie cracks open neatly into two parts, showing all too plainly that I am without fortune.

"Where is it?" Indrin asks.

"Not here." I show him both gaping ends of cookie.

"Ask for another one."

This cracks me up. "Oh yeah, I'm going to march back to the kitchen with my faulty fortune cookie and demand a refund. Nope, this is my fortune, Indrin. No fortune. The Goddess Fortuna turns her back on me. Really surprising, isn't it?"

Indrin pours more Chinese tea and I feel the heat seep into my fingers through the fragile china cup.

"So, what do you think we should do?"

My casual tone is not completely successful.

"We might as well find a place to stay."

Neither is his.

"What time does his bus supposedly come in anyway?" I ask.

"Six-twenty."

"That's pretty early."

Indrin pours more tea. Nothing means anything, we are both assuring ourselves, but we decide we are going to stay in a hotel tonight. It makes more sense. Easier than breaking camp at five in the morning. Gives us a chance to clean up. Relax. Catch up on what is happening in the wide world of TV news. You know. Handier, more logical.

So why the discomfort? We're certainly used to the close confines of a tent, and a hotel room only gives us a lot more space. But there's just something about the idea of "getting a hotel room" that changes the dynamic here.

Shutting off that train of thought, I go back to giving myself the pep talk about sense and logic and the practicality of it. I am still giving myself these lines when we pull up at the motor hotel and pick up the key to our room overlooking the highway, and I have a pretty good idea Indrin is giving himself the same speech because when we open the door to the room and throw our bags down on the respective double beds, I hear him mutter "Well, this makes sense anyway."

"What did you say?"

"Oh, just that this makes a lot of sense. It'll be good to sleep on a bed again tonight. Staying at the rectory spoiled us."

He throws himself down on the bed closest to the wall and I sit down on my bed, by default, the one by the window. Immediately, I am zapping my way through the channels. It is all very interesting if you don't mind watching the home shopping channel through a greenish snow. Or Cher selling cosmetics with the horizontal hold refusing to hold. I shut the TV off. So much for re-acquainting myself with world affairs.

"Mind if I take a bath?"

"No," says Indrin, looking up.

But then he sits up and suggests he take a shower first, since he'll be quicker.

"Fine." I turn my back as he starts to pull off his T-shirt and begin to flip through the magazines heralding the myriad of tourism attractions available in Kamloops. I'm about to turn to Indrin and make a smart-ass comment about the joys of fly-fishing when I hear the roar of water in the tub, then the change in pitch as the shower sprinkle starts.

Indrin has brought in his stuffed manila folder full of the photocopies he made at Lowrey's. The *doomsday papers,* I call them. I roll across the bed to pick up the tidy stash of gloom, intending to read some of the more ludicrous predictions out loud, but instead I lean back with the file on my stomach and stare at the ceiling, listening to the sound of Indrin in the shower. The echoing squeaks of his feet in the wet tub, the comforting warm sound of the rushing water.

I've shared hotel rooms before with the men in my life, but the occasions never demanded separate bathing arrangements. I think of my trips to meet Turner on weekends when he was playing with his band in Calgary or in any number of small towns. Those getaways had their little touches of romance even in the crummiest hotel with the lumpiest bed. In fact, even when he played late into the night, rolling into bed stinking of cigarette smoke and too many drinks, it wasn't unusual for him to haul me over to the window to try to get me to point out some of the stars to him, stars in constellations he could never pronounce properly.

Isn't that part of Cass-ee-OH-pee-oh?

Cassiopeia? No, that's Orion. See that? That's the belt.

Whatever. You're the expert, Randi. But it's great, eh? Look at that.

Then he would usually add one line too many, something slightly fake-sounding like, "But you're the only star I want to look at." Happily, I would shut the lounge-lizard tone of his voice out of my head and bask in what I just knew were his true feelings.

Then we would tumble into bed and the lovemaking would be gentle and sweet or passionate or both, but it was always the most effective lullaby, a potent dream potion. In the morning, which for us never dawned much before noon, there was always this golden time, me curled into his one arm, and Turner absorbed in the task of tracing pictures on my stomach with the other.

What's that?

A house.

No, a trombone.

You're kidding?

And then his finger, the artist's brush, would trace away again, drawing more pictures I was never able to guess. And even if I had guessed correctly, I am sure Turner would have changed the answer on me. For me to get it right would have spoiled the game.

The shower is still running. Indrin's feet are still squeaking. And I am feeling sad, like I do not belong here. I realize it is the sound of partnership that is filling my ears as the water pours into the tub. The sound of a man in my life. Suddenly it occurs to me that if I hear the sound of an electric razor I'm going to lose it, and so I sit up, grab the remote, and zap my way to the community announcements channel, where the audio serenades me with a strange uptempo string version of "Like a Rolling Stone."

I dump open the packet of papers and sit cross-legged on the bed, carefully placing cataclysms all around me: earthquakes on the West Coast, pestilence in Africa, and flooding in the heartland of North America. The destruction of New York now sits by my left knee, nuclear winter in Europe by my right.

A blast of humidity hits me when a towel-clad Indrin comes out of the bathroom.

"I thought you didn't care about any of that stuff."

"I don't. I'm just curious."

Indrin sits down beside me, dripping slightly with his wet hair exuding the scent of heavily-perfumed hotel shampoo.

"Hey, you're getting the bed wet," I say, leaning away from him slightly.

"So this can be my bed then. Did you read this one?"

Indrin motions to one of the sheets of Nostradamus's predictions.

"I haven't read any of them. I just opened them up."

"The Marian apparitions are in the other folder."

Beside the bed, sticking out the side of Indrin's tote bag, is another, even fatter, envelope.

"How many copies did you make?"

"Enough for quite a bit of bedtime reading. You should read about the Rwanda one." The dripping Wonder Boy gets up, tightening his towel around him, and goes to pick up his *Doomsday Papers, Volume II.*

"What I can't help wondering," he says as he slides out the neatly paper-clipped stash, "is if our refugee friend has ever heard of the Kibeho apparition. I mean, I wonder if it's common knowledge in Rwanda? Especially since the predictions began coming true."

Indrin's eyes look so credulous. Being open to the world has its merits, but this wide-eyed innocence makes me nervous. Always has. Faith might move mountains, but it seems to stop people. Dead in their tracks. Dead in their capacity for analytical thought.

"Do you honestly believe in all this?"

"I don't know about every prediction." Indrin re-tucks his towel sarong again. "But, yes, I think Mary is appearing to whoever is open to her."

"To give us pictures of doom and gloom."

"To warn us."

"So you think we're heading toward the end of the world, or something like that?"

"I honestly don't know. But you don't have to be a psychic to realize what's happening to the globe."

Indrin's appeal to a common ecological awareness doesn't get me off topic.

"Personally, I wonder how people emotionally prepared for the apocalypse the last time people figured the world would end. You know, back in the year 999. Without photocopies and mass media, it might have been a little bit harder to get the word out about the coming doom in time. I'll bet some people didn't even get notice until well into the year 1000. 1001, maybe. That "999" expiry date would have looked pretty silly then, wouldn't it have?"

"Hopeless," says Indrin, getting up. "You want tea?"

"I don't want to go out again if that's what you mean."

"No, I've got a mini-kettle and tea in my other bag."

The room is strewn with the bags and maps I threw down, but I only see one of Indrin's.

"In the trunk. Would you mind?"

Indrin waves his hands to remind me of his state of

undress. As if I needed reminding. "I'll make it if you go get it."

My feet are squeezing their way back into sweaty running shoes when the cable TV *muzak* serenade suddenly stops short.

"How can you stand to listen to that?"

"Age gap, I guess," I say as I slam the door and walk out onto the second-level walkway overlooking the parking lot.

Above the hills surrounding the city, the sky is clear and filled with a deep purple twilight on one side, a pale eggshell kind of yellow on the other. In between, it's like a watercolour painting where the colours gradually intermingle. Over in the east, it looks like India ink has rolled into a deep pool of colour, leaving a thinner wash of pigment streaked across the rest of the sky.

When I get down to the car, I look up to the motor hotel and see the yellow glow of the lights on in our room. What would happen if I just didn't go back up there? If I just sat myself down in the driver's seat and drove straight back to Edmonton, or headed off to Vancouver on my own? A sudden ending like that would be old hat to me, although it might be a bit of a shock to Indrin. Still, he'd get over it. I might not, but, yes, Indrin would get over it. And, once safely in the seminary, he would have good evidence to present to the other seminarians on why they were better off to have left the baffling world of women far behind them.

And me, strolling by myself on English Bay in Vancouver, or driving to the West Edmonton Mall back home in Edmonton, what would I have missed out on? What would be my story on the result of fleeing the baffling world of men? Or at least the world of this one perplexing male waiting for me upstairs.

The metal top of the trunk feels cool against my legs as I sit down. I should have changed from my shorts into jeans. *One reason to go back up there,* I think. My clothes. My possessions. My agreeing to help the fellow from Rwanda. And, okay, the big reason. My friend.

As the India ink continues to gather in the sky, the stars are starting to become more visible. Tiny points of light bleed through the dark canvas. Where *is* Cassiopeia tonight? It's been a while since I took a good long look. I look for familiar points in the sky. The constellations my mom and dad pointed out to me as a kid under vast prairie skies brilliant with stars. Stars filling the sky from one flat horizon line all the way across infinite space to the other horizon.

Infinity. I remember the night I learned what it was. Not just the adjective, but the full-fledged noun spoken aloud with my whole eight-year-old mouth. In-FIN-it-TEE. *Infinity.* And not just the word and what it meant, but the actual feel of it in my body. The physical sensation of it welling up from the ground, through my feet and stomach, and bursting from my head into that sky. That never-ending sky.

Never-ending.

Some people have told me they don't like to think about infinity, that the idea of it made them feel scared or anxious when they were little. Not me. Looking up at that sky and holding my father's hand exhilarated me. That soaring feeling of joy bulleting through me and rocketing straight up into the enormous sky made me want to jump up after it, made me dream of gravity vanishing, finally setting me free to follow it. But right now my legs are pressing hard into the metal of the car and the force of gravity has never felt stronger. I hear cars motor their way down the main strip of Kamloops. The neon hotel sign gives my legs an orange and purple glow and makes the stars too faint. The ones I can make out high above the hills do not look terribly familiar. I finally see Cassiopeia, and it has the right shape – has to have – but none of it is familiar. No joyful bursts, no jumping eight-year-old legs. Just tired me, sitting on the back of my car, straining to see the stars. And, as I sit here in the shadows in this parking lot, I wonder just how much my old happy excitement at the concept of infinity had to do with a little girl holding her father's hand in utter trust, if it had ever been the stars at all.

This makes me grieve, and what I am mourning is not the loss of my parents or the breakup with Turner, but the complete disappearance of that little kid. I am grieving the girl with the capacity to feel the whole universe inside her tiny body because it seems she is dead and gone. Without her, I know I will never feel infinity again.

"Can't you find it?"

The shout from the banister above the parking lot shakes me up.

"God Almighty, your voice is loud."

"What's happening?" Indrin is stuffing a T-shirt into his jeans and quickly moving down the steps. "Wasn't it there?"

"I haven't looked yet."

Indrin looks at me strangely. "I started thinking I left it back at Father Albert's."

My legs stick to the top of the trunk as I try to slide off. "Sorry. I got caught in a daydream, I guess."

"That's okay. Are you feeling all right?"

"Yeah," I say, but Indrin hears the doubt in my voice as clearly as I do. If I had a clear idea of how to tell him what I am feeling tonight, I am pretty sure I would try. Indrin is one of the few people in my life I have not been able to lie to. Not that I find myself lying often. It's more a case of lying to myself. The *I'm fine* and *That's okay, I don't mind* kind of lie. But Indrin reads my feelings well anyway, even without my words.

And how am I feeling?

Lousy. Thoughtful. Sad. Happy. Lost. As if I know.

Check here for all/none of the above.

Score 4 points for every word checked off and see page 56 of this magazine to see what the HOT QUIZ *results determine is* YOUR CURRENT MOOD.

The QUIZ *on page 57 will tell you what to do about it.*

"How did you get to know me so well, Indrin?"

"I don't know you well, Miranda."

Touché.

Okay, so he is only humanoid after all, not the *all-seeing guru master come to give direction to my life* that I keep trying to make him. If he does seem to pick up on my feelings from time to time, it is because I broadcast them loud and clear. Tonight, I am far from inscrutable. A woman alone in a parking lot, sitting on the back of a car staring up into the void, is not hard to spot as someone with a bit on her mind.

As I contemplate Indrin's sensitivity levels, he is preoccupied with strictly earthly concerns. He has got his entire torso bent into the trunk in his search for the tea and kettle. His foot kicked out for balance, he is pulling out a seemingly limitless supply of T-shirts and towels and dirty socks from his bag.

"Could you hold this?"

Suddenly I am holding a stack of the neatly folded T-shirts. The dirty socks he has thrown to the ground.

"You'll lose some that way."

"Here it is."

He pulls out the kettle and a plastic baggy full of tea bags in a gesture of triumph.

When we have packed away his belongings and make it halfway up the stairs, Indrin stops to look up at the stars. I almost want to point out my favourite constellations, but do not. I do not want to risk the chance of an infinite sky adding any more significance to this friendship.

No infinity here, please.

Maybe even if my little kid self were here to remind me of how infinity feels I would not want it anymore, not be capable of it.

Turning my head toward my feet, I watch them start stepping up the rest of the stairs.

"Hey, wait."

Indrin's head tilts back to see the sky, silhouettes the

shape of his neck and Adam's apple against the neighbouring hotel sign.

"What a clear night."

"I'm cold," I say as I keep trudging. "Have you got the key?"

"Yeah."

The steps shake as he bounds up and soon we are shutting the door on the night sky and moving into the comfort zone of tea and cloudy television and sleep.

~ ~

OR NOT SLEEP. It feels odd to share the same room as my fellow camper, yet watch him falling asleep far across the chasm between our separate beds. The air conditioner will not shut off, my feet are cold under the thin bedspread, and no matter how I try to pile up the pillows around me there is no camouflaging the wideness of this double bed. Across the great divide, Indrin's steady night-time breathing is audible, but I miss feeling it tickle my face. I also miss his sliding sleeping bag inching its way on to my bubble mat and the way his hair would manage to swat me awake when he turned over suddenly in the night.

The whole sensation of missing Indrin while still sharing a room with him makes me even more restless, so I finally give up, nod to the insomnia god with a good kick of blankets, and sit up facing the window. The hotel is quiet enough. Even if I listen intently, I can't find a single sound to blame for this. No partying soccer team. No baby crying down the hall. None of the many things I could focus my annoyance on had they been handy. I listen again. Okay, some muffled cars in the distance, but, yes, it has got to be the quietest hotel I have ever stayed in. Before my switch to a career in television, I worked in radio studios that were less soundproof than this. No, there is simply nothing keeping me awake except me. And Indrin's breathing.

The soft, inward rustling as he inhales.

The pause. The mysterious rest in the place between. Not anywhere, just between. The purgatory balancing on the knife-edge between life and empty lungs, between breath and death.

The satisfied sigh of his exhaling.

It is a soft, steady bellows taking in the air. And giving it all back. And in this moment, I love him for it. Just for his breath. The way its sound fills this darkened room.

I do not want to turn on the light and wake him up, so next I stand and try to turn my numb toes and flailing fingers into antennae and feel my way to the bathroom door. My fingers flick the light switch on only after I have got the door shut behind me.

The four tiny, tiled walls stare at me. So does the still damp tub. And so does my pathetic reflection in the mirror. Dark circles are gouged out under my eyes, which look more sickly yellow than hazel in this light, my hair is once again a short, fly-away bird's nest, and in this oversized flannel nightgown, I look like Wee Willie Winkie, sans the nightcap. I stare harder at my eyes. Sometimes I think they have always looked old. They looked exactly like this when I surveyed myself in mirrors even as a kid. There are a couple of faint lines, now, by the corners of my eyes, and one distinct furrow in my brow but, aside from that, nothing has changed. Not the hard, clear-eyed stare that allows me no escape, no vanity. Not their watchful surveillance of my perpetually mussed baby hair. Nothing. Even now, I'm still the selfsame skinny runt of a kid, with old eyes bored into a head that's topped with wistful, autonomous hair, hair that says *I won't co-operate,* and adds, *just try and make me.*

I squint my eyes shut for a moment and consider my options. Running a bath would make too much noise. Grabbing a book to read is impossible since I left the one Lowrey gave me down in the car and going to get it would make even more noise than running a bath, so there is nothing to take my mind off my sleeplessness unless I turn to Indrin's *doomsday papers.* That is the best choice, I decide, within the narrow field before me. Besides, I'm curious. I admit it.

I sneak out of the bathroom once again and nudge my way to the packet of predictions left on the desk. Without rustling the paper too much, I manage to get back to my hideout with a minimum of noise, one creak of the door, and no noticeable change in Indrin's breathing pattern. In fact, as I passed him, his face half lit by the light from the bathroom, he looked to be deep in REM dreamland.

The click of the door behind me sounds louder this time so I freeze for a moment. Still no sound. It would probably take a lot more than that to wake him, anyway, given the obvious depth of his sleep, the sleep of children and the innocent. Warier creatures like me and most cats and dogs I have known are a bit less committed to the netherworld, a bit more anxious to spring to alert attention, to stare down the intruder.

Wrapping my nightgown around my legs to seal out any air-conditioned cold, I climb up on the counter. Knees hugging my chest, my feet sit in the sink I am now filling with warm water. Kind of a mini-bath. The point is to get me sleepy again, to lull me into such a state of contentment and relaxation that I can barely plod my way back to the bed before closing my eyes and drifting into an undisturbed sleep. I lean back against the cold wall, adjusting my spine to avoid the awkwardly placed light switch, and slide out a few sheets of Nostradamus.

Trying to read the French version only wakes me up further.

L'an mil neuf cent nonante neuf sept mois,
Du ciel viendra un grand Roy d'effrayeur
Ressusciter le grand Roy d'Angoulmois,
Avant apres Mars regner par bonheur.

I am mouthing this, relying on the pronunciation I paid so much to brush up on only a few summers ago. Even at the time, I had a good idea the French I learned would not get me too far outside a Berlitz classroom, never mind the high-profile TV news-producing job in Montreal I had applied for. Still, I can usually get across what I want to say, even if my accent is clumsy, round-mouthed anglophone all the way. But nothing I learned in the course prepared me to figure out this maze of foreign vocabulary. My eye moves speedily down to read the interpretation in English.

> *In July 1999 a great, terrifying leader will come from the skies to revive the memory of the great king of Angoulême. Before and after war will rule luckily.*

Or *before and after war will rule by chance.*

Or *before and after Mars to reign through happiness.*

Whether any of those subtle clarifications makes a difference, I'm not the one to judge. But I am starting to get an idea of how wildly people interpret this stuff. As I flip through the sheets Indrin has got photocopied, I note that some see this predicting everything from an airborne invasion of France in 1999 to a new religious leader to arise in New York City, since Angoulême is apparently the old name for Manhattan. Myself, I figure any plane crash could fit the bill for *will come from the skies* and, as for war reigning before and after, it's a safe bet since the world has never been free of war and still shows no imminent sign of beating swords into ploughshares.

Time will tell, I guess. Nostradamus seemed to be pretty accurate on things like the assassination of JFK and of a military dictator he called "the new Nero" who would have the name *Hister* and would cause ovens to be built. That honestly did surprise me when Indrin and Lowrey gravely read those quatrains aloud to me. But make a few hundred predictions spanning a good five centuries and surely you will get a few right in there somewhere.

What I wonder about is what words like *apocalypse*

mean anyway. Phrases like the *end of the world.* It is all relative, as far as I can see, and it is not as if the world has never ended before. If I were a Jew who lived in Europe round about the Second World War, I would most certainly have witnessed the *end of the world.* And if I survived the holocaust, I would be that unique form of survivor. An *end of the world* survivor with a cataclysmically different view of the world, of life, of God, of humankind. If I were our friend from Rwanda witnessing one million people around me murdered within a month, I would also classify myself as an *end of the world* survivor.

Maybe it is no surprise good old Father Lowrey is so concerned with Nostradamus and the end of the world, I think as I flip through a few more predictions. This Michel de Nostradame sure does not seem to have too many happy times predicted for the Catholic Church in the years to come. He very clearly sounds a death knell for the old institution and heralds the end of that world.

This is a surprise? This is a problem?

Two weeks ago the idea would not have bothered me in the slightest. The end of the Church? After some of the stories of abuse I worked on, the end of that institution could not have come soon enough for me.

For everything there is a season and it's time to let some things die.

But now when I think of Father Lowrey quietly going about his work at the St. Francis of Assisi Parish in Revelstoke and diligently studying predictions for the world in the hope of steering people back onto a spiritual course, I feel somewhat more concerned about the old institution. Perhaps, more accurately, concerned about the people living in that world. My thoughts turn to Indrin sleeping in the next room, his dreaming head filled with thoughtfulness and sincerity and consistency, if also the odd bit of self-delusion.

I still do not think instincts can conflict, but then I am not the one choosing to become a priest, a vocation that demands the juggling of conflicting instincts and the smothering, or at the very least the refocussing, of physical desire.

The water has cooled off so I blast in some more hot water. This time, however, an unearthly groan emanates from the wall as the water shakes the pipes. Lightning-fast, I shut off the water and I freeze, once again, to listen for any sign of stirring in the next room. No sound. Just the dripping of the tap into the sink. I relax back into the light switch on the wall and flip through a few more notes on the apocalypse.

But the door creaks open.

"Hey, what are you doing in here?"

"I didn't want to wake you up. So much for that."

"That's okay."

Indrin closes the toilet seat and sits down, propping one foot against the tub. He is wearing shorts and a purple T-shirt with *Stop Violence Against Women* emblazoned across it; the guy is no end of sensitivity and political correctness.

His hair is spiralling everywhere. I notice his face looks a bit shadowy; he must not have shaved after all while I was outside surveying the stars.

"What's the matter?"

"Nothing. I just couldn't sleep."

"So, what's the matter?"

I blast a bit more hot water onto my feet.

"I was cold."

"Isn't there another blanket?"

"I didn't see one."

"I'll get one of the sleeping bags from the car," says Indrin, getting up.

"No, I'm all right," I say, waving him back down.

"Reading the predictions again?"

"Yeah."

"You're not worrying about them, are you?"

The idea of this makes me want to laugh, but out of consideration I turn the impulse into a smirk.

"I promise you it's not that. I was just cold, but this did the trick."

"It is cold, isn't it?"

Indrin's bare legs are covered with goosebumps.

"Why didn't you get right into the tub?"

"I thought it would wake you up."

"Oh. Thanks."

He blinks a few times and looks very much like he is having trouble leaving the netherworld and coming back into this dimension.

"What time is it?"

I look down for my watch, but realize it is not there and shrug.

"Can't help you."

The open bathroom door is evaporating any warm humidity that managed to gather and so I pull the plug on my mini-bath.

"Might as well give sleep another try, I guess."

Indrin pulls down one of the towels and hands it to me. As I wrap my water-wrinkled feet into it, he stands staring at me with his arms folded.

"I don't mind going down to get the sleeping bag."

"Honestly, that's okay."

Silence.

"Why don't you sleep with me?"

Indrin's tone is decidedly matter-of-fact. Too decidedly. Too breezy and casual for the level of awkwardness creeping into my limbs.

"I'm okay."

But his arm is suddenly around my shoulders, guiding me back to bed, his bed, and he is giving me a very *buddy, old pal* squeeze of the shoulders to tell me it is okay. *This doesn't mean anything.* Nothing means anything. We are simply going to sleep together. And I wonder if my heart will be able to withstand the imploding feeling that I know will build up when I am lying closer than ever to him, sharply awake, while he falls back to his happy, very separate dreamland.

"Hang on."

Indrin goes now to my bed, drags off the blanket and bedspread, and hauls them over to me in his.

"This has got to make a difference."

And soon we are covered up together, wrapped in the same sheets, folded into the same double layer of blankets. Through my cotton nightie I feel the heat of a powerful space heater. His body is blasting me with steady warmth and I shift toward him, moving almost close enough to feel his thighs against mine.

"You're a nuclear reactor," I say, with the same casual sitcom tone Indrin used with me. "Fusion furnace."

His foot checks mine.

"I can't believe you're still cold."

Indrin pulls me closer and I follow his body's lead until I am curved around him, my head pressed into his shoulder.

"Is this okay?"

"Fine," Indrin answers.

Despite his answer I am worried that this is not at all fitting for my guru friend, that my proximity breaks all the rules of future priestdom. But this is now, I think, not tomorrow or next fall. And he has pulled me in here, exactly where I want to be, so why argue?

And I kiss him. I just do it. I tilt my head up so I can kiss him squarely on the mouth, so long and hard he could not take his lips away if he tried. But I notice he doesn't try. All he does is push my lips with his and I finally feel his hot breath in my own mouth and all I want to do is be absorbed into him, feel my chest press into his, and feel us both dissolve.

And the kiss ends. It ends with Indrin moving his lips up to press another small kiss into the centre of my forehead. He draws his face away slightly, but keeps his arms around me, keeps me close. His eyes search mine, but I have nothing to say. Nothing to say, because if I never did find a way to properly describe the feeling of infinity rushing through me when I stared at the sky, neither could I describe this rush of speeding emotion. And nothing to say because even if I did, the words would not belong here. Not only would they be revealing, they would be dangerously premature.

My forehead is granted another careful, gentle kiss.

"Can I just hold you?"

Since that is what he is already doing and since nothing has felt more right or appropriate in the entire time I have known Indrin, I nod.

"I'd like to just hold you like this."

Just hold me. I realize he is making the emphasis clear and there it is, that familiar feeling of the imploding heart. Its giant expansion, supernova style, and immediate fiery collapse into a dense black hole. I would speak the words *I understand* if I were not absolutely sure they would get stuck in my throat and come out a sob. So I nod, but Indrin feels my hurt. My humiliation must have a scent, must wave flags as it rushes into my face with blood-red force.

"Hey?"

I nod again.

"You okay there?"

This is so ridiculous. So ridiculously immature. I am honestly shocked I have managed to get myself into this situation.

"Forgive the kiss."

There. My voice and my sarcasm are fully restored.

"Please don't say that."

Even in the dark I can see Indrin lean back, pull his arm behind his head, and stare at the ceiling. This is the exact posture of the most desperately hurtful conversations I have had in relationships. What is it about two people lying side by side in the dark that makes for such an inimitable form of isolation?

Silence.

We lie here. Me certain I have committed some sort of mortal sin and dangerous injury to the pride and morals of this bastion of purity, and Indrin, no doubt, shocked at himself and at what I now represent. *Sin.* What's maybe worse, *doubt.*

"I'm sorry. You must think this is so weird."

Indrin's voice is measured, restrained, and still directed to the ceiling, not me.

"It's okay. I get the picture. I'm just embarrassed is all."

"No, you don't get the picture. It's me. I'm sorry."

The next thought hits me hard. Is he gay? Could I have missed that? Me, who prides myself on being so observant. I lean away from him to squint myself some perspective on this possibility, but his arm wraps itself around me again and his fingers stroke my shoulder. Could he be a virgin? That is the likeliest possibility, I decide, and it may well be he wants to stay that way, what with entering the priesthood and all.

"It's not what you think. Lying here with you is driving me crazy. I just can't do this."

As always, when my flood of humiliation subsides, my vision clears, my humour returns.

"Take all this as a compliment, Indrin. I'm not trying to ruin everything for you. My God, me the sinner, trying to deflower a poor young priest."

"I'm not a priest, remember?" His tone betrays obvious fatigue at explaining this point. "I'm still a long, long way from that. And some days I'm a lot further than others."

"I was kidding."

His shadowy figure rolls over to face me. I tuck the messy mound of blankets around us both.

"I'm HIV-positive."

Now, this surprises me.

"Oh God, Indrin."

Up on my elbow now, I smooth out the blankets around him again and instinctively reach for his face. My fingers move into his hair, massage his head as I run my hand over it, and when my eyes fill I am glad it is dark because I do not know if I can truly say I am crying for him or for me and I am ashamed of that.

"My old girlfriend turned out to have a bit of a problem with needles. Heroin. She was messed up, but I didn't know how messed up. She tested positive six months ago."

Indrin.

Suddenly, it is a different Indrin I know. A person with fears larger than I could ever have imagined. A person I would like to enfold in my arms like a cloud engulfing a mountain, only I do not want to drift past and dissolve around him, I want to be a tangible blanket protecting him. A warm salt sea to rock him in. But I am only me, with my two awkward arms, and they feel too weak to carry him, too small to do anything at all.

Hope and the Facts of History

The facts are simple. Indrin may be HIV-positive. He may not be. Sure, his girlfriend tested positive, but the information I gleaned from him later last night seems to suggest Indrin only slept with her twice. He was reticent to talk about the details, but I have every reason to suppose he is educated enough to use a condom, so why worry in ignorance? In other words, why not go for a test?

"There's no point. I'm not going to be involved with anyone, anyway."

That is exactly what he said. This from *Follow-Your-Instincts Mr. Fearless.* This from my otherwise positive-thinking, almost New-Age-oriented friend. Throwing aside his usual assuredly optimistic approach to life, Indrin appears to be completely convinced he is HIV-positive. He believes he is healthy, that he could live happily for many, many years before ever developing AIDS, but, all the same, he says he feels this virus living in his veins, knows it is there, and cannot see the point of going to receive a doctor's verdict. Somehow, he thinks, a doctor's corroboration might weaken his resolve not to succumb to AIDS, and his resolve is the biggest thing he's got going for him at the moment. It's really all you've got when you're HIV-positive, or so says the new expert.

"But you could be perfectly fine," I kept saying. "In all probability there is absolutely nothing wrong with you."

I spoke these words to the mound of blankets beside me, tried my best to reason with the darkened face, but received not much more than a blanket-muffled "I think we should get some sleep" in response.

It's not as if I speak from wishful thinking alone; I've produced two documentaries on AIDS and an open-line phone-in show that dealt with the dreaded disease on numerous occasions. I could not help but pick up at least a few handy facts along the way and so my advice is straightforward: know what you're dealing with.

It's simple, Indrin. Just get a test.

And then we're back to the *there's no point* argument again. No sex, no worries. And now I'm wondering about just exactly what it is Indrin feels swimming in his veins. The dreaded virus? Or just the infamous Catholic-bred guilt. That is virus enough. It starts off small, ends up invading the whole system. I know how it goes. I have seen it in action more than once. It starts simply enough: *I am not worthy. Forgive me, Father, for I have sinned.* Then it moves to the bizarre, when the guilty party becomes convinced he is beyond saving, a black sheep who might as well go back to the bar after straying so far. Turner all over again. He may have claimed not to be religious in any way, but his Catholic guilt was a floodlit billboard as far as I was concerned. When you are not religious yourself, it is easy to spot the superstitious illogic of a *believer* a mile away.

A lifetime ago it was Turner. Now it's Indrin. I'm spotting the Church's handiwork everywhere and suddenly I'm crankier with the institution, in all its infinite wisdom, than I have been for at least a few days now. *Down with all of it.*

Just get the bloody test, Indrin. Spare me the facade of calm acceptance. You're mouthing the quiet wise words to justify your strange predicament, but there is a scream in you somewhere that would far rather be shaking your vocal chords. I can hear it. This is fear. Fear that makes you feel raw and unsure and desperate for justification and the pretence of control. But you've got it all wrong. It is not just the HIV that has got you terrified, it is the *sin of fornication.* A sin I didn't think even the Church took seriously anymore. Fuck it all.

Indrin knows I'm disgusted, but I do not think he truly understands why. It feels vaguely like he thinks he has disappointed me by not being some saintly-pure future priest.

The crime of sex. The gavel slams down with a crack. Guilty!

Does he forget I am well aware he is a member of the human race? I just assumed he was an intelligent member, so the wilful ignorance about his true medical condition astounds me.

Moments ago, I got up to get into the bathroom first without speaking to him, even though he knew I knew he was awake. But what do you expect? It is bloody five-fifteen in the morning, I have not had any coffee, and I am, once again, completely baffled by my strange travelling companion.

He seems to want to think he is HIV-positive and, while it might make his spiritual choice a touch easier for him, it sure as hell makes it more suspect as far as I am concerned.

The blast of hot water feels good on my skin. It pummels my scalp, drowns out anything but the sound of my own inner ears. I think I would like to spend the rest of the day here in the shower. Yup. You go find our Rwandan refugee, Indrin, I'll be here for the next few days. Happily drowning out everything that doesn't make sense in the world. You know how the song goes – washing a man right out of your hair. "Bali Hai," and so on and so on.

Through the din of my own personal waterfall, I hear a thumping on the door.

"Can I come in?"

"What for?" I yell through the shower curtain.

"I just need my brush."

"Come on in."

Easy, casual. The banter of an old married couple filled with a familiarity that can be used all too easily to prevent intimacy. My parents all over again – at least when they were at an impasse about one of my latest relationship disasters, my father not able to restrain himself from confronting me, my mother wishing only to let me figure it out for myself.

"I brought you tea."

The shouted words flood my ears and when I wipe the water out of my eyes I look down to see a mug of tea being placed on the ledge of the tub, just inside the shower curtain. A peace offering.

"Thanks, Indrin," I yell, but he's already shut the bathroom door behind him.

Yes, an old married couple. Desires unspoken, gratified all the same. Indrin remembers me telling him I am skilled in the art of drinking coffee in the shower before work. It is all part of my finely-tuned routine. The shower-spattered cup of caffeine and the water-resistant portable radio blasting news, weather, and sports at me. My first dose of the day. My anthem and prayer.

Give us this day our daily news.

Enough to start the day anyway. All I am missing are the piles of newspapers and the computer access to Associated Press and Reuters. That, and the familiar twisting in the stomach I get when I think about the stresses awaiting me in the newsroom. But when my stomach plays that game, the extra caffeine I gulp effectively kicks me into frenetic denial.

I'm fine. Let's get to it.

I am half-expecting to find a story meeting to greet me when I enter the other room wrapped in my towel, with my hair at least partly dried off and pushed into shape. Oh, the joys of ready-to-wear hair and an instantly assumable air of competence. Yes, I am ready for the day, ready to run the morning story meeting.

So Indrin, what are people talking about? What's the story of the day?

Well, Miranda, we've got a missing Rwandan refugee who's expected to show in, oh, about an hour. That would be our top story and we've got a good lead. The girl at the counter is willing to talk and we can get video of Rebero at the depot. We actually missed it the first time, but that's no problem. We'll just get him to climb back on the bus so we can get a good low-angle shot of him stepping down from the doors, throwing down his dusty bag, and gazing out at the hills to survey what lies ahead for him.

And what will our first sound bite be? Rebero, of course. We won't need a clip from the immigration authorities until later in the story, to give his plight some perspective. Better to start the story off with a bit of humanity – maybe a five-second clip.

Well, I'm here. Here I am. Brown-skinned homeless kid. Am I homeless or is the whole globe my home now? You decide.

Now, that is probably about a seven-second bite, but it will work. Then we'll run a clip from him over some pictures of last year's violence in Rwanda. Show just what he's come from. Contrast that with a few calm, safe, welcoming shots of Canada. Anything that shows *how lucky he is. How lucky we are. Thank God for our safe streets.* Dynamite. Great feel-good story.

Let's see. What to lead after the first commercial break? Why not another *story* on recent developments in the fight against AIDS? The risks. The need for testing.

The statistics on condom breakage. Community service type of story. The stuff our teens should know – and what they would know already were it not for the evangelical right-wingers concerned that knowledge of a condom will make innocent little Betsy rush right out and get laid. Right then. Holding the school pamphlet in her hot little hand.

See. See that. If only little Betsy hadn't seen that pamphlet. She'd probably be a good girl still, if it weren't for that pamphlet. Or if not, she'd at least have married the boy; it doesn't matter if you're pregnant first these days. Doesn't even matter if you're showing. Why, I saw one girl whose baby was carried right down the aisle, right behind the flower girl. And no one even blinked. Yes, poor Betsy.

"Are you not talking to me?"

"What?"

Here I am, wrapped in my towel and sitting on the bed, watching my hands fumble for the underwear I know I have in my bag somewhere. Indrin is looking at me from the chair by the desk. He is dressed and ready to go.

"I thought you weren't talking to me or something."

"No. I was just thinking, I guess."

"It's five-thirty."

"We're okay for time then, right?"

"I did want to stop by the Cathedral though, remember? Just really fast," he adds when he sees my expression.

Prayer? Already? And why does he have to go to the Cathedral for it?

"I don't need to get into the church. I thought I'd

just like to pay a quick visit to the little shrine outside."

"Fine by me, if you think we have enough time."

I start to hurry my pace a bit, but slow down again when I see quick movements jeopardize my decency. The towel is not tied that securely after all. Grabbing up my clothes, I head back into the bathroom to change. I am out in five minutes, too, by which time Indrin's got the car loaded. No need to stop at the desk since we put the room on my card last night, so we are off. Free to roam. Free to find Rebero. Free to go pray, if one is so inclined.

Indrin is driving when I ask him about the need for the church pit stop.

"So, does this have anything to do with me?"

With my heathenish behaviour. With my immoral sin of falling in love with this boy. Or my falling in *lust.* I am quite sure his Church would call it *lust,* not love.

"What do you mean?" is all he says.

But before I can answer, my eyes settle on the figure of a tall black fellow striding up the hill Indrin and I are driving down.

"Look. Over there."

Indrin is looking and coming to the same conclusion as I am. Across the street, the tall figure continues moving up the hill.

"He could be anybody," I say, eyeing the figure carefully.

There is certainly nothing in his appearance that says *Hello, I'm a refugee.* Far from it. The baseball cap, the L.A. Kings hockey jacket, and the confident stride all shout middle-class black kid from Los Angeles – at least one who has just walked out of the latest sitcom. You know, *Cosby, Fresh Prince,* all those typical examples of the Afro-American experience.

So where's his BMW, *then?*

Indrin pulls over, still a safe block uphill from the marching figure. Steadily ascending, the pedestrian does look foreign – but it's just *American* foreign, not a look from further afield. And I really only say American because of the L.A. logo on his jacket.

"What do you think?" Indrin asks.

"Well, I don't think we can walk up to him and say, 'Hey you're black. Is your name Rebero?'"

Suddenly we are spies on a stakeout mission, missing only disguises and a van with mirrored windows and empty coffee cups littering its interior. I try to watch him without looking obvious, waving a map around in case we look suspicious. After only a few awkward moments as undercover sleuths, Indrin and I agree it would be embarrassing to try to say anything. We should simply follow the original plan and arrive at the bus depot at the appointed time. With that, Indrin starts the car and we drive away from our short-lived sleuthing partnership.

At the church, during Indrin's shrine-stop, I decide to wait in the car and fumble aimlessly with the radio dial. Indrin's figure steps briskly across long, dark shadows stretching from the trees by the rectory door all the way to the pavement. He crosses to the small white statue.

The grass looks damp. The early morning's moist air feels cool coming in from my open window. Zipping up my windbreaker, I wonder if it was Rebero on the hill.

I wonder what Indrin is praying about right now and why he had to come here to do it. And as I wonder this I see Indrin lean forward and place something at the foot of the statue.

Whatever he placed there has to be small, since there was nothing noticeable in Indrin's hands when he left the car and, from my vantage point across the street, there is not a hope of figuring out what the object is. If it's a flower to add to the others, I don't know where he got it. Kneeling, Indrin pauses a moment before settling back on to the bench in front of the statue. His right hand crosses himself – automatic, as unselfconscious as breathing – and Indrin starts back toward the car. As promised, it was a quick pit stop. A drive-thru McPrayer stop.

This was his mission. To deposit one small, secret gift to his beloved Lady with the Sacred Heart.

Sacred Heart.

But aren't all hearts sacred? Even mine? I think, as I turn the key in the ignition halfway and blast the radio's sorry techno-pop louder to stop my ridiculous train of thought. How can I be jealous of the Mother of God, for God's sake? Odd, though, to have perfection personified standing in as my rival for a man's affection.

Shutting the car door, Indrin gives me a half-smile, eyebrows raised. The look is tentative, an *I'm testing the waters* expression.

"So, got your spiritual jump start?" I ask.

He nods and I add, "Guess I have to sacrifice mine."

His eyebrows push even further up his forehead.

"Coffee and a good thick newspaper. That's all I ever

need. But it'll have to wait." Indrin smiles again. It's still only a half-smile and it's distracted at that – but it shows me where we are. The water has been tested. We're not quite back in the swim, but I'm pulling hard to get there. I try to force a lighthearted chuckle to get us the rest of the way, but the sound is lost under the grind of my car's touchy ignition. So are all other concerns as we finally head off to meet our soon-to-be companion: the long-awaited, most mysterious Rebero.

~ ~

Two kids are dragging a third's duffel bag out the doors of the bus depot when we arrive. The sound scrapes the ears. The early morning still has that unique audio quality, the sound that has no discernible sound, even though we have all heard it. Our ears know it as unmistakable, even if we think we forget it. It has a completely different sound from night quiet. No one is quite ready to use their full daytime volume voices, and all hushed tones carry further than usual – like the chatting campers you can hear clear across a lake when the air is still. Everyone is an animal at this hour, ears perked upright. Footsteps click over-sharply, shoes scuffle across the asphalt, rasp the eardrums. Only the chirping of the birds I cannot see anywhere above me evens any of this out. The effect is morning white noise. This is the sound of silence, the sound of six-twenty a.m.

Actually, it is more like six-thirty-one. Indrin and I parked up the road for a few minutes before turning down the last stretch just in case our elusive Rebero *was* the figure climbing the hill. If it wasn't him, no problem, we are only a few minutes late. If it was, well, we will find out soon enough. No need to try to catch him at a lie. But both of us are still wondering why, if he did arrive yesterday, did he say he hadn't? And where did he go?

"Shall we go for it?"

"Right-o."

Rolling for sound. Action, sleuths.

A clapperboard of the old-fashioned movie variety snaps shut in my mind as we push on the glass doors into the small bus depot. The chalk words on it: *Rebero. Scene 1. Take 2.*

And yes. There he is. Our L.A.-Kings-jacket-clad morning walker. Our tall *I'm from the sitcom* friend, fresh from his morning stroll and sitting on his luggage – to be accurate, his one rather overstuffed, maroon-coloured nylon backpack.

There is no staring around the depot, making like we are looking for someone. We walk straight to him. "You must be Edmond," I say as introduction.

"Yes." He stands and, finally at close range, reveals an extremely impressive stature. He is a good four inches taller than Indrin, which puts him well over six feet. The flash of his smile is positively bold. It lights up his face with an unusual confidence, unusual in anyone and certainly not what I had expected in a refugee from genocide.

"You must be Miranda. Indrin."

The grasp of his handshake is firm, warm. His voice is gentle, with a soft-toned French accent.

Indrin nods and the next words spoken literally

shoot out of my mouth.

Steady, aim, rapid fire. "So how was your trip? What time did you get –"

Indrin shoots me a look.

Yes, yes, I know, Indrin. I just want to see what he'll say.

"Fine. Thank you. This is very kind of you."

And that is that. No hesitation. No incriminating pause. My eyes search for the girl who was at the counter yesterday or the guy she said was on duty before her, but all I see is a middle-aged woman talking to a grey-haired man with tired eyes. He is asking about taxis.

"There should be one outside or you can use the phones over there."

When she looks our way to point out the phones, her gaze stops at Rebero.

"So you got your bags, then, did you?"

The briefest wrinkle crosses Rebero's forehead, the rippling of reality you see when you look down a sun-baked highway and try to focus on the horizon and sky. Then, all poise and calm and graciousness, Edmond Rebero nods to the woman. *Damn good, he is.*

"We can go. This is all I have."

He points to the bag and I believe his words implicitly. For the first time in my life I am gazing at someone completely without root, home, or possession. Even tornado victims I interviewed in Edmonton had some ties, some reason to go back to the trailer park. Not this fellow.

Back in Revelstoke, Father Lowrey told us something of what to expect, and while he certainly did not do Rebero's presence or stature any justice, we did get a fair understanding of what this fellow had witnessed during the genocide in Rwanda. The brutal loss of everyone and everything in his life. His arrival in Canada just eight months ago as a refugee trying to convince immigration officials to let him make Canada his permanent haven. The horror of his young life only tempered with the hope that one brother may have survived and that, even after almost two years of displacement and refugee camps and utter silence, he might still be found.

And even what Lowrey didn't talk about directly, I remember all too well from the stories we ran. The video still plays in my head, vividly, as pictures that won't fade. Bodies floating in a river, churning in the rapids. Piles of machetes used to hack off the limbs of hundreds of thousands of Tutsis – of Rebero's family and friends. The even greater piles of hundreds and hundreds of thousands of bodies, of bones.

"How was tree planting?" asks Indrin. As Rebero opens his mouth to answer, I try to grab up his backpack.

"No, please. Thank you."

He looks embarrassed at my grabbing up the luggage, but I am strong for my size and he is the one who has had the long journey.

Or, should I say, the long walk up the hill from downtown.

"It's been good." He turns to Indrin. "I'm getting faster at planting."

"Are you hungry?"

This has always been a standard *ice-breaking* kind of question for me. Must harken back to some eastern European baba roots I know nothing about.

Rebero defers to Indrin, searches his face to see what we would prefer, then turns back to me. I give him nothing to read in my face, but I do answer the question for everyone concerned.

"Well, I need some coffee anyway."

Luggage loaded, we turn out of the parking lot. Rebero's knees are somewhere up by the ceiling, since the car is so small for him. No matter how you adjust a seat, height is height. Indrin tried to offer up the front passenger seat, but Rebero vehemently declined, insisting Indrin remain in his place – the place Indrin earned when he became the first member of my now tiny entourage. Still, Rebero looks comfortable enough and has folded to fit his allotted space amazingly well.

Indrin glances out the window, looking temporarily lost until Rebero begins to ask polite questions about our journey so far. When Indrin turns to answer, I start to look for a pancake house.

"It has been good weather, yeah. Hasn't it, Miranda?" says Indrin.

"Yes, good weather," my mouth says automatically as I change lanes. But I catch Indrin's eyes and as I do, more words float out from me, to Indrin, and then straight out the window to the sky where he looks after I redden. "I think it's the best spring I've ever known. Truly the best ever. I don't want it to end."

∽ ∽

Only two bites into the pancakes, I can hardly contain my curiosity. Rebero has made no mention of his secret earlier arrival, not even the slightest slip. In fact, with all his questions about me and Indrin and about our trip and the car and my job and Indrin's former job, Rebero has managed to learn a great deal about us while revealing almost nothing about himself. Nothing except what is supremely evident from watching this tall young man wiping his mouth with a napkin after a bite of blueberry pancakes.

Calm, intelligent – and with a quick eye – he sits here eating his breakfast betraying a truly considerate nature, not just a carefully learned politeness. My eyes so much as flicker toward the pepper and he is handing it to me. My head tilts back to drink from the bottom half of my coffee cup and he is already trying to make eye contact with the waitress. By the time I set my mug down after my last swig, Rebero is thanking the waitress for the refill she is poised to pour.

The idea of this composed young man crouched in the bus depot making whimpering sounds is starting to seem like a big mistake. Perhaps he just fell asleep. He might have snored just loudly enough to spook the kid at the bus depot counter. Maybe he suffered a nightmare, which would only be understandable, considering.

After being kicked out of the bus depot, this soft-spoken young gentleman of the old school would no doubt have been embarrassed enough to go wander on his own for a day and thereby avoid explanations, conflict, and further embarrassment. Just when I am hit with the temptation to bring all this out into the open with a straight-ahead question, Indrin, seeming to sense my gearing up for direct attack, steers us in a different direction.

"You must be pretty anxious to hear news of your brother."

Rebero nods, but before his spoken answer we sit in silence as he finishes a glass of juice. He sets down the tiny glass – tiny for the mega-price attached to it – and his fingers wipe sweat-like beads of moisture from it.

"It has been very hopeful to hear from him."

"Have you actually heard from him, then?"

My question is blurted out before I completely finish my bite of pancake and a soggy crumb flies from my mouth, across the table, and lands by the artificial sweetener. I quickly grab up my napkin to demurely tap my mouth, but the fact is, etiquette never works as neatly as an afterthought. I feel oafish.

"No," Rebero answers, carefully blind to the blob by his left elbow. "But Sister Fran in Vancouver hears of him. She hopes it is him. She wishes to bring him here, for him to meet me in Vancouver. Me myself, I do not know what to hope for anymore. If I am to see him again, I will. Life will take its course from there."

"I hope you get good news very soon."

This time I am not chewing or otherwise occupied and it feels important to let this Edmond Rebero know I mean that. I want to tell him I will pray for him or something, but the words sound strange forming themselves in my head. I do not pray, at least not what anyone religious would ever consider a prayer, and I certainly do not use phrases like that in everyday conversation. They belong to the foreign language of Indrin and Lowrey.

All this hanging around men of the cloth is starting to affect me. I will soon have to swear off the habit. After this holiday, no more picking up priest-wannabes for drives to Vancouver and absolutely no lounging about as a houseguest in small-town rectories.

So, what do I say to Rebero?

"I'm *wishing* it for you."

A wish. Sounds a bit feeble. Under normal circumstances, it certainly could not compare to *Indrin-the-shrine-visitor's* heartfelt prayers and requests of the saints, but in a pinch, with enough mental effort on my part, maybe my little wish could measure up to roughly the same thing.

I hope so.

I *wish* so.

Rebero thanks me for my wish. He looks me straight in the eye when he does this and I think he feels my intent, my awkward attempt at a prayerful thought. I feel I should say something more now, but the words get stuck. What would I say anyway?

Well, well. Rwanda. How are you coping with it all? Nasty bit of trouble, that.

Just what are the proper words for an occasion like this? I have no skills in post-genocide etiquette. I swallow all thoughts of further conversation with a swig of grapefruit juice.

"Please, to excuse me."

Rebero stands up, dwarfing us with his Mount Kilimanjaro stance over the table. Or Mount something or other. What famous mountains are there in Rwanda? As he walks away, I find myself wondering if there even are mountains there. For the life of me, I cannot remember if the country is marked by desert or jungle or savannah or snow-capped peaks. The landscape is simply not what I remember from last year's news footage.

"Are there mountains in Rwanda?"

Indrin wakes up from his daydream.

"Sorry?"

"So, where are you?"

"I'm sleepy I guess."

He looks wide awake to me, just preoccupied.

"What's the matter?"

"Nothing. I guess we should be getting on the road soon."

"Suddenly we're in a hurry?"

What has happened to my *time does not exist* friend. Twice I have seen him sneak a peak at his watch during breakfast.

"What's with you?"

"Nothing."

Indrin's uncommunicative side drives me wild.

"How can you just not talk?"

"What do you mean? I'm talking."

He stops talking and takes another sip of his coffee, which is not even decaf. Indrin is acting strangely.

"Listen, I'm sorry if I went on so much last night about getting a test. I guess I'm not good at veiling my opinions, but it's your life. Do what you want. Just don't shut off, okay?"

"I haven't shut off."

Silence.

Dark eyes. Sealed coffee-wet lips. Hair neatly drawn

back into a ponytail. He certainly looks shut off to me.

"Miranda, I know you're going to take this all the wrong way, but I've been thinking we probably should split up once we get to Vancouver. Head out on our own again."

"Oh," I say.

All there is here between us is silence. The words we speak can't even begin to lift the weight of it, although I do try. I try my darndest with whatever words come, before I have any idea what to say.

"Well, whatever. You know, if you think you better…you know, whatever."

The effort is futile. I twist my shoulders, try to straighten out my spine, crack my neck, but nothing eases the weight crushing down through my vertebrae.

Indrin then throws some more words on top of it all.

"It's just that there's that friend of mine out there and her family. I dreamed about them last night. I know it sounds weird, but I want to hang with them for awhile. It was kind of the dream, you know…." He trails off before lamely adding, "And you were talking about going back to work anyway."

There. There's something to take us out from under this crushing weight. He just thinks I want to go back to work.

"Listen, I don't know why I was on about that before. I'm not in any rush. I booked my three weeks. There's no point switching it all around now."

"It just makes sense. Don't you think?"

And there it all collapses again.

Sense. Since when did this guy care about what

makes sense in this world. Sure, pass just enough of your insane, quasi-spiritual philosophy on to me to get me happily wandering the roads of British Columbia without a care in the world, then dump a load of reality in my path.

"Thanks for the gravel."

"What?"

"Nothing."

Yup. A load of gravel. Thousands of little rocks that in themselves are nothing, but when piled up make a mini-mountain barrier on my highway. And never mind about the few loose pieces that are currently smashing against my windshield. How can you see straight when a fresh load of reality starts cracking up the tinted glass in front of you?

"To hell with it. Sure. Drop off the map if you want. Where's the nearest monastery?"

"Miranda."

I hate a pleading voice. The calm, veiled annoyance and sarcasm I got quite used to with Turner. *Be reasonable.* This morning, even the slightest hint that I should *be reasonable* makes me want to scream. Makes me want to drive straight into the fortress wall of gravel.

Interesting. I have not allowed myself to think too much about Turner over the course of this, my rerouted holiday, and I never did let myself dwell on his more negative side. To be fair, I know it was not his true nature. Being cruel was never the real intent of the sweet Turner who once showed up, amp and guitar in tow, to play "Happy Birthday" to me in the newsroom, nor of the guy who once sprang for a weekend at the Jasper

Park Lodge when I was so down about my parents I couldn't move. I know the coke was what messed him up, got him overcritical of little things.

But God, I put up with a lot of garbage along the way: *Be reasonable. Pay attention. You don't get it, you just don't get it.* Or sometimes when I allowed my intellect to out-manoeuvre his and he realized he might lose an argument, his dismissive response: *You're not an artist, you're just not going to begin to understand where I'm coming from. You can't intellectualize this. Now, can I have another fifty bucks for golf? I'm just a little low.*

"Need any money for golf?"

"What are you talking about?"

And it was probably never for golf either. The cartoon light bulb flashes on above my head.

"Oh nothing. Let's not fight. Our friend –"

I nod over to the approaching figure and Indrin does an *I give up* slouch back into his orange vinyl captain's chair.

As Rebero's tall frame steps through the room, the image of a giraffe comes to me. Tall, magnificent, and gentle. I've watched their soft fleshy mouths absently munching leaves in the Calgary Zoo. I've gazed into their large brown eyes. Giraffes even walk with a gentle grace – but I hear they have a lethal kick.

"Edmond, we were just trying to think of what kind of landscape Rwanda has. Is it more mountainous or more savannah-like?"

My tone sounds pleasant, conversational, even holiday-carefree. I am proud of myself. An observer could never tell I am hurt, angry and, most of all, baffled.

"Oh, very mountainous. It is called, sometimes, the land of a thousand hills."

"And you've got the famous gorillas, right?" adds Indrin.

"That is correct, yes. You have been there?"

"No, I saw a movie about them."

"I have never seen them too. Very *populaire,* pop–"

"Yes," I jump in, "it's almost the same word in English: *popular.*"

"Thank you. They are very *popular* with a kind of tourist."

"Eco-tourism?" asks Indrin.

"Yes, this is the word. Eco. They wish to protect the gorillas. Make sure they are not killed."

And suddenly I'm wondering why there wasn't any global ecological campaign to prevent the mass slaughter of Tutsi people. Maybe people aren't as sexy as seals or rare gorillas. I'd make a crack about it now, but Rebero's grave eyes tell me he's already made this particular connection.

The waitress comes around with coffee again, but this time I am able to wave her off. At home I just keep drinking it until it goes away, but when it keeps flowing like this it takes a little more willpower to stop. *Enjoy a bottomless cup. Freshly ground!* the sign says over an illustration of a steaming mug. And I would enjoy some more, but my legs are jumping under the table, bouncing to some internal caffeine-driven rhythm. The motion was unconscious until just now, but it feels too familiar and comforting to stop now that I am aware of it. Like jiggling my foot to help me fall asleep, all to the annoyance of anyone who has ever shared a bed with me.

I keep up the silent tapping of my heel. Indrin is probably right. Better to take all this nervous energy and plough it into acknowledging some hard reality.

"So. Want to head out?"

Hands start to reach for pockets and packs and wallets and the whole procedure embarrasses me, so I whip out my trusty credit card to put a stop to it all. The least I can do is give Rebero a breakfast. And Indrin. He will probably be sworn to a life of poverty soon enough. He may as well have a couple of extra bucks in Vancouver.

Their *thank yous* embarrass me more than the fumbling for money did. *It's cheap, for God's sake.*

"Forget it, you guys. Let's get going."

A trip to the bathroom. A breakdown of will on my part as I head back to the counter for one more coffee poured, this time, into my travel mug. A fill-up at the service station. Another necessary swipe of my credit card through the machine to stop money being waved at me for gas. Half an hour later, we are finally off. Only to stop again when Rebero sees a mailbox and asks if he could mail some letters.

"Of course."

We stop in the mall parking lot – unusually busy for this hour, I think, until I realize there is a large grocery store on this end of the mall and we are now in the thick of vacation season. There are barbecue grills to shop for now, coolers to fill. I pop open the trunk and watch Rebero dig into the side pocket of his pack.

He slides out four or five slightly bent postcards and one letter carefully folded in half. Indrin and I avoid the heat already building in the car and lean against the doors as Rebero walks over to the mailbox. When he gets there, he stands staring at the cards and letter in his hands. I never thought to ask if he had enough stamps. But he must, because he now pulls the handle and drops each one inside, one after another.

"I should be writing a few letters myself."

I say this more to myself than to Indrin. The last week and a half I have cut myself off from everyone normally in my life. The gang at work, my sister.

Not to mention Turner.

There was the one phone call I made to Julie to let her know I was fine, but I escaped awkward explanations since I called when I knew she would be at work and I would only have to lay out the barest of facts to her answering machine.

By the way, Julie, if you hear anything weird from Turner, this time it's true. Believe it or not, it's over. Honestly. I'm sure you'll be glad to hear that anyway. And I'm fine. I'm still taking my holidays. I really am fine. Anyway, how's the puppy? Hope he's not peeing all over everything – but I'm sure he is. I'm fine. I really am. Bye, Julie. I'll call soon. Maybe when I hit Vancouver.

In one sense, Julie would be happy to hear about the breakup, but she worries too much about me. I know I still could not handle the sympathy I'd hear in her voice if we talked in person. To her credit, she did try to be happy for me when I first started seeing Turner. Her words, "I guess dating a womanizer is like eating hot, spicy food." She figured it might be all right if I kept my wits about me. After all, spicy food – one of her very favourite things about living on this earth – is good in moderation. Warms you up. Makes you happy. Even seems to clear up colds.

I did not tell her that all it ever does for me is give me the hiccups – and that my doctor has already warned me about an ulcer developing in my stomach. Besides, although we had talked about Turner's reputation as a womanizer, I *knew* he was just misunderstood, just drifting a little, just looking for someone who understood him better. *Someone like me.*

At what point in life do women get brainwashed with that garbage? I was a very clear-eyed kid. But turn me into a grown woman and I start buying into crap my nine-year-old self would have shaken her head at.

I understand him.

Yeah, right. I understand him just fine now.

"Yeah, I should really write Turner."

For just a moment, I catch Indrin wondering whether he should ignore my last comment. But once again, he surprises me.

"You should thank him."

Indrin says this as he fiddles with the broken rubber on my windshield wiper.

"We should replace this," I say, trying to refuse the bait.

We? How have I single-handedly created a relationship here, I'd like to know?

"Okay, so why should I thank him?"

Indrin just stares at me. And laughs. Throws his head back, laughs and sits back down in the front seat.

Betrayal washes over me like hot wax in a car wash,

sheets of it streaming down, covering every window, every escape route. I stand, my back stiffened, feeling my stomach crushed from the inside out. My mind analyzes his comment and my eyes search his face, but neither can find any trace of malice. What remains is simply laughter I do not understand.

"I'm glad my life is so funny to you," is all I can manage to say through my hurt as Rebero walks toward the car, a grinning witness to what he perceives to be a little comedy scene.

"I missed…a joke?"

"Not one that I know of," I answer, more abruptly than I mean to. To make up for it, I plaster a forced smile on my face and add an overly cheerful "Hop in." As soon I blurt the words Indrin is off in full guffaw again. Even my fake smile is forced into something more genuine when I realize a *hop* does not at all fit the gymnastics routine Rebero requires to fit himself into the back seat.

"Um, or climb in. Whatever."

And Rebero clambers into the car, folding himself around the headrest to make way for his legs, as I give him a quick précis of how I met up with Indrin, how he helped me out, how I offered him a ride to the coast. But these facts are layered with a neat veneer of fiction. The story is a little easier to tell this way, a little more cut and dried.

I was just giving him a ride to the coast.

"Well, you're nearly there now," says Rebero.

Thanks for the encouraging reminder.

"Yup. Nearly there."

"And so you began your holiday with one man, and end it with two strangers?" says Rebero, his eyebrows raised playfully.

"That's about it, yes. One of you two want to get married? I was in the mood for it and everything."

"Thank you, no," says Rebero, smiling hesitantly. "I am not good mirage, mir –"

"Marriage," offers Indrin.

"Thank you, yes. I am not good marriage material. I have nothing."

"Don't let that stop you. Neither did Turner. See, I don't know how it works in Africa, but here in North America money has very little to do with it. Here we marry people we hate or will grow to hate. The people we love we push away. It's really a neat system. It keeps the divorce lawyers happy, the economy rolling with all those new wedding dresses needed every few years, and even the Vatican Bank swells with profit, thanks to the annulment fees."

This last bit I smile cheerily at Indrin. Yes, I am completely comfortable joking about my ridiculous life and revealing boundless cynicism where the optimism used to hide. But I do draw the line on revealing everything – the other suitcase at the back of the trunk entrusted with my own wedding dress, for example. Thankfully not a frou-frou mass of white lace and ruffles, but a classic navy crepe, no one will be the wiser when I wear it to a play or a relative's wedding or the next funeral I happen to attend.

Rebero smiles hesitantly, visibly wondering about the appropriateness of joining in the commentary on my personal life, but joining all the same.

"It is better this way. It is possible you should be thanking this Turner. You are too kind for this man, I think. Better you are free. Better you are here with Indrin and me."

"Can I hire you guys to look out for me? Or better yet, Edmond, could I officially adopt you both as the brothers I never had?"

The shy grin Rebero gives me I accept as all the official documentation I need. Indrin, on the other hand, looks away.

~ ~

INDRIN'S HEAD is leaning against the window and he looks dead to the world, but I know he is pretending. I have seen his eyes flicker a few times too often and his posture is just too upright and controlled. He is simply avoiding my glance.

Rebero, on the other hand, *is* asleep. He asked several times whether his sleeping would make me sleepy, whether I needed an extra pair of eyes on the road.

No. Absolutely not. I am awake. Wide awake.

To be honest, I am feeling over-agitated, no doubt partly due to the day's caffeine intake so far, and have trouble imagining myself ever feeling relaxed and sleepy again.

And with that, he crushed his head down into his jacket, carefully bunched up by the window, and tried to stretch his legs across the backseat and up to the opposite window, but settled for a deep fold at the knees. Then, with one last squish of his makeshift pillow, he promptly lost us in favour of the world of dreams or nightmares or simply deep unconsciousness.

Listening to his even breathing mark our steady progress forward, I catch myself insanely wishing my struggling little car will break down – nothing too serious, just enough to slow us down. Or maybe an obstruction. Any little thing that could prolong this journey, at least enough to talk to Indrin a little more. To find out what he is going to do. To hear about his girlfriend and to figure out why he refuses to get tested. To spend just one more rainy night in a tent with him.

Why?

The company. I know I cannot really be in love with the guy, but I am glad I met him. He has been good company.

But as I drive, there is nothing in the way. No gravel. No unexpected roadblock. Not even many cars this morning. Just the smooth Coquihalla highway stretching out before me. One long relentless piece of blacktop. And all I do is follow the road as it beckons us up and down.

Follow the yellow brick road.

I feel like waking them up – or at least the one fake sleeper – with a loud *la-LAH-la*-ing.

Hey, Scarecrow. Hey, Tinman. Some kind of Dorothy you've met up with, hey? We're not off to see any wizard though, because of course there is no wizard. It's all a sham and the Emerald City has a bad traffic problem, is due for a major earthquake, and the Munchkins are all probably homeless or doing heroin in the East End.

La, LAH, La, LAH, La, LAH, LAH…
But I'm just humming the tune in my head.

∽ ∽

With every click of the odometer, the temperature seems to climb. Now in the heavy heat near Merritt, my legs feel sticky against the car seat. The car is silent, save for the hum of the tires against the asphalt and the roar from my open window. Rebero is still sound asleep and Indrin and I are too heat-drained to talk. A hill or two back, Indrin did finally acknowledge his state of wakefulness by sitting up, nodding at me and pulling a water bottle from the day pack at his feet.

We are trading squirts from it now but it does not help much. A single drop of water on a forest fire. So much for quenching thirst. Even after draining the bottle, I feel no relief and Indrin has perspiration in a tiny row of beads just above his lip and across his forehead.

Seconds before it would have been too late, he suddenly points to a turnoff.

"There! Why not cool off? Turn here!"

I see bubbling white water to our left, but I am veering right onto the off ramp.

"Where?"

"There."

Somehow Indrin has already got the route figured and points to the underpass ahead. The curving road takes us through it, then turns to gravel as we near the river.

"Good homing device," I say, as I notice Rebero's

legs untangle themselves in the backseat and his head pop up between the front seats.

"Where are we?"

His face looks hot, the black of his skin taking on an almost flushed tone. His eyes are still blinking himself back to reality.

"There's a river to cool off in over there."

"I think it's just a creek," says Indrin.

"Whatever. It's wet."

When I shut off the car – parked in the only patch of shade I can see – we hear the tree-hushed tone of water shaking and tumbling its way across the earth. The sound of it pulls off Indrin's T-shirt as he steps out of the car. My own T-shirt is soaked under the arms and feels wet on my back. Rebero looks almost heat faint, standing in his dark and crisp new jeans and long-sleeved navy T-shirt.

"If I could open the car," he says by the trunk, "I would make a change of my clothes."

"Absolutely. This is ridiculously hot. We should have stopped a long time ago."

His arms reach for the backpack. I try to help him with it since he looks somewhat shaky. He refuses with a half-gesture, but still finds the composure to weakly smile his thanks at me before placing his bag on the ground.

"Are you okay there?" asks Indrin.

"Yes. It is just the changing of temperatures. It was very cool in Prince George yesterday and the day before. And now this."

"I know," says Indrin, wiping sweat off the back of

his neck. "You better get out of those clothes before you get heatstroke."

"This we're telling the fellow from Africa?" I joke.

I, with my mongrel but mainly British Isles breeding, have always understood people who cannot take much heat or sun. But this fellow? Our tall and stately African friend. Immensely funny.

Rebero laughs and crouches to pull off his running shoes.

"We can even get sunburnt you know. It is possible."

This makes me shake my head and chuckle as I stand waiting for him to change. Rebero seems pretty slow undoing his shoes until Indrin helps me realize it is modesty and not heat stroke that is slowing the process. The poor fellow has no intention of changing his clothes with me there to absently gawk at the proceedings.

"Come on."

Indrin claps his hand on my back and steers me to the river. Only then do I hear Rebero start to pull off his jeans behind us. Sometimes I forget I am not *one of the guys,* no matter how much I feel like it.

The breeze feels cool on my skin as Indrin and I walk into the ribbon of shade by the river.

"I should go back for my bathing suit," I announce, stepping into the cold water. The current pushes against my legs, making it hard to keep my balance even at knee depth.

"Why get your bathing suit? Just get in."

"You mean skinny dip? Yeah, right." I can still see cars motoring along the highway from here, not to mention my current state of discomfort with Indrin. Never mind the modest Rebero.

"No, I just mean your shirt is soaked anyway. You might as well swim like that. It'll feel good."

Indrin dunks himself into the water, jean shorts and all, then stands shaking himself like a dog. He bends over to dangle his head into the water and a sparkling curl of water arcs back from his hair when he flips his head back and stands up.

I stand squinting against the sun, seeing everything in the red-purple glow of half-closed eyelids, feeling the rush of the water against my legs. Dipping cupped hands into the water, I smooth icy handfuls onto my sunburnt arms, splash the back of my neck. When I plunge into the cold, the river current charges me with a fresh feeling, an instant springy vitality.

"Whoo! Why didn't we do this earlier?"

The cold has me gasping for breath. Never has feeling my lungs shudder with sheer cold felt more marvellous. I stop revelling in this icy relief just long enough to give Indrin a good splash.

When Rebero arrives, clad now in brightly-patterned shorts, he winces as we welcome him into the water fight.

"Bloody cold, isn't it?" I yell as I splash him.

"Welcome to the land of extremes," says a drenched Indrin.

We laugh and splash, lose our footing on the slippery rocks, keep dunking ourselves. The cold makes it impossible to remember what the heat felt like, exactly the way standing in the depth of a prairie winter feeling a cold wind bite your face, it is impossible to bring to mind the feeling of hot summer sun burning your neck. Or vice versa.

There is something for your theory of the *now,* Indrin. How the body feels temperature. How the body feels anything. I cannot recall anger. Anger either gradually fades until it is forgotten and far away, an *Oh, I was never really mad about that, was I?* kind of thing, or it is still there, as strong as ever, one thought of it conjuring the same cheek-burning indignation and adrenalin rush you felt the moment the anger twitched into existence.

Sorrow is never a memory either. It is either there, still hurting you, or it is gone. I know this, however, only in theory. For me, a sorrow is never gone. At the mere mention of their names, I'm right back in the very moment I heard my parents were killed. I'm still there, the *No, no, no* still in my throat, the gut-wrenching grief still twisting my insides. I do not have the slightest idea how to make that emotion fade. Time has not done it and I do not know what else could. Hurts collect inside me and pierce as sharply as ever if I let myself think about them. They pile up and gather like blackened clouds tumbling over each other and the only way I know to avoid the storm is to pretend the clouds are not there. Or to pretend I don't care.

Lying on my back now, I let the rushing current carry me a good twenty, thirty feet downstream. The cold water deep in my ears and the muffled shouts above the water's roar make the rest of the world disappear. There is only cold and clear water and me and the sky.

At least that is how it feels right now.

Right *now.*

~ ~

WATCHING THE WATER evaporate from my legs, I think about the relationships I have had in my life. How they have tended to vanish before I could even get a good look at them.

"Do you know I have broken up with someone every year for the last ten years, almost?"

Indrin positions himself on a more comfortable rock. Rebero is another three rocks over, absorbed in writing more postcards and completely unaware of us.

"Why do you look at it that way? The breakups? Why not, 'Hey, I've fallen in love every year for the past ten years.'"

"There is that, I suppose."

I do not feel convinced by this *look on the bright side* view, but I am willing to consider its comedic potential.

"So it could all be considered a determined optimism on my part. A *By God, that one didn't work out, could I love you, please?* sort of thing. Almost heroic of me, isn't it? When you think of it in that light."

Indrin just looks at me as he wrings out his hair.

"I'm tired of it all. If it has been determined optimism I don't think I have it anymore. I'm tired of all emotion and drama and hurt – and hope. I'm tired of hope."

"I don't believe you."

I look up to see Rebero, pen poised, looking at me.

Not staring, just gazing, but it is definitely a focussed gaze.

"It is impossible to be tired of hope," he says. "Hope is automatic. We cannot stop it or control it. It is there or it is not. If you have it, it is a gift."

What to make of this I'm not sure. The meaning is unclear to me, but it is coming from a context I am afraid to question, so I sit and say nothing. A shrugged-off sort of smile before he looks down to cap his pen tells me Rebero's words were not meant to chasten, only to correct.

"Maybe I just don't know what the word means – *hope.*"

"Maybe," says the man with the postcards, the man from blood-red Rwanda, the man who obviously does know. *Know well.*

All right, I am not tired of hope. I am tired of having hopes dashed. But the loss of my pathetic little relationships with men stands shrunken and inconsequential in comparison to Rebero's broken world and so there is no point in speaking aloud of my ridiculous hopes or disappointments. There was no reason to hope even briefly, for example, that Indrin and I could ever have had a relationship beyond being friends. For that matter, there was no reason to believe that a talented but coke-addicted womanizer ever meant it when he said he loved me more than he could believe and never wanted to lose me. He might as well have been repeating the chorus of one his pop tunes.

Love you forever, baby. Don't know what I'd do....

Yeah. *Yeah, yeah, yeah.*

Turner's idea of a wedding was just that, an idea, a fuzzy, far-off idea of something fun to do one weekend. The fact he brought the idea up on the phone after asking me for money should have been a clue as to its depth and reality. So should have been the fact he forgot his suit when we left for this holiday, the holiday in which we were going to surprise ourselves with a wedding in a park. We did not know what park, just that it would be a park. We didn't even care who the witnesses would be, although I had a sneaking suspicion I would call my sister at the last moment with the offer of a plane ticket to Vancouver.

Hope.

It is a funny concept. I am not sure what a person should hope for. I know you can never hope safely. Hope is inherently not safe. It refers to things that are not certain, so risk is an inherent part of the package. I hoped I could get back on track with my dad before he died. I hoped my mom would see us make up.

Maybe for some, hope is still a gift, but for me the risk only seems to lead to more disappointments and sorrows spiralling around in my stomach, the way they are now. Cruelly cutting into the middle of that mini-tornado is the lightning-bright thought that what I am truly sad about is never what I think.

Not Turner's dumping me so unceremoniously.

Not the loss of the wedding in the park.

Not even the loss of my parents on their way to visit me in Edmonton, where we might have had a chance to talk – to really talk.

It could be the feeling I no longer understand why I am living the life I am living, but even that may only be the by-product of the real cause.

It could be the cold, stark, frightening thought that hope is a cruel joke.

Right now I would relax back into the cynicism I feel welling up if I were not afraid that was the easy choice, the choice I always make. Instead, I wonder what gives Rebero hope and Indrin faith. Whatever it is, I hope it decides to come my way.

Hope.

Gift or no, at the very least I can see it is relentless.

My legs have dried off and are already prickling with heat, but my soaked T-shirt promises continued relief from the heat for at least a while. While I brush the sand coating off my feet, I notice Rebero looks quite comfortable in the heat now. Indrin's thick hair is still dripping but he goes back to the river's edge to douse himself one last time before we head back to the car.

While we throw towels onto the hot car seats we are silent and remain that way as we crackle down the gravel away from the roaring white sound, the bright glint of water on rock.

∽ ∽

"Ever noticed all the names? From Shakespeare."

Looking across me through to the passenger side window, Indrin points to the sign blurring by in a flash of green metal.

"Are you kidding, these were practically family shrines."

We pass Shylock Road, Iago, and variously named

exits. Exit Portia. Exit Lear. All so named by a Shakespeare-loving railway engineer named Andrew McCulloch. A man excitedly discovered by my father on our first family trip to the Coast when I was seven. McCulloch not only tunnelled the Kettle Valley Railway through a mountain of sheer granite, he regularly recited Shakespeare aloud to construction crews gathered by the campfire at night. *After my own heart,* Dad kept saying, as he read the tourism brochure aloud at the picnic table.

"Hello from Dad," I yell out the window.

A puzzled Rebero looks to me for explanation but before I can open my mouth, Indrin obliges.

"All those names are from Shakespeare. Miranda's family was very interested in literature. They loved Shakespeare and we were talking, earlier, about how he was...godlike to the family."

"Especially to my father," I throw in.

"Of course, that is normal," says Rebero. "Everyone has favourites. Molière, for example, is like Shakespeare in the French language."

Wheels hit a smooth stretch of new pavement and hum approvingly. We listen for a few seconds until my words pop out, like a bug against the windshield.

"It's amazing what we don't know about Africa."

"I was just thinking the same thing," says Indrin.

Rebero's eyes ask for explanation, but all he says is, "Yes?"

"I was just thinking that I don't think I could name a single African writer," says Indrin. "That if you hadn't mentioned Molière – who's French anyway, not African

– that I couldn't have guessed what you might have read in school. And now that you have, I can't – at least off the top of my head – I can't think of even one African writer."

"Camus lived in Algeria," I offer. I rack my brain further. "Then there's Nadine Gordimer. I saw an interview with her after she won the Nobel Prize. There's Alan Paton – I saw the movie version of *Cry, The Beloved Country.* That was good, even in grainy old black and white; it really got me. And I heard a lecture by Doris Lessing, once, on the radio."

But this is the full extent of my African reading list. And I realize not only are all the authors white, I still haven't read a one of them, except Camus. And even *The Stranger* is a foreign thing to me now, a book I read long before I got swamped with my work in TV, before the books in my house started to get dusty.

Rebero opens his mouth, perhaps to enlighten us further, but Indrin does not see it. He continues as he watches the rearview mirror for a fast-approaching Winnebago.

"I have a theory," he says as my little car hesitates up the steep incline, "that we think of the world like sections of history."

The car slows, seems to drift backward as the lumbering giant pulls out to pass us. Indrin shifts down to fourth gear with the least grinding my sorry clutch will allow, and the car finds its strength again. We continue. And so does Indrin.

"And for North Americans, Africa is either ancient history – ancient Egypt anyway – or the cave-man era.

It puts Africa just too far back for us to remember."

"Back?" asks Rebero.

"Exactly. It's lame, but we're taught about the cradle of civilization and the Nile and all that, so we have early history in our heads when we think about Africa, and then it kind of falls off. Europe takes over for medieval times and it stays in the forefront all the way into the eighteenth century – with the French Revolution and all. Then it kind of passes the torch to North America. Through both the world wars, America stays about tied with Europe, then America takes over. So the way we're taught, Africa is some kind of distant past that fell into decline, that we only care about in terms of who colonized what. Europe is the biggest part of history. And North America is the present and future."

"That's probably changing," I hear my voice saying to Rebero.

Damage control. You would think I were a P.R. flak.

"I mean, at least with media coverage of some of the major events in South Africa and Ethiopia – and Rwanda – I think people are getting a better understanding."

Yes, I sound like a public relations representative giving a talk at the local high school.

It does not impress Indrin.

"You've got to be kidding. I only see stories from Africa if there's a war or a famine. And even then you better hope there are some rock stars willing to take on the cause with a benefit concert. It's like the media doesn't even care about finding the truth, only about blasting out pat answers."

Why does this feel like a personal attack? What's got into you, Indrin?

"The media has not been making many reports of Rwanda?" asks Rebero.

Before I can answer, once again Indrin beats me to the punch.

"Let's just say none before the massacres. Before the genocide in '94, no one ever heard anything from there. I remember seeing one tiny article in the paper when a plane got shot down and some leader was killed –"

"Habyarimana," says Rebero.

"We just knew some African leader died – that's all it meant to us – and then suddenly out of the blue there's news reports of insane massacres, some weird war. Then nothing – no reports at all."

"That is simply not true, Indrin," I cut in. "We ran follows. We ran follow-up stories even a year later. And it's the kind of story where more will have to come out later."

"But the media reported it like it was tit for tat, you know," says Indrin, his mind obviously racing. "They gave it this first Tutsis, then Hutus spin. Like it was all even – or just some kind of crazy African war. But there's a genocide of a million Tutsis – and it takes place incredibly fast – how long did it take?"

"A hundred days," answers Rebero, quietly. "One million in a hundred days."

"And then a year later," continues Indrin, "when there's suddenly an outbreak of violence against Hutus in a camp somewhere, we're supposed to think of it as a war. But no one says the holocaust was a war between the Jews and the Germans. It's screwed, the whole way the media talks about it. Even our attention spans are screwed. I mean, people don't want to hear about all that stuff unless it's so horrific that we absolutely have to for a day or two."

Fine, Indrin. Your points are all fine. But they're nothing new. It's just so easy to hate the media while you are busy flipping channels, isn't it? Give me a break.

"Try running a news show, Indrin. Then maybe you'll be a little less paranoid and a little less critical."

I want Indrin to shut up. To leave me alone. This has nothing to do with the media or even Rwanda, it has to do with me. With my blabbing on about the AIDS test, with my blasting out my feelings for him last night. With my big mouth. My desire to kiss his. But that was my desire yesterday – not today. Today I want to forget all about it.

I want you to leave me and the media alone, thank you very much.

"The media is not all bad," suddenly offers Rebero. "I too do not have so great confidence in the radio, the newspapers. But you are too strong in your words, Indrin, for this country maybe. In Rwanda, it was a different story. There the radio made broadcasts telling Hutus to kill all Tutsis."

"They aired that, on the radio?" I'm stunned by this. This I know I've never heard before, in any of the reports we ran.

"Yes, *certainement.* It was on the radio," says Rebero.

And then the lanky young man with the finely chiselled face and the soft eyes leans forward between the front seats of the car much like a child might, an eager child anxious to tell the adults in the front seat exactly what happened at school. But there is nothing childlike about what Rebero recounts now, or how he recounts it. Calmly, steadily, he relates not only how Tutsis were described via *radio trottoir* – the word on the street – but what was actually printed, what was actually broadcast throughout his country just prior to and during an organized and pre-meditated genocide.

"Radio Milles Collines told all Hutus to exterminate the cockroaches, to kill the *inyenzi*. That was us," explains Rebero. "Tutsis were the cockroaches. And the music on the radio said this too – the pop songs. One song, very *populaire* – popular – sang that all should hate Hutus who had sympathy for Tutsis. *Kangura,* a newspaper, gave out the 'Hutu Ten Commandments.' The eighth commandment was that Hutus must stop having mercy on the Tutsis. It was like that in the days before," Rebero finishes, quietly.

I think back to the reports I know we ran at the time, some of which I put into the six o'clock lineup myself. They were big on horror, but obviously a bit short on facts. Until now, I'd never heard of this organized campaign of hate, of pop music blaring murder with every drumbeat, of radio that didn't even pretend to be objective – radio that issued deadly orders along with the soccer scores.

"None of that got reported," says Indrin. "None of it."

"I thought at first I met unusual people on the job site, planting trees," says Rebero carefully, still leaning toward the front of the car. "They knew very little about

Rwanda and what has happened there." He pauses. "I thought it is because they are not seeing television too much or they are not reading too much. Maybe not educated?"

He adds this last suggestion with an embarrassed half-smile, an *I probably shouldn't be saying this* smile. Indrin has the answer.

"No, sorry to break it to you, Edmond. They're probably typical. Absolutely typical. Mind you, like I say, it's our attention spans too. It's kind of a vicious circle. Why cover the stories if they're stories we don't want to hear about? The Yugoslavia thing is a bit weird though – the media has spent quite a bit of time on that, but then that fits my theory, right? I mean, it's in Europe."

Indrin as historical theorist is a new idea, but one which will probably fit in just fine with his desired vocation. *"Unusual sermon,"* the churchgoers will mumble to themselves as they shuffle from the church, squinting into the light, with new theories of history and the globe arguing in their heads.

If I were in a different mood or had any energy beyond what is required to lean my head against the window, I would try to defend the media a little more. I mean, how the hell can every story be told from everywhere on earth anyway? Not possible. I could give him more of the journalistic party line about how reporters are only human and how they work for finite news machines based in countries with their own interests and problems, and how, given all that, the vigorous open-mindedness of the press is actually remarkable. But I would weaken my argument by having to agree we could have stolen just a few minutes from the ongoing O.J. Simpson trial blasting from our sets every day last year.

We interrupt this celebrity broadcast to bring you a special news segment from somewhere in the world you do not normally hear from.

The revenue from the incredibly popular O.J. coverage could certainly have paid for a few extra plane fares to remote corners of Rwanda or Zaire or Burundi. The media, however, is just too easy a target for me to enjoy this debate, or whatever Indrin thinks this is. What the hell is news about the problem with news?

"I agree with you that the media could do a better job of covering stories in Africa, but it is improving."

My defense sounds as tired as I feel at the moment, but Indrin is oblivious to everything save his argument.

"You've got to be kidding. It's all getting even more superficial – and it was pretty superficial to start with."

His cheeks are tinged with red, his fingers pound out the rhythm of his words atop the steering wheel, and his elbows are jutting out, ready to oust anyone in his way. Although still not a speed demon, Indrin jerks the steering wheel erratically enough to make me sit forward in my seat and fix my eyes carefully on the road.

"No, I can't see how you think it's improving."

Seeing him grab this topic and tear into it with his jaws brings back an image of our news director terrorizing his latest reporter victim in front of the rest of the tensely gathered news crew.

You totally blew the live hit. We don't go live from a disaster scene to make our show look like a disaster. Quite frankly, you were worse than amateur. You were an embarrassment to me, to the show, and to the network.

And that would be just the warm-up to one of his critique sessions.

Like our station's resident psychopath, Indrin sounds relentless and autocratic; he is filled with the passionate intensity of a man who has no doubt of the superior nature of his convictions.

Finding a parallel between Indrin and the man my producer-colleagues and I refer to as "The Pit Bull" is not something I am comfortable with. Pit bull terriers are apparently dogs with a problematic gene, one that can flip out at any time, filling them with the unrestrainable desire to attack and kill. Once their jaws lock on to something, it is nearly impossible to pry them off. Years ago I interviewed some dedicated pit bull owners, so I know it is possible for people to love creatures with that unfortunate potential. Overall, however, the ability to hold an inexplicable and brutal deadlock is not generally considered a favourable trait. I do not like seeing it in Indrin.

"Okay, okay. News flash: TV news is superficial. Can we just drop the subject now?"

In the grip of the pit bull gene, however, one does not hear. The blood is pounding too loudly in the eardrums.

"You say it's improving," says Indrin, rapidly inhaling so he can rush to the rest of his argument, "which first of all I don't buy – but, the thing is, it doesn't even matter if it does improve. I mean, how can the media properly cover breaking news stories in Africa when, deep down, most North Americans can't imagine the African continent as a modern place where ordinary people live right now? It's only history to them, remember? Neanderthal Man. The search for the missing link. The rise of Egypt – a few magnificent pyramids – and that's it. Darkness."

"And genocide," adds Rebero.

"That's right, and now a new history lesson – genocide," says Indrin, his militant tone suddenly failing him on the final word. Even so, he regains himself in time for one more jab at the media. "You know, we didn't even hear about the appearances of Mary in Rwanda. I just found out about them – the ones at Kibeho. It's amazing, but I don't remember a single news report about the apparitions."

Indrin delivers this line to me.

Does he honestly expect a reaction here?

That Indrin could consider Marian updates and doomsday predictions on the same scale of newsworthiness as genocide is unfathomable to me. But if I'm ready to rudely point out his mistake, Rebero seems about to do so politely.

"It was reported on Radio Rwanda – the apparition, the last one," he says, hesitantly. "But I do not believe it."

"You don't believe it? Why not?" Indrin seems truly surprised at our new friend's reaction.

"They said she predicted the genocide," Rebero explains, "and that she gave it her blessing. Her final message in May – after a month of killing – they say it meant she supported it, the genocide."

"Who said that? That's insane." Indrin is sputtering now. "I don't care who interpreted or how they interpreted it. That can't be true."

"It was what people were saying. Me, I don't believe that. But I don't believe any of it. Not in God. Not in Mary appearing to her people. Not anymore. Pardon me," he adds, watching Indrin's grip on the steering wheel tighten into a deadlock.

And now I try to reroute our conversation – or at least to steer it off the topic of Mary and all her message's interpretations or misrepresentations.

"Kibeho," I say aloud, sounding out the word, trying to work out why it sounds familiar. Then it comes to me. "Kibeho – that's also where that massacre took place, isn't it? The one a year after the genocide. Wasn't that where a thousand refugees were killed in a camp or something like that?"

"Yes," answers Rebero dutifully, like a soldier trained to offer his name, rank, and serial number. "Yes, a thousand or more." Suddenly, his voice is barely audible. He swallows hard. "It was when they closed the camp. It went wrong, you see, for the army – the Rwandan Patriotic Front – it went wrong for them. It was not planned."

But Indrin, still white-knuckled at the wheel, breaks in now as if I need him to try to make sense of it all for me. "But they were Hutus, Miranda. Hutus. The ones who did it. That's mostly who got killed there, right Edmond? It was just...spontaneous revenge, right?"

"The authors of the genocide – *génocidaires* – many, many were in that camp because eighty-thousand

Hutus were living there. And yes, the *génocidaires* were Hutus, but not all Hutus were *génocidaires*, you understand? Some Hutus were good people, it is true; there were some, but not enough."

Rebero stares now at the gear shift, now at the dash – anywhere but at me or into the rearview mirror where Indrin's eyes await him. Then he straightens his back, raises his head. I see the giraffe in him again, the elegant line, the gentle eyes, before he adds, "But when those Hutus were killed at the camp in Kibeho, it was not genocide. It was…it was justice."

"Justice?" I blurt out.

"A desire for justice…that went wrong. After one million Tutsi people are murdered by their Hutu neighbours and bosses and doctors and family members, something is – how do you say? – *détruire* – destroyed. Something inside is destroyed. Justice too is destroyed."

Rebero leans back in his seat. Indrin starts to say something but coughs instead and, for the next few kilometres, we listen only to the hard-working chug of my car and feel the motor vibrate as we mount an upwardly winding road. I watch shadows, huge shadows, drifting across the valley, shifting to mould themselves into every crevice, every rise, every rooftop. The darkness comes and goes, exploring and moving on, but whatever light or dark plays upon them, the mountains remain unchanged.

I want to see parallels here. I want to find analogies for ignorance and hatred, for passing storms that are misunderstandings, that are war, that are slaughter, but I cannot. I can only see a vast, moving shadow and a cloud high above it, and this speaks of a harmless world. Harmless and dreamlike. Below in the valley, a brilliant light flashes, catches my eye. It is possibly the metal roof of some equipment shed suddenly revealed in a blast of sunlight, but from here it looks like a beacon. As we drive to a higher vantage point, the pure light flashing at me fades to something ordinary. Yes, a shed. And in the distance behind it, a deer. A deer or maybe one of a herd of cattle grazing before its trip to the slaughterhouse. At this distance, it is impossible to tell.

∽ ∽

SLAUGHTERHOUSES, AIDS, genocide, and the crashing of personal relationships. The topics of my thoughts over the last hour of driving.

Indrin is still at the wheel, still drawing out our journey by virtue of his by-the-book driving speed. The radio is blaring and the only two men in my life trade comments about music.

"Have you heard this?"

"No, who is that?"

"REM."

When the final notes of the song are interrupted by the overly warm and enthusiastic tones of the deejay, Indrin fumbles with the dial once again. For the next few minutes, we listen to a variety of different styles of static.

I know, I know. My stereo is archaic. Knobs to turn manually. It's hard to believe I'm from this century, isn't it, Indrin?

"What do people listen to in Rwanda?"

And now the car is filled with enough material for a winning quiz show, the topic: international music. Depending on the television writer hired to create the MTV-style show, its title would likely be something like "rockin' the borders," or "border rockin'." I am now the proud recipient of some truly international music knowledge. I truly did not know that good old Canadian rocker Bryan Adams was big even in Africa. And there are other surprises.

No, you're kidding? You mean the suicide of Kurt Cobain didn't have them weeping in the streets of Kigali?

Armed with trivia like this I could soon have new career opportunities opening up before me. With all the budget cuts in TV news these days, I should really just spiff up my hair with some heavy-duty hairspray, start wearing ugly, clumpy shoes with short, little-girl dresses and I would no doubt be snapped up in a second as a veejay.

Turner Mahoney? No, I don't think we want to play his video. It's too self-indulgent and forgettable. Instead I'll introduce you to the latest by U2, but first – I talked with Bono and....

"You're quiet, Miranda."

Indrin is trying to draw me into the conversation again. He has done this a few times now, but each time I have feigned fatigue or disinterest or whatever emotion came to mind. This time it will be scorn and sarcasm.

"I've decided to become a veejay."

"Oh?"

Indrin waits for the punchline. Rebero waits for an

explanation. Rebero wins.

"Someone who plays music videos on TV."

No, Indrin. No punchline. I do not want to play.

"Can we put on a tape instead of *this?*"

My tone and emphasis illustrate my opinion of the current bit of post-Seattle grunge rock screaming from my speakers. To my ear, it is also post-melody, post-lyric, and post-decipherable – despite what I used to try to hear in it for Turner's sake. No, if I am not hip to the best in modern alternative rock, I now make no apology for it. I like what I like.

"You're not going to make me listen to your Donovan tape again, are you now?"

Indrin's teasing is meant to remind me of all the joking banter of the journey thus far, but I do not feel like being reminded or playing along. In fact, I feel physically incapable of it.

"No, You don't have to listen to Donovan."

"I'm kidding, Miranda. Play whatever you want. The Beatles, John Lennon, whatever."

Already rummaging through the glove box, my hands sort archaic maps, a dusty hairbrush, and extra napkins from every fast-food place I have visited in the last year. Finally, tucked inside a warped *Map of the Western States and Canada,* I find the Leonard Cohen tape I was looking for days ago. Jennifer Warnes and Leonard Cohen, actually.

"This is something you should hear, Edmond," I say as I pop in the Montreal bard's music. "And it's *contemporary,*" I stress to Indrin.

No surprise, really, that the tape is cued to "Song of

Bernadette." I'm like that. Get on a kick for a certain song and play it ad nauseum. I'm about to flip the tape over to play the first side, but Indrin hears *she saw the Queen of Heaven once, and kept the vision in her soul...* and asks me to rewind the tape so he can hear the beginning of the song. This is fine until we come to the chorus.

so many hearts I find, broke like yours and mine
torn by what we've done and can't undo
I just want to hold you
won't you let me hold you
like Bernadette would do

And as the song continues my eyes fill.

Idiot, idiot. What's happening to my ability to control my emotions?

I turn into the window, pretend to get real interested in the exit signs to the town of Hope, but Indrin sees me, I know, and this just makes the tears bigger, fall faster. My throat tightens. I try not to swallow or breathe and concentrate on stopping this silent waterfall.

The water is rushing past me all over again, rivers and tears and time, all of them roaring and all of them beyond my control, beyond my comprehension. Ice-cold rivers behind us on the highway, like the one we swam in, the one I hoped might give us all a clean start. The rivers in Rwanda that ran red after the killings. My runaway, free-flowing grief that seems never to dry up, eternal spring that it is. This heartless river of asphalt.

I'm tired. So tired. And I don't care what Rebero says

– I think you can be tired of anything, even hope. And no, I have not lived through a genocide and I have a good job and people always say *you'll meet someone terrific* but I honestly don't want to anymore. Honestly. I want to be left alone by all manner of people presenting themselves as boyfriends.

But what I realize as I cry into the stupid, smudged pane of glass and as I feel the vibration from the car running from my elbow up to the hand on my chin is that I do not want to be left alone by friends, true friends, and that I do want – need – their arms around me.

Come on let me hold you, like Bernadette would do....

But how am I ever supposed to let that happen when it is always getting mixed up by the romantic thing, the sexual thing – the very thing that inevitably sends me back off into solo orbit. Solo orbit in a dark frozen universe, the murky universe of misunderstandings and hurt feelings.

Are you sure, Mr. Guru Priest, that you're chasing chastity for all the right reasons? I'd wear a robe too if it could spare me the political manoeuvrings of love.

Lies and the Past

The pace of exit signs picks up, one after another. We are entering a sprawling city of dreams, the destination point for everyone across this country who has visions of skiing and sailing and moving up the corporate ladder all at the same time, in the same day, maybe. At least, it's the destination of choice if they have enough money for the insane cost of living here and can afford their move up in the world – right up to a half-a-million-dollar rundown bungalow. Such are the costs of paradise.

"This is the only place in Canada where you'll find a flower garden growing at every gas station. My definition of paradise. Who cares if you're homeless, right? I mean, in a garden?"

Rebero smiles at this. Yes, even my new friend is catching on to my incessant sarcasm.

Indrin just watches the road. We are now well into

the land of speeding convertibles and newly-minted Jeeps, all aggressively driven and filled with young would-be yuppies in a hurry to get further into debt.

Let's get going. Move it.

Yeah, right. Let's hurry up and make our delivery. Sign right here for one very quiet, carefully enigmatic, new refugee friend.

Let us deliver him up to Sister Fran and the hands of the Lord.

Deliver him up and lose him to the wide, wide world.

I am actually going to lose both my travelling companions in a matter of hours now, but suddenly I can't stand the idea of losing Rebero without knowing something more about him. Because even though we have heard him talk about massacres and Marian messages in Kibeho, and radio stations blaring hate campaigns, we haven't heard a word about him personally. The survivor in our midst. There are pieces missing; I still don't know who Edmond Rebero is.

"Do you know what's going to happen when you meet up with Sister Fran?"

"I am not sure," he says, carefully. "I am afraid if they find him. For what I will do."

I puzzle out Rebero's twisted English and quickly twist in my seat to comfort him.

"There's every chance, I'd think, that your brother survived, that they'll find him alive. Especially if Sister Fran thinks she has tracked him down."

"No," he says. "She is not sure."

"Then, why come all the way out here…if she's not

even sure it is your brother?"

Indrin looks at me with a horrified clenching of his eyebrows and I instantly regret my bluntness.

"Sorry – I just mean.... What are you going to do when you get there?"

"I don't know. Sister Fran, she would like to speak with me more. To help find him."

"When did you last see him?"

Silence.

Silence, that is, except for the rhythm of the tires clicking across ridges in the asphalt every twenty feet or so.

"I didn't mean to...." I start, and stop at the same time.

My mouth is dry. Where is all the coastal humidity that is supposed to be here?

"It is okay."

Rebero's voice is soft and self-conscious. I watch his mouth choosing each word, holding onto it before it is spoken.

"It is very difficult. There were some very terrible things to see."

"I'm sorry."

"We don't want to pry," throws in Indrin from the steering wheel.

Shut up, Miranda, I hear him think.

And don't tell me you didn't think it, Indrin, because I heard you – plain as the green around us, plain as the Coastal Mountains looming up behind the city.

"It is okay. I don't like to talk about it at night, because if the pictures come into my head, I can't go to sleep. But right now, it is okay."

So it is amid the encroaching city, and the beauty of the trees and gas station gardens, and the new cars speeding along this expressway that we hear about machetes and gaping wounds. About hand marks in blood against a wall people thought they could climb to get away. About a child he saw, a boy of about seven, crouching in the bushes behind the limbless bodies of his parents. About another boy he saw, just eighteen years old, leaving a house filled with moaning, the bloody machete still clasped in his hand.

And it is here in this car, at the end of our journey, that we hear about two others: Rebero's escape to Burundi during the genocide in 1994 – and his trek back to Rwanda a year later to face a land of bodies still unburied and their living murderers.

On the way to Burundi, Edmond Rebero hid in underbrush and travelled at night. He returned in the daylight, trudging down dusty red roads filled with so many others – Tutsis and Hutus. Hutus flooded the roads as they left the refugee camps they fled to, fearing punishment, after the Tutsi army, the Rwandan Patriotic Front, ended the genocide. But Tutsis too filled those roads, both those who survived and those who had escaped and were returning, all of their minds filled with pictures of horror, all of them focussing on anything that could give them new visions of hope. Eyes searching crowds for family members, minds fighting to believe some loved ones miraculously escaped.

Yes, I think I saw her. Yes, I think she got away.

And so many of these hopes crushed by the blood-red, head-pounding images of those who did not.

No. No, I'm sorry. Alphonsine is dead. That man, walking over there, Gerald Ngeze, it was he who killed her. Her and her six brothers and sisters. I saw it all from the trees.

And always the questions – the questions a vast parched land, and the answers a disappointing spit of rain.

Your father, Edmond? No, he is not here. Perhaps he crossed to Zaire instead.

It was not true. But only later, in the rolling green mountains of the south, at Kibeho, did Rebero learn his father had not escaped to Zaire.

"My father," he says, "my father was not a bad man, not a good man, just an average man. An ordinary man – in life and death. I stared at his body. He looked no different than any other man."

Then, more than ever, Rebero had hoped. With every step, he listened for word of his brother. He watched the crowds intently for his brother's face. He knew he must find him. He *knew* his brother had survived.

His mother and sister had not. Rebero knows this too but cannot verbalize to us just how he knows, just what he saw to take hope of their survival away. But whatever he saw is firmly etched in his mind, in his eyes, like the red-blue negative of the sun you see inside your eyelids when you close your eyes after staring too long at the sky. It burns its way into your retina. The imprint fades slowly, a little more with every blink, and they say it doesn't leave a scar unless you look for too long. But how long would you have to look before a picture of agony was seared in your mind forever? And like the sun-branded shapes in your vision, no one would ever see the scars but you. Especially at night when you must finally give yourself over to the world floating beneath closed eyelids.

I watch Rebero's eyes blink away the passing cars and the sun-baked freeway.

He is never again going back. *Never.* He says this simply, quietly. No malice, no hatred. Just a statement of fact. He saw what the country was *before,* and he saw it after.

Another car rushes past us.

"No matter what happens, never. It is over."

There's your end of the world, Indrin. Your apocalypse, Father Lowrey.

Indrin either reads my thoughts or is simply on the same wavelength.

"The end of the world," he says.

"Yes," says Rebero. "But," he adds, "nothing is over for me – and for the other survivors. We continue even after the end. C'est ça."

C'est ça. That's that.

We continue.

So do we continue driving through this city. Me, the altar boy, and the refugee. The lost, the faithful, and the homeless. And crowding in beside us are cynicism, fear, and hope. It's a bit much for one car.

One freeway bridge too many, one accidental tour through the North Shore, and finally we are led on an involuntary race through the dark woods of Stanley Park.

All the while, no one speaks. We listen to the wind

rush through the open windows, the roar of muffler-less motorcycles, and the blare of other cars' radios. We listen to rap and easy listening and rock classics without ever turning on our own car stereo. The sounds are all too loud and somehow heartless and without point – and as I breathe in the smell of heavy gasoline fumes mixed with the perfume of the trees, my stomach feels slightly sick.

~ ~

Rebero said he didn't need anyone to see him in. He appreciated the lift, it was very pleasant to meet us, he just needed his bag and he would be fine.

Fine.

Goodbye and good luck, Mr. Survivor.

Indrin helped him lift his duffel bag from the trunk, and we watched Rebero make his way up the walk to the Catholic Charities Building, the old red brick of the building trying to speak something of solid old values into a gleaming chrome-and-particleboard new world. But I note that it seems to be a losing battle. Two craggy-faced men, probably only in their thirties but looking more like sixty years apiece, lean against the side of the building. One bumps into the other before sliding down to squat. Hands tremble. Heads shake. They are obviously drunk or high or both. Even a tried-and-true brick wall cannot hold back heroin and homelessness.

And AIDS.

Modern realities.

I watch the two men stagger around the red brick

corner into a door marked, MEN'S HOSTEL.

Not that this end of Vancouver is particularly grim. To the contrary, in fact. This end of town actually makes me feel welcome, like I know where I am – and that is because of the gleaming monolith sitting across the street from the old red brick Catholic Charities building. It's just what I need to feel comfortable – radar dishes, antennae, vans driving in and out of the parking lot filled with cameramen and reporters with their notebooks poised.

The Canadian Broadcasting Corporation. For me, a producer at a modestly budgeted private station in a good-sized market, I still view the old Canadian institution with a bit of awe. *Mothercorp. Canada's Public Broadcaster.* Even after all their budget cuts, I'm envious of the money they throw at certain current affairs docs – and amazed at the number of producers they manage to keep lurking in their newsrooms. The golden days are over, I know, even on the current affairs front, and the hiring situation no doubt as frozen as a Yukon lake in January, but it would still be worth popping in and making a quick visit of their newsroom. Never hurts to let people know you're still around.

Indrin leans against the car, nods to the CBC building.

"You want to go in?" he asks.

"Not like this."

No, if dazzling the producers in the Vancouver newsroom was my idea, I would certainly not get too far with my coffee stained T-shirt, wrinkled shorts, and legs in need of a razor. Not to mention my hair.

"So, what do you think?"

"I don't know, Mr. Prie–"

Indrin opens his mouth to protest but I press on.

"I just mean I don't know. I never have felt I'm steering this ship. I don't know who the hell is, but it's not me. For a while I thought it was you."

" 'Fraid not."

He slumps into the passenger seat.

Sure. No one is steering but it's my turn to drive.

"Well, I'm going to have to find a place to stay. You said you had friends here?"

"I should call them," he says.

So we find a phone booth and, from the car, I watch Indrin's lanky body lean against the broken plexiglass as he smiles and gestures and laughs, and then I stare at a bus gasping diesel as it trundles down the street. Above it, purple mountains gleam serenely against a pale blue sky.

Here the four elements stand plainly visible.

Water, sky, concrete, and fear.

Goodbye. So long.

Humming a line from the Family Von Trapp's getaway song – repeatedly, since I can't remember any other part of the tune and it has been just too long since I rented *The Sound of Music* – I serenade Indrin all the way to his friend's place. A stucco house with a broken window cringing alongside a rundown apartment block in East Van. Lovely. This is where we leave things?

"You didn't tell me I'd have to worry about your safety. Does this friend of yours have armed guards?"

"I'll be fine."

He pulls an overstuffed bag out of my trunk, then

reaches back to fish out a few loose socks that have spilled from it.

The sun is too hot. I wipe sweat from my forehead and onto my shorts. I reach to help him with the last bag, but he, like Rebero, is fine – *just fine* – without my help, and so I back off.

"Are you going to be okay?"

This sudden concern for me is more irritating and more humiliating than anything else he could have possibly said.

"What do you think?" I say, throwing myself back behind the wheel.

He comes around – probably my subconscious wish anyway – and stands by the driver's side window. This is one of those *I don't want to talk anymore but don't leave* scenarios.

"I think you'll be fine."

His brown hands grasp the side of the door and look browner – maybe greyer – than ever.

"Boy, do we need showers."

Yes, this is all I can contribute to a meaningful goodbye. Sometimes I astound myself.

"Yeah, I guess," he responds.

My next contribution to the conversation is a good stare at the dusty dashboard of my car.

"Gotta get this car washed too."

Bloody amazing, my repartee.

"Do you know where you're going to stay?"

"No."

I stare at him clear-eyed when I say this and I do not feel like embellishing my answer. Besides, I'm just being honest. I have no idea. There is no one I particularly want to call. At least not now.

"The world is my oyster, Indrin. I can stay anywhere."

There. See. I talked. I expanded my answer. Can't say I'm being uncommunicative.

"I'll give you my number then," he says, fumbling through his pockets for paper.

I hand him a pen.

"I mean, at least we can meet up in a day or two. Go for lunch or something. Or do you think you're heading back right away?"

"No idea, Indrin. I think I'll just follow my instincts."

I speak these last few words with an intended stab at his supposedly free-and-easy philosophy, but he doesn't take it like that. He smiles. One of his big – huge in fact – grins that have amazed me from our very first conversations. The smile seems to happen in slow motion – spreading wider and wider, like a wave breaking across his mouth – although I know, of course, that smiles are not tidal waves, *slo mo* or otherwise, and can disappear as quickly as they appear. But somehow this wave sweeps across everything I have been feeling and soothes me.

You're a sweetheart, Indrin. Thanks.

This, of course, is what I want to say. But what's new? Nothing comes out that way. At least I don't bring up bathing or cleanliness again.

"I should get going."

"Okay."

He hands me the address and phone number and I

tuck it into the pocket of my shorts.

"We'll talk."

He says this as a statement, but I wonder if he means it as a question. That's what I am wondering. Will we?

Yes, we will talk. Of course we will. At some point. About something or other. Maybe even tomorrow for all I know. But I also know it will not matter because I already feel myself shutting off. A casual hello over coffee, where we meet again as friendly strangers to chat about *that funny road trip* and leave all the important things unsaid, would feel worse than never seeing him again. I would rather lose him cleanly, with one knife-sharp goodbye, than allow this strangely important friendship to dwindle away into a casual *acquaintanceship.* So, for me, even if Indrin could handle moving into a *we must stay in touch, let's get together real soon* kind of relationship, this is truly goodbye.

And I don't care – or at least soon I won't. Soon I will be able to make Indrin as distant a memory as Turner – more distant since we never did actually *go out, date, get romantically involved,* whatever you want to call it.

One thing I have learned well is how to shut off when I have to. Sometimes it happens as abruptly as flicking a light switch. Other times it is a slower process, like turning one of those round fader switches that dials down the intensity of the light, dimmer and dimmer and dimmer – from daylight to romantic mood lighting to plain old stub-your-toe-darkness. And when that light is out, it's out.

Blackout.

Because there is no point grieving something once it is over, the blackout approach gives comfort. Surely

Indrin would approve, seeing as how the method allows one to leave behind all feelings that are no longer appropriate. What is in the past is gone – or at least forgotten.

Besides, being able to shut off the past has given me an inner reserve, an ability to carry on smoothly in the midst of any insanity. At those times, it feels like I am an engine running on a kind of super high-octane fuel.

After my parents were killed in the car accident, I only missed three days of work.

Shutting down, as I do, no doubt has its drawbacks. Although no one could say I'm anything but uncannily cool during a tragedy or a crisis, the blacked out, emotional void that keeps me functioning is very likely what is responsible for the lost, disassociated feeling I fall into afterwards. Sometimes I am a little afraid it has gained enough density to become a black hole, a high-gravity vortex of overwhelming grief that would destroy me if I ever decided to let myself succumb to it.

But I don't. I have no intention of giving in to it.

Admittedly, I came close ten days ago when Turner, that love of my life, chickened out and ran away. When Indrin walked me to the hotel that night and sat with me as I cried, I know I was dangerously close to letting the black hole swallow me up and crush me out of existence. Maybe it had something to do with Indrin, with his sympathetic eyes and silent guru sensibility, but a grief bigger than any disappointment over Turner was pulling me into it and, for the first time, I didn't even try to fight it.

At the time, I let myself believe the crying was a release, but I know now allowing my feelings that much indulgence was a dangerous thing. I have indulged them throughout this trip with Indrin, and it is high time that ended. Especially since so much else has. My feelings of shock, of disappointment, even my feelings for Turner, all seem like familiar tunes broadcast from a far-off radio station. The static-masked melodies rise for a few brief seconds, then fade once again, crowded out by strange voices from other stations in an endless chatter of news, open-line advice, and commercial jingles.

I don't remember caring for Turner. I know I did, but the feeling is so far away from me now it feels like it belonged to someone else. Someone loved that guy. I don't know who; I don't even know how. Some woman loved him but I can't quite make out her face.

Gone.

Both she and Turner entirely gone.

And Indrin, his dark eyes staring at me now, is quickly dissolving into a stranger right in front of my eyes. Did he ask me if we'll talk?

"Sure, we'll talk, Indrin. Whatever."

It really is not just a line; I truly have an uncanny ability to let emotions slide away and just not feel them anymore.

And I am proud of it.

"See you around," I say.

Then Indrin waves and I drive off, feeling cooler and more in control than I have in a long time.

~ ~

FOR THE LAST TWO HOURS I have been sitting here on the kind of giant driftwood you just cannot find anywhere but on an ocean coast. Grey-white, and completely smooth, as if it has been sanded, which of course it has, by Mother Nature herself.

I have seen the odd little spider try to make its way across the book I am reading, but otherwise I have been left completely alone and I am enjoying the peace.

Not that the beach is quiet. Peopled with all manner of tourists and teenagers and artists and wanderers, this is the English Bay I know as well as any twice-a-year visitor can know it. Water – a wonderful ocean full of it – and West Coast eccentrics galore. An elderly Elvis is sitting, complete with sound system, about thirty feet behind me on the sea wall.

Don't be cruel, he wails into his mike.

A tall man and his perfectly coiffed consort decide to get their picture taken with the sideburned, flashily pantsuited singer. They are all smiles and *isn't this a scream?* until he obviously asks them if they might give him a dollar or two for the *photo op.* And then they are off – off like a bolt of lightning with the image of Elvis floating on their camera film and their wallets safely intact.

Sometimes I think I hate people. Not some people, but people in general.

I turn back to my book. After passing a thousand or so bookstores as I walked up from my hotel, I finally decided to wander into one of them. All the doomsday discussions with Indrin and Father Lowrey had me lingering in the New Age section for a while too long, but after looking at book after book channelled by some spirit *on the other side* I got irritated and had to change sections. My crankiness lasted until well after I had moved on from the Travel section and, even while crossing through Reference, I shot an unnecessary sneer at a woman who accidentally bumped into me.

Why is being dead supposed to make these channelled spirits automatically wise and helpful and omniscient? Even if there is some form of life after death, my own personal view is once a nasty jerk, always a nasty jerk. In this life or the next.

Take, for example, the so-very-generous couple who hid behind their expensive sunglasses and could not be bothered to give a buck to a struggling Elvis, even after they had snapped his image onto the silver emulsion of their roll of film. Sure, it was just one negative, but some cultures believe that's all you need to capture the soul. With that in mind, you would think it a respectful gesture at least to pull out a dollar if requested. Self-important obnoxious folk. Now, let's just say they are killed in some awful boating accident. I am supposed to believe they are going to float around the spirit world all beaming with love and advice for our Elvis friend when he decides to expand his talents to automatic writing and channel them back.

Yeah, right.

And that's another thing: all those channelled spirits doling out advice you would never take seriously if someone alive and well tried to give it to you. It boggles the mind. No, if I am going to read a self-help book I want the author to be alive enough for me to write or phone if I decide his views are crap.

That cleansing diet you wrote about? Yeah, well, it made my ulcer worse.

Those handy tips for running a corporate meeting? You must have tested them on comatose executives, not unruly reporters.

Your guide to creative argument solutions for relationships? Here's the bill for my wedding dress.

No, after all my perusal of the New Age manifestos, I decided I could not handle one single, solitary second more of the sweet-voiced musings of saccharine spirituality. But do you think I could leave? It took me ages to get past the astrology and the tarot cards and the runes and the sleeping prophets. Maybe I was looking for that one little book channelled especially for me.

The Idiot's Guide to Personal Relationships.

You and Your Father: Mending Fences Beyond the Grave.

A Control Freak's Guide to the Erratic Universe.

Yes, I was looking for it all – answers to everything, all neatly bound in rosy-toned paperbacks just waiting for the next sucker to stare hopefully at the bookshelves with her eyes welling up. Embarrassing to admit.

That embarrassment is no doubt what fuelled my extra crankiness as I paced the store looking for something to get my mind off the New Age.

The bright colours of the Children's section finally caught my eye and I willingly took my escape – bolting there all the way from Canadian History to prevent myself from going back for a *Learn to Channel* guidebook from the *Be Your Own Psychic* series that caught my attention earlier. The first thing I saw was the C.S.

Lewis series Father Lowrey had in his office. *The Chronicles of Narnia* seemed a far enough cry from both the psychics and the international news journals I passed on my way into the store, so I happily plunked my money down for a book that had been read to me years ago, by my mom and dad.

This is what another little red spider just climbed across. And this is what is occupying my mind now, when I am not springing to the mental defence of Elvis impersonators. My very own copy of *The Lion, The Witch, and The Wardrobe.* As I turn another page, I remember every other night it was my dad who read the story to me and, as sweet as it was to fall asleep while my mom read aloud, it was he who made the book come alive. I still hear him in my mind, breaking up the story with his ad-lib sound effects, his lion's roar. And right now it feels so perfectly good to dissolve into the world of magical wardrobes and talking lions while the sun overhead moves in and out of the clouds, alternately illuminating and shading the pages, warming and then cooling my bare legs back into gooseflesh.

~ ~

OVER AN EXQUISITE little caffe latte with just the perfect amount of cinnamon and chocolate sprinkles floating on the foam, my eyes seem to want to hang around the phone on the far wall of this little café. Time after time I lead them back to the newspaper in front of me or to the LIFE STORY OF THE COFFEE BEAN poster on the wall beside me, but the phone always seems to win out.

Do I want to call Indrin? Somehow the idea of it bothers me. Not that I wouldn't want to talk to him round about now, but I do not like feeling this desire, or maybe even need, to talk to him. Especially not so soon. It hasn't even been twenty-four hours.

The desire to phone doesn't fit with the switch in my heart that is supposedly flicked in the OFF position. In fact, it feels like the switch has mysteriously snapped up again.

Why this insistent desire to seek out the companionship of my altar boy friend when only a few weeks ago he did not even exist in my universe?

The thought bothers me so much that when I finally do get to the phone and plunk in my quarter, I find myself spontaneously flipping the pages of my address book. The phone is now ringing into the apartment of one very, very ex-boyfriend. Namely, aspiring cartoonist Aaron Lee. He's actually been aspiring for a good thirty-seven of his forty-two years, but then I haven't spoken to him in about four so, to be fair, he may no longer be aspiring. He may very well have hit the heights of newspaper cartoon fame.

"Hallo."

The voice is slow and sleepy.

"Aaron?"

"Hm mmm. What time is it?"

Yep, he's still the Aaron I know. Straight and to the point.

"Eleven-thirty. So, I woke you up?"

"It's a.m., isn't it?"

I enjoy the consistency of some of my friends, I must say.

"This is Miranda."

"I know. I was expecting you to call."

Silence.

"Don't go into shock, now, Randi – I'm not psychic or anything. Your sister called all wound up about you. Said you'd probably phone."

There's something about family and their knowledge of our actions and inner psyche that I find both comforting and immensely disturbing. *I* didn't even know I was going to call Aaron until just this moment.

"Are you okay?"

There's that phrase I love so well.

"No, Aaron. I just choked to death. I'm dead."

"Well, so long as I know what's up."

A woman who shot me a plaintive look from her table when I settled myself into a comfortable lean against the wall moments ago now gets up, walks toward me, and stops immediately behind me.

"Listen, someone's waiting to use the phone. I've got to go."

"Where are you?"

"Right near English Beach."

"It's English *Bay,* Randi, you prairie kid, you."

"Right, all right. Bay. Whatever."

The woman behind me clears her throat, jingles the tiny bells attached to her earthy-style skirt. She makes pottery, I'll bet.

"I've got to go, Aaron. Earth mother alert."

"What?" he asks, certain the sleep slowly draining

out of him has caused him to miss something.

"Nothing. I just called to see if you want to get together."

"I can meet you. Want me to come by there?"

He sounds thrilled at the prospect of a morning outing. I can hear it in his yawn.

"No, it's okay. I'll pop by – you at the same place?"

"Actually, yeah. I was thinking about moving last year when they raised the rent, but it's such a hassle and –"

The woman is now glaring at me and I suddenly wonder if a person can be seriously injured by a well-aimed quarter.

"Listen, I've got to go."

"We haven't been talking long. Tell this person waiting for the phone to chill out."

"See you, Aaron."

"Right-o."

Click. And with that little click on the phone line, I feel as if I've taken a highway exit off my rolling, roving road to the future and detoured straight into the past.

~ ~

He has furniture, now. That is certainly the biggest change. Not a lot – I wouldn't go so far as to say the place is actually furnished. But he does have two chairs and even though the chesterfield is an ad-hoc arrangement of stretched-out sleeping bag atop foam, it shows he has made an effort. I see he still uses milk crates as his design cornerstone, but he has actually painted the board that sits across the two crates in the living room.

"Coffee table, eh? You are getting domesticated."

"Yeah, well. We're getting older, aren't we?"

"My *God,* you are cheery in the morning." I look at my watch. "Or afternoon – yeah, we're aging by the second."

"Why does aging scare you? I think you're aging well – you're what? Thirty-five now?"

"Please – thirty-three."

"Two years makes a difference when you're six, not when you're in your thirties, Randi. Anyway, why worry? You don't look older than that, anyway. Thirty-six, thirty-seven tops."

"Thanks a lot."

This conversation is taking place at almost shouting level as Aaron gets dressed in his bedroom. When I arrived he was dripping wet and seemed to want to make a quick getaway down the hall before I got a good look at the middle age spreading over the towel tied at his waist. But I did. And, yes, time is weighing heavy even on Aaron, the eternal adolescent.

Now he comes around the corner stuffing his T-shirt into a pair of definitely unstylishly torn jeans.

"Are you out to give the ladies a thrill?" I ask, as I nod pointedly at the wide tear in the upper thigh.

"Oh jeez."

He heads back to the bedroom. A bit of thumping around as he lumbers into another ensemble and out he comes in army fatigues.

Now he hugs me. One of his full-sized, grizzly bear

hugs. Finally, I know why I had to come here. I hug him back.

"It's good to see you. I still think in cartoon captions, you know."

"All right." He squeezes me harder. "My legacy lives on."

It's true. *Guru Boy. Minstrel Man.* The titles I come up with for everyone I meet are all thanks to the inimitable *Captain Cartoon.*

"Are you going to stay for awhile?"

He leans back and gives me a playful leer when he says this, but when I laugh he just gives me another friendly hug.

"Good to see you too, Randi."

"No girlfriend to mind all this hugging?"

"I've given up on them."

"My, my."

"No, seriously. I need to work through a few things first."

The grizzly bear arms unlock and proceed to rummage through a pile of papers beside the homemade drafting table in the corner.

"In fact, look at this. I've got a new project."

Thrust in front of me is a pen-and-ink cartoon of a man in pirate costume, sweating furiously as he rows a boat. One rather busty woman is spilling out of a kind of Viking-style teddy. She is obviously mutinying and is trying to paddle the other way. Underneath them is the caption *If this is a relationSHIP, why don't we paddle together?*

"Kind of cute," I say.

Cartoons – even Aaron's – have never really been my

thing.

"It's the cover of a book. Look."

He shows me a banner with stencilled lettering: *Smooth Sailing in Your RelationSHIP.*

"It's a cartoon self-help book," he explains. "Cartoons are fun to read, they're not threatening, and here I've got them illustrating all kinds of typical relationship garbage. See?" he quickly flips through a pile of cartoons. "It even ends happily with them heading into the sunset on a couple of SeaDoos."

"Separate boats?"

"I know, I wondered about that. I've got another version of them in a canoe together, but I couldn't figure out who I should put in the stern. I mean, if he's steering, women won't like that. If she is – you see? I can't win. Separate SeaDoos seem to be the answer."

"No, you're probably right. Separate SeaDoos – who woulda thunk it? The answer to the problem of modern relationships. Actually, it would probably be more realistic to get them onto separate oceans."

"I'd wonder about that extra venom in your voice, but Julie told me about the breakup."

"Well, then that's one thing we don't have to talk about, right?"

"I guess."

He sits down to stuff his feet into his running shoes. All his movements seem to be a little slowed down, but I can't tell whether it's just age and a few extra pounds or the after-effects of all the dope he used to smoke. In the mornings before work, even. No wonder he never has lasted long in the traditional workplace. But, fast or slow, he has always had a generous heart. That's how we got together in the first place. My heart was smashed up after a real doozy of a dysfunctional relationship and there was Aaron just to sit around and have a laugh with. Kind of took the hurt away until I could get into my shutdown mode.

"You finished with the bullies, at least?"

"Yes," I lie.

But it's not completely a lie. Turner never hit me. There was the one time he kind of slammed me into the wall when he thought I was too friendly to the buddies he had introduced me to that night. My role, I guess, was to smile at them – briefly – and then just stand back and bask in the glory of my hot musician boyfriend holding court. There was certainly not to be any hearty shaking of hands and happily heated discussion about the warm-up band, which is what did ensue. Even so, Turner apologized later. In a way. Said he wouldn't have gotten so mad, but I shouldn't have gone on so long with his friends. *Didn't I get it? How to act with his friends?* 'Fraid not, Turner. But I did know enough to pass it off as just one of his drug-induced states of paranoia.

The garbage I've put up with. And my sister, who has an uncanny ability for spotting signs of trouble like that even before she has met the boyfriend in question, never could understand why I'd stick around for it. After all, *she'd* leave.

Sure, it's easy to judge after the fact, but the Turners of the world don't go and act like that your first night out together, do they?

Anyway, I'm through with all of it. Turner was the

last. If I can't date a guy without having to dance around the angry edges of his ego, I just won't. Who knows? Maybe I should talk to Indrin. There just may be room for me to hide out in the Catholic Church too. That would shock 'em at work.

"Actually, I may be becoming a nun any minute."

Aaron's laugh is like a dog's bark, a big gruff blast.

"That bad, eh? Julie said Turner was a jerk."

"I'm glad you two had such a good chat about my life. God."

"Don't get all freaked out about it," he says, ushering me out the door of his apartment. "That's all she said – actually, she didn't even say that much. What she did say was more like, 'It's probably for the best,' or something totally noncommittal and discreet like that. I just know you, so I figured he was another one of your losers. You've had quite a string of them, you know. Present company excepted. Guess that's why you didn't take me seriously."

Aaron stops to lock the door behind us.

"Bagel or sandwich?"

"I don't care," I answer.

"Okay, bagels."

He wheels to the left and I follow and I want to kick him for saying what he just did.

"What do you mean *that's why I didn't take you seriously?"*

"Forget it."

I'm in kind of a white heat by the time we get to the bagel place and so pretend I'm just too engrossed in the decision between poppy seed and sesame seed to be able to speak. By the time we sit down with our toasted bagels and nicely melting cream cheese, we're a picture of some perfectly content couple on a Saturday morning. I, however, am not quietly content. Mixed into one big wave of emotion is pure, raging anger and disgust at myself for letting Aaron's pseudo-psychological surmisals about me and my love life bother me at all. Why did I even call this guy?

As I lick the cream cheese from my fingers, the wave subsides somewhat. Maybe what I am feeling is not so much anger directed at Aaron as it is at Turner and the whole assortment of bad-tempered louts in whom I ever had the misfortune to see redeeming qualities.

Aaron calmly chews and peruses the newspaper on the counter. I watch him, feel the anger surge back, and bite savagely into my bagel.

Just when I am about to start the conversation with Aaron up again to find out *what the bloody hell he meant by that* and *does he think I somehow look for people to treat me badly* and *how dare he assume it was all bad with Turner anyway,* he waves a newspaper at me.

"This is what has got me going."

The headline says, BATTERED WOMAN BELIEVED DEAD, POLICE SURROUND HOUSE. The picture shows an emergency response team guy, complete with gun, crouching in the trees.

"Oh, lovely."

"You didn't hear about this? It's been going on since last night. The lunatic husband, or boyfriend, or whatever, is still inside. Just before you came, I heard on the radio there had been another gunshot."

The newsprint holds his eyes, starts funnelling his attention into the narrow column. When he starts to turn the paper toward me, I wave him off. I don't need to read it. I could probably write the story myself here on my napkin. Controlling, abusive man starts to feel he's losing control – maybe because the woman decides finally, after two months or two years or even twenty, that she can get away, that she must get away. But, of course, dear hubby comes after her, all distorted with rage and hate, to prove her wrong. This is usually his final act of cowardice, since shortly afterwards he generally blasts himself to hell. At least, I hope it's hell. News reports like these make me wish I were a fiery-mouthed, God-fearing, fundamentalist Christian.

Dear Lord, punish our enemies that we may not have to torture them ourselves, much as we may feel like it. Keep us virtuous.

"What I hate is that this can scare other women enough to prevent them from leaving. A *look what happens when you try* kind of thing."

Aaron nods in agreement, keeps reading as he chews his bagel.

"Too much of this happening," he says before he takes his next bite.

He sets the paper down and stares at me, still munching. I know what he's thinking.

"Don't even try to make an analogy here...."

His eyebrows wiggle upward as I continue.

"...Because I'm a pretty good judge of character and

even when it was bad, it was never that bad. Never scary, lunatic bad."

"What about the break-in guy?" he asks me.

His eyes stare an open challenge at me, but nothing registers with me at all.

"The guy who broke into your place?" he prompts again.

"I've never been broken into."

"Yes, you were," he says smugly.

"I think I'd remember if someone broke into my place."

"You told me yourself."

Nothing. Not a shred of recall.

"I have no idea what you're talking about."

"That guy…." Aaron gives up and starts to talk while he chews, loosely holding up a napkin to bridge the etiquette lapse. "That guy who read your diary – who broke in to read it – and then claimed it was a break-in. Even helped fix the window."

He helped fix the window. This shatters the fortress wall around my memory. Yeah. Andy. Nice guy, Andy. Another guy Dad couldn't stand the sight of. Rightly so, apparently.

"I forgot about that. But I actually have no proof he was the one who broke in. It still could have been a real break-in."

"Thieves steal stuff, Randi. The money on your dresser was never touched, I remember you saying."

"Okay, okay, he was weird, definitely weird, but he wasn't dangerous. Not like that." I wave at the headline with the last bit of my bagel.

"He scared you. You told me that."

"He never hit me."

"I have reason to believe this guy," he says, pointing to the newspaper article, "never murdered her before. Yeah, it was probably just the first time."

Aaron goes back to the paper and, as I watch him read, I wonder if there will be a cartoon guide to escaping abusive relationships in this new book of his. Maybe a chapter, "When to abandon *ship*." With an accompanying caricature of a bearded maniac brandishing an uplifted outboard motor. Not funny. Not at all. But that's okay. I don't feel like laughing right about now.

~ ~

"I COME DOWN HERE to get ideas for my book," says Aaron, sitting on a bench overlooking the marina.

Gulls scream over a rapidly disappearing piece of doughnut beside us. Motorboats chug water and drip gasoline as they make their way out to the bay and people ramble past us on their way into Granville Island Market where they will fill their nostrils with the strong, raw scent of fresh salmon while they wander idly through the produce lanes.

We sit with coffees in hand, decaf for Aaron since he became a bit of a health nut about the same time he swore off women. Apparently he's completely off all poisonous substances.

"So where are the SeaDoos?" I ask, more tongue-in-cheek than actually expecting an answer. But he's got one.

"Oh, that was kind of an indirect inspiration. I was watching some people in the sea kayaks down there," he says, as he points to a woman struggling to stay upright in a kayak being buffeted by the wake of one of the motorboats. "So I started thinking maybe the book should end with them in those. But then I decided, hey, it's a high-tech world. I've either got to computerize this baby or get them into a trendier piece of watercraft."

I laugh while sipping my coffee and scald the roof of my mouth. For a few moments we sit in silence, me perusing the hundreds of masts sticking up from all the sailboats docked here in the marina as I feel for signs of a heat blister with my tongue. Aaron takes down a few notes.

"See that?" he asks.

"What?"

"That guy washing off his boat."

My neck cranes around so I can peer at an older guy, early fifties maybe, cleaning the hull of the boat he has in dry dock.

"That's an analogy. Everything's an analogy."

He stops to sketch a caricature of the boat cleaning. The rather slight man scrubbing rust stains is now a Herculean, muscle-bound Popeye-like sailor battling barnacles on the hull of a giant ocean liner. Each of the barnacles has a little scowling face.

"So what's the caption going to be for that?"

"I dunno. Something about people having to learn to care for their own *ship* before they'll be ready to sail off into a joint relation*ship*. Something like that."

He scratches out a few more lines with his pencil. A kid in a baseball cap that says *Vancouver Aquarium* peeks over Aaron's shoulder and says, "Aw, cool." Aaron smiles appreciatively at her before she runs back over to her family to tell them about the "artist" at work "over there on the bench."

"You know, I have a good feeling about this cartoon book. You can just tell it will go over pretty well."

"Absolutely, it will, Aaron."

There is no doubt in my mind. Sure, the cartoon approach is not really for me, but the self-help books I looked through the other day in the bookstore annoyed me because of their sweetly glowing self-importance. Given the choice, I would far rather flip through a few Popeye-style cartoons in the bathroom than read about how to contact the spirit world or listen to a sparkly-toned meditation tape, complete with synthesized bird chirps and waterfalls.

"Yeah, the analogies are everywhere," says Aaron, amazed at having spotted another inspiration. "I can hardly come down here without coming home with about twenty new cartoons."

He stops to scribble out a sketch of a father lifting his daughter's bicycle onto a sailboat considerably bigger than most of the boats in the marina. I glance over at the scene which inspired this latest creation and notice that this time he has kept it fairly similar. Except he has turned the roughly sixteen-year-old girl and her bike into one baby in a little sailor suit and, once again, the man's muscles are ballooned out with cartoon steroids.

"A good relation*ship* can carry little passengers safely

through the stormiest seas. I'll put something like that on this one, but I'll draw the storm later. Want to walk around a bit?"

It sounds good to me so we stand up, but not before Aaron stops to consider a group of gigantic gulls roaming nearby in quick, staccato steps, impatient for the next bit of dropped food. They look proud, aggressive, but a bit dim. Aaron seems to be sizing them up for how they might fit into his book.

"How about 'Make sure no unwanted strangers crap all over your boat?'" I suggest.

I was kidding, but he just says "thanks" and marks it down. As we stroll over to the art supply shop where Aaron wants to stop in, I start laughing, imagining Turner's *extra-relationSHIP*-lounge-singer-girlfriends as stupid, screeching birds shitting indiscriminately on everyone around them.

Maybe Aaron's *magnum opus* cartoon work of a lifetime will be a prize of a self-help book after all.

"Yes, you've definitely got a winner with this book, Aaron."

This remark prompts an affectionate squeeze of my arm, but I notice he takes his arm from around my shoulder the moment we enter the art supply shop. A girl – not woman, no, definitely girl, even though she does look to be in her early twenties – with blue-black, cropped hair and a diamond nose-stud, looks up brightly at Aaron and smiles a coy, pursed-lipped, Princess Di kind of smile.

"Well, hello. Back so soon. This is a nice surprise."

After a brief expression of concern at my presence,

she warms up to a full grin of delight with Aaron's next remark.

"I needed more inspiration. On why a sailor would come back to port."

Oh brother, I actually fell for this once?

I watch them smile at each other.

But it's true, Aaron has got an overeager, bounding-Labrador-retriever kind of appeal.

He introduces me to Sherry, who nods with a cautious but friendly head bob. Then, waving at the array of paper, acrylics, and brushes behind her, she tells me to let her know if I'd like anything. She can get me a twenty percent discount. After all, "Friends are friends," she muses to Aaron.

"Just don't tell anyone about the discount," she adds. "My boss, you know."

Since I don't want this young, starry-eyed girl to have to worry about her status in relation to me, I decide to make it simple.

"Thanks, but I'm no artist." I turn to Aaron. "This pal of yours is going to wait outside. Nice meeting you," I say to her and head out of the shop.

The jingle bells on the door see me out with a twinkle and I decide it won't be long before Aaron's back drinking caffeine again.

I also wonder how long it will be before this new friend of Aaron's moves in with him, how long before this *ship* will be launched. Perhaps a bottle of champagne will even be in order to crack across their heads – to crack some sense into them, I think – before they sail off into the sunset. Merrily, I imagine this cartoon, but then decide I'm lapsing into cynicism again and I really should fight the impulse at least now and then.

I'm off in the land of cartoon self-help, wondering whether I should offer to co-author this soon-to-be-bestseller, when I realize I am staring at a marmot.

My eyes refocus.

Shaking myself, I realize that, of course, it is not a marmot, only a poster of one, in life-sized, high-gloss finish, staring at me through the window of the adjacent shop. This marmot, with imploring eyes that I'll bet were touched up a bit by a graphic artist's pen, reproaches onlookers just above the caption, ENDANGERED ANIMALS – IT'S UP TO ALL OF US.

But there were scads of them up there on the mountain in Jasper, hundreds. There had to be. I remember the hungry hordes distinctly. Okay, maybe not hundreds, but more than I could count anyway. Glancing through the window of the art supply shop, I see that Aaron is still happily engaged in flirtatious banter with Sherry and decide I have more than enough time to check out this perplexing sign. I walk into the shop with the marmot poster and go straight for it.

"Vancouver Island Marmot," says the label on each of the rolled-up posters, still contained in cellophane wrap.

"We're out of grizzlies," says the guy behind the counter.

"Pardon me?" I ask.

"The grizzly posters. We're out of them."

"That's okay. I was interested in this one." I point to the poster child for the Save-the-Marmot cause.

"Well, there's lots of *them.* They never go as fast."

"I didn't even know they were endangered."

"Oh yeah, absolutely," says the guy, turning back to the newspaper on the counter in front of him. About thirty-five, he is dressed in too preppy a polo shirt to look the part of an environmentalist.

But then I remind myself it's all different here on the West Coast, that somehow the clichés don't always mean the same thing here. As I muse on this guy's brush cut, I decide the jingly-skirted earth mother I saw in the coffee shop the other day was probably head of a major law firm. That's the West Coast for you.

"I saw marmots in Jasper," I say to him. "There were a lot of them, I thought."

"No, it's the Vancouver Island marmots that are in trouble, just the ones on Vancouver Island. They're different, I guess. Maybe those other ones are fine."

"I hope so," I comment, staring at the poster and thinking of my spaced-out attempts to send mental messages to the marmots after Turner left the scene.

But, since clichés don't work the same way here on the West Coast, I decide I can be both pragmatic and believe in animal-world telepathy. And that is what makes me feel relaxed about sending another message now. A message that says *I'm so sorry. I didn't know your world was ending too.*

Because if it is ending for their cousins on Vancouver Island, connected as we are, it is ending for all of them.

~ ~

I AM TO GO BACK to Aaron's later and I'm still wondering why I agreed to that. It is not as if I have much in common with him anymore and, coursing through my caffeine-charged veins, there is not a single shred of nostalgia for *the way we were* or anything like that. It is just that he was so insistent. After Julie's phone call, I think he feels he has to entertain me and occupy my time to keep me from being alone.

Alone, I want to say, *is not the same as lonely.* But, as far as that goes, I don't know what my point is. I'm both at the moment, although the truth of it is I would still rather be on my own to sort it all out.

It's not as if I can't have a perfectly good visit here in town on my own. I certainly do not want any hand holding to help me get over the Turner thing. Or the *losing-my-new-friend-Indrin* thing. Or even the *what-the-hell-am-I-doing-with-my-life* and *do-I-even-want-to-work-in-TV-news-anymore* thing. But for some reason I said, sure, I'd go back and meet him later for supper. In the meantime, I am sitting here in the foyer of the CBC Vancouver building waiting for my producer friend, Karen, to show me around the plant, to tell me what she has been up to lately, and to give me some idea whether there is a hope in hell of finding a job in this place. In case that's what I want or need. Just a change of permanent scenery.

The glass door swings open and out steps one very bustling and extremely professional-looking Karen. I don't recall her wearing suits much, at least not back in our early reporting days, but then, as Aaron seemed so bent on pressing home to me today, we are getting older. Her hair, like mine, is now cut into what is supposed to be a short fuss-free style, but the bit above her left ear is standing out to the side like a strange little wing and the rest is decidedly straggly. Looks like it could stand a fair bit of fussing over right now.

"All hell's breaking loose, right?"

"Well," she says, "it's actually not a great time for a tour. That guy's still holed up in East Van and it's turning into a standoff. The province picks this time to hold a *newser* on sweeping health care reform and I've had two reporters go home sick."

"No problem. I'm around for a day or two."

I am?

"I could just give you a call tomorrow or something?"

"That might be better – but, hey, it's good to see you, Randi."

She gives me a brief hug, all light wool crepe and sweat. The familiar scent of newsroom stress.

"Hey, you know who's working here now?" she says in a tone of collusion before she heads back into the world of breaking news. For emphasis, she arches an eyebrow.

We're all gossips in this business.

"Jerry," she says finally.

"Jerry? Jerry *I've left-my-wife-for-summer-student-gal* Jerry?"

"She dumped him."

"What a surprise."

"He's quite bitter. It's made him a better cameraman, though. Not so easily distracted by a pretty girl."

We laugh a *good old days* laugh about good old Jerry,

who missed the only shots we needed of a certain prime minister's appearance because he lost track of the time shooting pictures of the demonstration outside. Never have seen so much footage of one protester. Halter top, minuscule shorts – poor Jerry never had a chance.

"I'll call you, Karen."

"Right. We'll do it tomorrow. If this wife-batterer thing settles down I might even be able to get away for lunch."

"Great."

I step out onto sun-bright white pavement blasting so much heat upward that it makes the skin on my neck and the underside of my chin prickle. The sky is truly a brilliant blue. People talk about the rain out here, but every time I visit I get the year's best weather. Clear, bright perfection in paradise. As I walk, trying to remember exactly where my car is parked, I see the little brick Catholic Charities building.

Why not? I wouldn't mind meeting this famous Sister Fran and I would certainly like to know if Rebero found his brother.

And so I step across the street and up the walk and into the cool front lobby. Cool in temperature, but definitely not in mood. A woman walks hotly across the lobby without noticing my presence and crisply shuts a door behind her. This is not a door slam, but it is the next thing to it. An overly emphatic clap of door and frame, borne of a brittle-burnt etiquette.

So much for finding a bastion of calm, a little fortress of spiritual tranquillity. Through the door, I hear words. These too are crisp.

"Don't say you don't know what I mean, I've seen it myself."

There is a murmur in response, but to my ears nothing intelligible.

"Don't lie. Don't lie to me."

This time the response is silence. Only silence.

The woman's tone strains itself back into a forced, tightened concern.

"I can't imagine what you think I'm able to do without your cooperation."

Silence.

The door opens again and the same woman bolts across the room, squeaking her rubber-soled loafers with every exasperated step. Naturally curious, I direct my gaze to the room beyond the open door, but all I see is desk, books, and crucifix.

She does not return. At least not for the length of time it takes me to peer around the front hall. Light wood panelling, probably veneer, 1950s-type squares of linoleum, streamlined seventies-style office desk. I consider leaving, but I cannot beat back the feeling that Rebero is sitting inside that room. In fact, I feel sure he is, but can't bring myself to actually waltz in and admit I just overheard their rather strange exchange.

"Can I help you."

Somehow this is a statement, not a question.

The annoyed woman is back. But if she is angry, she is also hiding it well. Her face is clear, even the wrinkles across her forehead and at the sides of her eyes betraying nothing more than about a half century passed with a considerable number of smiles.

"Um, I was hoping to find out about someone. A fellow I drove here the other day. He's from Rwanda."

It's back. The look of frustration.

"Well, maybe you'll have some answers then."

She turns sharply, almost a full pirouette on her heel, and marches back into the office. I guess I'm expected to follow and so I do, but when I actually reach the room I feel awkward. Yes, it's Edmond Rebero all right, but he is now a cowering primary school student, not the tall, regal fellow he was when Indrin and I delivered him here.

A tentative "Hi?" is my attempt to see if the old Rebero is there, hiding somewhere in his skin. But I do not see him anywhere.

I look from him to her and back. Edmond nods, gives me a thin smile, then refocusses his gaze on the empty wall beside him. I put on my best take-charge voice.

"What's going on here?"

"Not a lot, I'm afraid."

The woman sits back down at her desk and flips open a yellow file folder. The pages inside are neatly stacked and she turns them with efficiency.

"I'm sorry," I say to cut back into her awareness, "but we haven't met. I'm Miranda Tyler."

"Yes, thank you."

She keeps flipping pages.

"And you are?"

"Yes. Here it is."

Finally, she looks up at me, giving me a look I would expect to see over a principal's reading glasses – if we were in a school and if she wore glasses.

"My name is Fran –"

"Sister Fran?"

"That's right. Perhaps you can tell me about *this,* Miss...."

The clipped, accusatory tone stops short.

"It's Ms., actually. Tyler. But, please, just call me Miranda."

With a nod of acknowledgement, she raises a postcard, delicately pinched between her thumb and forefinger. This is *evidence.* She holds it the way you'd present the glove at the O.J. trial.

"I'm afraid I don't understand what's going on."

Rebero shifts in his chair, rubs his hands on his knees. He looks pained. I want to rescue this boy from the principal's office. As far as I can see he has no reason to *get it,* but it looks as if he is going to. I even have the feeling I could get in trouble myself over this. What *did* I used to say to weasel my way out of situations like this at school?

"Edmond has written this card. To his brother."

Sister Fran punctuates this last phrase with enunciation that could wound.

"Given the circumstances, I think that's only appropriate, don't you think?"

This Fran woman is starting to bug me. I straighten my spine, stand as tall as I can.

"I mean, wouldn't you expect him to write?"

"I would merely like to know where he is sending this mail. He hasn't filled in the address on the card. After two months spent on the phone to Africa – all over Africa, I might add, with the bill for it all going straight to this city's parishioners – and after endless correspondence with Red Cross workers all in the hope of locating this young man's brother, I discover he's known all along. He's just not telling us."

Sister Fran turns back to Rebero.

"You must believe me when I tell you that there is no need to fear for his safety anymore – if you think you're somehow protecting him. We can help him get here only if we know where to find him."

Her tone is sincere, if clipped, but it's met with silence. She stares, then wheels her body around on the swivel chair and turns her gaze back to me.

"We had located one boy we were told was Edmond's brother and I was so happy, just thrilled about it. I started making arrangements to try to bring him here immediately. Then the young man disappeared again, but not before telling the Red Cross worker who found him that he didn't know an Edmond Rebero. His Christian name was Théodore, the same as Edmond's brother, but I guess his surname was wrong. Also that young fellow was from the Hutu tribe, not Tutsi, like Edmond. So after all that work, we were back to square one. It was heartbreaking. And now it turns out Edmond has been writing cards to his brother, but for some reason doesn't want to let us in on where he is."

Sister Fran works up a resigned expression, but somehow this looks false.

"I don't know what I can be expected to do," she says finally.

And now I see she is close to tears, fighting them back with every flip of a page in the file she has just reopened.

"She's only trying to help, Edmond."

I try to make eye contact with Rebero as I say this, but it's no use. He is gone – as far away in interest and focus as he can get from us. At least, he appears that way until he speaks, his words directed more to the wall than to the two of us.

"I do not know. Please believe me. I sent them without an address."

An odd gasp erupts from Sister Fran.

"Don't lie to me. Whatever you do, please do not lie. I prefer silence to boldfaced lies."

Fran-the-truth-seeker looks back to me while her tone shifts to that of a presenter of evidence. Strictly the facts.

"I spoke with Father Albert Lowrey. He recalls Edmond sending letters as well. It hadn't occurred to him to ask where they were going. And of course it wouldn't have. He's a trusting man."

She says this last bit with just the slightest hint of condescension. As if to suggest that none of this would have happened if good old Father Lowrey were something more of a cynic.

"I never wanted to disturb you. Any of you."

The defeated boy stands up into a tall man of resignation.

"I am sorry if this has taken your time, but I never wanted this. Father Lowrey insisted on phoning you for help, Sister Fran. I told him there was no use. I can't give you any address for my brother and I can't think about this anymore."

Rebero moves to the door, but is stopped by Sister Fran.

"Now this will solve nothing. Where are you going?"

"To get my bag. It was kind of you to arrange for me a place to stay, but I will thank the family and go back to Prince George. There are buses," he adds when he sees that both Fran and I have looks that ask *but how will you survive?*

Sure, the guy can make it through a genocide, but naturally we worry about how he will find his way back to Prince George or even to the family that put him up.

"I can drive you, at least."

He nods. It's that easy to steer a rudderless boat – a few take-charge paddle dips, and you can get the situation in hand. Not that I'm thrilled about starting to think like a devotee of Aaron's self-help book. But so it goes.

Fran clumps down into her wooden chair.

"Well, this is completely unsatisfactory."

Over to you Miranda.

As in "Over to you, Northumberland High" from that old Canadian TV quiz show for teens, *Reach for the Top.* I saved my team more than once, usually in the current events category, but what I do with this reluctant refugee and the woman bent on saving him against his wishes, I really have no idea.

I look at the two of them. This Sister Fran isn't wearing your typical nun's outfit. Guess she's more of the modern nun school. Orange blouse, taupe A-line skirt that was already a bit dated some fifteen years ago – but who cares about style when you're dressing for the Lord,

I guess. Still, the orange blouse shows a bit of character. Is there a touch of the rebel here? If so, it is severely curtailed by the sensible shoes that really would have been better off with slacks instead of the skirt outfit. But who am I to criticize, anyway? Oscar de la Renta? Rebero is in what must be a borrowed T-shirt. It's got ST. JOSEPH'S MARAUDERS printed on the front, with a machine-wash-faded picture of a baby angel flying up beside a basketball going into the net. Nice to have divine help, I'm sure. I went to a public school with losing sports teams.

What to do with this situation? And a better question yet is what is it about me that feels I have to step in and help fix things up? I can't say it is altruism in a very pure form. No doubt it's ego mixed with a good dose of patronization. There is a terrible little feeling in me that people in general don't know how to get their lives straight, or their scripts, or even their daily perambulations through the world, without me there to point out the best way for them to take.

Talk about the blind leading the blind. But the truth is, while some wonder about where the hell I'm going with my own life, no one could argue I am not good at taking other people's problems in hand and making things work out. That is exactly why I am known as a good producer – one of the best, in fact – even if I do have a tendency to start looking pretty frazzled during ratings. But that simply gives the reporters something to talk about aside from their own miserable little scripts.

Tyler's losing it again.

I don't know how she can live that way.

I think it's important to have a life outside of work.

And they think I don't hear them.

The squeak of Sister Fran's swivel chair brings me out of my astral projection back to the newsroom.

"I'm sure we can figure this all out," I suddenly hear myself saying. "To start with, we may as well get Rebero's bag if that's what he wants. Come on, Edmond."

Backing my way out of the office, my eyebrows arching up to catch Fran's eye, I work my way around to get behind Rebero. The moment I make it out of the room, I duck in again.

"Just a sec, Edmond, I left my purse."

Of course, my purse strap is still comfortably perched on my shoulder, but I figure he didn't have a chance to notice that. What my feeble little lie does, however, is buy me a few seconds alone with Fran.

"I'll find out what I can."

She looks appreciative, somehow a little less severe.

"I'm staying at the Sylvia Hotel."

Then, just as Rebero peeks in after me, I throw out my name again in case it didn't register when I first told her.

"Miranda Tyler."

"Thank you."

And we're out. Walking down the sidewalk, I remember thinking only yesterday that Rebero's brief appearance in my life had ended for good. Not sure what to say, I watch our feet hit the pavement squares.

"It's hot."

Yeah, there goes my mouth with all the most apropos comments.

"Yes," he politely answers.

But only then do I notice how much I am sweating. How there are wide, dark circles under my arms and probably a wet streak up the back between my shoulder blades. I cannot see it, but I feel my top stuck to my skin there. Not the day for polyester, I see in retrospect, or for long pants either, especially not these jeans.

"Don't you wish we could be sailing today?"

Rebero's calm tone surprises me.

"I saw sailboats this morning," he continues.

"Yeah, sure. Sailing would be nice, I guess."

While Sister Fran's angry accusations are still knocking about in my head, making me feel uncomfortable and agitated, Edmond seems completely untouched by the third degree he has just received. He is far away, dreamy-eyed, thinking of oceans and sailboats. It strikes me that even I could take lessons from this guy on how to shut off my emotions. He's a pro.

Looking at him as we walk, I could swear Rebero looks taller than he did just a few minutes ago.

Typically for me, finding where I parked my car is an elusive quest, and today is no exception. Edmond does not seem to mind following my wayward navigation, but I am sweating more than ever as we double back down the block. Just when I remember parking near a Starbucks coffee shop – of which there are only about four hundred in downtown Vancouver – we are almost hit by a news van literally squealing out of the CBC parking lot.

"Hey, what the f –" I check myself and transpose my mouth into a "Mmrmph – damn!"

Should you use rotten language in front of new

refugees like Rebero? *Welcome to our country; we're rude and this is how we talk.* This is a dilemma I do not have the answer to, but I know I certainly feel inhibited thanks to a very strange sense of decorum instilled by my parents. Odd that it comes to me at moments like this, when I am in the process of nearly being killed by a news van that is acting like it's in some dramatic made-for-TV movie about a television news crew.

"Get real, you guys!" I yell. "Where are you going, city hall?"

The van backs up and *guess who* rolls down the window.

"Jerry, you bastard. I should have known."

"Randi?"

Jerry glances back at the impatient-looking reporter in his car. She looks about fifteen, it seems to me, and no doubt will soon be covering the Middle East by herself. That's the type they are hiring these days. Young, right-out-of-school cheap, with a model's face: blank, neutral, and familiar in a Sears catalogue kind of way.

"We gotta go," I hear her snarl at him.

"I'll call you, Randi. Where are you staying?"

"The Sylvia."

"Right on."

They speed off as I think about how grey his hair has become. At least he looks a bit more human than he did when he was trying to play Ken to *summer-student-gal's* Barbie. More evidence that time is passing.

As soon as I think that, I realize that time does not *pass* anymore. It surges forward, squealing through the universe like a car with spontaneous acceleration.

But I was just going to slow down and get onto the off ramp.

Not a chance, lady, you're driving a clock with spontaneous acceleration. Seems to be all they make nowadays.

I catch myself holding my breath again – my old childhood trick never did do much to freeze time in its tracks, but it sure ended up an unconscious habit. Suddenly my mouth gasps for air like a fish in polluted water. It startles Rebero but I make like it was just some kind of sigh.

"Let's go."

And we walk, for a good fifteen minutes, backtracking, until I finally remember where I parked – nowhere near a Starbucks after all, in fact at least two blocks from one – and Rebero climbs in to be delivered once again to a different point on his wheel of fortune.

The car is an oven.

As I push in my stubborn clutch and wipe the back of my sweaty neck, I notice Rebero calmly gazing out the window, already settling into his new life direction. Manoeuvring my way into the traffic jam, I think about how his future seems to be ever-changing, completely unpredictable, truly lived on what could be termed *Indrin-approved impulse,* and I marvel at how calmly he accepts this ever-evolving fate. If I had to abdicate all control over my own life, there would be some kind of nuclear core meltdown inside me.

Is this life lived on the buffeting winds of destiny? Or is it still willpower somehow that steers it all from inside? While I cannot be sure, what I do see is that there is nothing linear about Rebero's life, only stimulus and response – and even that is not neat and straight ahead. Nothing that could be plotted on the science class graph paper I imagine when I try to make plans for my own life. Admittedly, my own life rarely conforms to the graph paper approach, but I do keep working at it. Someday, maybe.

The car moves forward. I am almost ready to shift into second when the brake lights in front of me blink, then stare. Stopped again, I decide that Rebero's life is simply what life is like after the end of the world. The end of any world you knew and loved and understood. And in the vacuum that follows, there is no time and no reason and no point, except to move along and do what feels right and hope you'll be left alone and in peace for at least a little while longer.

War Zones

Not until Rebero went to pick up his bag from the family of do-gooders who agreed to put him up did I flick on the car radio. No surprise that I tuned in for the news, that being what has motivated me for the biggest portion of my life. No surprise either to start hearing the all-too-familiar details of the police showdown surrounding the house of the battered woman. Yeah, they figured she was dead, but nothing was confirmed. He was still inside, but dead or alive they were no longer certain. As for the child, police weren't speculating.

Clips from neighbours punctuated the familiar story about another abusive relationship gone over the edge. These were divided. Half of them suspected all along there was *something weird* about that quiet guy, even if he had always been civil enough to them. They should have known this was coming. The other half had *no idea.* No reason to suspect he was not just a typical guy in a typical neighbourhood.

This was, therefore, the typical news item on the typical battered woman murder.

What was surprising was the follow-up report with its recording of a chorus of little kids singing just behind the line of emergency response team sharpshooters.

Bad boys, bad boys, whatcha gonna do....

Their voices were high-pitched with excitement, singing the theme song of their favourite cop show. For them, this was great. Just like TV. It didn't take long for the kids to get cleared back from the intensely-charged situation, the reporter explained, but the fact is, they had somehow managed to get dangerously close, "the situation's appeal understandable in a world where violence has become merely another form of entertainment."

Bad boys, bad boys....

The reporter neatly ended her story with a fading out of the children's chorus, giving the listener the eerie feeling that pop culture has truly pushed us all over the edge. From *To the moon, Alice, why I oughta...* to this. What's a crime scene without the proper theme song? A bit manipulative, a bit forced, but the story made its point. Likely a West Coast Award winner for finding the "human" side of a tragedy.

But as surprising as the little kids' voices were, singing the theme song, it didn't match the chilling realization that this, the top news story of the week, maybe the month, maybe the summer, was unfolding almost exactly where I had dropped off Indrin.

And that's where I'm heading to now. I don't care if it's crazy to worry. Even if there is no reason to believe he is in any danger, I just know I have to get there. There's no way I got this far in the world of TV news without having a certain trust in my gut feelings. No, they are not the high-minded spiritual instincts of altar boy Indrin; they are nasty, uncomfortable feelings in my gut, not my stomach, but my gut, wherever that really is in the human anatomy, and the only thing I know for sure is that I trust them when I get them.

Mr. Winds-of-Fate Rebero seems to have no problem with this. It all makes sense to him. If I hear a report that has me scared for Indrin's safety, as far as he is concerned the only thing we can do is to go and make sure he is okay.

As I drive, freely cursing aloud now, Rebero is flipping through my daytimer to find the little scrap of paper with Indrin's temporary address and number. In the meantime, I remember the way fairly well. Not too far off Hastings, I think it was, past a crumbly old hotel on the corner and then a few blocks south. Somewhere around there. But Rebero still can't find the paper and I'm trying to drive while simultaneously reading over his shoulder and flipping the pages for him.

"Here. No. It was part of an envelope. Torn off. That's it! No. Here."

The stoic survivor of the world's most recent genocide is now looking tense with me and I guess I am compromising our chances of seeing tomorrow with all limbs intact, so I lean back to where I should be sitting behind the wheel and start concentrating again on where the hell the house was. Why didn't I get the last name of Indrin's friend from him? Then it would be as simple as looking it up again in the phone book. Just when I am losing hope at recognizing any landmarks at all, I see a familiar 1960-ish square box hotel on the corner. Its crumbly concrete and broken step tells me I am, in fact, on the right track. And, when I turn the corner, I see my gut has served me well once again.

Police cruisers surround the very house where I dropped Indrin off.

"God. Oh God."

This is not happening. This is not happening.

Rebero's hand comes down softly on my shoulder.

"We must back up."

He sees the police officer acting as traffic cop waving us away from the line of orange pylons. Rebero is calm – as I usually am myself in tense situations. I have covered murder scenes complete with fresh blood, grieving parents making television appeals for the return of their kidnapped children, as well as traffic accidents with victims still groaning beside frantic, screaming mothers, and never have I lost it. Sure, I've drunk a few too many beers after the fact, but never have I lost it in a tight situation. I know better.

So, off duty and well removed from my old reporter role, maybe it's only fitting that I feel the fear and horror building up and making me sick and angry, almost like I'm going to throw up any second. Instead all the crap in my guts comes surging up out of my mouth in the form of words.

"I need to fucking talk to someone here."

The officer starts strong-arming me back into the car I've started to climb out of even before taking it out of gear. That's why the car lurches forward, stalls itself, and throws me to the ground, but not before slamming me into the police officer first. My knee feels smashed up from hitting both the car door and the pavement, and the officer is now backing away from me like I'm a drug-crazed freak. He stares at Rebero like he's O.J. in the Bronco.

"I have to ask you to clear the area."

"What's going on in there?"

I hear myself screaming the words at the officer and don't even care that I'll die of shame later, since now I see Jerry and his little blond reporter consort pushing through the swarms of officials to find out what other news story there might be breaking on this side of the roadblock.

"Ma'am. I have to ask you to get back into your car."

The officer is stiff with tension and authority and efficiency and I don't blame him. I did come on like someone crazed, someone potentially even armed.

"Randi, what's going on?"

Jerry, bless his soul, has set down his camera despite nudgings from Little Miss I'm-National-Material to keep rolling. He helps me up.

"I think my friend is in there."

"Who?" Jerry looks puzzled. "You knew the woman?"

"No, the guy."

"The murderer?"

"No."

Rebero has now stepped around the car to the driver's side and is politely slipping in to back the vehicle up. Relief shows itself almost imperceptibly through the severity on the officer's face. Is that what moustaches are for? To help hide emotion?

Bizarre thoughts like that always hit me in times of crisis. I remember asking the policeman what kind of car killed my parents when he broke the news to me over the phone. I even asked what colour it was. Now I choke back the desire to ask what Jerry thinks about moustaches, realizing the question only comes from the way my mind rambles when it is trying not to acknowledge the old familiar black hole of anguish taking over my heart. Like a high-tech car radio in search mode, my mind quickly skips over a thousand possible places to dwell. Where it finally tunes in may be based in no logic whatsoever.

Jerry motions to the reporter to mind the camera as he guides me gently along, following my retreating car. By the time Rebero parks it and shuts off the motor, I feel myself calming down.

"There's nobody else in there," Jerry tells me.

"Nobody?"

"No. A guy goes nuts and freaks out on his ex-wife. We figure they're both dead by now. There's a kid, I guess, but no one has heard anything about her so she may not even be in there. But there's nobody else in there."

"No?"

But my insides still feel queasy and knotted and sharp at the same time. I don't believe Jerry and I want to find Indrin and hug him and tell him he's not crazy about following instincts, because I know he's in there and I don't know how to explain it.

Rebero touches my shoulder and hands me the keys.

"Sorry, Jerry. This is Rebero. Sorry – I mean Edmond. Edmond Rebero."

"Hi's" are exchanged, along with a few nods about how terrible the situation is, how tense everyone is – police and reporters.

"We roared down here to join the other news crew because we heard they were going to storm the place immediately. Now it's all on hold again for some reason. You know for sure your friend went in there?"

There it is – the broken window I noticed the other day, the same stucco finish on the house. But aren't there a thousand houses just like this one? I could be wrong. I have to be wrong.

"I don't know. I thought it was there," I start.

Then Rebero produces the missing scrap of paper.

"I found the address you were looking for."

Jerry takes it and holds it a few feet from his face to read it. My old pal is aging.

"It's the same address," he says finally, through a squint. "Sorry, Randi," he adds, when he sees me take a clumsy step backward.

None of this makes sense. There has been no report of anyone else in the house, but now I know for sure that something has gone terribly wrong and I am mad I ever left Indrin here. I am mad at anyone or anything that could hurt Indrin and his sweet wanderings through life. And somehow in the midst of all this rage,

I am mad that I ever met him.

The only thing I want in life is to be left alone and undisturbed and to leave all the violence and freaking hysteria for reports on the news. Fill my TV screen with life's garbage, but don't come near my life. I'm through with loss and grief – any of it brings the phone call about my parents surging back into my stomach and makes me feel I can't cope with even the smallest things. So I want none of it. How the hell did I know giving a lift to some would-be priest would make this sickness come bursting back into me?

The little blond reporter is back. She is leaning her head to the side, stroking her hair as if absentmindedly, but it's all for effect, of course. *See my pretty hair, pretty even when rumpled by this bit of breaking news in progress.*

Easy to see through. She's as transparent as her eyes.

"Jerry?"

Her mouth is left hanging open in a fake expression of concern for me.

I cut right through it.

"I'm Miranda. I used to work with Jerry."

"Oh?"

Turns out her name is Tara Tomson, an assumed TV moniker if ever I heard one. Or maybe her wealthy parents had big plans for their precious little baby right from the start. And I know she comes from wealth, what a person like her would insist was merely *comfortable,* but what anyone else would know for what it is. Her short, stylish leather boots and matching thick leather Holt Renfrew purse slung over her shoulder, along with the expensive but casual Roots-style *I'm a serious reporter* sweater and pants, tell me she is slumming it in this reporter job. None of this could she afford on a reporter's paycheque alone. Not the subtle gold earrings adorning her ears either.

"We have to get back to work here, I'm sure you understand," says this clone of a Young-Ambitious-Journalist-not-Reporter in a tone hinting she believes I could never understand. "This is a very tense situation and the police don't want spectators getting in the way. I'm sure you understand," she repeats, to help me on my way.

She stops to do her tousled hair thing again as she gives me a surveying look. Her eyes burn into the sweat stains on my shirt.

"So just *where* did you work with Jer?"

From the look on her face, I know she expects me to say I was a fellow burger flipper back in high school or maybe that I was the janitor in his former newsroom. But it's all framed in a sweetly innocent little question.

I cannot stand syrupy tones. She is a wheedling little creature, it's plain to see. Give me someone direct any day over this saccharine attempt at femininity in the workplace. She strokes her hair again. *God.* Femininity doesn't equal fake and affected, or has someone forgotten to inform our new young sisters about the meaning of equality and feminism in the workplace?

"I'm senior producer at CFQR in Edmonton."

Okay, I'm actually current affairs producer, but our news director, liar though he's known to be, did promise me I would be senior producer by the fall. And it *could* happen. I mean he could have a heart attack in one of his pit-bull-attack modes, allowing fairer minds to prevail. Besides, I kind of enjoy the look on Tara Tomson's face at hearing the words *senior producer.* Suddenly, I am someone she might need someday.

"Oh? You're number one in that market."

I watch her trying to peg me. How does she reconcile this lunatic woman standing before her with the image of the station she has in her head? Still, she knew our placement in the market. Ambitious. Watchful.

The dislike I have for this girl fills me with the control and emotional distance I need to talk about Indrin.

"I dropped a friend off at this building yesterday and he may still be in there."

The officer acting as traffic cop has now walked up to us, and Tara Tomson tries to take charge. First, a seemingly unconscious hand through her hair, then an officious-sounding statement.

"This woman believes she knows the gunman inside. She brought him here yesterday."

My mouth blasts a gasp of frustration and I flail my hands. I hope to God this gal uses more journalistic skills in her actual reports. But it's not like I'm optimistic about it. Heaven help the folks who will be tuning in to hear the truth about Saddam Hussein or Bosnia in the years to come. And that era is coming, believe me. It's already here. I've worked with this new young school of "journalists."

"You know the man in question? Jeffrey Allen Baker?"

The officer whips out a notebook.

Gathering up all the professionalism I can muster to

help the lunatic image fade from the officer's mind, I begin to answer. With a pointed and withering stare at you-know-who first.

"No, I don't know any Jeffrey Allen Baker. I do know an Indrin Krishnayya who I dropped off here yesterday. He was going to stay with a friend. I haven't talked to him since."

"Could you spell that please?"

I start but realize I am only guessing at Krishnayya. Yes, I have spent my holidays with this guy, shared tents and even a hotel room, but darned if I know how to spell his name.

"I believe it's...."

I give him the spelling that makes sense to me and hope I am roughly right. The police officer doesn't question it, just marks it all down with a quick, efficient scratch of the pen, and turns to leave.

"Wait right here, please."

He's off now to join the other boys and girls in blue. There is a group of them, all very grim, standing in a tight circle behind one of the cruisers. When he returns, he is followed by one of the group, a policewoman in her mid-thirties with curls poking out from under her cap and surprisingly heavy eye-makeup. Blue eyeliner and the whole bit. Every aspect of this is surreal, a Fellini film sequence.

"Could I ask you to step this way, Ms.?"

"Certainly. I'm Miranda Tyler."

"Thanks, Ms. Tyler. I just have a few questions."

She leads me to the back seat of one of the cruisers, where her questions are punctuated every few words by the squawk and squall of the police radio.

How did I know Mr. Krishnayya?

Squrawk. Dispatch 196, we've got another code 6....

How long did I know him?

CcrssshAck. Please report to the command post...

Did I know his next of kin and how to reach them?

KraLAHax. Lawson is the officer in charge...

Just when the line of questioning is bringing the sick surge of panic back into my stomach, we are both stopped by the sudden movement of emergency team guys coming around the side of the house. And just when they round the corner and the paramedics are waved up the lawn, I start talking again. As fast and as furiously as I can. Talking as if my words could preclude anything frightening, as if they were a shield flying up against what is moving toward us. But this convoy of officers and paramedics just keeps moving forward and nothing stops it. My words only seem to slow it all into slo mo, this train of officers and medics and white stretchers, and the legs running all gangly beside the wheels.

"From Calgary. He grew up in Calgary. His father's a doctor and I think his name's Rajiv."

The train moves closer.

"He's Catholic," I add feebly when I can't think of what else to say. And then I look down at the pavement and know I cannot look up again because I have already seen his long dark hair on the pillow even from this far away.

~ ~

It's hard to describe the feeling I had when I thought the priest gave Indrin the last rites. Turns out they don't even call it that anymore and it was actually more of a precautionary prayer or something, but I didn't know that and for the first time in my life I thought I was going to faint. It was not going to be an easy dropping-away-from-it-all either, like a good swoon in the movies. The darkness moved in from the sides and filled me with a hot, prickly feeling that slowly enveloped everything I saw and heard. Indrin's mother took my hand then and led me outside the hospital room and when the feeling finally dissipated it left me ashamed that I had dragged her away from her son at that moment.

She is petite and has the same dark hair and eyes as Indrin. His father is not nearly as slim, but through the pear shape – what I call the *businessmen's silhouette* – I can still see the young man who fathered Indrin. In his mother, I can see Indrin's calm, even if this has been tempered with the tension of the moment and the rushed trip to Vancouver as soon as they got the call.

"Thank you, God. Thank you, God," she kept saying when the doctor explained that, grave though the situation was, Indrin's condition was now stable.

It turns out Anila and Rajiv – both went straight to their first names at the introduction – knew a surprising amount about me. Somehow it never occurred to me that Indrin was in contact with his parents over the last couple of weeks. I can't remember him phoning even once. But just outside the room where Indrin's still form lay hooked up to intravenous, here was Anila asking me if I was well over my flu and saying she had been sorry to hear about the traumatic experience with my fiancé.

She is back in Indrin's room now, along with her husband and the surgeon who removed the bullet. It blasted its way into Indrin's shoulder and lodged precariously close to an artery, which prolonged the delicate surgery. Indrin lost a lot of blood, but not as much as the little girl, Daria, who was hiding in the storage closet with him. She is still in critical care.

Her mother, Lynn, was dead even before the police showed up. The gunshot that came later, and that continues to be played as a sound bite in all the radio reports, was the shot that Jeffrey Allan Baker turned on himself after his day's work. And in those same radio reports come the stories, now, about the bitterly controlling sicko who used to go into rages over the smallest and silliest things, rages that often ended up with Lynn getting punched in places hidden by her clothing. Never anything obvious like a blackened eye. No, he never truly blew his cover as a *normal, regular guy* until this. After all, she *had* left him. His suspicious jealousy was confirmed when, watching the house from down the block, he saw "some Paki" go into the apartment. That's when his gun left the trunk.

Rebero sits beside me. Twice he has suggested he take me back to the hotel so I can sleep, but I don't want to go anywhere until we hear something more about how Indrin's doing. Maybe more to the point, I don't want to leave until I hear that Indrin is happy and healthy and ready to go for a stroll to his favourite shrine or to get on a roll talking about conflicting instincts or prophecies and prayer.

Truth is, I simply don't want to move. I am afraid if

I do, the bottom of the world could drop out again. I just want to sit here and feel the hospital floor under my feet and know it's not going anywhere. And Rebero understands, I think. In fact, I have been afraid this is bringing a lot of awful memories back to him, but when I suggest that, in a roundabout kind of way, he brushes off my comment with a grimace that pretends to be a smile.

"We never waited in a hospital for news. We knew who was left alive. And who wasn't."

Then he picks up a magazine, some five-year-old back issue all about fishing tips, so I know he doesn't want to talk about it.

And we sit. I'm onto another coffee, just lousy stuff from the machine since I didn't want to go all the way to the cafeteria again. And I forgot to press *black* so I am sipping double-cream-and sugar like the person who plunked money in before me. My mouth is all stale coffee aftertaste and oversweet.

Just where did you go in Kamloops?

This is what I want to ask him, what I'm going to ask him. What I'll ask him soon. Maybe even now.

Perhaps it's the fatigue, the plain old emotional exhaustion, or the fact I think I have just decided something important. I am never, ever going to play along with something I do not understand if it means playing dumb – and that goes for regular life as well as the truly dumbfounding world of relationships. There has always been a reason for me to avoid the awkward question, a coke habit or a tragedy in the family or something – always something to make me squelch my gut feelings.

After all, I had to be understanding. I had to give a person space. I had to give a situation time. I had to be patient. I had to understand where the guy was coming from.

This time is no different. There are a thousand reasons to leave poor Edmond Rebero alone.

For starters, he is coming from an out-and-out genocide, truly hell on earth – as if hell could be anywhere else – so on that ground alone, how could I possibly justify forcing him out of his self-imposed silence?

But sipping my sweet, creamy coffee, worse now that it is cooling off, I decide all the old *understanding* was a kind of cruel joke. Far from meaning I *understood* anything at all, it just meant I was too timid or cowardly in the truest moral sense to trust my own natural-enough questions and feelings.

You're right about instinct, my dear guru friend. Do you hear me in there? Through all the anaesthetic and dreamy layers of prayer surrounding you? You were right. And my instinct now is to speak the hard words. To ask the tough questions.

Funny that what is second nature in the newsroom is so difficult for me in the murky, awkward world beyond the TV set, far from the indignant eye of the Betacam. In a scrum around a politician it is all too easy to shout the obvious question.

So the decision to allow development in that previously protected wilderness had nothing *to do with your son's plan to develop a ski resort?*

And hey, Mr. Cameraman, did you get my question on tape? I can use that with his "no comment" to make myself sound smart, sharp, and smug.

Not so easy out here in raw, unedited real life to state the questions directly, to cut straight to the heart of the matter.

As I am about to do now.

Yes.

Now.

"Where did you go in Kamloops?"

I voice the words in a carefully gentle tone.

Rebero's eyes lock onto the fishing magazine.

I feel my stomach get queasy. The last thing I want to do is create pain here. It feels wrong to impose even the slightest discomfort into his world. I feel mean, transformed into a screeching, strident caricature of Sister Fran, so I listen again carefully to the echo of the words in my head. No, they were soft-toned, even resigned.

For a moment I think we both wonder if the question will simply evaporate, but suddenly I am filled with a certainty that today, in this moment, here in this hospital waiting room, I cannot let that happen. And the realization feels much bigger than a decision to ask a simple question should.

"I guess I'm prying here. But we saw you that morning on the street before we got to the bus depot. And they had seen you there the night before."

Might as well let him know I'm sure. Now that I have opened it up, I want to avoid the possibility of any embarrassing attempt at a fib. Unlike Sister Fran, I am not horrified by the idea of a lie – it's generally the route I take myself if I think I can avoid an uncomfortable conversation – but here, today, I realize I do not have the energy required to keep good lies afloat anymore. Besides, I truly want to know.

He's still not answering. His hands, smooth and a beautiful chocolate black, rest motionless across the colour photo of a rushing northern river. The water sprays white in a freeze-frame splash against the dark green trees on the bank.

Maybe one reason I've backed off from this kind of straight-ahead question in my personal life is the obvious distress it now seems to be causing in Rebero. With boyfriends, however, it wasn't so much to avoid that kind of distress as it was to avoid the backlash of anger that would be turned on me if I did dare to lay down the gauntlet of reason. Or speak the obvious question.

Why?

I saw you.

Or maybe *I saw her.*

I was always trying to keep the peace – false though it was. But what a lot of effort it took *not* to say it all. Or to believe the long involved explanations if I ever did lay out a question.

To break the silence between us, I cough, as if adding a pointless sound could dislodge an avalanche of words. But of course it doesn't. Rebero does not look angry, just helpless. He looks as though he is waiting for the explanation as much as I am.

His fingers are moving now, absently running over the northern river and smoothing the pages out over his knees. Oblivious to the staples in the middle of the page, his hands trace the banks of the river, flow to the edges of the magazine, and then move back to start the journey again from the centre. A funny symbolism occurs to me. Rebero caressing the river. Caressing the world.

And just as I think that, his hands stop.

If he weren't so indomitable looking, so regal and proud, I would reach for his hand now – just place mine over his. Instead, since I don't feel I can, I start to imagine my hand on his so clearly I would bet any money his fingers are icy cold right now. That's how they feel in my mind.

His smooth, straight fingers suddenly curl up. He tucks them under his knees, then turns to look at me. He doesn't speak, just stares, but there is nothing piercing or angry about it.

"I didn't know if I was going to meet you. I couldn't decide."

"Where did you go?"

"Nowhere."

He looks away, back to the magazine, to the water I can almost hear roaring.

Nowhere? Don't deflect me, Edmond. Not now.

"Really," he emphasizes.

He forces a smile at me to break the tension, to make *me* feel comfortable.

"Nowhere."

The magazine is closed and tossed onto the coffee table in front of us. We sit in silence. My eyes ask him for more.

"At first I didn't think I would come," he says finally, his voice rising at the end of his sentence, as if he is asking me to understand not just his words, but what he means.

"I wasn't sure if I would take the bus at all, even come to Kamloops, but I did. And I came early so I would have time to think about what to do. Then, after I arrived, I decided it was a mistake, so I left my bag and walked for a while."

"They didn't ask you to leave?"

Sorry, Rebero, I see your face wince and the embarrassment flood in, but I have to ask.

"I thought someone asked you to leave."

For a long moment we sit in silence, but I get the idea this is not deflection or avoidance, it is just Edmond growing comfortable with the idea of talking to me. He is listening in his mind for the right words to say.

"I told you I see pictures in my mind sometimes," he tells me in a voice that sounds consciously calm and controlled.

"I see pictures that sometimes I can't stop. If I am busy or with people, I can make them go away. If I am by myself, I shake my head, like a shiver, and then I try to make myself think of something else. But at night it is more difficult. The pictures came that night and I couldn't make them stop."

This time, my hand does not wait for my mind to tell it what is appropriate, it just moves to his, in fact, pulls it into mine, and as I feel the cold of his fingers seep into my palm, I take heart that some of my warmth may be moving into him. Both of my hands, now, clasp both of his, rubbing them the way my mother did with my hands to warm away the numbness when I came in from a wintry day of skating. It always hurt, the flesh reawakening, and so I tried to resist my Mom's hands until the blood coursing back into my frozen fingers left me no choice but to feel again. And so, now, I do the same with Rebero – clasp and rub and massage his hands intently, insistently.

And as I do this, Rebero speaks, finally gushing words as steadily as the blood I trust will soon start surging through his fingers.

"I couldn't see my mother, but I could see the blood and I saw – around the corner, I could see – an arm. And I couldn't go in. I didn't know if it was my sister's or my mother's at first, because they'd both been there. I couldn't go further. I ran around the side of the house, to get away, and I got almost to the banana trees before I heard her screams. My mother's. And that was when I knew I could have gone in because it hadn't been too late. She was still alive. She was alive until the sounds that came after her screams.

"Later I saw a boy – a boy we knew. He was eighteen, a neighbour from just north, and he came out from the house – I saw him. The boy knew us all. Our family thought we knew him well. And his father. We knew his father well. His father was not a bad man, but he was not strong. And this boy was *interahamwe* – youth militia – just following his orders to kill all Tutsis.

"I saw him walk away. Just walk away, as if he'd butchered a cow, and was now walking home for lunch. From the trees I could see him join a group of others, all with their machetes swinging, and then they ran, clapping each other on the backs like a soccer team after a game.

"I don't know why they didn't see me when I ran. I

don't know why I am alive. And I don't know why I went back into the house. If I'd gone in before, maybe it would not have been too late. But by then it was. I should have run, just gone away. But I could not. I went back into the house, the house of my family, the house where we shared meals with neighbours – Tutsi and Hutu, to see walls smeared with blood. And on the floor, my mother, my sister, and her baby. What was left of them."

Rebero is completely motionless, speaking without the slightest movement anywhere in his body. If his lips were not moving, I would swear this was a disembodied voice, coming from somewhere near the fluorescent lights looming surreal above us or from the fake fig tree behind his chair.

"There is nothing human about the body when the spirit has left. That's what I kept thinking, what I tried to think. That this was not them. I prayed to think it. *This is not them.* Not Anthalie and her little Jean-Marie, not my mother. They had been human. These bodies were not. Their killer was alive, but he was not human either anymore. Everything human was destroyed in that room. And me, I didn't feel human either anymore. My spirit left too in that room. I am not human. I don't remember what it feels like to be alive.

"My own father would not recognize me. He did not. And my own brother, he would see nothing in my eyes. If he looked, he would fear as my father did. He would fear for the future.

"The picture of my mother and sister in that room is what came into my mind in the bus station when I closed my eyes to wait. I couldn't stop it and I couldn't stop the sounds I started to make and, when they asked me to leave, I left. I walked on the highway. A large truck was coming down the hill and I watched its headlights, deciding. I would have walked in front of the truck. I truly thought I would until I realized dying would make no difference to me. I am already dead."

He stops speaking and there is nothing for me to say. Me, feebly holding his frozen fingers, me with friendly North American reassurances of *you'll be okay* springing to mind and choked back just as quickly. How to find a life after death? A world after the end of the world? My comfortable Canadian upbringing has not shown me how.

It'll all be okay.

A spoiled teenaged consciousness to the rest of the planet's hardened adulthood does not have appropriate answers, only immature questions.

Why can't I bring warmth here? Why can't I massage his fingers back to life, bring Edmond back, bring his family back?

I wish I could.

Wishes are futile. They change nothing. Especially when what I want to change is already etched into the relentless rock of history. Carved into memory and flesh and time with both the irrevocable precision of a surgeon's knife and the raw, random swing of a machete.

But still I wish. I wish I could believe wishes made a difference. And that wish is so strong, it is a tangible thing in my hands, hands that are now growing cold. The ice from Rebero's fist spreads outward. I feel it seep into my bones.

Warmth is suddenly all I can think about, an emblem somehow of every wish running through me, so when my glacier-numb fingers finally acknowledge their uselessness and let go, I feel a frantic kind of despair crush my chest from the inside. I clench my hands in my own lap now, studying their pale, purple-veined surface. The knuckles are white. I can see the bones through my cold, transparent skin.

Where else can warmth come from when the body fails? I wish my mind could bring it here, create it like some giant sun, and pour out all the warmth Edmond Rebero would ever need. But ice is all I feel in my hands and in my heart and I wonder if it's true, if you can catch death while you are still alive.

~ ~

ANILA AND RAJIV took us to dinner before dropping Edmond and me off at the hotel. They are on their way back to the hospital and despite my desire to go with them, I know I am not family and this time is theirs. The acknowledgement is reluctant and, while logical, feels like a lie.

I am family, Indrin. We are family.

The hospital feels two thousand miles too far from me tonight and I want to be there, keeping watch over Indrin. Not that I would do any good, but there is certainly no great benefit to my sitting here feeling worried and lost and tired and not at all interested in getting ready for bed.

Edmond is across the hall in the room I insisted on

getting for him. What is one more charge on the old credit card anyway? Especially when I know I need some time alone. Edmond too. He could have crashed on the couch in my room or we could have called for a rollaway cot, but it is better this way. He looked as relieved as I felt when the front desk called up to tell me they had another vacancy after all.

A stack of phone messages sits in front of me on the desk. From Aaron, Karen, even Jerry, and two from Sister Fran. *To hell with all of them* is what I am feeling at the moment. Not with them, I suppose, just with the demands inherent in these little pink sheets of paper.

Call me. Call me. Call me. Explain what's happening please. Explain it now.

What a distance I have travelled. From being able to happily handle the stresses of daily news in our pressure-cooker newsroom with my pit-bull boss to this, to feeling overwhelmed by a handful of pink phone messages. It strikes me that I will need a year off to recover from this strange little holiday.

How I Spent My Summer Holidays.

The title of the essay I can write for the shrink I'll need.

Tonight, sitting with Anila, Rajiv, and Edmond at dinner, I realized how alien I feel. As if I had spent far too long in the wilderness away from civilized society. I hadn't had a "normal" conversation with anyone in a long while. My rambling trip with Indrin was far from any kind of normal summer holiday break. More and more it seems like a mirage to me, a magical wandering through some mythical, mystical world. A world of prophecies and priests and lying in tents talking about instincts and God. If it weren't for the fact of his parents chewing food beside me tonight, I might be tempted to believe that Indrin himself had been nothing but a myth or mirage. But no, he was very real, very mortal. All too mortal.

Innate dignity. That is the best description I can come up with to explain what Indrin's mother has in spades. Anila has a distinctly gentle nature, but it is a deceiving one. For starters, she is not at all a person given to outward displays. In fact, the way she calmly chatted about the flight, and how many travel points they had gathered so far – only one more short flight would give them enough for two tickets to India – and her new job as a florist – it's the humidity and perfume of the flowers she loves most – you would never know her only son was a few miles away recovering from a gunshot wound. She is not at all cold, but she does have one very cool exterior that seems to act as the counter-balance to her husband's extreme emotions.

Several times throughout the meal, Rajiv's eyes were telltale red or actually welling. He kept glancing at his watch and actually swallowed only about three bites of his meal, which was certainly the best and hottest curry I had ever eaten. Anila's hand continuously caressed her husband's hand on the tabletop before the meal. After it arrived and her hands were occupied, her eyes took over, constantly searching his to encourage him to take just a bite or one small sip of tea.

Throughout the meal, little things annoyed him. The napkin wasn't folded properly. The water was in the wrong kind of glass. The music was too loud. The restaurant was too cold. The table next to us was too close.

Anila made all those concerns drop away for him. Like a child whose scraped knee can only be healed by a kiss from Mom, only Anila could sweep away Rajiv's frustrations.

I was fascinated watching the two of them. Years ago, on my one and only backpacking trip to Ireland as a student, I was surprised to have so many people greet me with friendly smiles and handshakes and the words, *I'd love to meet your mother.* Always "your mother" – not your father or your brother or your sister or your pet iguana, but your mother. This, apparently, was the key to truly getting to know someone. They wouldn't know me until they had also met my mother. And I find myself now believing the same thing. I had not known Indrin until tonight, until I had met his mother.

She was obviously well skilled in running interference for Indrin in regard to his father. Even tonight, she carefully began asking Edmond about his tree planting job after he had innocently brought up Indrin's intention to become a priest. I saw how quickly her hand flew back to calm Rajiv's. She switched the topic so subtly and lightning-fast, her manoeuvre was seemingly unnoticed by her husband. The very moment the conversation had been safely steered to non-controversial ground, the annoyance in Rajiv's face dissolved and he found himself taking the first bite of his meal. Deftly handled, I thought, but rather precarious too. Here was a woman who trod minefields daily as a matter of course, who was highly skilled in avoidance and ready to defuse upon request.

The whole thing reminded me how relaxing it is not to be involved with a man.

Hats off to you, Anila. Even when I try to step deftly, I seem capable only of setting off bombs.

Because even when I have tiptoed as softly as I could, the ground has always given way to rows and blowups with the men in my life – the biggest war with my father because he couldn't stand to see my tippy-toe ballets in the first place. He'd have preferred me to clomp my way through life in army boots than to see me taking the mincing, faltering footsteps I've taken – all to avoid shaking the worlds of insecure boyfriends. But somehow their worlds got shaken anyway. It occurred to me, as Rajiv realized with horror that there was a lipstick mark on his untouched water glass, that the mines are everywhere and they never were all my fault.

As for the biggest war – with my dad – all his annoyance over my boyfriend choices, which only ever convinced me that he didn't care about what I wanted, was maybe just frustration that I didn't want enough.

Perhaps if I'd realized that sooner, my mother wouldn't have had to spend her life acting as an arbiter of truces between my father and me.

Anila, I could see, isn't setting the terms of any truce here, between her husband and a world that never measures up to his exacting eye. She's a diplomat, preventing the wars and skirmishes from beginning in the first place. Given her expertise and comfort with the role, she has obviously had many years of practice. And so from Indrin's mother, and the way she handed Rajiv the new, sterile glass from the waitress, I could see clearly that Indrin was raised on the brink of war, that he played in a sandbox of toy soldiers à la late 1939. Thanks to his mother's careful diplomacy, Germany never invaded Poland – a considerable feat, but tension remained all the same. No wonder Indrin sought out a spiritual solution, a religious retreat.

Rise above the concerns of the world. Pretend the minefield isn't there.

Peace be with you.

This is just my take on Indrin's upbringing. It is wildly generalized, put together after just meeting his parents, and largely based on my own habit of dating men who need to be coddled and placated. It probably isn't true. But if it is not an accurate portrayal of Indrin and his family, it doesn't matter. All it shows me is that I see warfare wherever I go, always have. All I ever hear about are wars and rumours of wars and never before has it made me feel so heartsick.

I am the one who has been living in a war zone. I don't think I have ever really believed a person could live anywhere else. I fought wars as a reporter; I fought on the other side as a producer. I even fought for peace within relationships with as much justification as any soldier in any holy war, that veritable institution and oxymoron. The whole bloody world seems like a war to me. Every part of it. Relationships, newsrooms, you name it. There are wars where little kids fight to stay alive after a freak kills Mom. Other wars in which the walking dead fight to make sense of genocide. There are my own wars. Wars where I fight to find out why I stuck around with jerks, where I fight to believe that life is not random, where sometimes I fight to believe it *is* random just so the hurts won't matter so much.

Tonight, if I could gather a peace rally to protest in front of my own heart for awhile, I would do it. I would gather thousands and would paint every picket sign myself.

Miracles and Ceasefires

Edmond has disappeared again. Sister Fran has called four times and as I shuffle and fold a new batch of little pink message sheets into dismal origami, I still don't know what to tell her. I have not yet thought out the safest lie. What I believe is that he may have gone back to planting trees. This is the likeliest possibility. He did tell me once he hoped to save enough money to go to university in Montreal, where he could study in French. Planting trees could help him save up at least enough to get him started. Or perhaps he is on the hunt for a job here – moving boxes or cooking food, pouring coffee or doing something, anything to help lose himself in the vast Vancouver area. Of course, I really don't know where he went or why, but I do know one very important thing. He did not leave in despair.

This gives me a certain consolation. The funny thing is that I know I watched the decision to leave cross his face the moment it occurred to him. I just didn't understand what it was at the time. Never had I seen him look more peaceful. His features visibly softened and more than anything, I felt an instant ceasefire. Whatever it was before that gave me the feeling he was constantly on guard simply vanished. Like one silent but almost ecstatic sigh.

War is over.

I witnessed this change yesterday afternoon, but the difference in the new Edmond Rebero was still apparent last night, just before we went into our rooms for bed. Even at the time something felt very final about it. It should not have, since we were simply saying goodnight, but it truly did feel like a parting goodbye. Maybe this is just how I see yesterday's events in retrospect. Maybe not. All I know for sure is that, although we did speak one more time and share a hug after that *goodnight* in the hallway, Edmond was trying to say goodbye even then.

When I called his room this morning to meet for breakfast, I found he had checked out. Then I saw the note thanking me – not thanking me for paying for the room, or for giving him the ride, or for anything in particular, just thanking me. The note was folded and slipped under my door.

Thank you. Your friend, Edmond Rebero.

And I know that his thanks were as much for Indrin as they were for me. Perhaps more.

I know this because of what happened earlier in the day.

Yesterday was the first day Indrin sat up and began to

seem a little more like the fellow I met on top of the mountain. Anila was out searching bookstores with Indrin's list in hand, a variety of books recommended by Father Lowrey when he phoned that morning. Would Vancouver bookstores have the most recent works published on the Marian apparitions in Rwanda? Anila was off to find out.

Rajiv, lost without Anila there to make his world smooth and trouble-free, had just had a ridiculous argument with the entire nursing staff about the mopping of the floor.

"The smell of that stuff will make my son sick. Are you wanting to make him sick?"

"We'd all get sick if the floor was never mopped. Sir."

The nurse made the title *Sir* sound like an insult and all hell broke loose. His arms flailed, a vein in the centre of his forehead bulged, and when he came back into Indrin's room, his son miraculously exhibited his mother's skill at calming rough seas.

He was fine, he assured his dad. Yes, the smell was strong and certainly his father was right, they should not use that stuff, but he was truly fine. It would dry in a moment and he was glad it was so clean and wouldn't his father like a cup of tea, he'd be perfectly fine visiting with Miranda and Edmond. His father could use a moment to himself.

So that was how Edmond and I came to have our first time alone with Indrin in the hospital. Just time enough to hear his strange story.

There had been an apparition.

Oh, Indrin. The drugs are working overtime. Can't you see that?

But you don't blurt out reactions like that to an earnest kid in a hospital bed, only just back from the brink of death, who speaks the words to you as if they were sacred text.

"She appeared to me. The Blessed Mother."

The doomsday papers have pushed him over the edge. I never did think they were a good idea.

This was what was going through my head. Edmond, if he was skeptical, did not show it. In fact, his face never did reveal much, I realize now. Edmond sat in his chair quiet and clear-eyed.

According to Indrin, the miracle – the most intense spiritual experience of his life – had happened in the house, after the shooting. He was in the storage closet, bleeding all over the little girl, Daria, in his arms, and praying the rosary.

"I used my fingers as the rosary beads, but I couldn't keep anything straight. It was like I'd forgotten how to count, and then I realized I was saying the *Hail Mary* all wrong – I was getting the words all mixed up. I started to cry. *Now and at the hour of our death* was what I was forgetting. It was like I couldn't say those words, just couldn't say them."

Now this is where his handy-dandy Virgin Mary apparition comes in. And excuse my irreverent tone, but it just seems all too convenient and understandable that this overly religious kid would imagine *just* what he needed to see in his hour of need. At least, that is what I made of the apparition at the time, maybe what I am still trying to make of it.

Edmond, on the other hand, seemed to get something completely different out of Indrin's description of the events.

"The closet completely filled with light and Mary appeared where the door had been. As soon as the light appeared, I lost the feeling of pain in my shoulder and Daria kind of sighed and fell asleep. Her head leaned against me and her breathing got regular, and a tremendous feeling of love welled up inside me – I can't remember ever having such a feeling of happiness. It was an intense feeling of joy that seemed to radiate straight from Mary, into my heart, and then into Daria.

"Mary stood, kind of floating on a mist just above the floor, and she was holding the baby Jesus. She was tall and beautiful and dressed in robes that were bright and multicoloured – orange and red and blue – just like the cloth the baby was wrapped in. And while it seemed completely natural at the time, what seems surprising now is that she was black and so was the baby.

"Finally she spoke, but what she said wasn't for me. It was for you."

I stiffened uncomfortably in my chair until I realized Indrin was looking past me to Edmond.

"To me?" was all Edmond said quietly.

"Hm hmmm. I guess maybe that's why she appeared the way she did. She said, 'Tell Edmond not to cry.'"

"Not to cry," Edmond repeated.

"Then she smiled, and I must have passed out because she didn't seem to vanish, it just felt like I slowly dissolved away. And then this."

Wincing, Indrin cut short his attempt to motion to the hospital room around him.

"Hey, take it easy there," I said. Then I asked if he had told Father Lowrey about the incident on the phone. Surely Lowrey, even with his belief in miraculous apparitions, might suggest this one was nothing more than an understandable, anaesthesia-related reaction to trauma.

"My Dad was in the room and he doesn't know. I couldn't really get into it. Dad was annoyed enough that a priest was phoning."

At that point, Indrin's father returned. He seemed in a brighter mood – apparently the woman in the cafeteria was very nice and had sympathized with Rajiv about the cleaning fluid.

"She was saying the very same thing, that it is bothering her many times," Rajiv said, while he promptly sat down in the chair Edmond had just vacated for him.

I rose too and Edmond and I said our goodbyes, ostensibly so father and son could have their time together, but more because both of us could feel the vague dislike Rajiv seems to have for me. It is very politely suppressed and mixed, I think, with a certain enjoyment of the fact Indrin has at least been travelling with a woman, namely me. All the same, he doesn't know quite what to make of me. I get the feeling he wants his son to have a girlfriend so he tolerates me as a step in the right direction while hoping for more. *My son could do better* is what I read in his eyes.

Rajiv, I know you all too well.

Just before we got out the door, however, Edmond turned back to Indrin.

"Thank you," he said, and smiled a pathetically heartfelt smile – pathetic in that it revealed such a lack of pretence, such an open, freely admitted hunger.

Indrin smiled back, and that was when the look crossed Edmond Rebero's face. An unclouding. A relaxing. A return to life maybe.

I still don't believe in miracles, the kind written up in books about people saved by angels and that kind of thing. What I guess I do believe in is what I think happened when Indrin told his little story. Whatever went on inside Indrin's head in that closet while he was bleeding, he ended up with an experience that meant something to him and that gave him strength. In telling us about it, Indrin then gave something important to Edmond, and if that is a miracle, it's the kind I wish we could have more of in this world.

Later last night, long after Indrin had told us about his "apparition," after Edmond and I had left the hospital, and several hours after our strange "goodnight" that felt like a "goodbye," a knock at the door woke me up.

It was Rebero.

He did not step from the hall into my room, just stood there awkwardly for a few long moments until he spoke.

"Sorry to wake you, but there is something I should tell you."

I asked him if he wanted to come in, but he shook his head.

"It is about my brother," he said.

I nodded.

"He does not exist."

I thought for a few moments, then told him I had figured as much, that I was terribly sorry his brother had been killed too.

"No, he was not killed. He is not alive. He does not exist. I have no brother."

My eyes searched the face of this person, this stranger once again. Questions tried to formulate themselves in my mind, but none of the tangled thoughts could move to my lips smoothly enough to voice. For once, not a word could come to me.

"I am sorry for your trouble," Edmond said gravely.

And still no words seemed able to escape from me – Miranda, queen of conversation.

He turned to walk back to his room, but I finally recovered my voice in time to stop him.

"Could we talk, Edmond?"

My voice cracked.

"Could we just sit down and talk?"

But no, it seemed Edmond had nothing more to say.

"Do you believe in what Indrin said? The apparition?" I found myself asking suddenly.

Was it just to make him stay a moment longer?

"I was raised Catholic," he said. "But I don't know what I believe anymore. Not all the priests in Rwanda were good men."

"They're sure as hell not all good here," I said, my voice rising with a bit of its old confidence.

"Some turned against the Tutsis too," he continued. "But that is men, not God, I know."

"I'm sorry I asked."

"No, it is okay."

"It's just that telling you not to cry seemed like such a stupid thing to say."

Rebero stood considering this, or considering his shoes or the carpet or something, until he told me he did not think it was stupid, that it was exactly what his sister would have said.

"Your sister?"

He nodded. And as I looked at him I realized he believed a woman and child had indeed appeared to Indrin, but a different woman and child.

"They are still alive. In spirit. I know this now."

Time stretched during the next few moments, every second lengthening as I looked into Edmond's eyes.

"Are you okay?" I finally said.

There was that old, dreaded catch phrase, born again with heartfelt concern in words that caught at my throat.

Yes, he nodded. "Are you?" he asked.

The tears that came into my eyes surprised us both. That he, Edmond Rebero, the walking wounded, survivor of the end of the world, should share his miracle and then ask about me, care enough to ask about me, broke a giant wall inside. One enormous crack, and the concrete dam exploded and all the rivers of the world suddenly poured through it. That was when I hugged him, or he hugged me, or both. And that was when I felt a weight lift off me just as I had seen it lift off Edmond himself earlier that day in the hospital.

My body shook, and tears rained down, and for a moment I hoped no one would come down the hallway, but suddenly, as quickly as that thought crossed my mind, I realized I wouldn't care if they did, if an entire news crew complete with sound man came upon us now.

If the black hole I carry around inside me is still there, last night it lost its force. Its relentless gravitational pull was released in the hallway with Rebero, and now the darkness can simply exist, benignly floating inside me. It feels harmless, like it will never be able to draw me into it again.

War is over.

I could hear the words being sung in my mind as Edmond hugged me, the words sung in John Lennon's voice since I never could carry a tune.

War is over.

~ ~

I'M GETTING USED to the unusual. Maybe I'm habitually suited now to the bizarre, exotic, and strange.

"I think she cured me," is what Indrin whispers to me while his father is out in the hallway, arguing with yet another nurse.

"Who?"

"The Blessed Mother."

I sigh. I don't know how to talk about these things. Yes, I may be getting used to them, but that doesn't mean I have the vocabulary to match. Or the will.

"I know you lost a lot of blood. I know the surgery was tense. Who the hell knows? Maybe she did. I'm not the one to discuss it with."

"Not that," he strains through tense vocal cords, "the HIV."

"Oh good God, you've got to be kidding, Indrin."

"Fine."

He settles back onto his pillow, his long black hair splayed over the white cotton like a Rorschach blot. Back to the enigmatic quiet he is so comfortable with. Silence is a country he is definitely more suited to than me.

His certainty frightens me sometimes. It is frightening me now.

"Well, what do you mean?" I ask finally, as a burning knot makes itself felt in my stomach.

But Rajiv walks back into the room and we spend the next twenty minutes listening to him go on about the lack of discipline on this ward, how he would never put up with it at his hospital, how the nurses are rude to people – *yeah, to some people, I think* – and how he will get his son back to Calgary as soon as he is well enough.

"And not a moment before. I will not be having you shuffled about and jostled through an airport before you are absolutely well enough to make the journey."

It is not until Rajiv is convinced he wants another cup of tea, this time by Anila, who has walked back into the room after some short-notice peacemaking efforts with the nurses, that we find ourselves alone again.

"I asked for a test. An AIDS test," he whispers.

"Well, finally."

"It was negative."

"See? I told you your chances were slim."

"Even after Larissa?"

"Larissa?"

"My ex-girlfriend."

"Yes, even after Larissa."

"I was HIV-positive before. I know I was."

There goes my stomach again. A tightening, burning knot.

"Indrin, it doesn't just go away. If you had it, you'd still have it. That's what's such a big deal about this little disease they call AIDS. If it just disappeared all of a sudden, people wouldn't be so scared of it now, would they?"

To ignore the facts and place a problem like AIDS in the hands of superstition and old-world religion seems to betray a loose grip on reality. On the reality I know, at least. And this reality is something I still grasp with enough force for bones to show through the skin on my knuckles.

"She healed me," continues Indrin. "I know how I feel, how I felt before. My blood feels different."

"You can feel your blood?"

"Yes, as a matter of fact I can. At least I could. And I'm glad I never got the test before. I might not have had enough faith to be healed if a test handed me a death warrant."

Sun shines in through the window, casting long shadows from the chair legs, shadows that are blurred by the fluorescents overhead.

Something appeared to Indrin and, even if it were only a powerful dream image, it was important enough to change the world for Rebero. Why couldn't it change

Indrin's world too? And why, when I plan to concede this with one sigh of incredulous acceptance, does my mouth form a sarcastic quip?

"So this is proof positive, then, that ignorance is bliss?"

Ignoring my comment altogether, Indrin continues.

"What I didn't tell you yesterday is that I was praying the Rosary about the HIV. Because I was bleeding all over little Daria and I didn't want her to get AIDS."

So Indrin had set his mind on this request, laser-focussed his wish with every prayerful word he uttered.

Why shouldn't prayers be answered if they are voiced with the kind of assurance Indrin has? Whether that of a sublimely wise guru or a quick-witted altar boy, the mind is a powerful thing. There have been reports aplenty about mysterious cases of healing when sheer willpower seems to be the only reason for it. I myself did a story on a guy whose brain tumour completely disappeared, leaving the doctors at the cancer clinic with broad baffled grins and shaking heads.

"Well, maybe it did go away, I don't know. You have incredible willpower, I know that."

"It wasn't willpower," says Indrin intently. "It was a gift."

His eyes pierce mine to see if I understand. There is nothing I can say but, yes, I know what he means.

A heavenly gift of faith.

My understanding can go only this far. I know what he means – my mind knows – but I cannot get my belief around it.

"A gift of faith." I mouth the words clearly, honestly,

but without any emotion at all. The words I can speak, but somehow they still do not register.

"Why can't you believe me?"

As I stare into his brown eyes, the answer comes to me.

"It would clash with my universe, the universe that keeps me alive."

And yes, I believe the sudden act of agreeing that Indrin is spending his days talking to the Mother of God and being cured of incurable diseases would be a little too hard for me to accept, could even do me some damage. It would probably throw my body into shock, a little like the way deep-sea divers who come up from the depths too soon get the bends and die. None of this miracle stuff fits particularly well into the world in which I was raised, where time is linear, and dead people like my parents stay dead and don't show up in people's storage closets, and where I'll have a good shot at seventy or eighty years to make something of my life before ending my days as a bunch of enzymes or fertilizer or whatever it is that feeds the grass in the graveyard.

"I'm not ready for my world to end," I announce to Indrin.

"Worlds are always ending, Miranda. That *is* the world."

Indrin's eyes fill up with humour the way other people's fill with tears. They are positively mirthful.

"What? You're laughing at me?"

"No. Not exactly. You're just funny is all."

"Yeah, yeah. My whole life is a riot."

So what if miracles were a part of my daily life? What

then? What if I believed in them, even expected them?

But I end this line of questioning and decide I would rather remain safe from uncomfortable answers.

That's the beauty of denial. If I decide not to recognize miracles as such, even if they are actually there, then they do not exist, at least in my life. The denial simply makes them vanish.

Troubling miracles gone.

Gone.

And this denial method of mine is tried and true and practised around the world.

∽ ∽

WE EXCHANGED ADDRESSES before the Krishnayyas left for the airport yesterday. There was no point in my going along since they had rented a van and, as much as I'd have wanted to follow them out and have Indrin to myself for one more drive, they were now travelling as one family unit. It may be just as well; I work Monday and have to clear up a few things here before I head back. First on the agenda today, to sit down here on the sand at English Bay with my mug full of caffe latte and simply stare. I haven't seen Elvis yet, but it is still early – not even eight-thirty yet. I have checked out of the hotel. The car is loaded. I even have a few more tapes to serenade me on the trip home and they all happen to be by John Lennon. That's what I'm humming now.

I'm just sitting here watching the wheels go round and round.

I know I'll never be quiet and calm and enough of a

dropout from society to really relate to the song – I'm too driven and type-A or whatever the hell the classification is – but there is something in the song I needed to hear, that makes me hum it like an anthem this morning.

The tune popped into my mind after I carefully hugged Indrin goodbye – hard to avoid that shoulder – and watched him get rolled along the sidewalk in the wheelchair. He said he was well enough to walk – which I think he was – but Rajiv had argued for that wheelchair and Indrin was damn well going to sit in it all the way to the rental van, all the way through the airport, and right up the driveway to his parents' home. And Indrin had even managed to look remarkably good-natured about his concession to sit in the chair.

When I kissed Anila's cheek, I gave her hand a squeeze and wished I could tell her that I see her strength and appreciate it. I can't say I want to emulate it, but it is a pretty clear indicator to me of what I am not willing to work at anymore. Surely not *all* men need constant placating, I always found myself wondering around her and Rajiv. Thankfully, her son allows me a certain, tentative faith that, yes, it could be better than that. Anyway, if Indrin's mysticism is even half-real, I think Anila received some extra strength from me for continuing her peacemaking efforts. I certainly tried to send it, care of the mental messaging system I seem to have so much confidence in lately.

I still feel Indrin's last hugs, the one his arms

enveloped me in and the one in his words.

"You're going to be okay. The newsroom won't recognize you, you know."

He said it mid-embrace. I didn't want to let go, but had to when, just behind Indrin and in full view to me, Rajiv looked pointedly from his watch to me to the van. Right then, I remembered I forgot to put on my own watch and laughed out loud.

"Better get going, Indrin," I said, nodding to his Dad. "Time's a-wasting."

There's no question my eyes were smarting when they pulled away. My emotions were surging all over the place for most of the day afterwards, but somehow I feel more of a calm this morning, like no goodbye ever has to be quite as final as I have feared in the past.

After they left for the airport, I went to see Daria. She is still in a coma and while there is supposed to be some hope, I can't help thinking about Indrin's story, his description of her sigh and gentle falling asleep when Mary or Edmond's sister or Indrin's imagination materialized in that storage closet.

Her grandparents arrived just as I was leaving. They are quite young, neither could be more than fifty-five years old, and they both have only touches of grey in their hair. As we spoke briefly, hush-voiced there in the hospital halls, I wondered for a moment if I should tell them about Indrin's story, but couldn't bring myself to mention it. Somehow it felt too final, too much a story to ponder at a funeral, and these two people, who had already buried a daughter, were praying for awakenings, not peaceful eternal sleep.

Aaron and I tried to get together for brunch later that morning, but somehow we missed each other. Maybe I went to the wrong side of the Granville Island Market, maybe he just slept in – but when I talked to him later on the phone I could have sworn I heard a female voice asking him something, so I assume he has launched himself into another *ship* – safely, I trust.

Good for him, I thought.

Bon voyage, Aaron and Sherry. Bon Voyage. Here's to smooth sailing.

A limitless supply of bravery, the guy has, and optimism. Maybe I will just have to wait for his book to hit the shelves so I can put all his cartoon tips into action.

In the meantime, no more pirates. No more bullying pirates. That's a new rule of my own.

Have you got a song about that, John Lennon?

I drain the bottom of my styrofoam cup, lick the foam from the underside of the lid, and rethink my plans for today. The idea of touring the CBC newsroom is starting to make me feel nauseous, but that may have more to do with what lies just across the street from Mothercorp. Sister Fran sitting in her office at Catholic Charities can no longer be avoided. I did leave two messages on her office machine, shrewdly at midnight both times, but I will have to face her today.

Still no Elvis in sight. A golden Lab barks further down the beach, trying to scare off the giant freighters moored out on the bay. The air is cool and moist this morning and there is a heavy bank of cloud weighing down over the city and hiding the mountains. My hair is ringletting in all this humidity.

Terrific. Little Miss Shirley Temple gets to meet the Executive News Producer.

When I want to look mature and experienced, I rematerialize as my grade ten school picture, all curly-locked and awkward. When I want to look sexy or glamorous, even with all the lipstick and mascara I can muster, I wear the entire week's news stories under my eyes. Go figure.

~ ~

FRAN pushes her chair back and bites her lip.

"Oh dear, I'm so sorry."

"Don't feel bad. How could you have known?"

"No, it's obvious. I should have seen it. The poor boy. I never meant to sound so harsh. God forgive my tongue."

Her face is very grave and I can literally watch the tide of guilt flood in. This is making me shrink in my chair.

"Listen, Edmond just didn't know what to say. Once he had talked about his brother to Father Lowrey, the ball just started rolling and he didn't know how to stop it."

"Well, of course. It would have been so very painful for him."

Her hands, older looking than I had remembered, close a file folder on her desk.

"But why would he say one had survived?"

"I don't know."

And that is the truth, the first completely true thing

I have told Sister Fran this morning. I honestly cannot begin to sort out Edmond's motives, what drove him to create a brother, what drove him to finally tell me the truth, and what drove him away.

"Sometimes we say things to believe them, I guess."

"I guess."

"It had something to do with hope, I think," I blurt out suddenly. "I'm not sure."

Now that Edmond has gone, there is probably no point in my lying to Sister Fran. I'm not completely sure why I didn't just tell her what Edmond told me. But I didn't. And after I leave I know she will start saying prayers for Edmond's poor dead brother.

"Thank you for your help," she says to me.

Don't thank me. Please don't thank me.

I try to turn it around. "I know Edmond would have wanted to thank you for all your work. I think he was just too embarrassed by the whole thing."

"Perhaps I should try to contact him."

I quickly discourage this. No, Edmond wants to disappear, just get back to work. He has Father Lowrey's number. He'll be okay.

Sometimes we do say things just to believe them.

He'll be okay.

He'll be okay.

∽ ∽

SHIRLEY TEMPLE got her tour of the Vancouver newsroom. No openings at the moment, I quickly learned, but the executive producer seemed to like me and I didn't pick up on any pit-bull tendencies in him. It'll be worthwhile staying in touch.

By the time I met Jerry for coffee in the cafeteria, the newsroom-inspired nausea was finally subsiding. The more I talked to him, the more he reminded me of Aaron somehow. There was that documentary film he was going to make – just as soon as he could get the money together – then he was leaving. *Outta* there. That was that. Just leaving the Mothercorp and going independent.

It wasn't that I didn't believe him, it's just that I got a flash of Jerry at sixty-five, reluctant to retire from his job as cameraman because, despite all his talk of independent filmmaking, I think he actually loves his job.

"That reporter asked me if she should send you her résumé." He seemed to broach this remark with caution.

"Which reporter?"

"Tara *this-woman-knows-the-killer* Tomson."

"Oh yeah?"

I smirk.

"Can't say I got a great first impression."

"She's okay."

I give Jerry a good hard look. He reddens slightly.

"No, it's not that. Give me a break. She's just a little insecure. Got a summer contract, but there's nothing for her here come the fall."

"What the hell? Tell her to send it to me."

"I'll be out in Alberta in August. Family reunion."

"Yeah?"

"Maybe we could have dinner."

"Well, give me a call."

The guy has a history of spinelessness, this I know. But he is no bully and we've always been friends. The boyish awkwardness in his face when he asked about dinner tells me there is something new going on in his mind when it comes to me, but I can handle that. Not that anything will happen, but if it did, a good fourteen hours between us by car would ensure no more intimacy than I could handle.

Separate Sea-Doos, Aaron. Separate Sea-Doos.

I'm learning.

~ ~

THE ROUTE OUT OF VANCOUVER was such a bottleneck that by the time I got up past fifteen kilometres an hour I had no intention of stopping, except for getting gas, until I had reached Salmon Arm at least. But about twenty minutes outside Kamloops, I realized I was just too curious to drive past without looking. The church and the statue and Indrin's last secret mission here were simply too strong an influence to resist.

It was small enough to fit into his hand, so I know it's not the candle or the bouquet, but nothing else seems to be here. I sit back on the bench and face Our Lady of Stone veiled in shadows.

So did you show up or what?

Indrin left something here at the foot of this statue the morning before we met Edmond. I saw him leave something – I'm sure of it. But what it was I still can't figure out. The fact that it's dark isn't helping, either. Even with the moon as full as it is, I can't see worth a damn.

Back to the trunk to find my mini-flashlight. Yes, it's a bit faint, but at least it's working and may have enough juice left to do the trick.

I walk across the damp grass and shine my light methodically across her feet, then the base of the statue. And finally, poking out beneath someone's soggy, wilted bouquet, I see something.

My fingers pull out what looks like a two-inch school photo of a young girl. She either has a nose-ring or there is a bit of dirt on the picture. When I turn it over, I see smeared ink, still readable enough.

To I., Love from L.

Larissa. It was the ex-girlfriend with the death sentence he handed over into Mary's safekeeping. No real surprise, I guess. But it makes Indrin's apparition thing that much weirder.

So what is the deal with all these apparitions, Mary?

As far as I can see, they didn't do a thing for Rwanda. Yugoslavia still came apart at the seams even after all her appearances at Medjugorje. Her warnings at Fatima in Portugal didn't prevent the Second World War either, despite the thirty thousand people who managed to see her there. And in that apartment in Vancouver, Indrin and Daria had already been shot. The damage had been done. So what was the point?

The water on the bench has soaked through my jeans, but I'm still not moving anywhere. It is not as if I expect answers to come from this neatly carved bit of stone, but then again, at this stage in my life, I am open to answers wherever they may come from. Maybe I'm not as choosy as I was, when it comes to sources. Maybe I'm just a little less afraid.

And so I ask.

Why do people see you?

Do you have any answers for me?

But I hear nothing.

A picture pops to mind. Tommy, my next-door neighbour when I was five, dressed up as Joseph and wandering across the stage in the kindergarten Christmas play. On that momentous occasion, I got to play Mary, a source of great pride at the time, although I knew I had upset the teacher by forgetting the baby when we left Bethlehem. I did run back to grab up the doll, but I guess after the way I carried it, and dropped it from time to time, that was no consolation to pretty Miss McKee. It really wasn't my fault. The swaddling clothes were complicated and the ends kept unravelling. The doll would just slip out.

The memory is out of context and utterly meaningless. But it won't go away.

Yes, there is Tommy, with the blue towel over his head and the cardboard staff in hand, right beside the papier-mâché cow. He is looking quizzical, perhaps perplexed at how I had managed to drop the baby Jesus yet again, perhaps in awe of the number of parents gathered there to watch in the kindergarten hall.

His brow is furrowed with concern and his eyes are searching mine for answers, yet he looks truly hopeful that whatever mysteries are perplexing him will soon be untangled. It is an expression probably not unlike the one the real Joseph had, way back when Mary first talked about a heavenly baby.

My heart suddenly goes out to both Josephs, both of them caught up in scenes far grander than they could imagine, both of them dwarfed by the responsibilities they shouldered, by the mysteries they wished to understand and would in time.

∽ ∽

PURPLE AND GREEN sunlight wakes me up, the light stained that way by the strange set of plaid curtains in the motel room. When I walk over to look out, I see I left the rain somewhere back around Shuswap Lake. Revelstoke sits under a clear blue sky this morning, still slightly pale at this hour. I wish I could sleep in. It's only quarter to seven, far too early for getting in at close to three, but that is my lot in life, I guess. Maybe I'm afraid I will miss out on something if I sleep too long. Or maybe I am just uncomfortable with my voyages through dreamland and subconsciously try to keep them short.

Last night the dream had been about Indrin again. What was it? I lay my head back down on the pillow and close my eyes to slip back into that dream feeling. Something about seashells and blood, altars and my dark-haired friend. That's it. Yeah.

Indrin was dishing out communion from a seashell and I was lined up like everybody else. But when I saw blood dripping from the shell, I stepped out of line and sat down, kind of disgusted, over to the side.

Suddenly Edmond Rebero is there, sitting beside me – he looks just like Indrin, but I know it's Edmond – and he puts his hand on my shoulder and says my sins are forgiven.

Then I'm swimming in the water with Indrin again. Deep in the ocean somewhere. And it seems like Edmond is there somewhere, but I don't see him. It just feels like he is there with us.

∽ ∽

LOWREY was thrilled to receive the book Indrin sent with me. Indrin finished it in the hospital and knew good old Lowrey would be happy to see this newest collection of Marian sightings. In fact, at the moment, Lowrey is politely trying to avoid reading its pages in front of me. He glances, flips, glances, looks up and tries to remember the thread of what we're talking about.

"Pardon me?"

"I asked if you really think Mary is appearing to people around the world."

"Oh, maybe not every case is authentic, but there are a great many that have the ring of truth, as far as I'm concerned. I've just begun reading about a fascinating example in Ireland."

Come Back To Me, is the title of the book he picks up from the table at his side and waves at me.

"And wherever and however she happens to appear, her message seems to be the same. It is always to pray, and pray hard for faith and guidance during the cataclysmic times to come. The world as we know it is ending and she urges us to prepare."

Enter Jan who has lost not a grain of her deeply-ingrained skepticism.

"You're not still on about all that, are you Father?" Then to me, "As Catholics, we don't have to believe in the apparitions. It's not required."

"I'm fine anyway," I answer. "I'm far from Catholic."

Chuckling, Jan pulls off her windbreaker and sits down. She is wearing sweats and running shoes, the attire for her morning speed-walking workout, she explains. When she saw my car parked outside, she decided to make a detour and say hi.

"And you thought she came back for an apparition update, did you, Father?"

"Actually Miranda brought up the topic this time," he says, with a bushy eyebrow firmly raised. At that, he takes the opportunity to sneak another peek at the book I brought from Indrin.

I am bursting.

Indrin's vision.

It's all I can do to restrain myself from telling Father Lowrey all about it. I would like to know what he would make of what Indrin saw in that closet after he was shot. I would even like to know his view of how Edmond interpreted it for his own life. Nevertheless, I realize telling this story would rob Indrin. He would want to tell Lowrey about it himself. Still, I am tempted and know I probably would give in to it, if it weren't for Jan's presence. I am pretty sure Indrin would not want to share his *blessed* experience with a diehard skeptic like her just yet.

Frankly, I am surprised he told me. For the first time, I truly wonder why he told me about it.

Suddenly, and with obvious reluctance, Lowrey sets his new book down in the centre of the coffee table, the only way for him to avoid its temptation. Just as I start thinking about how I could word a safe question, a kind of "how would you react if *someone* you knew were to claim they had seen the Virgin Mary" kind of question, Lowrey brings up Edmond.

"By the way, I've done a bit of checking. Our Edmond has phoned the tree-planting outfit. Apparently he'll be able to get back on with them. I might arrange to bump into him up there at some point."

Then we talk for a while about Indrin, and the little girl, and the horrific prevalence of that kind of domestic shooting, before we circle back again to Edmond.

"He's a survivor, praise God."

There is so much I want to talk about, but I force a gag on my mouth full of miraculous secrets and incomprehensible lies – about Indrin, about Rebero's non-existent brother – because none of it is mine to tell.

"I was certainly very sorry to hear about his brother's death," continues Lowrey. "He did speak of him very strangely, but of course I thought it natural under the circumstances. I'm sure I wanted him to be alive as much as Rebero did. He sounded like a wonderful fellow."

"Oh?"

As far as I know, Edmond never said anything specific about his phantom brother to anyone.

"Oh, yes. What happened in Rwanda took a terrible toll."

And then I begin to hear about Edmond's brother, Théodore.

Théodore Habizi.

When I ask why his last name is not Rebero, I learn that neither name is a surname as we think of them here; Rebero and Habizi are Edmond and Théodore's respective African names.

"In Rwanda," explains Lowrey, "each member of a family is given their own African name rather than taking the name of their father. I only found this out recently myself, while trying to brush up on Rwandan culture. It's too bad. I wish I'd known earlier."

Apparently, right from the first, he and Sister Fran had been searching with the wrong name.

"We kept telling our contacts his name was Rebero," Lowrey says, shaking his head. "I mean, we told them the names Edmond gave us, what we thought were only his brother's first and second names, but we always stressed *Rebero* as the name to look out for. If we'd only realized, it could have saved Sister Fran a lot of time and effort. I'm sure we would have learned the truth about poor Théodore's death much earlier. It would have spared Edmond much embarrassment."

For a few moments, Lowrey, Jan, and I sit in silence while staring at the carpet. They, no doubt, are pondering the mystery of a survivor who would pretend his dead brother was still alive. For me the mystery is stranger still. Constantly clearing my throat, as if I could cough up the lies stuck there, I wonder if I should finally tell them what Edmond told me: that Théodore Habizi is not dead, he is a fiction that simply never existed.

Then, Lowrey breaks the silence.

"Yes, it's all such a shame. I don't blame Edmond for pretending his brother was still alive. It is always hard to admit someone is gone. And Edmond had lost so many others; perhaps his brother is the last family member Edmond saw alive."

Next, I hear what an appetite Théodore apparently had for banana beer. I hear what a laugh he had, a laugh that could always make laughter erupt in others. I even hear where he lived.

"Just to the north of our Edmond. He lived with his father."

"His father?"

"Yes, Edmond's parents lived apart. Edmond stayed with his mother and sister and her child. His brother, Théodore, lived with the father." Lowrey stops to shake his head. "Broken families are everywhere, it seems. Théodore and his father moved out not long before the genocide. If only they'd known how little time they would all have together."

"His father was Hutu, you know," adds Jan in explanation.

Lowrey stares at her.

"Hutu? No, Jan, Edmond is Tutsi," he says.

"Yeah, he's definitely Tutsi," I confirm, with a nod of agreement to Lowrey. "I'm sure of it."

Jan shakes her head while she finishes biting off part of a fingernail. I figure this is a newfound habit to replace the chain-smoking I don't see her doing this morning.

"No, Edmond considers himself Tutsi, because of his mother, but he's actually half Hutu. He told me so." Her tone is relaxed, but firm. "So I'd assume his brother Théodore felt more Hutu than Tutsi, for him to have moved out with his father."

Hutu.

"I had no idea," says Lowrey incredulously. "A mixed marriage. Hutu and Tutsi. I obviously have to do even more reading on Rwandan culture. The mysteries abound."

But, for me, things are becoming less mysterious, more disturbingly understandable.

Théodore Habizi.

Hutu.

Théodore Habizi.

Brother. And neighbour.

Suddenly, I am trying to remember exactly what Edmond told me that day in the hospital. About the boy of only eighteen. The boy who knew Edmond's home and all its inhabitants. The boy who slew them anyway. The boy, no longer human, who walked away from a house of blood down a long road in a land now alien to its countrymen, now blind to its brothers.

And I wonder. Which is the truth? Which the lie? Edmond Rebero, the young man with no brother, who created a fictional one to help him understand the genocide, perhaps so he could keep changing its ending at will. Or the Edmond Rebero with a brother, a brother he could no longer admit he had after such a bloody, brutal act, a brother who had to be erased, if only in his mind, in order for Edmond himself to continue.

The fiction is easier to accept, in fact, begs to be accepted. The fiction is what I would surely try to believe if I were Edmond.

∽ ∽

FATHER LOWREY would not let me go without making a thermos of tea for me.

"Never you mind. Return it the next time you're through this way."

I drove off in a mental fog, waving goodbye while breathing in the steamy, spiced scent of black currant tea. The fog was still thick enough that at Lake Louise, where I should have headed for Banff, then Calgary, then Edmonton, I turned north to Jasper. Half an hour down the road I realized my mistake, but by that time decided it didn't matter. I decided I would rather drive through the mountains a little while longer even if it did add some time to my route home.

I arrived in Jasper by four.

My head was still thick.

But not so thick that what I did next was any accident. As I stared at the shadow of the gondola darkening the treetops, I realized I had probably planned this ascent from the moment I left Vancouver, maybe from the moment I left here in the first place. That I planned it unconsciously made it no less a plan. I had to come back. I'd known it all along.

Maybe it was even more essential because of what I

was feeling in front of the statue of Mary at the church in Kamloops: that I was looking for answers, that I was truly looking hard for them, and didn't really care where they came from anymore. I just wanted them.

Maybe it was a textbook psychology-class case of someone wanting a little closure on a chapter in her life.

Maybe it was a physical need to feel a change in altitude, to rise up above everything in the world, to feel my ears pop, once and for all, and to feel my head clear.

Whatever the reason, I came back.

When the door of the gondola swung open, I climbed out and, already focussed on my hike, sidestepped the guys working in the Tram station and all the slowly strolling tourists. I headed straight into the bracing air and up to the very top of the mountain, along the path that winds high above the teahouse. I was feeling pretty proud of myself, too, as I climbed, until I saw some seniors happily and healthily marching their way down.

But I'm not here to prove anything. I'm not here to make peace with anything.

Neither is it a matter of feeling I have to face anything up here; there is absolutely nothing to face. Turner is long gone. The clear-headed girl I feel back inside me now would never have given him the time of day in the first place. Indrin is gone too, but not the same way. I love him as a lifelong friend and think it's a fairly safe bet I'll always feel this way; I just don't need him to fall in love with me to feel I'm worth loving. And that realization stops me short, where I now stand staring down the sheerest drop of all.

But there's still nothing to face up here, nothing but a stiff breeze.

No logical reason I can see for having to be here, for needing to stand and stare out at this vast expanse of blue mountains and never-ending sky.

I think all this through, all my non-reasons for being here, until the cold wind rushing into my ears makes my head ache. Suddenly, the thought of hot tea floods my mind and pulls me back down the path. Just before I make it into the teahouse, I hear a piercing series of whistles and stop to watch the marmots darting among the rocks as one avid tourist, clutching a disposable camera, stumbles too close for comfort. A few seconds later the peace settles again and the marmots are as busy as ever with their regular routine. They peer out from the massive boulders, sit on their haunches in expectation of a sunflower seed or a peanut, and when it doesn't come forth from empty-handed me, they scurry off to potentially more generous tourists. Again and again they do this.

Hello. Do you have something for me?

No?

Hello.

And so on.

They are occupied simply with the business of being alive. With breathing. With scampering for food and whistling away danger. And suddenly I imagine every breath they take – every warning whistle they sound – isn't theirs alone. Because if they're feeling the wind bristle their fur and the cool stone surface of the rock underfoot, so are their endangered marmot cousins hundreds of miles away on Vancouver Island.

Hello, I think.

Hello.

One of them stops to eye me. He looks up for only the briefest moment. It's impossible to think of this as proof of any conscious connection, as anything more than a childhood desire to feel a Peter Rabbit kind of brotherhood, a Beatrix Potter brand of solidarity with the animal kingdom. But he looks.

Then I march inside the Tram building, right into the gift shop section, and buy a dozen postcards and a book of stamps. I lay down the money like I'm a little girl again, buying something on my own for the very first time. I take them back to the cafeteria, present myself with another eternally-preserved muffin, and sit down to write them out.

I start with mountain scenics for the most recent men in my life – one to Turner, to Rebero, to Indrin, and to Father Lowrey. Then I write my mom and dad on a card with a single alpine wildflower. I write things I never thought I'd dare speak, much less set down in ink. I even write Mary, with a special greeting to Joseph, on one of two cards featuring aerial shots of Jasper. The other, the one I start to God, I tear up. That is going just a bit too far, I think, for someone who still feels safer believing she is agnostic. Besides, I'm not sure I'm ready to face what I might have to write on that one. Instead, I write Rebero's mother and his sister and her baby, all together, on a card with gondolas ascending Whistlers Summit, and, finally, on another identical card, I write Edmond's brother and father. On theirs, I ask only a question.

Then there's Jan's to consider. For her, I choose the Maligne Lake card, all turquoise and tree-lined, and somehow hers is the hardest card to write so far. I want to be able to tell her what a rare thing it was for me to talk to her like I did and how glad I am a woman like her could be my Mother Confessor that day in Lowrey's kitchen. Instead, I only manage to tell her I'm okay and that she's in my thoughts. But I also ask her to tell Sister Fran I'll send her a note soon, too. The truth is, I won't get away with a note. It'll have to be a long letter, a letter telling Sister Fran the whole truth as far as I know it.

Finally, I write my sister, Julie. She gets the only extra-large scenic I bought, the one giant panoramic view of everything here, the one I maybe should have tried to write the day Turner first went catapulting out of my life. It's not too late, though, for this card. It's not too late for any of them, I'm realizing. And so, on hers, I ask how the hell she knew I'd phone Aaron, how it is she's always known me better than I know myself, and, suddenly, scrawling fast now in huge, incredulous letters, I also ask her why I never realized before just how much like our mother she is.

As I sit and read the cards all over again, I realize everything I've written is just a variation on *goodbye,* the kind of goodbye that is usually left as a thought, floating in the air and echoing in your mind. And it doesn't take all that much space to write what I have to because the real goodbyes are always the shortest. They include only what's essential. No matter how many words you use, they can only ever say one thing.

When I pick up the last card, a card with a marmot

on it, I write myself. I write myself in the future. I send myself good wishes and good news and I start to wonder if all this is a prayer somehow, a prayer asking for the big things, release and forgiveness, even for the mother of all things, the belief a prayer like that could make a difference.

Then I feel just the slightest stirring through my body – a motion toward the sky – as if I'm stretching inside after a long sleep and trying to feel what I used to, out with my mom and dad looking at the stars, that wonderful old feeling that I could leap toward infinity, that I could feel it inside me.

And now, here I am.

Now.

A tourist in a coffee shop staring at cards on a table.

None of the postcards are addressed. They will not be. But they will be mailed. I will deposit each and every card into the mailbox and the postcards will slide through the chute and fall through infinite space, continue falling, until the messages, if not the cards, are delivered. Suddenly, absurdly, I have no doubt they will be received.

The altitude, the thin air, the lightheaded, dizzying spin of the world might explain it all away. But as I sit here, licking stamps and pressing them on, I think I have never felt so light, as if gravity is hardly holding me to the planet.

ACKNOWLEDGEMENTS

I WISH TO THANK Bertin Muhizi for his grace and courage in speaking with me about the genocide in Rwanda and for his friendship. I will always be grateful for our first and fateful conversation on the bus to Calgary.

Philip Gourevitch has my deepest gratitude for his important writings in both *The New Yorker* and his outstanding book about the genocide in Rwanda, *We Wish To Inform You That Tomorrow We Will Be Killed With Our Families.*

More people than I can name provided me with helpful information and moral support; among them are Dorothy Abernethy of the University of Saskatchewan's St. Thomas More College Library, Father Ed Heidt, also of St. Thomas More College, Shirley Brown at Vancouver's Catholic Charities, Father William Laurie of St. Francis of Assisi Roman Catholic Church in Revelstoke, and Ron Marken of the University of Saskatchewan.

Louis de Bernières offered helpful comments on an early draft while he was the University of Calgary's writer-in-residence. Pamela Faye Finlayson generously shared her story of the injured rabbit. Christian Eckart and Bob Feldman gave me both encouragement and insight. Martin Morrow helped me to believe in the novel at a crucial time. Edna Alford has proved to be a perceptive and sensitive editor.

I would also like to thank my mother, Mona Webber, for her limitless faith and encouragement, and Jill Webber Hrabinsky, Rob Hrabinsky and Joan Webber for their equally immeasurable love and support.

And, finally, I thank Jonathan Forrest, who defies gravity himself and whose gentle nature and loving soul continue to open my heart.

Jennifer Wynne Webber can write knowledgeably about the world of television – for more than a dozen years she has been a television reporter, writer, researcher, and producer in Edmonton, Calgary, and Saskatoon. In addition, she is an actor and playwright. Her first play, *Beside Myself,* was recently produced in Saskatoon. She is also currently working on a screenplay with her sister Joan Webber.

Born in Ottawa, Jennifer spent her early childhood in Calgary and Montreal. She moved to Saskatoon at the age of nine, after the death of her father. She graduated from the University of Saskatchewan with a B.A. Honours in History before an oral history interviewing job led her to a career in journalism. *Defying Gravity* is her first book.